Shagpile

Also by Imogen Edwards-Jones

My Canapé Hell

IMOGEN EDWARDS-JONES

Shagpile

FLAME
Hodder & Stoughton

First published in Great Britain in 2002 by Hodder and Stoughton
A division of Hodder Headline

A Flame Book

2 4 6 8 10 9 7 5 3 1

A CIP catalogue record for this title is available from the British Library

ISBN 0 340 76737 5

Typeset in Palimpsest Book Production Limited,
Polmont, Stirlingshire
Printed and bound in Great Britain by
Mackays of Chatham plc, Chatham, Kent

Hodder and Stoughton
A division of Hodder Headline
338 Euston Road
London NW1 3BH

For Kenton

ACKNOWLEDGEMENTS

I would particularly like to thank my family for their help with this book. My mother and my step-father for all their sartorial advice, my father for his very good memory, my brother for his humour and especially my sister for reading it through, correcting things and pretending she enjoyed the whole process.

I would also like to thank Daisy, Sean, Alik, Claudia, Ciara, Katya, Candace, Ant, Gay, Xander, Laurie, Cathie, Tom, Beatie, Sarah, M&M, Peter and Seb who have coped wonderfully with my lack of humour, conversation and money throughout all of this.

And finally I would like to thank the marvellous Simon Trewin for his hours spent on the telephone, his delightful emails and the occasional cocktail. As well as Phil and all at Hodder (esp George) for their help, guidance, and deliciously themed lunch parties.

Shagpile

Prologue

Liz is laughing loudly at one of Larry's lewd jokes, while his wife, Madeleine, serves the starter. Larry and Liz have been lovers for a couple of years now. It is not a terribly romantic relationship, the sort that is peppered with weekends away, ostentatious bouquets of flowers and long sighing telephone calls. It is more along the lines of frantic penetrative couplings in other people's utility rooms, and the occasional quick one in the toilets at the Golden Cross. But they like it that way. Cigarette in her left hand, Liz's right is firmly cupped around Larry's balls. The vice-like grip is perhaps not as erotic as she intends, but Larry doesn't seem to notice. Neither, indeed, does his wife. For Madeleine is entertaining. It is 10 June 1976, the night of her thirty-second birthday, but she has little to celebrate . . .

I

It is the beginning of the long hot summer of 1976 that sweats in the memory, and Madeleine has been in the kitchen nearly all day. Radio 4 is on full volume and various pots and pans are steaming away. The atmosphere hums with hysterical creativity. It's her thirty-second birthday and she has been doing battle with an avocado ring all afternoon. She is overtired and emotional by the time her husband, Larry, comes home from work. Up to her elbows in grated avocado, gelatine, Hellmann's and prawns, she looks more like a vet wallowing with the contents of a cow's stomach than someone following a cordon bleu recipe with naïve, yet Masonic zeal.

In Solihull society Madeleine is not known for her culinary expertise. With little interest in food, thanks to the amount of amphetamine-based slimming pills she takes, she tends to exude enthusiasm in the first furlong, only to lose interest and eventually burn things. So much so that Larry has recently sent her on a cookery course in the hope that some improvement in the home entertainment department might help him further up the corporate ladder.

As he comes in through the front door Larry – unlike his other half – is rather pleased with himself. Hurling his summer checked driving jacket in the vague direction of the hatstand, he almost trips with delight up the hallway towards the kitchen.

Larry is not the most attractive of men. In fact, truth be known, in his expansive middle age, he is possibly the most unattractive of men. Wide girth, wide arse, wide thighs, mean mouth, he has the sort of fat-boy forearms more genetically suited to pulling pints. He is pure Birmingham. Well, more of a heady cocktail of Black Country and Redditch, or just plain Solihull, depending on whom he is talking to. Solihull to Madeleine's parents and Norfolk friends, not that they can distinguish the subtle nuance of this white lie. But Larry persists anyway. Birmingham to the other swingers in tyre trading circles, and Black Country/Redditch down the pub. Where he is, often. As Larry has a backside bar stools are made for. His well-padded buttocks make it possible for him to spend whole evenings knocking back pints of unreal ale with gin-tonic chasers, without much need for movement, save for a return trip to the fag machine and/or an infrequent toilet facility break.

And he is ginger. Not the sort of sandy ginger that generous people would call strawberry blond, but the sort of fluoro ginger that requires heavily smoked sunglasses on a summer's day. Fortunately, or unfortunately depending on your gingerist point of view, Larry also has lots of hair. On his head, legs and chest. The fact that his collars and cuffs match is one of his favourite cocktail boasts. He has thick, heavy sideburns that reach towards his layered chin like splayed fists, and a leftward-leaning fringe that covers his forehead in a soft feathered line to just above his eyebrows. He also sports a bushy, almost fecund, David Wilkie moustache that squats like some flavour-saving device on his top lip, dipping and dunking itself into soups, sauces and alcoholic beverages with such frequency that it is nearly always moist. His daughters hate it, and refuse to kiss him unless he dries his mouth first.

'Hey,' he says. 'Guess what?'

Madeleine looks up with a faint smile, a sweaty blonde curl in the middle of her forehead.

Larry grins a wide smile and chucks a fistful of one pound notes up in the air, letting them fall around him like confetti. 'Can you believe it!' He laughs. 'Bloody love . . . bloody British . . . bloody Leyland.' He leans against the door frame, slightly exhausted. 'Can you believe it,' he repeats, inhaling and exhaling over-exaggeratedly. 'Got the order of a lifetime this morning; well, this afternoon, over lunch in fact. Want more tyres down Leyland's,' he gasps. 'The Rotarians are splashing out. Shifting more Princesses a year than they thought. So we, my dear, are rich,' he pronounces.

Larry raises an imaginary glass in the air and then hugs his wife. He squeezes Madeleine so tightly that she feels much like the piping bag of whipped cream she is now holding. With her nose and cheek in Larry's armpit, she inhales the suburban cocktail of body odour, stale cigarettes and slops. It makes her feel quite queasy.

But she is actually, genuinely pleased for Larry. He's been working at J&C Rubber Company ever since he moved south to Solihull from the Black Country almost twenty years ago. Starting out on the shop floor, he is now deputy managing director and doing rather well for himself. No, she is pleased. Really pleased. But there is still a rather stiff plastic Charlie's Angels element to her smile. Since Larry has managed to get himself rather over-lubricated at lunch, the new tyre deal will obviously be the only topic of conversation at dinner. Her birthday dinner. The dinner she has spent all afternoon cooking for.

And she is worried. For Madeleine knows just how much the subject of heavy industry makes Angela's skin crawl. Angela is the Johnsons' neighbour, in so far as one actually has neighbours when you are rich and live in seventies Solihull. She and her husband live just up the road in Lapworth, in a heavily interior-designed, mock-Elizabethan manor. Angela talks about money constantly, but finds it vulgar to discuss where it comes from. Her neck stiffens and those endearing little acronyms just come careering out at a ROK – rate of knots. Truth be known, Angela only gets on with Larry when she is tight. But since Larry always fills her full of drink every time they meet, it is normally only a matter of cocktails before they finally bond.

'You know, Larry,' she usually insists, holding on to her plaited hairpiece as she leans forward to light a cigarette from the long, thin, orange, tapered candle ensemble, organised into a crown motif, that *everyone* is decorating their tables with in 1976. 'You're QSAA – quite a scream after all,' she pronounces, taking a drag from her fag through her lip-lined pan-sticked circle of a mouth, and exhaling like a pair of industrial bellows. 'But no . . . but no . . . really,' she repeats. 'QSAA.'

The main problem, however, is Angela's husband James. Quite like Larry, in a sort of new-money, rabid Tory type of way, he has the affected chinlessness of someone who has been to a minor public school in Oxfordshire. An insurance broker, he finds the subject of money more distasteful than his wife, yet at the same time seems irrevocably drawn to it. So instead of letting the subject drop like most polite people do in polite company, he becomes fiscally competitive. He will boast about the size of his garage, the amount of glass in his greenhouse – which mutates into a conservatory depending on whom he is talking to. His latest was the expense of his wife's pedigree toy poodle. It was almost worth buying stock in, the amount the price went up in one evening.

Madeleine is therefore determined to calm Larry down a bit before the guests arrive. 'Why don't you go and have a Badedas bath?' she suggests, leaning over the sink to pick up her spare cigarettes and green plastic daisy lighter from the windowsill. 'The girls are in their nighties. You could go and tell them the good news, read them a story or something, and get ready before everyone arrives.'

Larry looks strangely stunned. He even wobbles slightly in his slip-on pumps. He never reads his daughters stories. Why on earth should he start now?

'What?' he asks, recoiling slightly with the energy of his protest.

'Oh, I don't know,' mutters Madeleine, lighting her cigarette. 'They're coming in an hour. Just go and get ready. Or organise the drinks tray. Make yourself useful. I've got the rice to do yet and the table to lay.'

'Ah,' says Larry, sticking his finger in the air. 'Drinks tray. Good idea.' And he is off with the enthusiasm of a lab technician assigned some very interesting mixing to do.

Madeleine heaves a sigh of relief and leans back against the kitchen unit. She smokes her cigarette and looks down to check out the sharpness of her hipbones. How did she end up here? she wonders, inhaling deeply.

A shy, skinny, middle-class girl from Norfolk, under-educated, under-optioned, never employed, she married flash Larry because he asked her, and she thought she had no other means of escape. He was the most glamorous man she had met in her short and sheltered life. He earned his own money and drove a soft-topped car. He smoked small short cigars, wore sharp suits and smoothed his side-parted hair with some sort of pomade. And her father really disapproved of him, which, of course, more or less doubled his charm. A product of fifties parenting, where girls were taught nothing and told to dream small, the idea of anything other than motherhood terrified her. Hitched at nineteen, pregnant in the sixties, Madeleine has never really been young. Like thousands of other women before her, she married for necessity yet dreams of love. She understands mother love. Mother love tears at her very soul when either of her two daughters is ill or unhappy, but romantic love has well and truly passed her by. She sees young couples in the street, giggling, holding each other's hand, and stealing kisses as they walk along. Her eyes follow them with a wistful longing and suffocating tightness in the pit of her stomach. Hedonistic love doesn't happen to people like her. Mad passionate love doesn't happen to suburban housewives in Solihull. So Madeleine watches films, reads books, pops her slimming pills and loves her children more than ever.

Breathing in, she lifts up her maroon T-shirt and verifies the gap between her stomach and her hipster jeans with flared ankle insert. Two babies and still thin, she thinks, smiling to herself. 'Not bad, not bad at all,' she reassures herself, stubbing her quarter-smoked cigarette out with a sizzle in the kitchen sink. She fills her ring mould with avocado mousse, puts it in the fridge, then goes upstairs to change.

Larry is predictably at the drinks tray when Madeleine reappears. She has bouffed up all her hair on top of her head, using a whole packet of Kirby grips and one faux doughnut ring hairpiece. She has also tonged three fair strands of hair into curls on either side of her head. She is wearing a lethal pair of silver sandals that make her slip slightly as she teeters rather tentatively into the sitting room. She looks amazing.

'Mummy, you look lovely,' says Lara, as she helps herself to a handful of the salted cashews Madeleine has put out for the guests.

'You look like a real princess,' adds Sophie, so over-excited at the prospect of a party that she has both fists full of cocktail eats, and can't decide which to shove into her mouth first. 'Daddy?' she says, covering her father's navy light cotton slacks in a fine mist of moist cashew bits as she bounces up and down near him for attention. 'Doesn't Mummy look just s-o-o-o pretty?'

Larry looks up from the gin martini he is concocting and checks out his wife as one might do a new motor: up, down and round the back. 'Not bad,' he says, tweaking his moustache and handing over what is effectively half a pint of gin with silver cocktail onion garnish. 'Who's coming then?'

'I told you this morning,' says Madeleine, taking a slurp and whistling a gentle 'wow,' through her teeth as she swallows.

'I know, I know,' admits Larry, bent over the silver-plate drinks tray again, trying to get the correct amount of vermouth in the glass. 'But I can't remember. You organised the whole thing. It is your birthday supper after all. Angela and James?'

'Angela and James always come,' replies Madeleine, looking round for her cigarettes. 'Liz and Geoff . . . and Valerie,' she continues distractedly out of the corner of her mouth.

'Valerie?' Larry snorts his cocktail. 'You could've told me she was coming.' He frantically brushes his slacks. 'I'll have to go and change now.'

'What ever for?' says Madeleine with an innocent smile. 'You're not rich enough for Valerie. New deal or no new deal, you simply don't have enough flexible friends to keep Val happy.'

Larry, of course, knows this to be true. He doesn't have a slush puppy's chance in hell of getting anywhere near relieving Valerie Roberts of her underwear. And although he is most certainly joking, a bloke could dream, couldn't he?

'C-o-o-ey?' comes a familiar shout from the kitchen. 'Anyone home?'

Angela and James have arrived.

Madeleine knows it is them. Angela and James are always first and they are always early. They march straight into the living room and after some cursory kissing take up their usual positions: James next to Larry at the drinks tray, and Angela in some tantrically skilled cross-legged position on

9

the leather pouffe beside the glass-topped table, where she can stash her cigarettes and alcohol without moving. Wearing an extraordinary scarlet, feather-fringed jerkin with matching feather-trimmed bell-bottoms and a silk shirt whose collar reaches to her nipples, Angela is so thin and so overdressed that she looks like a highly decorated gift shop pencil.

'Oh, gosh, nearly forgot,' Angela exclaims, flicking her smooth blonde bob and leaping up from the pouffe. 'Here you are, Maddy, happy birthday, darling. Happy birthday,' she says, proudly holding aloft the sort of itsy bag that is normally reserved for diamond rings, or a box of four truffle chocolates.

'Oh, thanks, you shouldn't have,' replies Madeleine, brushing cheeks and squeezing shoulders. Putting her drink down on the table, she opens the packet with theatrical trepidation. 'Oh . . . wow,' she says enthusiastically.

'Let's see, let's see,' chime in Lara and Sophie at the same time, tugging at their mother's cheesecloth ensemble.

'It's a . . .'

'Sellotape-end finder,' pronounces Angela, flicking her ash purposefully, obviously thrilled by her own generosity.

'Is it?' says Madeleine. 'Oh? Of course it is. How silly of me. Look, girls,' she continues valiantly. 'A Sellotape-end finder, isn't that great?'

Lara and Sophie are unimpressed. Aged eight and six they have yet to acquire that social veneer that allows people to mask their true feelings. They lost interest almost as soon as they saw it tumble out of the bag and embarrasingly are already back at the sideboard digging in to the nuts and crudités.

'Larry?' says Madeleine, using an especially high-pitched, jovial voice. 'Look what Angela bought . . .'

Larry has been showing off about his new tyre deal to James. James has been monosyllabic in his responses, running his hands through his blond flyaway hair, staring at the drinks tray, secretly willing Larry to shut up and make the gin martinis more quickly.

'What?' says Larry, looking up and over his shoulder.

'A Sellotape-end finder.'

'Where on earth did you get that?' says Larry, laughing. 'It's—'

'Lovely . . . very, very, kind and very, very lovely,' interrupts Madeleine. 'Angela bought it.'

'Oh, so it is,' says Larry quickly. 'Um, lovely . . . Drink anyone?'

'Oh, JWTDO,' says Angela, settling herself back down on the pouffe, arranging the feather fringe on her bell-bottoms attractively.

Larry looks confused.

'Just what the doctor ordered,' repeats Angela, pronouncing each word as if Larry were some aurally challenged relative.

'R-i-i-i-ght,' he says. 'Onion?'

'What?'

'Oh, silver cocktail onion garnish?' he embellishes.

'Please,' replies Angela.

'Nuts?' offers Madeleine.

'Oh, Lord! No,' says Angela, patting her Twiggy-slim stomach and reaching for her packet of JPS. 'A moment on the lips, a lifetime on the hips.' She laughs heartily at her own well-worn joke, disturbing her blow-dry in her enthusiasm. She lights a cigarette. 'So,' she says to Larry. 'Business good?' She takes a slurp of her gin and whistles through her teeth as Madeleine has done before her. Larry's cocktails are always too strong.

'Funny you should ask,' says Larry, puffing up his paunch with pride. 'Today the most amazing thing happened—'

'Was that the front door?' chimes in Madeleine breezily. 'Larry? Off you go, don't want to keep our guests waiting.'

'Tell you in a second,' says Larry, pointing his finger in the air on his way out of the room. 'And I promise it really is worth waiting for.'

'Ooh, how exciting,' replies Angela, mincing in her seat with anticipation. 'I do so enjoy a good story. Don't I, James?'

James doesn't reply.

'James? Don't I enjoy a good story?' she repeats at greater volume.

James pretends he can't hear and wanders over to the eight-track cassette player, where he flicks through the Neil Diamond and Demis Roussos collection. 'These are all terrible,' he complains. 'Whose are they?'

'Mine,' replies Madeleine. 'You say that every time you come, James,' she says, looking at her collection protectively. 'Why don't you just put *Ipi Tombi* on and be done with it?'

'Oh, I love *Ipi Tombi*,' pronounces Angela from the pouffe. 'Went to see it in London. Such a hoot.'

James fumbles through the stack of tapes for a minute and finds a dark green cassette with a pair of naked breasts on the front. He momentarily peruses the cover with the clammy frustration of a pubescent. His flyaway hair flops forwards as he slips the tape on.

'Hey, look who I found outside,' announces Larry, coming back into the room holding an empty glass. 'Liz . . . and her lovely husband, Geoff.'

Madeleine smiles. She is trying hard to enjoy herself.

'Oooh, new necklace?' says Angela, tugging at her jerkin as she stands up.

'What d'you think?' replies Liz, offering up her gorge for group appraisal.

'Looks terribly expensive,' says Angela, getting indecently close.

'From that new shop in Stratford,' announces Liz.

'Jewellery quarter in Birmingham,' whispers Geoff to Larry as he smooths down the sleeves of his lemon-yellow sports jacket and pulls the sweaty waistband of his trousers up around his girth. He turns and pops a carrot and cream cheese combination in his mouth, ruffling Lara's hair as he does so.

'Secret's safe with me, mate,' says Larry, winking to Geoff. 'Gin martini?' he adds in an extra loud voice.

'Don't mind if I do,' replies Geoff, as if he's some extra in the village panto.

'Gin martini?' Larry asks Liz.

'Just tonic for me,' she replies, making a steering-wheel motion with her burgundy-tipped hands.

They all stand, hold their drinks and smile pleasantly at one another.

Liz and Geoff are relatively new friends of Madeleine and Larry. Although their children all go to the same fee-paying prep school, Pankhurst, in Henley-in-Arden, they met about two and a half years ago at one of Angela's famous Conservative lunch parties. It was fitting that Madeleine should meet Liz and Geoff at a Conservative do, because they are known, countywide, for their fund-raising efforts. When it comes to finding cash for the Tories, Liz and Geoff try to help out as often as they can. Liz and Geoff are rich. Villa in Spain rich. Cottage on the south coast rich. Large six-bedroomed Georgian house in Aston Cantlow rich. Liz loves to boast that they are a two-Jag family. They also have a swimming pool (always the colour and consistency of pea soup) and tennis court (with a fine crop of very rare grasses).

Liz is special bestest friends with Angela and, much as Angela likes to be the epicentre of Solihull society, so too does Liz. She is a marvellous committee member and is even, very occasionally, seen manning the Oxfam shop in Stratford herself of a Saturday afternoon. And if she can't spare the time, Liz is sure to make it known that she gives ever so generously. Always immaculately turned out in the latest fashions from London, Liz is especially careful to change her make-up of an afternoon – darker shades for darker daylight tones – just like the Avon Lady, who calls round every couple of months, told her.

Geoff can smell a deal in the next-door building and anything he turns his rather short-fingered hands to makes money. He enjoys talking about the ups and downs of the stock market, and he loves the buzz he gets from playing around with other people's money for his firm of brokers in Birmingham. Larry, although he quite likes Geoff in a men-round-the-barbecue sort of way, dislikes his line of business intensely. He often, when tight, calls him a 'parasite' that 'sucks the blood out of heavy industry – the real employers of this country'. But Geoff and Larry get on, most of the time; they share pissed-up secrets over lunch at their gentlemen's club, the Pastures, in Birmingham. Although Geoff, like Madeleine, has no idea that Larry is sleeping with his wife.

'Well, this is nice,' says Liz, making her way over to the sofa. 'Your girls look well, Madeleine. Are your girls well? Lara?'

'Yes, thank you, Mrs Richmond,' says Lara.

'Richmond-Adams,' corrects Madeleine.

'Yes, thank you, Mrs Richmond-Adams,' repeats Lara and then looks puzzled. 'When did you add the Adams?' she asks.

'No, no, not added,' replies Liz, sounding distinctly peda-gogical. 'It's been in the family for generations. We've just decided to resurrect it. With a hyphen and everything, you know.'

'Food, anyone?' asks Madeleine, attempting to circulate at her own party, indicating to her daughters to do the same.

'Love your dress,' says Angela to Madeleine, as she pincers a carrot stick off the hors d'oeuvres tray. 'DIY?'

'Er, no, actually,' says Madeleine, with a tight keep-it-together smile. 'Hipsters in Warwick.'

'Ooh, ever so ethnic,' comments Angela. 'Never go to Hipsters myself, they simply don't do clothes small enough for me. When you're as tiny as I am . . .'

'That's a shame,' replies Madeleine, 'because a lot of their stuff's very nice indeed. Don't you think so, Liz?'

Liz is sitting, intently watching Larry at the drinks tray, while teasing her new necklace around her neck and hasn't actually heard the conversation. But Madeleine can tell by the cut of Liz's navy-blue silk flares that there is no way she shops at Hipsters. They are so expensive, they make her look at least half a stone lighter. Unless she's had another op of some sort, that is. Liz had her stomach done a couple of years ago. According to Angela – and she'd apparently heard this in the strictest confidence – they'd whipped Liz's navel off and popped it into a side plate in the operating theatre. Then they'd gathered up all the loose flesh and sewn the navel back on again. Not dissimilar, so she'd said, to tying up a freezer bag and snipping off the excess. Anyway, they hadn't done that brilliant a job because Liz still looks rubbish in a bikini – or so Angela said – and as a result she only ever wears one-pieces on holiday.

Just as they were running out of things to say to each other, Valerie arrives.

'Oh, hiya. I did knock,' she says, surprising everyone as she snakes her way into the sitting room. 'But you know, the back door was open and all I could hear was loads and loads of male laughter.' She smiles and pauses for dramatic effect, quite conscious of the impression she is giving. Tall and blonde with a big Farrah Fawcett hair do she is dressed in a tight – very tight – baby-pink, scooped-neck T-shirt top, her bosom so underwired she could lick her own cleavage. In fact, as she minces across the room to greet Larry, he is so mesmerised by the gently vibrating mass of rounded flesh that he forgets to close his mouth. Her dark purple platform sandals match her ankle-length skirt, unbuttoned so high at the front that, if you look hard enough – and both Larry and Geoff do – you can see the white gusset of her pants.

'Great knickers,' says Larry with a clammy-lipped smile, only discernible from the changing angle of his moustache which, for some strange reason, is looking a rather odd mustard colour under Madeleine's new candle-effect bulbs.

Valerie giggles. Oh, Larrr-y,' she says in her childish high-pitched voice, lilting up at the end of every sentence. 'You're so racy. Madeleine,' enthuses Val some more, turning round to flash a neatly waxed bikini line. 'Your husband's ever so racy.'

'Isn't he just,' says Madeleine, looking heavenwards.

Valerie means well. She always means well. She is what Larry calls a tart with a heart. Madeleine, needless to say, had never heard such an expression until she came up to the Midlands. But Valerie is – and even Madeleine has to admit this – nice. Extremely nice.

In fact, against all the odds, she and Madeleine are really rather close friends. Valerie was the first person to be friendly to Madeleine when she arrived in the Solihull area. Sensing something different about her, Valerie had taken her to her rather ample bosom and had tried to make Madeleine her partner in crime. But after the first couple of girls' lunches, it became apparent that Madeleine wasn't the unfaithful kind. Yet somehow they gossiped and joked and Valerie delighted in shocking Madeleine and Madeleine was delighted to be shocked.

Valerie is fun and naughty and flouts convention. Indeed, she is so entertaining she's managed to bed half of Warwickshire and still be invited for dinner. She has this enviable knack of making best friends with wives, while simultaneously fucking their husbands. But Valerie has changed tack of late and is smartening up her act. She's had it with other people's husbands and is now only after the rich, more loaded, version of the male species. Realising, as a piece of bruised fruit, that she only has limited time left on the shelf, she is cutting her losses and going after the cash. Val has always had a touch of the shiny car showroom about her, and she knows that nothing tarnishes more quickly than solid brass, so she is entirely single-minded in her approach towards upward mobility.

She was once married to Adam, a BMW dealer from Selly Oak. Poor bastard. He was completely taken in by Valerie's big bosoms, long legs and beguiling manner – he was only human after all. And it wasn't until she started coming home with fur-trimmed mini-coats and silk push-up bras from Janet Reger that he started to listen to all those whispers. But by then Valerie didn't care. The big boss's son at Rangers, the sports wear manufacturers, fancied the expensive lace pants off her and she was already helping him to renovate his mock-Tudor pile in Hockley Heath before the divorce came through.

She is currently living at Five Chimneys in Hockley Heath, where Christopher, the heir to the Rangers' fortune, is oblivious of her infidelities because he is so tied up with work that it takes an all-out strike to get his attention. Consequently, Valerie behaves exactly as she pleases. With Christopher always away on business, she has what most of her contemporaries consider the best deal of all: money and the freedom to do what she wants. But it isn't enough money. Val wants a much bigger lump sum and she also wants marriage. Not because she has a big roman-tic vision that she'd look fabulous in white – she knows that is the case already – but because she wants and needs the security of a gold card before everything suddenly goes south.

★   ★   ★

'Right,' says Madeleine calmly. 'Now that we're all here, shall we have dinner?'

There is a general murmur of group approval before they shuffle next door to the lime-green-painted dining room.

Solihull wives pride themselves on their fabulous culinary ability and there is quite a lot of stiff, some would even say aggressive, competition between the households. All done with good-natured, manicured smiles, of course, but it is a competition all the same. So when Madeleine's mousse arrives at the table, all fat and plump and wobbling like a baby's arm, dressed with a delicate tomato sauce, the silver-plated forks are drawn. Madeleine wafts around in her cheesecloth frock, serving with the fixed game-show-hostess smile of someone only recently confident of her own ability. There was a time when she would have gauchely apologised for everything in advance, in the hope of soliciting compliments. Now, however, she brazens it out. Val is, of course, the first to comment.

'Crikey, Madeleine,' she enthuses, just remembering to cover her mouth while she chews and speaks at the same time. 'It's as good as being at Lambs. Actually I'd go so far as to say it's better – ever so nice.'

Geoff looks up, placing his lemon-yellow elbows on the table, pointing his short retroussé nose towards her. 'Didn't know you were a Lambs girl, Valerie?'

Lambs is a name that Madeleine has only ever seen on her husband's credit card slips. The connotations of it being a venue for illicit sexual encounters have completely passed her by. Discreet, equidistant from Birmingham and London, with a five-star hotel in drunk-driving distance, it is *the* affair restaurant. But all Madeleine knows is that it is a very smart place for food and takes Valerie's comment as the greatest of compliments.

'Just like Lambs, you say,' she mutters, finally serving herself the smallest of portions, appropriate to someone who has been cooking all day. 'That's very kind of you.' She smiles. 'Darling?' she adds, trying to engage her husband through the candle crown table decoration. His mouth is so obviously drunkenly dry that he is having great difficulty in swallowing his food.

'What?'

'Wine?'

'I think you'll find you're nearer,' he says, forking his starter, not moving.

Madeleine springs to her feet. 'Blanc de blancs all right with everyone?'

'Actually,' says Angela. 'Would it be terribly contrary of me to have rouge? White is to acid for me,' she adds, putting down her fork on her barely touched plate. 'Delicious, darling.' She smiles mechanically to Madeleine. 'Anyone mind if I have an intercourse?' She reaches for her packet of JPS before anyone can object and lights up.

Madeleine dishes out half-pint goblets of her husband's store of KWV South African wine and soon everyone is having intercourse.

'D'you know,' announces Geoff, 'I was in the dentist the other day in Edgbaston.' Geoff is never very good at telling stories. 'And I came across this article in an old *Cosmopolitan* about Michael Parkinson and his vasectomy. Extraordinary.' He chuckles, extra loudly. 'It was all about how it was the most beautiful thing a man could do for a woman. Have the snip. I mean, Parky of all people. I always though he was the biggest swinger in town.' His whole body shivers with laughter, and as he throws back his meanly pointed chin, the whole table can see his nasal hair.

Madeleine collapses into her seat. 'I could think of many more beautiful things a man could do for a women,' she pronounces. 'Like take her to Venice, on a gondola, with roses and things . . .'

'Or buy her a big fat diamond,' says Liz.

'Or a sports car,' quips Angela, blowing a blue cloud loudly across the table in the direction of her constipated husband.

'Well, I think it's very modern and rather considerate,' says James, in a manner that takes the whole table by surprise. Despite his ability to boast about money, James rarely joins in group conversations and never normally ventures an opinion.

'Ma-a-te,' says Larry, leaning forward, tweaking his moustache with horror at James's terrifying sympathy for the women's movement. 'You can't be serious. Mate, tell me you're not serious?'

'Well, actually, I am.'

'No-o-o,' says Valerie, mincing in her seat with confusion. 'James? You? Really?' Sounding unnaturally interested, she smiles at him.

'Um,' says James, raising an eyebrow and running his hand through his thin blond hair. 'Actually . . . um, it's a joke.'

There was a brief silence and then everyone laughs, for just a bit too long.

'Oooh, ma-ate,' says Larry, whipping a false tear from his eye. 'You had me going there.'

'Yeah, yeah,' says Geoff, joining in the lie. 'Me too.'

Madeleine thinks about clearing the plates but decides to half-smoke a cigarette instead.

'Talking about amazing things for women,' says Valerie, resting her breasts on the table. All the men pay attention. 'Have you heard about the new dish who's opened up the furniture shop in Henley?'

'No,' says Liz, immediately interested both in the idea of retail and some new flesh in town.

'Oh, I've heard rumours,' says Angela, pretending to be in the know.

'Like what?' says Val enthusiastically, keen to glean as much as she can.

'Oh, you know . . . this and that.' Angela smiles, taking a timely puff.

'Why, what have you heard?' says Madeleine, stubbing out her cigarette, standing up and beginning to scrape all the starter leftovers on to one plate.

'That he is quite simply to die for.' Val grins. 'He's got one of those smiles that can fell a pair of panties at forty paces.'

'Really?' says Liz. 'He sounds wonderful.'

'That's just gossip,' mutters Madeleine, stacking up the plates.

'Well, I haven't actually seen him yet,' agrees Val. 'But the woman who does my hair says he's just gorgeous; kind, sexy and funny,' she adds for good measure. 'You know, movie-star looks with a personality.'

'He sounds TGTBT,' pronounces Angela. 'Too good to be true.'

'Well, I think he sounds like a total arsehole,' says Larry, getting to his feet. 'Who wants another drink?'

Brushing past his wife as she carries the plates into the kitchen, Larry fishes around in the fridge for some more wine. Madeleine loads the dishwasher and brings out some more plates for the rice plus chicken and mushroom in a white wine sauce.

'D'you think it's going well?' she asks her husband.

'Seems fine to me,' proffers Larry by way of bland approval. 'You know the same old . . . same old . . . Val seems to be on good form.'

'She always is.'

'. . . anyway his name is Max,' announces Val, as both Madeleine and Larry come back into the dining room.

'Who's that?' asks Madeleine, placing the heavy copper-bottomed pan of chicken and mushroom on the hotplate.

'The dishy man.' Val smiles, raising her eyebrows in anticipated pleasure.

'Not him still,' complains Larry, pouring the wine. 'He's probably got a cock like a white wine cork.'

'Oh, God, Larry,' says Val. 'Stop judging people by your own standards.'

'How would you know?' replies Larry, halfway round the table with his bottle.

'Oh, we've all heard the rumours,' smiles Val sarcastically.

'What rumours?' asks Madeleine, sounding endearingly concerned.

'I'm only teasing,' says Val, with probably a bit too much zeal.

'Yeah.' Liz laughs.

Madeleine is not really listening. She dishes out her portions, two hearty spoonfuls each for the men, the size of a quail's packed lunch for the women. One martini and she is already zoned out of her own party. The company does not exactly enthral. Apart from Val, she doesn't find her guests terribly appealing. They are mainly Larry's friends, most of whom he has known for the majority of his forty-four years. Actually, if she were being honest, they are entirely Larry's friends. Madeleine doesn't really have any of her own. When she first moved to the Midlands she kept in contact with a few of her girlfriends back in Norfolk – telephoning, writing, sending the occasional postcard – but they all went on to get married, move away and she lost touch.

So now she contents herself with Val and Liz and Angela. Val is lovely, and the other two women are all right. It is just that when they gather together as a group, in the same breath as being unpleasant about their husbands they show off about how well they are doing. It's strange and disloyal behaviour; not a starting point that Madeleine understands.

Geoff and James are agreeable enough in their own way. They both talk about business. They are both excited by cash. Geoff once pushed her up against the wall at a New Year's Eve party. Painfully grabbing her left breast in his right hand, his short nose pressed against hers, he asked her to go to bed with him. She refused, very politely, and has avoided being alone in his company ever since. Occasionally she catches him looking at her, his top lip moist with desire. She looks the other way.

As she serves the food she hears Liz flirting with Larry and James talking to Geoff about a new client he has just found near Stourbridge. Angela is boring Valerie stupid about the last time they were all on holiday in Greece.

'God, I never knew you were so-o-o funny . . .' More rice with that, thinks Madeleine. '. . . and then they said five grand and I said no way . . .' She hands round the plates to general murmurs of appreciation. 'I got so burned I couldn't sit down for weeks!' She only really hears vague words and phrases. Whole sentences seem to float through the air like party streamers; it is like someone was trying to retune a radio using her brain. '. . . and the amazing thing is that no one else knows you like I do . . .' She drains her glass of white wine. She pours herself some more. '. . . I mean it's like he's got money to burn . . .' She mops up what she's spilled with her napkin and takes a swig. 'I was so-o-o brown they had to check my passport photo twice!' She rests her head in the palm of her hand. '. . . so I said . . .' '. . . we swam . . .' '. . . five thousand . . .' She is spinning in a wheel at the fair. 'Scream if you want to go faster.' She is enjoying the feeling. '. . . me . . .' '. . . they . . .' '. . . gold . . .' She closes one eye completely. '. . . I . . .' '. . . you . . .' '. . . I . . .' '. . . me . . .' '. . . me . . .' '. . . me . . .' Madeleine pulls herself up straight.

'Would anyone like any pudding?' She is definitely slurring

her words. She is quite aware that she's pushed it too far. But no one appears to have noticed. Nearly everyone in the world holds their drink better than Madeleine. And tonight is no exception.

The conversation around the table grinds to a halt. Everyone looks up to her end of the table. Madeleine smiles.

'Don't tell me you've had to bake yourself a birthday cake?' asks Val.

'No, actually it's profiteroles.' Madeleine smiles, thankful for her friend's concern.

'Oh, God, not for me,' says Angela, sucking on another cigarette. 'I'm quite full enough already. It was really delicious though. Must get the recipe.'

Madeleine now clears away the food she's prepared and brings in the pudding. A great mountain of choux pastry covered in liquid chocolate, she's put a small wax candle in the top for good measure.

'Larry, darling, could you dim the lights?' she asks.

'I'll get them,' says Valerie, leaping from her seat, taking her uplifted cleavage with her. She dims the candle-shaped bulbs with drip-wax effect and starts to sing. 'Happy birthday to you . . .' she chants.

'Happy birthday to you . . .' Angela joins in between inhalations.

'Happy birthday . . .' says James, in a deep baritone.

'. . . dear Madeleine . . .' adds Geoff, with a smile.

'Happy birthday to you . . .' Larry finally makes it in the last line.

Everyone claps and Madeleine blows out her one candle.

'Make a wish . . . make a wish,' insists Val. Her enthusiasm for the ephemeral and romantic is contagious.

'But what should I wish for?' asks Madeleine, genuinely at a loss.

'Oh, something lovely and just for you,' smiles Val.

'Careful,' says Larry from the far end of the table. 'We don't want her getting ideas now.' He laughs. 'Caribbean cruises are off limits.'

Madeleine crosses her fingers and screws up her face, concentrating on her wish. Whatever it is, it is obviously something complex and heartfelt. Larry looks on, momentarily intrigued, but is soon distracted by Liz's breasts and pouring the wine.

'Do share,' says Angela.

'Don't tell anyone,' reminds Val, offering up her glass for more wine. 'Otherwise it won't come true.'

'I bet it's to have another baby,' announces James, taking a sip.

'Jesus, James, don't be ridiculous,' says Angela. 'She's got two and that's quite enough for anyone. I bet it's that Larry finds her G spot before she's seventy-five.'

'G spot?' says Larry, looking puzzled. 'Isn't that near the carburettor?'

'Ooooh, Larry,' squeals Liz, flapping flies away with her hands. 'You're so funny.'

Madeleine would have laughed except she knew he wasn't joking. Larry was about as sexually exciting as a spider plant – genetically made to breed entirely on his own.

'Who would like some of this?' she asks instead, with a strained wifely smile on her lips.

'That looks just fantastic,' says Geoff, pulling at his trousers as he walks the length of the table to collect his serving. Slipping his hands around Madeleine's waist, he presses his crotch against her hips and kisses her on the cheek. 'Almost as fantastic as you . . .'

'Oi, mate,' yells Larry from the other end of the table, his hand cupped around his mouth in exaggerated jest. 'Leave my bird alone.' He laughs. 'Otherwise it's car keys at dawn and I'm taking yours home with me.'

'Oh, Larry,' says Liz, laughing like a schoolgirl, her hand rubbing his thigh.

'That's so revolting,' opines Angela, flicking her ash on her side plate. 'I've read that some people actually do that . . . Frightful . . . The whole wife-swapping thing. They throw their car keys in a circle and go off with whoever's they pick up . . . It's so vulgar . . . I mean for Christ's sake if one's going to screw around, wouldn't one like a bit of choice in the matter?'

'It's your choice that can often get you into trouble,' says Val.

'Now that's certainly true,' agrees Liz.

'Sometimes it's better to have no choice at all,' adds Madeleine, passing a plate along to James.

'Oh, I don't think that anyone could still believe that in this day and age,' says Valerie. 'What with women's lib and that.'

'Jesus Christ.' Larry yawns. 'You don't believe any of that shit, do you, Val? Nice-looking girl like you?'

'I don't know what you mean,' she replies.

'Oh, God, you know, not wearing bras, that sort of thing,' he says.

'It's a much more interesting and important philosophy than that,' she says. 'The women's lib movement—'

'Yeah, yeah, yeah,' dismisses Larry. 'They're all lesbians who can't get laid, simple as that.'

'Larry Johnson, I can't believe—'

'Shall we have liqueurs in the sitting room?' interrupts Madeleine.

She can see that Val is now irritated by Larry. Her bosom is shaking as she tries to control her temper and stop herself from shouting at her host. But Madeleine knows that arguing with Larry is one of the more pointless of pointless exercises. He never listens in arguments. In fact, he sneers. But, unfortunately, he knows an irritatingly small amount of facts and

26

figures that he uses to great effect. He speaks with confidence and what he doesn't know he makes up with equal confidence. So unless you are extremely well versed in your subject, it is difficult to catch him out. In short, he's a bully and not worth the effort.

'I think it would be rather pleasant if we all retired to the other room and I'll put the coffee on,' Madeleine continues. 'Is that okay with everyone?'

'*I'm OK, You're OK,*' jokes Geoff.

'Oh?' says Angela sounding impressed. 'Have you read that, Geoff? Such a marvellous book, you know . . . Do you like all that self-help stuff? I think it's simply fabulous . . .'

As they wander back to the sitting room, Madeleine remains at the table. Staring along its length at the carnage – the half-empty glasses of wine, the great mound of chocolate pudding, the full ashtrays – she wonders why she bothered with the evening at all. No one is really enjoying themselves. They are simply going though the motions. Sitting around the dinner table, drinking too much wine and toying with the food is just a way of filling time before they are allowed to go home. She realised about halfway through the evening that she was more or less going through the motions herself. Smiling here, laughing there, serving out more food. Larry seems to be enjoying himself. Flirting with Liz. He likes that. She reciprocates, which is more than Val does. Larry knows that Val is out of his league. That's why they normally end up arguing. It frustrates him that she doesn't find him attractive, so he resorts to picking fights just to gain her attention.

All Geoff and James are interested in is drinking as much alcohol as possible, at someone else's expense, the only difference being that when Geoff drinks he becomes one of those sexy pinchers you don't want to sit next to, while James just thinks he's sexy. So he sits and flicks his thin blond hair like a horse trying to rid itself of flies. Angela simply wants to

27

prove how clever she is. She once did a year of night school at Stratford College, studying English literature. She missed a lot of her classes due to social engagements, so it was impossible for her to finish the course. But she is still very opinionated about Thomas Hardy and can even quote a word or two of his poetry. Madeleine can hear her holding forth about the philosophy of literature as she sits down at the glass table.

'Are you all right?' comes a voice from behind her. It's Val. Standing in the doorway, back-lit by the hall lighting, she is all legs and curves. It's easy to see why she has half of the male population of Warwickshire eating out of her hand.

Madeleine nods.

'It's just that you seem a bit down,' continues Val.

'You know, another year older . . .'

'God, you make it sound as if your life is over.' She laughs.

'Sometimes it feels that way,' Madeleine says dramatically. She has had too much to drink and is feeling sorry for herself.

'Don't say that.'

'I'm being silly.' She smiles. 'I've got two wonderful children and I wouldn't change that for the world. And they are wonderful.'

'They are.'

'So what have I got to complain about?'

'Nothing,' answers Val. 'So come and have another drink . . . you can leave all that clearing up for the morning.'

'Aaah,' say all the men in unison as Val and Madeleine walk into the sitting room together. Angela is cut off mid-flow and Liz mid-flirt.

'Where have you two been?' says Larry.

'Nowhere.' Madeleine smiles. 'Everyone got everything they want?'

The three men raise large birdbaths of cognac in response.

Both Angela and Liz have a Tia Maria. The drinking becomes more serious and intense, as does the conversation, although the level at which the subjects are discussed does not.

The oil crisis comes under some scrutiny.

'Terrible,' they all agree.

The Cod War.

'Terrible,' they all agree again.

And there are endless theories about inflationary recession.

'A very bad thing indeed.'

It's nearly 1.45 a.m. by the time they all leave. Madeleine is exhausted. She wanders up stairs to check on her children. Both sleeping soundly in the same bright yellow room, they move only slightly as the shaft of light from the landing disturbs their calm. Madeleine thinks about kissing them but decides against. She doesn't want to sully their sleep with the smell of booze and cigarettes. Instead she goes into her bedroom and, throwing all her clothes over the back of the chair, puts on the pale pink nylon baby-doll nightie that Larry gave her that morning for her birthday. She stares at herself in the full-length mirror. The three rows of frills barely cover her behind, the coarse material scratches her skin, the giant bows on the shoulder make her feel ridiculous. She looks like some sad male Sandra Dee fantasy.

'Fucking hell,' says Larry as he rolls over in bed and sees his wife. 'Get your arse in here right now; that is the sexiest thing I have ever seen.'

Madeleine dutifully does as she is told and climbs in the other side under the sheet. It barely takes a minute of foreplay before Larry is on top of her. His rough moustache rubbing away at her face, he flaps and flails around like an overweight plaice short of air. Madeleine lies there, letting out the occasional mandatory moan and sham encouragement of a sigh. Larry ups his tempo for a few seconds and then is done.

He lies heavy breathing in her ear, his whole weight collapsed like a corpse on her body. Oh, God, there has to be more to life than this, thinks Madeleine, as he rolls off. She lies there quietly and pretends to go to sleep.

2

Days in Solihull are quite difficult to fill, especially if you don't have children. Fortunately for Madeleine she has two and therefore her life is pleasantly regimented. Perhaps not regimented exactly, because mornings at the Johnsons' are particularly chaotic. At the moment especially because Madeleine doesn't have a nanny. She has had them in the past, lots of them, both with uniforms and without; some were properly trained, others did not know one end of a baby from the other. But she is currently between nannies. Having lost the last Danish girl, who was a dab hand at potato printing, to a French student who worked as a part-time tour guide in Stratford, she has failed to find anyone suitable despite advertising in the *Lady* and has decided to make do for the summer without one.

'Okay, okay,' she says, flip-flopping around the orange Formica kitchen in her slippers. 'Who wants toast? Who wants cereal? Who wants eggs?'

Lara and Sophie are sitting on a low, brown linen padded bench underneath the window. Both still slightly too short for the height of the seat, their legs swing in unison. Blonde and freckled, dressed in the purple and white striped school uniform summer dresses with white lace socks and Clark's sandals, they are old enough to get themselves ready in the morning. Lara is two and a half years older than her sister, and is often involved in the fine-tuning of her sister's outfit. Today, as Madeleine stands with a loaf of bread in one

31

hand and a packet of Rice Krispies in the other, Lara is correcting the buttoning-up on Sophie's grey cardigan with purple-striped collar and cuffs.

'Thanks for that, darling,' says Madeleine as she watches. 'You two are so grown up these days. It's quite amazing.' She smiles.

'I'm not that grown up,' complains Sophie, her bottom lip plumping out. 'I'm still the baby.'

'Course you are, darling, course you are,' reassures Madeleine. 'Toast and Marmite then?'

'In soldiers?' says Lara.

'In soldiers,' agrees Madeleine.

Larry has long since gone to work. It takes him over an hour and a half of vigorous commuting to get to his factory in the north of Birmingham. Although deputy managing director, he is one of three, and there is still a rather sanctimonious boss to impress, who as a teetotaller abhors anything other than fresh-faced punctuality. Despite the amount he drinks, Larry makes it his business to be on time, even early, and always leaves the house before 7.30 a.m. He is not normally back until about 7.30 or 8 p.m., which leaves Madeleine a full twelve hours every day, more or less, on her own.

The first part of the day is spent doing the school run, which Madeleine usually does in her nightie. Part of her reason for doing the journey in a state of undress is laziness, but the other part is a sort of social deviancy. Most of the mothers use that early morning children-depositing sortie as a form of display: a way of showing off their new cars, coats, hair-dos, tans. It has been known for some of the more opulently kept to arrive on, say, Valentine's Day in full diamond earrings with matching solitaire set ensemble, for appraisal and appreciation by the group. The school run in the Solihull area is the social equivalent of a nineteenth-century trip to the opera. And Madeleine, by her obvious non-conformity, contributes to her own alienation.

Not that she cares particularly. She loves the drive to school. She plays her music loud, sings along, and enjoys the wind in her hair. The car is where she fantasises and she often pretends that she is somewhere else: in a French film, wearing Capri pants on the Riviera, drinking Pastis and being sophisticated. Not that she has seen any French films, or ever been to France for that matter. But she's heard a few Serge Gainsbourg records and seen stills of Bardot in magazines. She once saw Alain Delon on television, and couldn't believe such handsome men existed.

So as Madeleine speeds up the long gravel drive of her children's school, deep in thought, flicking ash out of the window, the last thing she needs is a reality check when she deposits her daughters in the school yard. The idea of being brought down to earth by the group of women huddled together in the corner near the netball posts, exchanging intimate tittle-tattle about people they hardly know, does not interest her. In fact she often thinks, as they ignore her yet again, that all one has to do is rewind the world about twenty years, and the same group of girls would be doing the same thing, in the same place, talking about the same people, only the level of scandal would have decreased.

The nightie wearing was a bit of a joke to start with, to give them something to talk about. But it has since become a convenient habit that Madeleine finds hard to break. One less thing to think about between cereal and satchels. The nightie is thus the norm, except on occasions such as today when, having dropped off the children, she is going straight round to Angela's for an all-girls tennis tournament.

The Neil Diamond tape finishes just as she pulls up outside the school. Madeleine stops singing and gets out of the car. Her slim-fitting green and white tennis dress barely covers her behind as she turns to let the children out of the back. The netball-post cabal is thinner on the ground than usual. But then Madeleine is later than usual. The lack of a nanny in their household is beginning to show.

'Now, you two, be extremely good for Mummy,' she says, squatting down to Lara and Sophie's height to kiss them goodbye. 'No being naughty in reading, Sophie?'

'No.' Sophie smiles, her stomach and her bottom lip both plumping out with attention.

'Make sure you wait for me to come and collect you later,' insists Madeleine.

'Course we will.' Lara grins, kissing her mother back.

'Bye, sweetie,' she says to Sophie, running her hands over her almost white-blonde hair that Madeleine has plaited and then double-backed on itself to make a loop on either side of her head.

'Bye,' replies Sophie. 'I've got art this afternoon, so I'll make you something nice.'

'Can't wait,' smiles Madeleine. 'Off you go. Love you . . . have fun!'

'Love you right back,' they both trill as they turn towards school.

Madeleine gets back into the car, and leans forward, resting her chin on the steering wheel as she watches her two daughters, their white knee socks held high with garters, sprint into school. Their satchels hit them repeatedly on their backs as they bob along the path. The door slamming behind them, they vanish inside the building. It is quiet. Madeleine gazes into the middle distance. The high angelic singing of a prep school at worship gently drifts across the playground. She listens and, half closing her eyes, she sighs.

The thought of going to Angela's doesn't exactly fill her with delight. Taking place on an almost weekly basis,

Angela's tennis tournaments are famous for their competitiveness. They always start out as a sort of jolly girls' gathering, where people are supposed to compare frocks and racquets and balls, and always deteriorate into a seriously hard-fought battle, with tempers fraying and, on more than a few occasions, tennis racquets being thrown across the court. Fortunately, or perhaps unfortunately, Madeleine is rather good at tennis; her mother was an extremely good sportswoman, with long legs and strong lean arms, and that was one gene she was determined that her daughter should inherit. Consequently, Madeleine was given every coaching lesson going. So she rides well, plays tennis well, water-skis well and is even quite good at swimming. But sometimes being that good is not to her advantage. Winning only makes the other ladies tetchy and irritable and less well-disposed towards her, so she fluffs a few serves and deliberately hits a couple of balls too long.

Personally, Madeleine blames the drugs. Of the party of six or sometimes eight women who play regularly at Angela's tournaments, over three-quarters of them – and this includes Madeleine – have been to see Xander Paul, the pill doctor in Edgbaston. A discreet dietician, he dishes out Apesate to those who can afford them like they are Hermesetas sweeteners. Consisting almost entirely of amphetamines, these pills speed up the metabolism, while at the same time handily suppressing the appetite. Most of the time, therefore, Madeleine and her mates are wired. This in itself is not too difficult to deal with – it just makes them all slightly hysterical and somewhat hyped – but combine this cocktail with thick, black, kidney-killer coffee, copious amounts of cigarettes plus exercise and the resulting combination is combustive to say the least.

As Madeleine crunches up Angela's heavily gravelled drive to her heavily interior designed mock-Elizabethan pile, a toy poodle runs out yapping to meet her. Narrowly missing two hundred quid's worth of inbred dog, Madeleine parks her huge Vauxhall in the row of soft-top Stags, jaunty MGs and expensive shooting brakes. Retrieving her racquet from the boot, she walks through a pink-rose-covered doorway, to be greeted by the strong smell of coffee, the gentle thwacking sound of a ball on catgut, and the occasional shout of 'Shot!'

'Ah, there you are,' announces Angela. An inch length of ash on her JPS, she has pulled her smooth blonde hair into bunches and is wearing a pair of white shorts that are so tight around the crotch they form a camel's hoof shape at the front. 'All the others are warming up. There's coffee on the table over there, and a couple of rolls, if you need one.' She indicates with her JPS, the ash falls on the grass.

'Have you decided pairs yet?' asks Madeleine, anxious not to be with Liz.

''fraid so.' Angela smiles. 'You're with Liz.'

'Oh, right,' she says breezily. 'Do you know where she is?'

'Having a roll I don't doubt,' says Angela.

'Great,' says Madeleine. 'How long before we draw lots and get started then?'

'About five minutes.'

Madeleine sets off in the direction of the court, the coffee, the rolls and her partner. Weaving her way through some rather badly designed topiary that looks like it has been executed by an alcoholic gardener, she finds the group. Liz is bent over the refreshments table with a mouth full of roll, wearing a very expensive-looking tennis dress that plunges at the front and is cut high at the back to show off her trendy Teddy Tinling frilly knickers. She waves, unable to speak, and does a 'you and me together' sort of sign at Madeleine, who smiles and turns to see who is knocking up on the court.

It's the usual group of ladies who come to Angela's tennis mornings. Candida is at the far end about to serve.

Large-legged, small-busted, she always sports virulent pink lipstick and a salon-coiffed hair-do. Rich and powerful and a scrap-metal heiress in her own right, she has a small weasel of a husband who agrees with everything she says. Her partner, squatting by the net, is Anne. Plain-faced, with neat hair and a smart appearance, Anne is a Stepford wife if ever there was one. Polite and kind, she is very good in a crisis, if slightly over-keen to please on other social occasions.

At the other end, receiving, is Patricia. With a long neck and no chin, not only does she have a laugh like a Canada goose, she also looks like one. She comes from an old Oxfordshire family who fell on impoverished times and sold their rambling pile to a country hotel chain. Madeleine finds her entertaining in a rather hearty way. Her partner is Barbara. With a mass of blonde curls, short legs and plump arms, Barbara is all of twenty-one years old, and has just married a second-time-round divorcee friend of Angela's who is in his fifties and worth a lot of money. No one knows where she comes from, but they suspect a dating agency of some sort. Either way, she is perfectly pleasant if a little young.

'Have you lot finished warming up?' shouts Angela as she walks towards the court.

'Not quite,' booms back Candida from the other end. 'Just got to get a serve in.' She hurls the ball in the air and comes down on top of it with all her weight. It flies past Patricia who, stretching her long neck, makes a valiant attempt at connecting with it after it miraculously bounces in.

'IN,' shouts Candida, with an ungallant punch of her pink-tipped fist. 'I think we're more or less ready, aren't we, Anne?'

'Whatever you think, Candy.' Anne nods, with a pleasant smile. 'I'm easy.'

'Okay, okay,' commands Angela. 'Gather round. Candy, you and Anne are on first with Madeleine and Liz, while the rest of us will sit out. I should be on there with you two, instead of Liz and Mads, but Valerie is late as per and I really don't know how long she will be. So we'll have a bit of a relax while we wait for her to turn up. You may as well get the competition started, don't you think?'

'Yup, too right,' says Candida, galloping sideways towards the court in her enthusiasm.

'Um, rough or smooth?' asks Madeleine, preparing to spin her racquet on the ground.

'What would you like, Candy?' asks Anne nicely and politely.

'Christ, everyone knows I like it rough,' announces Candy, star jumping at the back of the court, hard hair still holding.

'Don't we all?' honks Patricia, cradling a cup of coffee.

'It's smooth,' announces Madeleine.

'Oh, shit,' shouts Candida. 'I'll receive then.'

'D'you want to serve first?' Madeleine asks Liz.

She nods and, pulling her pants out of her behind, tries to bounce up a couple of balls with the side of her foot. Failing that, she bends down, picks up two, and puts one in her frilly knickers. She bounces the first ball five times on the hard court, stops, throws it up in the air, makes as if to strike it and then lets it bounce again at her feet. Candida lets out an enormous sigh from the other end of the court.

'Even Borg does that sometimes,' apologises Liz. 'The wind's a bit gusty today.'

The whole process is repeated again, except this time Liz hits it, swatting it like a fly. The ball sails over the net painfully slowly, barely capable of managing a bounce; it does so in the tramlines.

'OUT,' shouts Candida. 'SECOND SERVICE.'

In a state of panic, Liz serves the second speedily and without a thought straight into the net.

'FIFTEEN love,' scores Candida from the other end. 'Oh,

actually,' she adds, running hard pink fingernails through her hard brown hair. 'That's LOVE fifteen, because you're serving.'

And so it goes on. Liz, for all the loveliness of her outfit and expensive equipment, really can't play. She has been known to fluke a few shots here and there, but on the whole, despite last summer's tennis coaching with some South African hunk called Wade, with whom she was rumoured to be having an affair, Liz is really rather poor. Especially when she plays opposite Candida whom she finds intimidating, making her fluff and blunder more than usual.

Liz and Madeleine lose to love. They manage one rally where Candida returns the ball, except Liz, stunned that her first serve is in, is so busy congratulating herself she forgets to be ready for the return. Madeleine knew this was going to happen. Every time she plays with Liz it is the same story: fab outfit, crap shot. She should really give up the game altogether.

Next to serve is Candida. Anne did make some sort of genteel yet hopeless muttering about going first 'to get it out of the way', but Candida pushed herself forward.

'Ready down there?' she says, leaning in, bouncing the ball like a professional.

'Fine when you are,' replies Madeleine, swinging side to side ready for the serve.

Candida throws the ball in the air and hammers her serve like her life depended on it. It flies past Madeleine, barely scraping the baseline.

'Shit,' shouts Candida, scolding herself more than anyone else.

The next ball is launched into the air. She comes down on it with the same amount of force, yet this time it's in. Madeleine sends it back. Anne, all squat and ready at the net, volleys it into the far back corner. Liz runs. A sight to behold: layers of pitted flesh rippling in unison. She prepares herself for a smash and frying-pans it into the middle of the court. It's over the net. Madeleine can't believe it.

'Good work!' she urges.

'Mine!' shouts Candida.

'Yours!' agrees Anne.

Candida is so close, but misses it by such a gaping margin she stops to check she doesn't have a hole in her racquet. 'Shit,' she shouts. 'Okay, Anne, THIS is the one that bloody well counts.'

As so often happens in tennis, when those playing are neither gifted, talented, nor capable in any way, the score does not go with serve. So by the time Madeleine's turn to serve comes, the score stands at one all. At this stage she normally doesn't know what to do. A better player than everyone else on the court, she usually decides to play socially rather than competitively and today is no exception. All her serves go in, at a gentle but accurate pace. Liz leaves most of the returns to her and as a result they are two to one up in the first set. Although they only ever play one set at Angela's tournaments. Most of the ladies aren't fit enough to play for longer and those sitting on the bench get too bored of waiting for their turn.

Against all the odds and Angela's expectations, Liz and Madeleine win and are through to the next round. Candida huffs around a lot. Not only is she cross about losing the match, she has also broken a nail. Anne is terribly apologetic and promises to try harder next time.

'There won't bloody be one,' announces Candida in a loud voice. 'Anyway, Christ . . . I need a pee.'

They come off the court at the same time as Valerie arrives. She's playing 'Jesus Christ Superstar' in her soft-top MG at such a volume that half the county can hear her as she pulls up outside the mock-Elizabethan manor.

'Phew,' says Liz, mopping her brow with one of her bright white sweatbands, taking care to avoid her eye make-up. 'That was exhausting.' She plonks her behind on a bench by the court and takes a packet of cigarettes out of a shoulder pocket especially designed for the purpose.

'It was great fun,' says Madeleine, who actually played quite hard to ensure victory at the tail-end of the match.

'Hiya,' shouts Valerie, waving to the crowd as she turns the corner through the topiary. 'So-o-o sorry I'm late.' She does one of those exhausted fake sighs that indicate trauma. 'Car wouldn't start and I had to wait an age for the AA.'

Everyone knows she is lying, but it's always easier to go with the flow rather than pick her up on her story.

'Val, you're just in time,' says Angela, inhaling a JPS. 'You and I are on court right now.'

'Terrific,' says Val, putting her tennis bag down with dead straight legs, showing her nicely toned behind to the group. 'One sec, I've just got to tell Madeleine something.'

'Hurry up,' says Angela efficiently, the sight of Val's pert behind irritated her.

Val sprints over to Madeleine who is lying back on the bench, eyes closed, her legs and face in the morning sun.

'Hey, God, you'll never guess what?' whispers Val so loudly in Madeleine's ear she gets quite a start.

'What?' she says, opening one eye.

'I've just been to see HIM,' Val announces, her eyes wide open in her enthusiasm.

'Who?'

'Max.'

'Max who?'

'Oh, my God, what d'you mean "Max who"?' whispers Val. 'Max from the other night Max.' Madeleine obviously still looks blank. 'Christ, the guy I was telling you about. The Greek god who has opened up the furniture shop in Henley.'

41

'Oh, right, him,' nods Madeleine. 'And?'

'And he really is a Greek god,' she confides. 'That's why I'm late. After all I'd heard I had to go and check him out. You know, for research purposes, professionally speaking, of course. I keep telling Christopher that we need some new furniture and stuff.'

'Quite right.' Madeleine smiles, lying totally still in the sun's hot rays.

'Anyway it's just fabulous—'

'What, the furniture or him?'

'Oh, my God, him. I have never seen such a specimen.'

'Careful,' says Madeleine, shifting in her seat.

'He isn't married.'

'How the hell do you know?'

'I asked.'

'You did what?' Madeleine is now bolt upright, staring at her friend in disbelief. 'You are a terrible—'

'I know.' Val smiles. 'Isn't it great?'

Angela is becoming irritated by her partner's gossiping. 'For Christ's sake,' she complains. 'If it's such a hoot, let us all share in the gossip; if not there's a whole game to play, Val. Hurry up.'

'Coming,' shouts Val, sprinting towards the court. 'Sorry, sorry, I'm here now. Okay, rough or smooth . . . anyone?'

Barbara and Patricia win the spin and go to the other end to serve. Hot, squat, all pink and blonde, Barbara looks like a slightly chubby dolly as she trots along after Pat to take up their positions. Madeleine sits back in the sun with a cup of thick black coffee and thinks this will be an interesting match.

For a start, Angela is a good tennis player, if a little lazy; actually very lazy. She has been known to run for the ball, but only in the tightest of match point spots. Although not exactly a keen asset to the team, she does have the advantage of knowing all the holes and hillocks in her own court. And she can serve. Patricia, in her big old-fashioned mid-thigh-length skirt and Aertex shirt, was obviously once quite a good player. She had her own court as a child but has grown a little rusty over the years. Truth be known, she might actually play a little better than she does if only she would stop talking, honking and giving a running commentary on her each and every move. Barbara has all the enthusiasm of youth, but no accuracy. Consequently she often sprints only to sky the ball, or hit it over the baseline. While Valerie, on the other hand, is possibly the most erratic player on the court. She oscillates from moments of pure genius to the totally half-witted. Angela spends as much time in each game praising her partner as she does sighing out loud and telling her to concentrate.

Liz comes to join Madeleine on the bench to watch the match.

'Gosh,' she says, flicking crumbs off her thighs as she sits down. 'Who do you think will win?'

'It's hard to say, isn't it?' replies Madeleine, taking a sip of coffee, her thin hands shaking due to over-stimulation. 'But I think if I were a betting woman, I'd put money on Val and Angela.'

'Mmm,' muses Liz. 'It depends really if Val's mind is on other things.'

'Quite possibly.'

'Thanks for dinner the other week,' continues Liz. 'It was such fun. Larry was on such good form.'

'Wasn't he just?' agrees Madeleine, with a hollow smile looking straight ahead.

'And your food was so . . .'

'Much better?' helps Madeleine.

'No-o-o,' says Liz, overly protesting. 'It was delicious. Really delicious.'

They both sit in silence.

'Ru-u-n!' comes a shout from the court. Val is urging Angela on as she teeters towards Patricia's lucky drop-shot. She misses.

'NQOTBD,' she says, by way of apology. 'Not quite on the ball, dear.'

'Game!' announces Patricia, applauding herself on her tennis racquet.

'Phew, it's hot,' says Liz after about three minutes of silence.

'Mmm.'

'No . . . but I'm really hot.'

'Mmm.'

'I've never known a summer like it,' she continues. 'All the ground by the swimming pool is cracked and crying out for water. I'm sure they'll be calling for hose-pipe bans soon.'

'I know, it's amazing,' agrees Madeleine, pulling her skirt slightly higher to brown her thighs.

'Second service.'

'So what's Valerie's gossip about this Max man then?' says Liz, lighting a cigarette and inhaling. 'I couldn't help overhearing.'

'God, you must have a bionic ear,' mutters Madeleine, relaxing her shoulders against the bench as she tries to calm her slightly speeding heart. Angela's coffee really is strong.

'Well, she doesn't have the quietest of voices, even when she's trying to whisper or be discreet.' Liz laughs.

'I agree with you there,' smiles Madeleine.

'So?'

'So . . .'

'So what's he like then?'

Liz is finding it difficult to contain her curiosity, while Madeleine is rather enjoying being ahead of her in the gossip-mongering stakes. It is a rare position indeed.

'Oh, I don't know. You'll have to ask Val.'

44

'But I'm asking you.'

'Well, apparently . . .' reneges Madeleine.

'Yes?' Liz leans in.

'Apparently he is drop-dead gorgeous, single and some of the stuff in his shop is even worth buying.'

'Oh, my God.' Liz swoons back on the bench. 'How gorgeous?'

'Drop dead apparently.' Madeleine smiles. 'But you know, Val is prone to exaggerating.'

'Mmm.' Liz isn't really listening. She is fantasising about some nebulous matinée idol coming to rescue her from the suburban hell of her own making. He is wading though her shagpile carpet, his crotch in skin-tight pants leaving little of his potency to the imagination, his chest a swathe of fecund hair, his head a luxuriant demi-wave. She lets out a sigh. 'I'm going to invite him round for Sunday lunch, you know,' she announces, with great determination.

'But you don't know him,' points out Madeleine.

'Yet,' she insists. 'I don't know him yet. That, my friend, is easily remedied.'

'Oh, yes,' says Madeleine, intrigued.

'Well, he owns a shop, doesn't he?' she says.

'Yes.'

'Well, then, I think I might just become a very interested customer.'

'What d'you think Geoff will say?'

'Geoff? What has he got to do with it?' replies Liz, exhaling cigarette smoke.

'Well, you are married to him.'

'Madeleine Johnson,' says Liz, sitting up straight. 'You are so-o-o old-fashioned. I can't believe you think things like that matter in this day and age. It just means that you have to be a bit more discreet that's all.' She laughs.

'Game, set and match,' shouts Patricia. 'To you lot.' She

canters towards the net, hand thrust forward, ready to shake. 'Crikey, that was a close-run thing.' She laughs, louder than a pair of mating swans at Slimbridge. 'I, for one, could certainly jolly well do with a sit-down. Lord, look at the rings of BO I've got under my armpits!'

Everyone wanders off the court, a sheen of sweat glowing on their arms, shoulders and legs. It was quite a hard-fought match.

'Excuse me . . . um, Angela,' asks Barbara hesitantly. 'Um, is there any chance of a soft drink instead of the coffee?'

'Oh?' says Angela, sounding put out and patronising at the same time. 'Um, I wonder? Oh, yes,' she adds. 'There's some R Whites or cream soda in the fridge that I keep for visiting children. It might be a bit old, but you're welcome to it. It's on the right in the door. Help yourself.'

Barbara walks off in the direction of the house.

'Christ,' says Angela. 'Where the hell did Trevor find her?'

The others pour themselves large cups of coffee. Liz is the only one who has milk and sugar; the rest curl up their noses, like they'd been offered something genuinely appalling.

'Oh, Val,' says Liz as nonchalantly as possible. 'Um, where did you say that new furniture shop in Henley was? Next to the bank?'

'D'you know, I don't think I said,' says Val, raising her eyebrows.

'Oh, don't tell me Liz is interested in Val's new discovery?' stirs Angela, sitting down on the grass, her knees tucked under her in anticipation. 'Surely it's finders keepers at a time like this? We are all far too dignified to sink to a cat fight.'

Madeleine is fascinated. She has no idea who this poor man is, but she is sure he has no notion that his future is being organised in such a fashion. He is being parcelled up like a piece of steak, and not only is he ignorant of it: there is nothing he can do about it.

'Who are you all talking about?' asks Patricia, striding up like a weird Egyptian god, half Amazon warrior in her pleated skirt, half long-necked bird. She has a cigarette stuck uncomfortably between her fingers.

'Oh, some new man who has arrived in Henley,' says Angela, not bothering to turn round.

'Oh, yes?' prompts Patricia.

'Oh, yes,' says Madeleine, with large smile. 'Apparently he's drop-dead gorgeous and owns a furniture shop.'

'What's his name?' asks Pat, exhaling cigarette smoke.

'Just how handsome is he?' asks Candida, looking in her hand mirror and tweaking her lipstick.

'Very handsome,' says Val, enjoying being the only person who has actually met him.

'What his name?' asks Pat again.

'He's got black hair down to about here,' continues Val, indicating just around the shoulders. There's an audible sigh in the assembled company. 'And he's got these thick eyelashes that are long and curl and look like he's been crying.' They sigh again. 'His eyes are blue – yet green in direct sunlight – and he has a voice that makes you want to take your clothes off there and then.'

'It's Max, isn't it,' announces Pat. 'His name is Max, isn't it?'

Everyone turns to look at her. She shrugs, inhales on her cigarette. 'Known him for years,' she says, exaggerating somewhat. 'He's an Oxfordshire boy.'

'What else do you know?' asks Val, flopping down on the grass at Pat's feet, looking up in expectation.

'Um,' says Pat, slightly put on the spot. She corkscrews her breasts around in her Aertex shirt to buy some time, and blushes a little.

Max is, in fact, the older brother of a girlfriend she knew nearly twenty-two years ago, when she was about ten. She remembers him because he made a fantastic impression on her, even then. About five or six years older than her, she and Max's sister put on some sort of show for him and his mates, using the gramophone and a dressing-up box. It is embarrassing to think about it now, but she supposes that Max is probably her first crush. Not that he ever noticed her, of course. But she held a candle for him right up until her first kiss at the age of seventeen. She always kept her ears open for any information about him. He disappeared for a long while, probably travelling. She heard a few bits and bobs on the grapevine: that he was back, he'd gone into antiques and had opened a shop somewhere. But she had no idea that it was in Henley. The description, however, of a dark-haired dish into hard furnishing was unmistakable.

'Gosh,' Pat says. 'Um, what can I say?'

'Where's he from in Oxfordshire, for a start?' quizzes Liz.

'Oh, a small village just outside Woodstock,' explains Pat. 'His parents are something to do with the Heythrope and they own a big pile in the area. To tell you the truth,' she says, finally coming clean, 'I haven't seen him for years. He's from some enormous family. I think he's the eldest son of five sisters, something like that. My friend Constance was number three. A bit younger than me, she was extremely beautiful and rather sophisticated. I think his grandparents owned tea plantations in northern India. They could even be Typhoo or Twinings or something like that.'

'How romantic,' says Madeleine.

'How rich are they exactly?' asks Val.

'To be honest I don't really know,' continues Pat, rather enjoying the undivided attention of the group. 'They did have this fabulous house, but you know quite honestly it was always a bit chilly and damp. You got the feeling that they had fallen on hard times. Nouveau poor, so to speak.'

'Well, he can't be that well off if he's running a shop in Henley,' asserts Candida. 'Speaking as someone who has made money in trade, I know that that sort of trade makes no money at all.'

'Maybe it's a soul thing?' suggests Madeleine, beginning to have rather romantic cinematic ideas about Max herself now that everyone is talking about him. She likes the thought that he might have suffered or be suffering. The thrush with the broken wing. The beautiful man who has fallen on hard times: in her eyes, there is nothing more attractive.

'Soul thing? You must be joking,' scoffs Liz. 'No one does soul things round here. The rents are too high for a start.'

'Oh, I don't know, he looked fairly soulful when I saw him this morning,' says Val, sticking up for her friend.

'So that's where you were,' says Angela. 'Waiting for the AA breakdown man, my foot.'

'Ooops.' Val giggles. 'But think of the fun we've had out of my encounter.'

'Fair enough,' concedes Angela. 'But enough of Max. I think we'd better get back to the game in hand.'

'Can't I just hear a bit more about him from Pat?' moans Liz, peeling her sweaty thighs and nylon-knickered arse off the bench, keen to get out of the heat and stop playing tennis.

'Wait till lunch,' says Angela. 'And then we can all hear.'

'Just as well I'm not playing,' roars Pat. 'I better get the old thinking cap on and see what else I can remember.'

Madeleine and Liz lose the toss, and Angela and Valerie elect to serve. For once Angela finds her competitive edge and runs for every ball. Valerie seems to be concentrating and manages to find shots and lines she never knew existed. Liz, needless to say, with so much sexual excitement raging around the coffee and rolls table, is unable to keep her mind on the job. She misses shots, hits others long and the easiest of volleys into the net. She is playing like a rabbit in possession of a butterfly net and doesn't seem to care. In fact, she is willing the game to finish so that she can move on to lunch and some more gossip. Even Madeleine is distracted. She can't work out what is bothering her. All that silly talk about the handsome Max. She hasn't heard a group of women so feverishly over-excited since David Essex appeared in *Godspell*.

She and Liz eventually lose the set two six, much to Angela's delight. She tries to hide it, of course. To win one's own tournament, in one's own house, on one's own court is not exactly the politest behaviour. But she is so thrilled, her voice sings with sated adrenaline and she almost skips into the house to prepare the lunchtime leaves.

'Okay.' She smiles as she comes back out again, swinging her hips in a positively pubescent and jaunty fashion. 'Who wants to eat in and who wants to eat out?'

'I think it's out, don't you?' says Candida in such a manner that few could refuse her.

'Jolly good idea,' says Anne with a simple Stepford smile, already moving garden chairs into a more attractive circle. 'It seems such a shame to waste the weather.'

'It's been like this for weeks,' complains Liz. 'So much so that we've even had to have the pool cleaned. The children were complaining. I do so hate it when they swim all the time, because it ruins Chantal's hair. I don't mind about Christian's so much – he could do with some highlights – but with Chantal I spend a fortune at the hairdresser in Henley and then she just ruins it.'

'Oh, how is Chantal?' asks Madeleine. Their daughters are in the same class at Pankhurst.

'Very well,' says Liz, blowing her smoke over her right

shoulder. 'She got some love letter at school the other day.'
She laughs. 'Isn't it amazing how young they start these
days?'

'So, outside then?' interrupts Angela.

'Absolutely,' says Val, already in a prime position, rubbing
oil into her slim, sleek shins as she toasts them a darker shade
of brown in the bright sun.

If anyone can put on a spread, it's Angela. For someone so
slim and swizzle-stick-like it's extraordinary that she should
have any interest in food let alone what appears to be an
obsession. Except Angela's obsession only extends to the
preparation and not to the consumption. Backwards and forwards she goes to her well-equipped kitchen, which is blessed
with every modern whizzer and splicer and wipe-clean service
available in Rackhams in Birmingham. Everyone offers to help
but Angela refuses insistently; she enjoys the martyr act and
knows the appreciation of her marvellousness would be halved
if anyone else joined in.

Out come great wooden bowls filled with crunchy lettuce
salads. Next are flat, frilled-edged dishes of tomato salads.
Dipped in boiling water, the tomatoes have been relieved
of their skins, doused in olive oil and white wine vinegar
and sprinkled with chives. After the tomatoes come the
avocados, laid out in circles of new-moon-shaped slices, two
huge round platefuls to Liz's obvious delight. There is also
a platter of water-thin ham, so transparent you can see the
plate design through it, one stubby French baguette, and a
large bowl of burgundy cherries still wet from being washed
under the tap.

Angela lays it all out on a table underneath an apple tree,
between the topiary and the tennis court. She flaps out a
lemon-yellow and white check cloth, brings out bottles of
chilled blanc de blancs and some half bottles of Perrier
water. Her final touch is a bunch of pale yellow roses in

a cut-glass jug and a few more essential ashtrays for the assembly.

'Right,' announces Angela, standing back to admire her own handiwork that looks as though it has come straight out of a magazine, which it has. The May issue of *Harpers & Queen*, or was it *Tatler*, she can't quite remember. Anyway, she'd seen it in the hairdresser's, thought it was JTD – just too divine – torn it out and placed it in her large leather file that she keeps for such occasions. 'Right,' she says again, indicating that she is now amenable to appreciative noises.

'Gosh,' says Anne. 'Angela, you really are terribly clever.'

'Oh, it's nothing,' says Angela, flicking one of her bunches as part of her preening process.

'Shit, that looks great,' says Candida, having a bit of trouble with her Dunhill lighter. 'Really very glamorous indeed, darling.'

The women gather round a table groaning with salads and tuck in with varying degrees of enthusiasm. Liz unwittingly takes half the baguette, then, rapidly realising her mistake, rips off the end and replaces the rest of it on the plate before anyone is any the wiser. Patricia, although finding the display attractive enough, is more of a meat girl and, suffering from an irrational hatred of tomatoes, she helps herself to three slices of ham. Hiding her indulgence under a lettuce leaf, she disappears like a dog with a stolen bone to the edge of the group and sits cross-legged on the grass. Angela, Valerie and Madeleine stand in the queue taking a small spoonful of this, a slither of that.

'Xander Paul?' says Valerie, looking at Angela's plate.

'Isn't he divine?' says Angela, her eyes rolling in delight. 'There is nothing I like more than a crooked doctor, don't you?'

'Couldn't agree more,' smiles Valerie, trying to separate one avocado slice from another to return one to the bowl.

'Don't you find they make you a bit irritable?' says Madeleine, debating whether she can manage that many tomatoes.

'Oh, God, darling,' says Angela. 'CATS – cross as two sticks – but, you know, as they say in France *il faut suffrir pour être* . . . slim.'

'I just wonder sometimes what those pills do to our insides – and my relationship with my children,' rambles Madeleine, making herself a spritzer. 'There are days when I'm so irrational I know that they're giving me a wide berth, or are just desperate to get away from me.'

'There is one advantage to not having children then,' laughs Angela.

'God, Christopher wants me to have some of those,' says Valerie. 'I think he hopes it's a way of tying me down, chaining me to the stove.'

They all lie down on the grass, lounge in deckchairs, perch on benches, or relax on the rug. Large glasses of chilled white wine are drunk, packets of cigarettes are smoked, and salads are played with, and occasionally eaten. It's a baking hot afternoon. The air is almost completely still. The isolated efforts of a breeze transport the odd trace of honeysuckle from above the open conservatory window. Lubricated by alcohol, the gossip moves from conspiratorial pairs, to sub-sets and then eventually to the whole group. Who is sleeping with whom? Who is supposedly sleeping with whom? Who fancies whom? Whose marriage is going well? Whose is on the rocks? Who behaved badly at the last Conservative do? Who has done up their house? Where to get nice fabrics? Where to find the latest Biba lace frilly shirt? Did you know that Marks do a great push-up bra?

'Did you read that article in *Cosmo* the other day?' says Angela, lying back languidly on the rug. 'About how you are supposed to sit on a hand mirror and familiarise yourself with your bits in order to be better in bed?'

'God, how hideous!' exclaims Candida, pouring some more wine. 'Can you imagine if you got caught?'

'How awful!' shrieks Patricia. 'What would you say to your husband if he walked in on you squatting down in the bathroom. Yuk. It hardly bears thinking about.'

'Oh, I don't know,' says Valerie, flicking her cigarette into a handy rose bush. 'They might have a point.' The whole gathering stares at her. 'Wha-a-at?' she says, shrugging her shoulders. 'I was only making a suggestion. I mean with all this talk about the multiple orgasm, who round here has had one?'

There is a general silence as everyone shifts uncomfortably and avoids eye contact.

'I think I'll help clear away some plates,' says Anne, springing to her feet.

Barbara gets up to join her. This is all a bit too liberated for Anne and rather embarrassing for Barbara.

'Oh, no, you don't.' Val smiles, her hands in the air as she rises to her knees. 'Okay, who here has even had an orgasm let alone a multiple one?'

'Does a horse count?' asks Patricia rather bravely.

'Who the hell are you? Bloody Catherine the Great?' asks Angela, leaping up from her lotus position in shock.

'No, no,' mutters Patricia, immediately regretting the wine and her consequent frankness. 'You know, nothing like that. Just canter, canter, jump, up in the air, and whack down on the saddle and hey presto . . .' She smiles, imploring someone to share the same experience. 'It was a very long time ago.'

'Well, I'm bloody taking up riding,' announces Candida, breaking the atmosphere. 'Sounds bloody marvellous to me.'

'That explains the smug expressions of all those women at the Badminton Horse trials and stuff,' says Angela, squatting back down again in relief.

'We're off the point,' says Valerie, returning to it swiftly, much to the irritation of the rest of the group. 'Horses, no – unless that's your only experience; if so then yes, because technically you've had one.'

'Well, I'm afraid it's just the horse,' says Patricia.

'Any advance on the horse?' says Val.

'If we must play this game then I've had a few,' sighs Angela. 'I know James looks about as potent in bed as an over-boiled carrot but when we first married he made an effort. Put it this way, Dr Alex Comfort and his bearded man used to be our rather good friends.'

'Really?' says Val, sounding impressed. 'It really is the only gourmet guide worth buying.'

'Absolutely,' smiles Angela looking unreasonably smug.

'Madeleine?'

'Oh, my God, don't ask me,' she says, crossing her legs and squirming with embarrassment.

'You've got two kids.'

'So?'

'So . . . ?'

'I've no idea, ask someone else,' she says eventually.

'I'll take that as a no then,' says Val. 'Liz, you've also got two kids.'

'Loads,' replies Liz, gloating and grinning with contentment.

'What, with Geoff?' queries Val, sounding indecently surprised.

'Who said they had to be with one's husband?' says Liz. 'What do you think tennis coaches are for? Anyway, little Miss Robert Robinson, how about you?'

'Put it this way,' smiles Val, 'I sat on a hand mirror a long time ago and weekly, if not every other day, I get its rewards.'

'Reap its rewards,' corrects Angela chippily. 'You "reap" rewards, you don't "get" them.'

'All right then,' says Val. 'I "reap" about two or three times a week.'

Barbara and Anne look stunned. Neither of them has reaped in their lives let alone two or three times a week. In fact, as it happens, Val has out-reaped them all. Madeleine thinks she might have once but isn't really too sure, and the last thing she wants to do is to share her lack of experience. They think her quaint enough as it is, without divulging a not-really-that-certain reap to boot. Candida and Liz look slightly put out; they both think they have reaped enough to be able to hold their heads high in the sexually liberated stakes, but apparently not.

'Christ, is that the time?' asks Candida. Always loath to be beaten at anything, she decides a sharp exit is preferable to being forced to confess her mediocrity. 'I've got a child to collect.'

'God, and so have I,' say Madeleine and Liz in unison.

They all thank Angela for the fabulous day. The lunch was amazing, the company splendid and they all promise to come back next Tuesday to do the same thing all over again.

'I'm going to make it a much more regular thing,' explains Angela, getting up from the rug. It's been a bit disorganised before, but I'm going to phone round later in the week and fix a day we can all do and then set it in stone. What do you think?'

'Great,' says Candida. 'Just so long as it's not Friday as that's my golfing day. That's been going for a couple of years now, and I couldn't change it. Or Monday when I play bridge.'

'I'll bear all that in mind,' says Angela, waving them off.

Candida roars off in her Mercedes shooting brake, spraying gravel in every direction as she goes. She lives south of Stratford in a fantastically large house and educates her son

Robert at some very expensive private boys' prep school in the middle of Stratford.

Liz and Madeleine dally by their cars, while Liz takes the roof off her Stag. 'That was fun, don't you think?' she muses as she pulls at the big press-studs.

'Fine,' says Madeleine. 'Although to be honest I could have done without all that sex stuff at the end.'

'I know what you mean,' says Liz, heaving her roof around. 'Val can be a bit tactless sometimes. We all know she fucked half the county but there really is no reason to rub our noses in it, is there? I caught Geoff looking at her once, you know, in a certain way. I gave him the bollocking of his life.'

'Mmm,' says Madeleine, not really knowing what to say.

'Hey, oh, my God, I've got an idea!' says Liz, spinning round in her tight tennis ensemble. 'Let's go antique shopping on the way to school.'

'What antique . . . antique shopping?' queries Madeleine.

'Course!' Liz smiles, her eyes shining, slightly bloodshot with booze.

'I couldn't,' says Madeleine.

'You could.'

'No, really I couldn't.'

'Just follow me,' smiles Liz, leaping into her car with the renewed athletic vigour of sexual excitement. 'It'll be fun.'

3

Liz is as good as her word. As Madeleine drives on past, Liz beeps her horn and waves frantically for her to stop outside the furniture shop opposite the hairdresser's in Henley High Street. Madeleine laughs out loud as she watches Liz in her rear-view mirror getting out of the car and smoothing down her hair before she walks into the shop. You have to admire her single-mindedness, thinks Madeleine, as she sits at the traffic lights, beginning to sweat in the hot sun. The woman knows what she wants and has gone out to get it. She wonders what Val would think.

As news of Liz's rendezvous seeps out, Val, it transpires, is furious. Not that she is particularly interested in Max, but it is the rather puerile fact that she has seen him first and, by rights, she has first refusal. She and Liz have apparently exchanged a couple of heated telephone calls on the subject where Liz told Val to grow up and find her own new flirtation. Angela knows all that is going on, of course, and regularly keeps Madeleine up to date on the gossip whether she likes it or not. As does Val.

'I mean, Christ,' says Val about ten days after the tennis tournament and Liz's clandestine liaison. 'Talk about bloody loyalty. Liz and I have known each other since childhood. I mean, she already has some . . .' She pauses. 'Jesus, have I ever screwed her husband?'

'Um,' replies Madeleine, not quite knowing which way to go on this question.

59

'Well, have I?'

'Um . . . no?'

'Exactly, no. And it's not through lack of bloody opportunity either. He's all over me like a cheap suit, with his short nose, every time I bloody well see him. I'm practically fending him off with a bloody hot poker half the time. And I mention, in passing, that I've met some bloke that I might possibly fancy, and she is off like you-know-what off a bloody shovel and . . . and . . .' She has exhausted even herself.

'I know, I know,' says Madeleine, not really knowing but trying very hard to pretend that she does. There is a pause in the conversation. 'Well,' she says, by way of filling the silence. 'Have you ever thought that he doesn't like her . . . you know, um, fancy her, if you see what I mean?'

Madeleine is finding the whole conversation a bit difficult and embarrassing. She is normally fine having these girls' talks with Val when she doesn't know the people involved. Val is usually hilarious, telling stories about leaving her silk pants behind in married men's bedrooms because their wives have come home while they were at it. She has this tale about keeping a spare pair of knickers in the glove compartment of her car, which she naturally locks in case Christopher finds out. Madeleine always thought she was joking until one day, when Val offered to take the children ten-pin bowling as a special treat, she noticed them scrunched up in the front while Val looked for her de-icer spray.

Madeleine does, of course, feel a bit sorry for Christopher. His girlfriend provides executive stress relief to half the county and he seems to be the only person who does not know. But then again, he is always so out of the picture. Madeleine could probably count on her fingers the times she has met him, he is away so much. Val always insists that he must have a mistress stashed somewhere.

60

'No male could go that length of time without sex,' she says, to explain her own behaviour. But whatever the case at their home, and no one ever really knows what goes on behind other people's closed doors, theirs is a relationship that seems to work.

This time, however, Val seems to be a lot more serious about Max than she has been about anyone else. She is serious enough to fall out with Liz anyway. She is also serious enough to make a bit of a scene about it, which is very unlike her. Sex is usually something rather trivial and amusing for Val. Something to while away the time between shopping, drinking with the girls, trips to London and expensive dinners with Christopher. Max is also, by all accounts, not very rich. Madeleine really cannot understand Val's interest.

'Oh, my God, you could have a point there,' screeches Val down the telephone. 'Maybe he doesn't fancy her in the slightest and he's rather embarrassed by her advances and is just being polite; now that is very possible.' She breathes a huge sigh of relief. 'I love you, you know,' she says. 'I'm off to buy a bloody pine chest of drawers with hand-turned handles right now.'

So this is the state of affairs as Madeleine dries her hair, waiting to use the bathroom on the Sunday morning just before Liz's barbecue lunch party. Larry is having a shave and the girls are lying on the bed trying to work out what their mother should wear. Madeleine is not really listening as they suggest one ridiculous outfit after another for a casual lunch.

'The long blue silk jersey dress,' says Lara, rolling around on the sheets.

'No, no, the silver one,' insists Sophie.

Madeleine is much more interested in meeting the magnificent Max than working out what she should wear. Liz has

61

also invited Val as some sort of peace offering. Val has already interpreted this as meaning that nothing is going on between Liz and Max and as a result she has carte blanche. Madeleine is not sure if this is actually the case, or whether Liz is simply feeling confident enough to ask her love rival. Either way, it will certainly prove an entertaining afternoon, she thinks, as she smooths her hair into a sort of bouffed ponytail.

She walks into the bathroom to check her hair and make-up in the full-length mirror down one side of the avocado-tiled room. The smell of her husband's early morning bowel movement and heavily spiced aftershave makes her eyes water slightly as she inspects her reflection. She has huge round brown eyes the colour of honey in certain lights, plus fine eyebrows that she has plucked into an even finer new moon above each eye. She has a short straight nose and plump bow of a mouth that makes her look alluringly innocent and eminently corruptible at the same time. All this, complete with thick blonde shoulder-length hair and slim hips, means that Madeleine regularly turns heads while out shopping in the new Solihull commercial centre.

Today she is wearing a skirt that she altered after making a mistaken purchase at Hipsters in Warwick. She'd bought a floor-length green and orange patchwork skirt with a split to the knee that frankly made her look like she was about to pass out at Woodstock. So she cut it to knee length and put some buttons up one side. Teamed with an orange scoop-necked T-shirt and green cork platforms, she could almost out-Val Val, were it not for the uncalculated way she had put the outfit together.

It is about a twenty-minute drive to Liz and Geoff's house from Madeleine and Larry's rather ramshackle modern home just north of Henley-in-Arden. And as they pull into the drive behind the church in Aston Cantlow, Madeleine is struck by how truly beautiful the (Richmond) Adams house is.

A six-bedroom, red-brick Georgian house with white sash windows and a walled herb garden with outbuildings and stable blocks, it reminds Madeleine of the houses she used to visit as a child.

'I always forget how big their gaff is,' says Larry as he parks his BMW next to Liz's Stag. 'It's amazing how much money parasites make these days.'

'What's a parasite?' asks Lara.

'Oh,' says Madeleine, looking heavenwards in a see-what-you-have-done-now sort of way. 'It's a technical term for things that live off other things,' she explains as breezily as she can.

'How can they earn lots of money then?' continues Lara.

'They can't really, darling. Daddy got that wrong.'

'I didn't think that daddies could get things wrong,' says Sophie.

'They don't,' replies Larry, pulling on the handbrake. 'Come on, out you get. And don't forget your swimming stuff from the back.'

Liz's front door is open. Opulence is probably an under-statement when used to describe how Liz has decorated her house. The long flagstone floor of the hall is covered in the fluffiest, whitest collection of shagpile rugs Madeleine has ever seen, like delightful clouds on a summer afternoon. She practically has to restrain her children from diving into them. As she turns right at the end of the hall into the drawing room, she looks at the open French windows leading into the garden: the frills on peplums, on tiebacks, on frills of the lined and interlined curtains almost take Madeleine's breath away. The clotted-cream-coloured carpet is so thick you can see the footprints of the people who made the journey before you.

The elegant fireplace is crammed with china objects with a Persian cat theme, all on top of each other like some porcelain orgy. Liz has six cats with a varying purity of Persian blood, which are her pride and joy and often, on very dull days, her sole conversational topic. There are three leather sofas covered in so many cushions it's difficult to see that they are made of leather at all. In the far corner sits a nest of glass-topped tables covered in more catifacts and a foot pouffe of magazines just by the door.

As they walk through the French windows out on to the terrace, the sweet smell of clematis mixes with the charcoal smoke that is floating across the lawn.

'Over here,' shouts Liz, waving in the largest, roundest, darkest sunglasses Madeleine has seen since JFK's funeral. Obscured from view every minute or so by rogue columns of smoke from the barbecue, she is dressed in a giant floppy white hat and a diaphanous floating thing that Madeleine thinks is supposed to make her look like a nymph but only succeeds in making her look pregnant 'Come and join in the fun.' She grins expansively rather like some ebullient countess.

Lara and Sophie need no further encouragement and, breaking loose from Madeleine's grip, they are off in the direction of the swimming pool, trailing their bathing costumes behind them as they go.

Larry, in a navy terry-cloth short-sleeved shirt is already complaining about his beige long trousers. 'Christ, it's hot, Mad,' he says. 'I knew I should have worn my shorts.'

'Mmm,' she says by way of reply, thinking how she's saved the world a view of his neon-white office legs with purple veined marbling effect, more complicated than a lot of hotel bathrooms.

Approaching the barbecue area, Madeleine looks around at who else is either almost entirely horizontal in their deckchairs, or totally horizontal on the large checked rugs, or, failing that, hanging around the cooking area in a manly fashion. The first person she sees is Angela, cigarette in hand, in a short yellow sundress that matches her hair, bent over the Pimms table, serving herself what looks like another long drink. Lying back in a deckchair is Val. Wearing a pink bikini with hip belt and padded bra top, she is covered in suntan lotion, laid out like a steak waiting for a good grilling. James and Geoff are by the barbecue. Both in tight brief blue shorts and slim-fitting T-shirts, they look like overweight schoolboys around a campfire. Each has a drink in one hand and a fire-prodding implement in the other. It takes Larry two minutes to find both essentials before joining them at the fire.

'That's a great outfit,' says Madeleine as she sits down next to Val, making her jump slightly in the process.

'Oh, hi to you too,' she replies, sitting up and depositing a rather creamed kiss on both Madeleine's cheeks. She smells of baked skin and Nivea.

'So where is he?' whispers Madeleine, out of the side of her mouth like someone out of a cheap spy movie.

'Up by the pool,' replies Val, doing the same.

'Why aren't you there?'

'Playing it cool.'

'There's cool and missing the boat altogether,' says Madeleine, lighting up a B&H.

'He's with Christopher.'

'Oh, my God!' squeals Madeleine a bit too loudly.

'What?' says Larry, turning around from the barbecue.

'Nothing,' she replies.

'Oh, yes,' says Val, through her teeth 'Christopher said he wasn't coming, that he had to be in Frankfurt on Monday so was going to leave this afternoon. But when he saw how lovely the weather was, he decided he'd change his flight, enjoy the weather and go early on Monday morning instead. Like it's been bloody good weather for weeks anyway; if anything it's too bloody hot. Anyway, we got here about half an hour ago and they disappeared off together up by the pool. Max said he'd teach Chantal and Christian how to dive and Christopher said he'd go and bloody well watch. Liz is up and down that path like a rat up a drainpipe, but I don't really have the maternal excuse.'

'Oh dear,' says Madeleine, smiling slightly.

'It's not bloody funny. I had a bikini wax and my roots done on Friday just in case.'

'I know,' says Madeleine, trying to sympathise. 'You can just never plan these things. The course of true love . . .'

'Piss off.'

They both sit there in silence and watch the men round their fire. Larry is laughing heartily at Geoff's joke; James is staring at his feet, shuffling from one to the other, smiling but obviously not understanding what is quite so hilarious.

'M-a-a-te,' says Larry, patting Geoff on the back. 'It's damn hot; do you have any shorts or anything I could change into?'

Larry in shorts has to be Madeleine's nightmare. When she sees his short white legs she finds it hard to contain her revulsion.

'Course I have, mate,' says Geoff, patting him back. 'I've got a pair of trunks somewhere you can borrow.'

'Um, shall I go up to the pool and get him down for you?' says Madeleine to Val quickly. Anything not to see the tight line around Larry's calf where his sock has been.

'That's a brilliant plan,' says Val, pushing her giant pink sunglasses on to the top of her head. 'And if you're not back in ten then I'll come and get you.'

Liz goes inside looking for a pair of trunks for Larry, and Madeleine walks up the path towards the pool. Lined either side by a heavily scented climbing rose garden mounted on posts, it is an airless and heady walk. The sound of splashing and children screaming indicates that she is going the correct way. She pushes open the small gate to the pool area designed to keep out dogs and very small children.

'Mummy!' shouts Lara, running around the edge of the pool pulling her bikini bottoms up with one hand while waving with the other. 'Look what Max has taught me.' She runs the length of the diving board, leaps into the air with total confidence and lands in the water in a sort of L shape, head and feet at the same time, her bottom a short while behind. There is an enormous splash, as she empties half the pool.

'Dive in head first, always head first,' says this tall slim man standing with his back to Madeleine, about ten feet to her left, by the side of the pool. 'It's all about confidence, believe you can do it and then take the plunge.' He laughs. 'Ready?'

Lara runs around again, and stands dripping wet, glistening like a seal waiting for his command.

'One, two, three, go!'

She runs, jumps and executes exactly the same performance with exactly the same results as last time.

'That's great,' he enthuses. 'So-o-o much better.'

Even from behind Madeleine can see what all the fuss is about. Dressed in a black T-shirt and jeans, he has long, slim, muscled brown arms and bare brown feet. He has a strong straight back and an edible backside. His hair is indeed dark, wavy and shoulder-length. It's lovely, thinks Madeleine as she stands and stares. Even his shoulders are lovely. She must have made some sort of noise, because he turns round. Back-lit by the sun, she can't see his face but she knows he smiles.

'Madeleine, is that you?' comes another voice, from her right. She turns. It's Christopher perched on top of the bank, wearing a pale yellow shirt, a pair of pistachio slacks and a Panama hat. He's smoking a small fat cigar. 'Come and sit up here,' he says, patting a patch of ground next to him. 'I haven't seen you for a very long time. How delightful. How

67

very delightful to see you again.' He gets up as Madeleine approaches and plants two moist kisses on her cheeks, clipping her mouth as he does so. 'Very delightful,' he repeats.

They both sit down.

'So,' says Christopher. 'What have you been up to?'

'Not very much really,' mutters Madeleine distractedly.

'Ah,' says Christopher. 'Um . . . planning to go away this summer?'

'No.'

'Oh, that's a shame. Valerie and I are thinking about going either to Greece or Puerto Banus in Spain. If I can find the time that is. I'm terribly busy at the moment, you know, what with . . .'

Christopher is off, recounting tales of his expanding business, lucrative contacts here and trips abroad there. Madeleine is incapable of listening. Never before in her life has she seen such an amazingly handsome man, with so little sense of his own attraction. Even the children are fighting for his attention. He praises and smiles at them as they hurl themselves time and again into the water just to please him. Their devotion is extraordinary. He moves with such grace and athleticism. He is not affected in any way. Madeleine is hypnotised. All she can do is stare. Every so often, aware of her looking at him, he glances over his shoulder and grins.

Christopher's monologue dries up. 'He's a popular man,' he says, following Madeleine's stare.

'Who?' she says.

'Max,' he replies.

'Oh, right,' she says.

'He's got all those children wrapped around his little finger and he's only been here about half an hour.'

'Yes.'

'Have you met him yet?'

'No,' she says, sighing quite unconsciously.

68

'Would you like to?' asks Christopher like he was offering round a particularly good cheddar.

'Yes, please,' says Madeleine, weak with enthusiasm.

'Max!' shouts Christopher. 'Come up here a minute, old chap. There's someone I'd like you to meet.'

He turns and walks up the slope. It is as simple as that.

As Madeleine watches him walk towards her, his bluish-green eyes catching the sun, a wide smile on his face, his hand outstretched ready to shake, the rest of the world appears to fall silent. She can no longer hear the screaming and splashing from the pool, she no longer hears Christopher's voice rattling on in the background. She doesn't notice Valerie appearing at the poolside gate.

'Madeleine, this is Max. Max, Madeleine,' says Christopher, his hot pink hand moving from one to the other.

'Hi,' says Max, shaking Madeleine's hand. 'So where exactly do you fit in around here?' He smiles and sits down next to her, looking towards the pool.

Madeleine is still revelling in the touch of his hand and smell of his skin as he sits so close to her. She feels hot and flustered; the erotic charge that has shot right through her body, awakening its very core, makes her aware of his slightest movement. The way his shoulder brushed hers as he sat down. The way his knee now touches hers as he turns to address his question.

'Now there's a question.' She laughs, embarrassed. She is finding it hard to maintain any sort of cool.

'Those are her two there,' intervenes Christopher, helpfully pointing out Lara and Sophie.

'Two,' says Max, sounding slightly surprised. 'You've got two children.'

'Oh, yes,' continues Christopher, talking across Madeleine. 'Her husband Larry is a helluva bloke.'

'Really,' says Max.

'Oh, yeah, one of the blokes . . . wicked sense of humour.'

'I'll look forward to meeting him.'

'Darling,' says Christopher, suddenly seeing Valerie at the gate. 'There you are; come over here and join us. I was just introducing Madeleine to Max.'

'So I see,' says Valerie, swinging her bikini-clad hips towards them. 'And how are they getting on?' she asks in a slightly patronising tone.

'Famously,' says Max, standing up and running his brown hands through his thick dark hair. 'In fact,' he says, turning to look down at Madeleine still rooted to the spot. 'Um, Madeleine.' Her name curls off his tongue like shaved chocolate. 'Shall we go back down and join the rest of the party? I could really do with a drink. It's suddenly got rather hot up here.' He leans down and offers his hand.

She takes it without question, reply or protest in any way and follows him to the gate.

'Yes, yes, exactly,' agrees Valerie. 'I was coming up to get you all. The food is nearly ready and there's gallons of Pimms to drink. Come along . . . um . . . darling, you've been away from our hosts long enough.'

When the party reaches the other party, walking down the heavily scented rose path, it is obvious that the food is far from ready. The flames from the barbecue are still high and bright and lapping above the grill, the trestle table for the salads is only half laid. Geoff is mixing more Pimms, James is sitting smoking and Madeleine is greeted by the sight of her husband sitting in a deckchair, wearing a pair of washed-out navy swimming trunks. His short white legs are wide open and the string bag containing his balls has slipped out of the left-hand side.

'That bloke over there, with the red hair, is Madeleine's husband,' announces Christopher, putting a matey arm around Max's shoulders and directing him towards the seated ball-bag-displaying Larry.

Madeleine's heart sinks. The reality of her situation is there for her to see, as the long languid Max walks over to meet the short stout Larry. Larry gets out of his chair, and pulls his trunks out of his crotch with his right hand before proffering it to Max.

'Ma-a-ate,' says Larry, shaking vigorously. 'I don't know what you've got but I want some of it, I can tell you. I've never heard such a bloody fuss about some bloke opening up a bloody furniture shop in my life. It is furniture, isn't it?'

'That's right,' says Max, withdrawing his hand.

'Jesus Christ,' laughs Larry, checking out the competition as subtly as a Jack Russell sniffing another's arse. 'You've got half the ladies of the county in a total bloody tizz. I bet trade's been brisk since you opened.' He hoots again. 'You'll be the breaking of all of us.'

'Max, darling, there you are,' calls Liz from across the garden. Her chin lifted so she can see beyond her hat, she is obviously struggling with two large wooden bowls of salad. Max immediately turns away from Larry and jogs gently towards Liz, offering to help carry things to the table.

'Poof,' mutters Larry under his breath.

'Do you think so?' says Christopher, with his usual incisiveness.

'You'd better bloody hope so, mate,' says Larry, stubbing his cigarette out on the lawn and in search of another drink.

'Will you stop it,' hisses Valerie in Madeleine's ear.

'Stop what?'

'Staring.'

'Oh, God, am I?' replies Madeleine, gauchely turning away. 'I didn't realise I was. It's pathetic, isn't it, but he really is divine.'

'Don't I know it,' sighs Val, sitting down in a white plastic chair. 'We've never seen anything like it round here.'

'That's true,' says Madeleine, sitting next to her. 'Even my girls like him.'

'They are female,' laughs Val. 'I have a feeling that it's a given where Max is concerned.'

'Over here, Max, over here,' trills Liz, enjoying her moment of triumph. 'You are just such a wonderful guest, you can come whenever you want. In fact, move in!'

'No, he bloody well can't,' says Geoff, laughing, in a manner that means he is not really joking.

Max ping-pongs his affection around the group until lunch is served. Each female he pays any attention to lights up like Christmas decorations on Oxford Street. Even Angela, who is usually immune to basic emotions, finds it hard to resist his charms. As soon as he sits down one of the children is on his knee. Madeleine suddenly decides the whole thing is rather embarrassing, and elects to take a back seat in the proceedings. She finds sycophancy unattractive at the best of times, but when performed with so much hair flicking and pouting and giggling it is positively revolting.

First Liz runs after him, asking him to help her with little chores. Just as the poor man is about to sit and enter into a conversation with someone, her coy high-pitched calls float across the garden from the kitchen.

'Oooh, Max,' she cries, leaning out of the window. 'Just one more bowl of bits if you can.'

Up he gets again. He seems extremely good-humoured about the whole thing.

'No, really, seriously, Liz, it's fine,' he says. 'I'm from a large family myself and I have five younger sisters. I'm absolutely used to everyone mucking in.'

Except everyone isn't mucking in. It's just Max and his pert arse that are making the journey back and forth from the kitchen. Every time he is back, anywhere near the terrace, it's Val who takes over. Propped up on a beach towel, quietly marinating in sun oil, she beckons him over on the pretext of talking about furniture.

'Christopher is really quite rich, you see,' she says out of earshot. 'And between you and me, he'd very much like to invest in some very expensive furniture.'

Max just smiles and remains fabulously noncommittal.

Meanwhile, Larry is almost horizontal with booze. In fact if Larry downs one more of Geoff's glasses of fizzy pop, he'll be in that chair until way past sunset. James is fussing around the barbecue with Geoff. Together they are cremating the chicken wings in the middle of the grill, while the ones around the outside would take a nuclear holocaust to cook. Candida and her husband, Alan, are late arrivals and have come back from depositing their rather plump, rather spoiled only son, Robert, up by the pool. Built like a walrus in a pair of emerald-green briefs, he refused to go on his own in case it was 'boring', and insisted that both his parents accompany him.

'Shit,' says Candida, coming along the path, a cigarette between her bright pink nails. 'That has to be the worst bit of barbecuing I have ever seen. Max!' she yells, pursing her pink lips and shaking her hard hair. 'Be a love and get a bottle of water next time you're in the house, will you?'

'Darling, I'll go,' says Alan. 'Give the man a break.'

Max sits down, looking politely grateful, while Alan, the size of a National Hunt jockey, trots on into the house eager, as always, to carry out his wife's assignment.

With Candida in control, the lunch looks increasingly promising. To maintain the salon hardness of her hair, she has requisitioned a headscarf from somewhere and, with tongs in one hand, a cigarette in the other, she is issuing orders and sorting out the food. Alan acts as sous-chef, ready with plates and a bottle of water, and hovers at Candida's elbow awaiting her command.

'Shit, shit, okay, Alan,' she says, flapping away some flames that have just discovered a supply of chicken fat. 'Water . . . Water now!'

Alan's there in a flash, splashing fistfuls of water on to the fire.

'Stop!' she says, holding her tongs like a policeman's baton. 'Go!' she commands. 'More now . . . I said now.'

Alan is back with his hands full of water.

After some more sizzling, turning and tweaking, Candida eventually announces that lunch is ready. Geoff seems remarkably relaxed about the revolution at his own lunch party. His own ousting as host has either passed him by, or he was bored enough of barbecuing and his lack of drinking to be positively conspiratorial in his own usurpation. Either way he has jollied up considerably and, with another jug of Pimms in his hand, is doing the rounds. He even feels jovial enough to pop an ice cube into Valerie's navel while she poses – much to the amusement of Larry and James.

'Ma-a-ate,' says Larry. 'Top joke!' He chortles. The joke is apparently funny enough to enable him to rise from his chair and join the queue for food behind Angela, goosing her as he does so.

'Larry Johnson,' she shrieks in return. 'I swear there should be laws against men like you!'

'Let me tell you there are,' replies Madeleine dryly, as she walks away from the table with just a chicken wing and a few leaves on her plate. She has obviously been at the Apesate again.

'You are far too thin to be eating just that,' says Max, gliding up behind her.

She starts slightly as he moves alongside and places another wing on her plate.

'Where are you going to sit?' he asks with a wide white smile. 'And do you mind if I join you?'

'I rather had my eye on the swing seat, over there in the sun,' says Madeleine, not really knowing why she is agreeing to his plan. It is rather against her nature to be so forward.

'The swing seat it is,' he says. 'Would you like me to get you a drink on the way?'

'A Pimms would be great.'

'Then a Pimms you shall have.' He wanders over to the drinks table, and manages to balance carefully the two drinks and his plate, then walks back to the swing seat and sits down. 'So, Madeleine,' he says, as he picks up some chicken thigh and turns to meet her eye. 'How long have you been married?'

The directness and abruptness of his question embarrass her. 'How long have you been in Henley?' she replies, clipping an edge of her wing with her front teeth.

'Not long actually,' he responds. 'About six months.'

Undeterred by her swift side-stepping, Max maintains firm eye contact. He can't help himself. Not exactly unversed in the ways of the world, he doesn't comprehend what interests him about this mother of two. But there is definitely something about her. He likes the way the dappled sun finds so many colours in her hair: red, gold, yellow, and darker stripes of brown. He likes the way her eyes change colour as they move. First they look at him, then they glance down in shyness, frightened to meet him head-on. They are brown, then honey, then right in the middle they have shiny amber stars. He is transfixed. He has always been a lover of beauty and this woman is most certainly beautiful. She commands his total attention. She draws him towards her. The effect is hypnotic. He chews his chicken thigh so slowly it is almost as if he has forgotten he is eating it.

'Six months, you say,' she says, twitching her head slightly, trying to shift his stare. 'What a strange little town to have chosen.'

'I've driven through it a few times before in my childhood,' he says, blinking slowly in the sun. 'And I thought it sleepy-looking enough for someone as financially untogether as me.' He smiles. 'You know, not very much competition.'

'You're certainly right about that,' she says, smiling back. 'There's no competition for the likes of you round here.'

'Really?' he says, raising a dark eyebrow flirtatiously.

'I mean furniture-wise,' she continues, steadfastly refusing to go down that line.

'Well, that's what I was hoping,' he replies.

They sit in silence for a while, neither feeling the need to talk. Candida's loud laugh rolls around the lawn; Angela's acronyms pepper incomprehensible snippets of conversation. Max starts to rock the seat. Slowly at first, he moves it back and forth, simply using the tips of his toes, pushing them against the grass. Madeleine can see his brown feet flexing and relaxing as the seat slowly and almost imperceptibly swings. She can see the long bones, the dark hair on his toes and the whiteness of his nails. She ignores the movement at first, playing with her lettuce with her fork, taking a sip of her drink. Soon the whole of his foot starts to move. She can feel him staring at her, a playful smile on his lips, as he swings the seat with greater force and increasing speed. The breeze as they move through the air starts to ruffle her hair. She takes her feet off the ground so he can go faster. He pushes harder; they fly higher.

'Stop!' she laughs.

'One more,' he says, and, with a final thrust using both his feet, they do one giant swing, which makes Madeleine scream like a child, before they come gently back down again.

Madeleine looks flushed. Max grins.

'Are you always this badly behaved?' says Madeleine.

'Only when I think I can get away with it,' he replies.

'Well, I don't think you have,' whispers Madeleine, pointing out a rather perturbed and proprietorial-looking Geoff sitting on the edge of his chair, his short nose pointing straight at them.

'Careful with that seat,' he warns with a drumstick. 'It's new this year. I had to replace the last one after a group of children did just that to it.'

'Sorry,' shouts Max. 'It won't happen again.' He turns to face Madeleine once more, his back towards the rest of the party. 'Now where were we?' He smiles.

'We were talking about furniture,' says Madeleine.

'Were we really?' replies Max, his mellifluous voice loaded with pathos.

''Fraid so.'

'Oh, okay, furniture it is.' He sighs.

'Can anyone join in, or is this a private conversation?' says Val as she snakes towards the swing seat, a drink in one hand and a cigarette in the other. She makes as if to sit between them.

'Oh, no, sit here,' says Max, shifting along the cushions, right up close so that his thigh touches Madeleine.

'Only if I'm not interrupting,' says Val, sitting down. 'You two are looking very cosy over here.'

'Nonsense,' says Madeleine as breezily as she can. 'We were talking about furniture.'

'Really?' says Val. 'Max knows what a big fan of furniture I am, don't you, Max?'

'You certainly are,' says Max, turning to face Val. 'And you have no idea how much it shocks me.'

'Max, don't be silly,' teases Val. 'I've been to your shop enough times to prove how keen I am.'

'Course,' says Max. 'So tell me, Val, what's your favourite period?'

'My what?'

'Period.'

'Oh, that . . . um, I'd say that the Victorians were rather nice,' she says tentatively.

'I find them a bit ornate and heavy myself,' says Max.

'If a little ornate and heavy like you said,' she continues.

'So your favourite is?'

'D'you know,' she says, putting her hands in the air. 'I love it all.' She laughs. 'Well, all the stuff you have in your shop anyway . . . um have you been there, Madeleine?' she says, changing the subject as quickly as she can.

'Where?'

'To Max's shop.'

'Um, no,' replies Madeleine, wondering how much longer she can cope with the feeling of Max's thigh rubbing against hers.

'She's coming to lunch on Monday to have a look round,' says Max, edging further along the cushions, and placing his hand on her leg.

'I am?' Madeleine's voice has definitely risen an octave.

'She is?'

'Oh, yes, she is,' insists Max. He turns to her. 'You promised.'

'I promised?'

Val looks put out, Max looks pleased and Madeleine is flustered to say the least.

'M-U-U -MMM - MY,' shouts Lara, running from far across the lawn, panic in her voice. 'I think Sophie's trod on a wasp . . .'

Madeleine is up and out of her seat before she had finished the sentence. Guilt is streaming from every pore as she runs towards her daughter.

'Where? Where is she?' she panics.

'Down there.' Lara points at her younger sister lying on the grass, collapsed in a pool of tears.

'Sophie darling, Mummy's here; it's all right, Mummy's here,' says Madeleine over and over again, reassuring herself more than her daughter. 'Where does it hurt? Show Mummy where it hurts.'

Sophie turns to look at her mother, her huge eyes full of self-pitying tears. She thrusts a small foot curled in pain into the air. 'There,' she says.

Madeleine strains to see if there is anything there. She takes the foot gently in her hands and twists it into the sunlight for closer inspection. There, embedded in the soft tissue of the pad of her big toe, Madeleine spies the thinnest and smallest of splinters. Transparent, she only really manages to see it when it catches the sun.

'I don't think that it's a wasp sting, darling,' she says as she pulls the spike out with her fingernails. 'That looks like a nasty old thistle to me.' She kisses the sole of her daughter's foot. 'The nasty old thistle has all gone now.' She smiles. 'Does Sophie feel a lot better?'

Sophie nods and rubs her dimpled hands across her flushed wet face. 'Thank you, Mummy.' She smiles. 'Thank you, I'm lots better now.'

'Is everything all right down here?' comes Max's effortless voice, sounding concerned.

'Oh, my God where did you come from?' says Madeleine. 'How long have you been standing there?'

'I've just arrived.'

'No, you haven't,' says Lara. 'You've been standing watching from over there.'

'I don't think I was.' He smiles, cuffing the back of Lara's head. 'Anyway,' he says, changing the subject, 'how's the patient?'

Sophie's face lights up at all the attention, particularly

from Max. 'I'm much better now, thank you,' she mumbles, turning her head on one side and blinking her wet separated eyelashes. 'Max?'

'Mmm?'

'Can we go swimming?'

'Darling, I don't think Max wants to go swimming, do you, Max?' says Madeleine.

'Oh, I don't know.' He smiles. 'A bit of a dip might cool me off; it's a rather hot and sweaty afternoon.'

'Mummy, will you come?' says Sophie, knowing that she is pushing her luck somewhat.

'I don't think so, darling. You know Mummy doesn't do swimming on occasions like this. She doesn't want to ruin her hair.'

'All right then.' She sighs.

'Why doesn't Mummy forget her hair and come swimming with the rest of us?' asks Max.

'Yeah,' say Sophie and Lara.

'Let Mummy have a think about it,' replies Madeleine, turning to walk back to the party.

'Don't think about it too hard,' says Max, taking both the girls' hands and walking up towards the pool.

Back around the terrace area Val has been wondering what's going on. As soon as Madeleine turns the corner round the magnolia tree, she breaks off her conversation with the sort of enthusiasm never reserved for enquiring about the health of someone else's child.

'So . . . all okay then?' she says, her eyes rapidly scanning the lawn behind Madeleine, looking for Max. 'On your own?' she asks, as casually as she can.

'Yes,' says Madeleine, pulling a deckchair into the sun and collapsing into it with a long languid sigh. 'God, it's hot.' She smiles. 'How long do you think this will last?'

'No idea,' says Val distractedly.

'They say it'll be weeks.' Madeleine stretches in her chair. 'It's quite stifling at night, don't you think?'

'Um,' says Val, becoming increasingly twitchy. 'Max not with you then?'

'No,' replies Madeleine, her eyes half closed.

'Right.' Val nods. Then after a pause she adds, 'Any idea where he might be?'

'Who?'

'Max.'

'Oh, him,' says Madeleine, smiling to herself. 'I think he might be up at the pool.'

'Oh,' says Val. 'Up at the pool . . . what a very good idea. Darling?' she says to Christopher, who is deep in conversation with Geoff, flicking his cigar ash as he talks. 'Darling,' she repeats. He looks up. 'Um, I think I might just pop off up to the pool.' She makes a fingers-walking sign in his general direction and he nods back.

'D'you know I might come and join you,' smiles Madeleine.

'Oh, don't be silly,' says Val. 'Stay down here with the grown-ups. Liz,' she shouts. 'Liz, for Christ's sake look after your guests, will you. Madeleine is so bored she is thinking about having to go swimming.'

'Oh, my God, darling, how ghastly for you, you don't want to do that,' she says, sounding genuinely perturbed underneath her giant hat. Liz has never swum in her own swimming pool in the fifteen years they have had it. She tears herself away from Larry who turns and looks over his shoulder.

'What was all that drama about earlier?' He yawns.

'Oh, Sophie stood on a thistle,' replies Madeleine.

'That all,' says Larry, stretching in his chair to his very fingertips and belching through his back teeth.

'Now, Madeleine,' says Liz, wandering over, finally removing her large floppy accessory. Her shiny dark hair is stuck to her scalp. 'What can I get you?'

'Nothing, actually.' She smiles. 'I'm very happy here, you know. I've having such a lovely day.'

Liz pulls up a pink plastic sunbed and sits down in the middle of it. She lights a cigarette and takes a sip of her Pimms.

'It's been fun, hasn't it,' she says, running her hands through her hair, removing some of its hat shape. 'Isn't Max just divine?' she leans and whispers. Liz is slurring her words slightly so that she sounds like she is saying one long complicated German word. 'I mean, isn't he really amazing?' She smiles, reminiscing on remembered favours and errands performed for her all afternoon. 'I mean, Geoff, even when he was desperate to get me into bed all those years ago, was never that charming. God . . .' She exhales. 'Do you think he's a good screw?'

'Um . . . probably,' replies Madeleine, rather taken aback at Liz's frankness. 'He seems rather good at most other things.'

'Now that's true, that is most certainly true,' says Liz. Her eyes aren't focusing too well and as she holds her finger up in the air to indicate her agreement, it bobs around in a faux, yet tempestuous, breeze. She sighs out loud again. 'Where is he?' She turns her face to look around the garden, an exaggerated frown furrowing her forehead.

'I think he's up at the pool,' says Madeleine. 'He's swimming with the children.'

'Swimming, you say?' says Liz. 'Let's go!'

'I don't think so,' says Madeleine, suddenly sitting up with concern. 'And I don't think you should either.' She smiles. Liz must really like this man, reflects Madeleine, if she is prepared to get into water for him. What has he got that makes even the most grown-up and together of females totally humiliate themselves for a moment in his company?

'Yeah, you're right,' says Liz. 'Anyway, I'm too pissed to

do anything about it.' She laughs. 'But,' she adds, with inebriated seriousness, 'watch this space. I'm telling you, watch this space.'

Almost before she could finish what she is saying, there is a loud screaming and shouting noise as a dripping wet Max comes careering down the hill clutching both Lara and Sophie whose shiny, slippery legs are wrapped tightly around his waist.

'Aaaah . . . Max . . . Max . . . Max,' they squeal together at the top of their voices.

The entire assembly turn round to stare. Candida's pink-lipped mouth forms a perfect circle. Geoff and Christopher stop talking. James and Alan look up from the drinks table. Angela forgets to smoke. Even Larry manages to sit up in his seat.

'Jesus Christ,' he mutters.

Max is in his jeans. They are soaking and sticking to every inch of him as he hares along the rose path. His chest is brown and slim and covered in damp curls. His stomach is flat and toned; you can see all his ribs.

'Beware . . . Greek god approaching,' announces Angela sarcastically as she finally inhales on a cigarette.

Max comes to a stop just by the terrace and slips on the grass with his wet feet and extra load of giggling girls, dissolving into a tangled mess of wet children and jeans.

'Your children are incorrigible,' laughs Max, horizontal on the lawn. 'Can you believe it? They threw me in!'

The girls giggle, Madeleine starts to laugh, as Val also comes running down the path, letting off a more self-conscious yet audible Indian yell.

'Aaaaah,' she cries, waving her arms above her head. She too is dripping wet, her pink bikini is transparent, her nipples and pubic hair clearly visible; her blonde Farrah Fawcett hair hangs limply around her face, her eye liner has run in tracks creating an Ordnance Survey map on her cheeks. 'Oh,' she says, pulling up fast as she reaches the terrace, her breasts taking a whole second to come to a halt. She starts to laugh, a sort of hysterical teenage giggle, before she collapses on to the grass with Max and the children, trying to worm and squirm with the rest of them.

'For Christ's sake, Val, will you behave yourself,' mutters Christopher, standing up, still holding his cigar, his teeth gritted in irritation. 'What the hell do you think you are doing? Running around after some man . . . at your age.' He pauses, almost too outraged to speak. 'I mean these are our friends. Have some respect.'

Everyone else is stunned. No one thinks that the bizarre scenario merits such a public admonishing. Liz actually feels sorry for Val.

'Don't be silly, Christopher,' she says with a laugh, trying to smooth things over. 'It's only a bit of fun.'

'Yes,' agrees Madeleine. 'I think you're overreacting.'

'Madeleine, stay out of things that don't concern you,' he says, politely but very firmly indeed.

'Valerie, will you say goodbye to your hosts, we are leaving. I have a busy day tomorrow and I really don't need this sort of hassle.' He is treating her like a child and she reacts exactly like a child.

Sheepish and contrite, she gathers up her things and, covered in bits of damp grass, follows her partner like a well-behaved five-year-old.

Max does not know where to put himself. He tries to laugh and joke his way out of the situation but Christopher is not prepared to acquiesce.

'Honestly, it is not your fault,' says Christopher finally as they walk towards the house to go. 'See you around, mate.'

As they close the French windows behind them, Liz is the first to react. 'Jesus Christ,' she says, pulling herself up as straight as she can. 'I have never seen such an overreaction in my life.'

'Shit, I mean really?' opines Candida. 'What is that man on? Or what should he be on, more likely?' She laughs.

Larry suddenly gets up and decides that it is time to leave. Wandering around in his swimming trunks, he tries to find the clothes he arrived in. Meanwhile Madeleine starts drying her children, and searching for their sandals and socks which have been deposited all over the garden. By the time she is back at the terrace, Larry is raring to go.

'Come on, everyone, say your goodbyes,' he encourages.

The girls do as they are told. Both of them rush to hug Max.

'See you two soon.' He smiles. 'You must both come by the shop on Monday,' he says breezily to Madeleine and Larry together.

'Yeah, yeah,' says Larry as he turns to leave. Madeleine simply smiles. They walk back through the garden and across Liz's fecund shagpile. 'Sure, mate, absolutely.'

4

Madeleine never makes the Monday meeting with Max. Not that she doesn't want to, because she does. The man intrigues her. And he is devastatingly attractive. Who wouldn't want to walk into his shop and pretend to look at nests of tables? But she is far too nervous. She's a married woman with two children to think of. The idea of rocking the boat is far too frightening. Anyway, the reaction to Valerie's drunken ebullience is enough to put anyone off. It is savage to say the least. Christopher, not normally a witness to his girlfriend's bad behaviour, leaves for Frankfurt the next morning without exchanging a word. And that is only the beginning.

'I mean, all he bloody well kept on saying was we should use this time apart for me to start seriously looking at my own behaviour,' says Val two days later on the telephone. 'Uptight little bastard. Hasn't he ever got a bit tight of an afternoon and showed off?'

'Probably not.' Madeleine laughs.

'Anyway it's not as if he caught us doing it or anything like that,' she snorts. 'The poor bastard doesn't know the half of it. I mean the things I've done in the past and he's all bloody uptight about a see-through bikini and me looking slightly bloody foolish. The arsehole.'

'Is that what he's upset about?' asks Madeleine, really quite curious.

'Oh, yes,' parrots Val, her head wobbling in her irritation.

'That and he's convinced something went on up by the pool.'

'Did it?'

'Are you kidding?' She laughs. 'Not through lack of trying on my part, I hasten to add.' She laughs again. 'That's what is so annoying,' she adds. 'I can do it on the bonnet of a TR7 on the roof of the multi-storey in the centre of Birmingham and he's none the bloody wiser. A bit of horseplay in a mate's pool, which consisted of me trying to push Max in, which I achieved – with the help of your girls – and then jumping in afterwards, and Christopher hits the roof. I have all the flirtatious sophistication of your eight-year-old daughter and he's worried!'

'I know,' says Madeleine, pathetically relieved to find out how little happened. 'Who was it in the multi-storey?'

'God, no one of any interest,' Valerie says dismissively.

'Oh, all right then.'

There was a pause. 'Oh, go on then,' giggles Val, 'Xander Paul.'

'What, the doctor?'

'The very same.'

'But he's one of Christopher's best friends.'

'I know.' Val laughs. 'That's bloody irony for you.'

Irony is far greater than either Val, or Madeleine, realise. For Val, or so it appears, has made a more terrible gaffe than the two friends would believe. Val, with her semi-naked cavortings and well-lubricated tomfoolery, has overstepped the mark. She is right in one way, that you are allowed to be taken any which way you please on the bonnet of a TR7 in a multi-storey in Birmingham of a sunny lunchtime and effectively get away with it. It hurts no one, so Solihull logic goes, and no one need ever find out. Furtive and secret affairs are fine, so long as they remain just that. Flirting is also fine, so long as it remains within the realms of reasonable conversation. What Val did that Sunday afternoon, however, was none of these things. She made a fool of herself and her partner in public. She showed up her host and embarrassed another guest with her sexual enthusiasm. She went too far. Rules are rules, and rules are not meant to be broken. How else can you have people round to dinner when at least two of the couples are sleeping with each other?

Val isn't aware of this yet. Although normally well versed in this game, she is beginning to suspect that she might have lost her cool. In the week after that Sunday, while Christopher is away, her telephone rings remarkably less often. The tennis invitations are fewer. Actually there is none. The girls' lunch invitations also fail to materialise. As do the bridge calls, the requests for shopping trips into Birmingham and Warwick. Even her beauty day with Angela is cancelled. Nevertheless, her male friends still call and flirt on the phone. And in a fit of boredom and pique, she even rings up Xander Paul for a lunchtime quickie in the car park just to amuse herself, and wreak some form of revenge on Christopher.

Although, perhaps, in comparison to everyone else, Christopher has not been that unpleasant. He had not asked her to move out. He had made it clear that she was on borrowed time and that he expected a 'well-behaved live-in girlfriend' when he returned in ten days. But apart from that, he'd been quite magnanimous. In fact when he does get back ten days later, it takes him all of half an hour to forgive her totally. Val is charm itself and he simply can't resist.

The women however are a different story. Val is suddenly no longer seen at Angela's tennis tournament days. It isn't that Angela doesn't want to invite her because she does. Val is SGV – such good value – but it's that some other women will not come if they know she will be there. And Angela really can't tell a lie on the telephone when they ask. She has known Val for years, but she realises that when it comes down to a choice between a well-populated socially successful tournament and Val, there's no competition.

Madeleine has yet to find out who all these women are, because every time she raises Val's name at one of Angela's dos the reaction is the same. 'Oh, we so miss her,' they say. 'Where is she these days?' they add, 'Anyone heard from her?' And Madeleine is the only person willing to admit that she has. Even though she knows that Val has had lunches with Liz and Angela, neither of them says a word about it when her name is mentioned.

'Oh, it'll pass,' says Larry, when Madeleine quizzes him about it one morning. 'It's a female thing,' he adds, shaving very carefully around his moustache.

'But it seems so odd,' says Madeleine. 'One minute she's the social epicentre then the next it's like she has died. I can't understand it.'

'It'll pass,' he repeats.

Larry is right of course. Val goes through nearly four weeks of social ostracism, until almost the end of July, before the phone call comes.

'It was Liz who called,' says Val, all over-excited at her sudden and triumphant rehabilitation. 'She had some nightmare with her Conservative dance thing. The hotel where it was supposed to be has double-booked and Christopher and I have the only house large enough to cope with her two hundred or so guests.' She laughs. 'It's amazing how humble people are when they need something.'

'That's great,' says Madeleine, genuinely pleased.

'And she apologised for the incident,' says Val, sounding victorious. 'She says Max has never forgiven himself.'

That is all she needs to say and Madeleine instantly feels sick. How can the mere mention of someone's name produce such a reaction? She has fantasised about him for weeks now. Handsome Max. Gentle Max. Divine Max. So much so that he has ceased to be the real Max at all. He has mutated into some sort of nebulous concept indicative of longing. Still dark and lean and essentially highly potently male, his face is more blurred and increasingly less defined in her daydreams. The perpetrator of random acts of kindness or swooningly romantic gestures, he has constantly been in or around her thoughts since that Sunday.

At first she found any excuse just to drive past his shop, finding herself vacantly taking the long way round, on the off-chance that she might glimpse him through the plate-glass window. She'd slow down to a crawl, a dangerous ten or fifteen miles an hour, her head straining to peer into Wright Furniture. Just to look at him. She thinks she might have managed to see him once or twice. The sight of his shadowy form was usually enough to make her shiver with delight at the good fortune of her day. She's seen Liz's yellow Stag outside a few times. But she herself would never dare go in. She even found herself wandering up Henley High Street at lunchtime once or twice, hoping that she might bump into him either at the delicatessen buying a sandwich, or popping out for a light lunch with a client in one of the many pubs or the few restaurants in the town. She has sat on the war memorial, sunning her legs, keeping a close eye on the shop door further down the street, hoping that fate might send him across her path just one more time. The window of opportunity she was leaving was surely wide enough for the most unstellar of star-crossed lovers to meet? But he never showed.

Then, in a matter of weeks, frustration commuted to anger. Their lack of chance meeting stewed in her brain and mutated into a personal affront. The fact that Max had not contrived to bump into her was indicative of his superficiality and lack of interest. It was a snub that he too wasn't at the war memorial, sunning his legs, waiting for her to drive by. He was obviously as trite and as shallow as the rest of them. Why wasn't he hanging around, lounging against the door frame of his shop on the off-chance that he might see her pass by? The bond they had had at Liz's party must have been a figment of her imagination. The man was a flirt. You only had to see the way he behaved with Val to work that one out. Like a firefly attracted to the brightest light, Max is only interested in whoever gives him the most attention. That great big ego of his needs massaging all the time, thinks Madeleine as she drives slowly past his shop again on the way to the hairdresser's.

Since that Sunday, Larry has noticed a change in his wife's behaviour towards him. He hasn't pinpointed the precise date of the shift but he has certainly been aware of a difference. She is vague and distant. She has developed a selective deafness which means he has to repeat himself when he's talking to her. She doesn't appear to be able to follow a conversation particularly well any more and is prone to sighing out loud a lot. She has even refused him sex, twice. He puts it down to the new batch of Apesate pills he picked up the other day. She is always a bit odd when she takes those pills and she seems to be on them more and more these days. If Larry weren't so busy he might worry a little more. But he is very busy at work these days. He is very busy with his new big order. He is busy being nice to his boss to try and secure a promotion and he is busy on Tuesday and Friday lunchtimes with his new secretary, who is very compliant indeed. It is just the constant sighing he finds irritating.

'You've gone and bloody done it again,' he moans, tucking his light green frilly dress shirt into his red Y-fronts.

'What?' asks Madeleine, sitting at her dressing-table, back-combing her hair to give a bit of height and lift to her do.

'Bloody sighing,' says Larry, pulling the end of the shirt down each of the legs in his pants. 'All you bloody do these days is sigh. Can't you pretend to be in a good mood? I have spent a small bloody fortune on these tickets for this bloody party, you know.'

'I didn't realise I had done it.'

'Well, put a bloody lid on it, will you?'

They continue to get dressed in silence. The two children, sensing the increasing tension between their parents, are downstairs watching television. They aren't dwelling on it too much, however, because there is a distinct possibility they might be allowed to stay up to watch *Starsky and Hutch* if they are good. So they have eaten all their supper, drunk their milk and brushed their teeth so they can go to bed 'straight afterwards'. They are the picture of innocence, sitting in their brushed-cotton pyjamas, making almost no movement or sound at all, in the vain hope that the babysitter will forget they are there and let them stay up all night.

It was a last-minute decision to go to Liz's Conservative dance. They aren't really Larry's things – Conservative dos – but as soon as he heard his boss was going to be there he rang Liz and just managed to buy one of the last couple of pairs of tickets. Madeleine has been to a few of them in the past, mainly out of loyalty and to help Liz. But Larry complained so bitterly about the last experience – old birds with blue rinses stinging him for cash at every opportunity – she didn't dare suggest it this time round.

'I am not going to get pissed tonight and blow a hundred quid on the bloody tombola like I did last time,' announces Larry, pulling up his trousers and trying to squeeze a cummerbund around his expanded waistline. 'Why the hell these things have to be black tie in this bloody heat, I don't know.' His voice is strained as he holds in his stomach and pulls the piece of bottle-green velvet around his girth. 'Has this thing

93

bloody shrunk at the dry-cleaner's again?' he barks. 'I told you to take it to the specialist place in Birmingham and not that shit-hole in Henley,' he continues. 'You never bloody listen. How many times do I have to advise you on the basic running of this bloody house?' He pulls at the fabric again, wheezing his breath in. 'That's unwearable now,' he says, throwing the cummerbund on to the bed and stomping back to his cupboards. 'Too bloody hot anyway.'

Madeleine is not really listening; she is much more interested in trying to attach the blonde hairpiece she bought yesterday in Stratford. A thick plait the same width all the way down and exactly the same colour as her hair, the effect – if the thing would stay in – is stunning. Dressed in a floor-length sky-blue silk jersey dress, low at the back with a twisted knot at the front and a slit up the side, she looks great, even if she does think so herself. The blonde plait swings around her buttocks and she completes the outfit with a long gold chain that is tight around the neck, like a choker, and then hangs to her hips. Larry puts on his green velvet jacket. It is highly inappropriate for a July evening, but his other black jacket is even smaller and utterly unwearable.

By 8 p.m. the traffic around Five Chimneys in Hockley Heath is backed up right past the deep-freezer centre and beyond. There is some sort of steward, sporting an extravagant-looking bright blue rosette, standing at the left-hand turn just after the pub. Occasionally, rather officiously, he stops the through traffic to let the party traffic cross. Christopher Rangers' house is not in the centre of Hockley but about a mile and half outside. Effectively in the middle of nowhere, he has built what could be described as a modern stately home. In keeping with the mock-Tudor style of a lot of the houses in the area, he has simply taken the standard black and white gable-styled five-bedroom hacienda template and more or less tripled it. Surrounded by a high ginger red-brick wall, which rises in points, decorated with large concrete spheres, Five Chimneys is an imposing place. The original gravel drive has recently been replaced by tarmac, after Christopher found the former too high-maintenance with all his work commitments, and the two large balls on the pillars at the front are now rampaging lions from a garden centre near Redditch.

'You can drop the lady off at the front if you want, sir,' says some buck-toothed teenager with a downy moustache through Larry's opened car window. 'But all parking is in the field area to the right, if you'd like to carry on.'

'The queue for the house is way too long,' announces Larry. 'I think we'll go straight to parking.'

'Very good, sir,' says the youth. 'Down there and to the right; if you'd like to follow the Rover in front of you.'

'Larry,' says Madeleine, 'I've got my Kurt Geiger silver sandals on. Would you mind?'

'Jesus Christ,' snaps Larry, his face a dark shade of pink. His pale green frilly shirt is striped with sweat in dark bands across his stomach. 'Bloody get out here and walk then if you want, and I'll meet you in there.'

Much to Larry's surprise she doesn't sit there like she normally would, in a meek and non-combative way, waiting for him to park the car and then accompany her into the party. For both of them know that Madeleine finds it very difficult to walk into a large party on her own. Instead, she is out of the car before she has even had time to think about it. She spins around, slamming the door behind her, forcing her plait to make a whole tour of her body before swinging against her hip and then coming to rest down her spine.

The buck-toothed youth can't believe it. She smiles while he stands more slack-jawed than usual, watching her march into the party, the red bronze of the evening sun warming her shoulders.

Not until she is inside the large marquee that smells of damp grass does she realise quite how pleased she is with herself. Larry's sniping succeeds in undermining her confidence so much that she sometimes forgets she is capable of making her own decisions. She helps herself to a glass of not very chilled sparkling wine and looks around the party at some one hundred to one hundred and fifty revellers. She can see Liz in an enormous baby-pink ball dress that looks like a lampshade. Flitting from group to group doing her hostess bit, she is constantly hoicking it up at the front. It really does nothing for her large loose breasts and upper arms the consistency of cottage cheese. Angela is wearing black. Or at least Madeleine thinks she is. But the woman is so thin that she keeps losing her in the throng. Val, tanned and blonde in a yellow sheath dress with a triangle front, looks sensational and knows it. Far from the discreet re-emergence of Val that everyone was hoping for, she is milking the moment for all it's worth.

Madeleine smiles as she watches the male reaction to Val. Some puce old boy to her right can't quite believe the vision of yellow before him and slowly pours his drink on to his own shoe, until his wife digs him in the ribs to bring him round. But it is not until Val has wafted by that Madeleine realises it's not Val or Angela or Liz for whom she is scanning the crowd. It's Max.

He must be here, she thinks, taking another sip of sparkling wine. It is one of the biggest social gatherings of the year, so surely he would come? Maybe he votes Labour? But then so do half the people here. It's just that the Tories give much better parties. She can't imagine that Liz has not invited him. Perhaps he can't stand their little social gatherings. Coming from Oxfordshire he might be more sophisticated and find their parties bourgeois. The Val thing hasn't affected his social fluidity; she knows that for sure because Liz keeps showing off about having him round for dinner every time they see each other. So where is he? Madeleine scans the marquee again. The terrible thing about black tie is that it makes all the men look the same. Well, almost, she thinks, looking at the range of flash jackets on show. Red brocade, golden with black collars, a couple of guests have even turned up in white jackets, making it difficult to distinguish them from the waiters. Still she can't find him. Then she thinks she's seen him and snakes her way through the crowd, wearing an expectant smile, only to have to continue on to the other side of the marquee when she realises her mistake.

'Jesus Christ, there you are,' huffs Larry as he finally finds his wife. 'I've been looking all over for you. No one knew where you were.' He stands looking over her shoulder and absent-mindedly helps himself to the glass of wine in her hands and drains it. 'Phew!' he says, taking a handkerchief out of his pocket and patting it across his sodden forehead. 'That's better. What a walk!' he continues, picking up another glass from a passing waiter. Madeleine does the same. 'Where did you run off to then?' he asks. 'I even ask that wanker Max where you were but he had no idea.'

'He's here?' asks Madeleine, coughing into her drink. The bubbles go up her nose. Her eyes water.

'Yeah,' says Larry, patting his pockets for his cigarettes. 'Got a very sexy bird in tow as well.'

'Who?'

'I don't know,' he says. 'Never clapped eyes on her before in my life, but she's certainly worth a squirt or two I'd say.' He laughs, thwacking Madeleine on the buttocks.

She smiles stiffly, the energy slowly seeping out of her like a punctured party balloon. The shine slips from her eyes and her shoulders round slightly. The glimmer and sheen of the evening have disappeared. As she stares vacantly over Larry's green velvet shoulder, everyone's laugh seems more laboured, everyone's dress less attractive; even the sparkling wine tastes nothing like champagne. The string quartet that had earlier made the party sound slightly decadent and delicious are now off-key and playing Elgar. What could have been a romantic, ardent evening has become another one of those parties you just manage to get through on the correct balance of alcohol and nicotine. Madeleine lights up another cigarette.

'I know, let's go and buy some of those raffle tickets you're so fond of,' she says, wanting to move from her depressing spot, where inertia has pinned her to the floor.

'What, already?' says Larry.

'I think it's best,' she replies. 'Strike while we can, before they run out of all the lucky numbers.'

'Tell you what,' says Larry. 'Why don't you piss off over there with this wad of cash and treat yourself to some tickets, there's a good girl.' He snakes around his tight trousers, moving his hips left and right, making room for his puffy hands in his constricted pockets. Pulling out a wodge of notes, his licks his thumb and begins to count like a market trader. 'Here,' he says. 'Twenty-five quid. I'll be in the pay bar area if you need me.'

Ordinarily, Madeleine would find Larry's rude and patronising behaviour upsetting, but she is relieved at his departure. Incapable of banal conversation, she wants to be left alone to drink too much and wallow in her disappointment. She picks up another passing flute of sparkling wine and lights another cigarette and starts to wander through the throng.

'. . . and then I said to him how much?' laughs a woman with a family of chins. Madeleine carries on through. 'Brenda, have you met Dennis and I'm very sorry I can't remember your wife's name,' guffaws a pink walrus in a red bow tie. 'Of course! How lovely!' agrees a thin brown woman like a stick of vanilla. '. . . anyway as I was saying . . .' Madeleine stops and drops her cigarette on the floor matting, spinning it out with her sandal '. . . and they're supposed to be lovers . . .'

She looks around to see if she can spot anyone she knows. Val, with her bronzed shoulder and yellow scooped dress, is about two groups away. Madeleine downs her drink and starts to weave her way over there.

'Oh, hi, darling,' she says, exhaling her cigarette smoke in Madeleine's face and then frantically flapping it away. 'I've been wondering where you were.' She kisses Madeleine's earlobes and squeezes one shoulder. 'Great, isn't it?' She grins.

'What?' says Madeleine.

'My party, you fool, my party.' She can't stop smiling and nodding at people who walk past doing the same. 'Hi,' she says, with a hand jangle of a wave. 'Thanks,' she adds, with one of those 'Who? Little me!' shrugs.

'He's here, isn't he?' says Madeleine in a loud stage whisper in Val's ear.

'Who?' she says, still smiling and waving.

'Max.'

'Yes, he's here.'

'With some gorgeous woman.'

'She is rather, isn't she . . .'

Val isn't concentrating on her friend or the conversation. Nearly four weeks in social Siberia is enough to make anyone desperate to enjoy the warm glow of social encounter. But Val is positively bathing in its heat. The party of the year is taking place in her house, and she can't flick her long blonde hair enough for all the attention she is getting. Even Christopher walks past occasionally planting possessive moist kisses on her shoulder, like a terrier marking its own driveway. Liz and Val are also such good friends tonight, exchanging, little waves, knowing nods and the odd anxious hostess glance in the direction of the catering tent. Madeleine is on her own tonight and she feels it.

Madeleine leaves Val to her own marvellousness and, picking up another glass of sparkling wine, looks around for somewhere to sit down. She finds an empty white plastic table near the canvas corridor to catering and slumps down. The fizzy wine is making her feel slightly unwell, but she carries on drinking it all the same. In fact she concludes she couldn't have chosen a better spot, for rather than having to move for booze the alcohol comes to her. She is the first to get it as it comes out of the tent. This tickles her slightly and she laughs to herself as she places a cigarette in her mouth and looks around on the table trying to see where she put her lighter.

'Finally! We have found you,' comes the unmistakable voice of Max.

Madeleine looks up. He is as attractive as she remembers him. The same handsome brown face, straight nose, with a curling smile and those pale eyes. His long dark hair is clean and shiny and has obviously been washed for the occasion. He is dressed in an old-fashioned, slightly too loose, black tie ensemble probably from the 1920s or 1930s that even from where Madeleine is sitting smells of naphthalene and must surely have belonged to his grandfather.

'Well, you have found me,' she says, lowering her head, trying to coax her lighter into life with her suddenly shaking hands.

'God.' He sighs. 'We've been looking everywhere for you.' He laughs, sitting down next to her. 'Let me do that,' he says, getting out his square petrol-powered lighter. 'I've been boring the arse off Heather all evening saying that you must be here somewhere, haven't I, Heb?'

'Heb?' says Madeleine, looking up to see this tall, lean, glamorous, blue-eyed redhead standing in front of her in a simple but classic black evening dress.

'Yes. Isn't she lovely? She is number one.'

'I am . . . number one.' She smiles apologetically, shrugging her shoulders.

'I bet you are.' Madeleine smiles, flicking her ash, and draining the rest of her glass. 'Everyone's bloody number one,' she mutters.

'I thought it was about time I introduced at least one of my sisters to the group.' Max smiles, running his hands through his hair. 'Otherwise you'd all think that I was lying about having any at all. And what better way to start than with the eldest.'

'That's me-e-e.' Heather giggles as she pats her breasts with both hands.

'That's yo-u-u,' says Madeleine, laughing with relief as a giant knot of tension unravels and leaves her body, making her feel quite weak. 'Ooh,' she continues, catching her breath and suddenly feeling rather drunk. 'It's nice to see you.'

'It's nice to see you,' says Max, moving his chair in closer.

'So you're Madeleine,' says Heather, also sitting down slowly. 'Max has mentioned you.'

'He has?'

'Yes.' She smiles.

'Oh.' Madeleine can't manage much more.

'Are you all right?' asks Max, sounding concerned.

'Fine,' bluffs Madeleine.

'I think you might need to go outside,' he suggests.

'I might?' she replies.

'Heb,' he says. 'Go and grab us a glass of water. I think this young lady needs some air.'

'Young lady,' says Madeleine, snatching at Max's shoulder, finding it tricky to stand. 'Young lady . . . I am a mother of two, you know.'

'And they are a lovely two,' he says, threading his arm around her waist.

Madeleine is determined to do this on her own. She pushes

his hand away so that his grip around her is not so strong and, with her jaw in the air, she heads for an opening in the marquee. Her steps are unsteady like a foal just about getting it together to walk. Although determinedly direct in her route, she occasionally trots off at an angle that fortunately Max is there to rectify. She has a beauty-queen smile fixed on her face, and looks as if she'd like to 'travel, horseback ride and help handicapped children'. She nods a couple of rigid 'hellos' as she goes, taking care not to move her head around too much. The excitement of making it through the crowd and out of the tent makes her relax enough to tumble over slightly on her left ankle.

'Jesus Christ,' she says, as Max catches her under the armpits. 'How the hell did I get this drunk? I wasn't even trying. Well, maybe just a bit. It does that, doesn't it . . . alcohol?' she says, trying to turn to face Max, who has her in a vice-like grip from behind. 'It takes you unawares . . . very . . . very . . . unawares.'

Madeleine isn't an unattractive drunk. There are some women who should patently never touch alcohol. It makes them strident and aggressive and puff up as if they've been sitting on a bicycle pump all afternoon. Candida is like that. With her hard hair and hard manner, she would have castrated her husband long ago, after half a bottle of whisky and a couple of brandy chasers, if the ramifications weren't so inconvenient. But Madeleine is not like that. Madeleine is rather sweet. Or at least Max thinks so as he steers her towards the trunk of a rather mature-looking elm. She is floppy, and slightly giggly. Her large round eyes are even larger and rounder, and all sophistication has fallen from her face. He props her up against the tree and makes to sit down next to her. But as he eases himself down on to the grass, she slides down the side of the tree.

'Oh, my God,' she sniggers. 'I'm falling down the tree.' She grins moronically as she slides. Just before she hits the grass she manages to get her hands out in front of her to break the fall. This seems to bring her to her senses somewhat. 'I am sorry, Max,' she says, stumbling over her words. 'I was fine until you came along, quietly sitting in my corner. I mean I'm sure I've only had about five or six glasses of that wine stuff . . . but you know I don't . . . I don't really drink that much normally . . . not normally.' She seems to find this a very interesting fact and furrows her brow as she lies in the odd cat-like position on the grass.

'Um,' suggests Max. 'Have you actually eaten anything today?'

'Course I haven't.' Madeleine laughs. 'Max, darling, you should know by now that women round here don't eat.'

'That would explain it,' he says, kneeling forward, taking her by the shoulders and propping her up against the tree once more. She starts to slip down the side of it again. 'This is useless,' he says, standing up and placing himself between the tree and Madeleine so she is sitting between his legs, her head resting on his chest. His arms are around her shoulders. His thighs run alongside hers. Her soft blonde hair is tickling his face, as is the strange blonde plait thing she is wearing. If he leans forward, he can feel the skin at the nape of her neck against his cheek. It smells of the sun. He inhales and exhales. He can feel his heart beating faster. He is in heaven.

'There you are,' says Heather. 'I've been looking for you for about half an hour.'

'Half an hour?' says Max, surprised.

He did not realise he'd been there that long. He had not moved or said a word. Madeleine had been making inconsequential chatter, none of which he'd been listening to. He'd just sat there, quietly, and very still, frightened that if he had drawn attention to himself she might have moved and disturbed his silent ecstasy.

'Anyway,' continues Heather. 'Here's the water you wanted and some bread to help soak up the booze.'

'Oh, hello,' pipes up Madeleine, thrusting her hand out as her eyes come into focus. 'Have we met?'

'Er, yes,' says Heather. 'Um, Max,' she whispers. 'Does her husband know she's out here?'

Max shakes his head.

'Shouldn't I go and tell him?'

'My name's Madeleine—'

'Yes, I know, we've met,' says Heather. 'I just think he might be a bit worried and you, young man, you should be careful.'

'Do you have to tell him yet?' says Max. 'Couldn't you give me ten more minutes before you tell him?'

'Five.'

'Seven.'

'All right then, seven.'

As Heather leaves, with nothing more to focus on, Madeleine lies back into Max's arms. She lets out a long and relaxed sigh, eats her bread and drinks her water.

'You're just lovely,' she says afterwards, her face snaking up his chest towards his shoulder. 'Really, really nice; and really, really lovely.'

Max knows that it is not the done thing to take advantage of drunk girls. He has five younger sisters whom he would deck any man to protect. But this woman has been on his mind. In fact he can't get her out of his mind. Everywhere he goes, everything he does, every time he stops to think, pause for a second from what he's doing, it's her face he sees, her laugh he hears, and her skin he smells. Ever since he met her that Sunday, all he's been doing is working. He hasn't been able to concentrate, but at least when he is seriously

104

working for a couple of minutes it stops him from thinking about her.

He can't resist. She is finally here in his arms. What else can he do? He tries to stop himself. She is someone else's wife. But he can't. Maybe she won't remember it in the morning if he kisses her now, while no one is around to see it. It won't matter; it is only a kiss after all.

He takes hold of her chin and pulls her towards him. Madeleine seems to understand what he is after and twists to face him. He slowly lifts her chin and brings her face alongside his. He traces the line of her cheek with his lips, bit by bit, as he moves closer and closer towards her mouth. They are both breathing heavily. Her mouth opens. They inhale each other as they finally kiss. It is better than Max ever imagined. He feels light-headed and aroused and slightly out of control. She tastes delicious, her lips are soft, her mouth divine, he can hardly stop himself.

Madeleine draws away first. Her lips are still parted and her eyes are closed. She slowly opens them to stare at Max.

'Oh . . . my . . . God,' she whispers very slowly. 'That was amazing. I have never been kissed sober before. I feel wonderful. You . . . are wonderful.'

Madeleine's whole body is tingling. It feels alive for the first time in about ten years. She feels so turned on she doesn't know what to do with herself, or where to put herself. She exhales from what sounds like the very depths of her soul. 'My God,' she says. 'I think I'm in love.' Standing up, she smooths down her dress and, running her hands through her hair, leans against the tree, her body like a rag doll.

'Madeleine, is that you out there?' Larry's voice cuts through the balmy night air like someone has just opened an industrial freezer. 'I've just been told you're pissed and puking or something to that effect.'

'No, no, I said, not very well,' corrects Heather, running along behind. 'Madeleine, I promise I said not very well.'

'That you there, Max?' says Larry. 'Thanks very much, mate, for looking after her. Total pain in the arse, women, can't hold their bloody drink. Anyway, Madeleine, are you feeling better?'

'Fine,' says Madeleine, inhaling and shaking her hair.

'She really wasn't that unwell,' insists Max.

'Yeah, right.' Larry nods, giving Max a conspiratorial slap on the back. 'Not that unwell. Don't worry, mate, I'll take over puke duty from now on.'

'No, but really,' says Max. 'She isn't that drunk.'

'Thanks anyway,' says Larry.

'It was a pleasure,' says Max with a smile, bowing slightly before he walks into the darkness with his sister.

'Totally underestimated that bloke Max, you know,' mutters Larry, taking Madeleine by the arm. 'Great bloke . . . great bloke. Anyway,' he adds, 'you all right? Or are you going to let yourself down again?'

'I feel wonderful.' She smiles. 'Shall we go back to the party?'

Madeleine walks unsteadily beside her husband across the uneven ground, but with tension and adrenaline restored to her body she is a lot more sober than she was ten minutes ago. In fact a few more glasses of water and a load more cigarettes and she will soon be on a par with the rest of the party. Except that she will not be. She is floating a rather elegant ten to twelve feet above them all, not engaged by any of the conversations she is having. She is laughing freely at jokes she hasn't really heard, smiling blissfully at people she has only met a couple of times, and generally exuding a confident contentment and glowing radiance that she has never done before.

'Your wife is on form, mate,' says Geoff, pulling up his

trousers and breast-feeding on a cigar. 'What have you done to her?'

'I haven't done anything,' replies Larry, cradling a glass of whisky from the pay bar. 'She's done it to herself, mate. Pissed as a fart, she spent most of the first part of the evening outside getting air, she was that far gone.'

'Really?' says Geoff, sucking away. 'You should get her pissed more often. It makes her very sexy.'

'Do you think so?' says Larry, staring at his wife. 'Worth a squirt I suppose.'

Madeleine is sharing a joke with Liz and Val, all three of them laughing about something the men haven't heard. Angela arrives to join the group.

'Have you seen the GC, gorgeous creature, with Max?' she announces, raising a conspiratorial eyebrow.

'It's his sister,' all three women say together.

'Ooh, Madeleine Johnson, since when have you cared who Max Wright has on his arm?' replies Angela, looking Madeleine in the eye, inhaling on a cigarette.

'I don't,' she says rather too quickly. 'It's just that he introduced her earlier and I know how you do so love to be kept in the picture.' She smiles through her rambling. 'Doesn't do to spread untrue gossip now, does it?'

Angela smiles. 'QRD, quite right, darling,' she says. 'If it really is untrue, that is.'

At that point someone announces that the buffet is now open and there is a masculine stampede for boeuf bourguignon with rice and bread rolls. Most of the women stand back and smoke and wait for the jazz band to strike up, which they do at about 11.30 p.m.

Over in a small marquee on their own with a special wooden floor, the jazz band is a six-piece ensemble dressed in low-slung dinner jackets surrounded by banks of lights. Red and green, they flash in time to the music. At the apex of the tent there is a rotating mirror ball that Val had insisted on after reading an article about Studio 54 in New York. At the first note emanating from the jazz tent, groups of women start to wander over. They stand at the edge of the parquet square, shimmying their shoulders in the hope that some man will ask them to dance. Some of the younger members of the party had been hoping for some disco music, but the committee had plumped for jazz as their 'please-all' toe-tapping option. And they were right, for after half an hour the dance floor is almost full.

Madeleine dances with James, who flicks his flyaway hair and stiffly corkscrews both his legs on the spot in the hope that he looks a bit like Elvis. She dances with Geoff, who grabs the opportunity to push his penis up against her thigh and then rubs his short nose against her cheek as much as possible. She then dances with Larry, who half-heartedly jumps up and down on the spot flapping his hands like a toddler desperate to pee. As she snakes and sways in her figure-hugging dress, she can feel Max watching her, but doesn't dare catch his eye. Angela is not the only one who has eyes in the back of her head. But as Larry approaches his first coronary and the end of his first dance, it is he who sees Max.

'Ma-a-te.' He waves and beckons him over. 'Do me a favour. You look like a good mover to me.' He smiles as he looks Max up and down. 'Give her a run for her money, will you. I'm desperate for a drink and want to go to the tombola draw.'

'If you insist,' says Max. 'I'd be delighted.'

'I do bloody insist,' he says. 'Get on with it,' he adds, walking off the dance floor, mopping his forehead with his handkerchief.

Astonishingly, and a rare event, Larry's observation proves to be correct. Max is indeed 'a good mover'. He holds Madeleine by the waist and whisks her round the dance floor in such a flash, well-choreographed manner it is almost embarrassing. She doesn't care, of course; but every other woman in the room does, as they do their damnedest to dance with their overweight husbands who move with all the elegance of hippos in jam. As she comes out of a particularly dramatic spin, she meets Val who has been running through the crowd trying to find her.

'You've won, you've won, you've won,' she repeats in a flap. Her voice grinds to a halt when she sees whom Madeleine is dancing with. 'You've won,' she states.

'Won what?' says Madeleine, slightly breathless.

'Um, the raffle,' says Val, staring at Max.

'What have we won?' says Madeleine.

'I don't know,' says Val with a sudden haughtiness. 'You better go and ask your husband.'

It is 2 a.m. and Madeleine sits back in the car, her face towards the open window, letting the warm night air blow through her hair. What an amazing evening. The dancing, the talking, the winning . . . the kiss. Her eyes half closed, a smile on her lips, she thinks about the kiss, his kiss . . . his face, his lips, his skin, the way he smells right up close . . .

'Did you have a nice evening?' says Larry, trying to engage his rather distant wife.

'Yes,' she replies, still staring out of the window. 'One of the happiest of my life.'

'Really?' says Larry, sounding surprised.

'Yes.' She smiles. 'It was fantastic.'

'Why?' he asks, really rather bemused.

'Um,' she says, turning to face him, trying hard to think. 'Well,' she smiles. 'I've never won anything before.'

'What, that bloody revolting Teasmade thing?' He shakes his head. 'I'll never understand the opposite sex,' he snorts. 'Bloody mystery to me.'

5

It takes Max nine days to get Madeleine into bed. It's the longest it's ever taken him to sleep with anyone and there are times when he finds it rather frustrating. Like all extremely handsome and charming men, Max is used to getting what he wants.

Brought up in a family of five girls, he is not only the sole son but he is also by far and away the cleverest. The pride and joy of his parents, Alice and Alexander Wright, he is showered with all the attention at family occasions; fêted at Christmas, his birthday is the only date starred on the large calendar in the kitchen. When he passed Oxbridge and won a scholarship to Trinity College Oxford to read Classics his parents could not have been more thrilled. They threw a drinks party to celebrate in their large Cotswold manor house just outside Moreton-in-Marsh and invited all their friends. The five younger sisters handed round Ritz biscuits, while Max languished at the epicentre of the party, receiving compliments and fending off passes from middle-aged women.

At Oxford Max did start to rebel. But with the family money coming from tea – a company they had long since sold, but tea none the less – everyone thought it marvellous and highly appropriate that Max study a bit of Sanskrit on the side. The long hair and the flowered shirts were just something that everyone was doing in his year in the late sixties at Oxford. The pot smoking and the experimentation with LSD were not things that Max shared with his parents. So they were only too delighted to finance his trip to India and his six months on an ashram in Rishikesh. Six months became nearly three years and he came back quite a different person. There were many in the county, including Patricia's parents, who thought that he would never come back. So his idiosyncrasies, his glazed eyes and the strong aroma of strange tobacco that emanated from his room were all tolerated with pleasant middle-class smiles and total denial.

Eventually Max got bored of getting stoned in his old bedroom in Oxfordshire and decided to move up to London where he shared a house with a mate from university just off the King's Road. It belonged to his mate's parents who lived abroad. Max tried and failed his Foreign Office exams. They knew as soon as he walked in smelling of a hangover and sweating old drugs that he was not suitable material for the Diplomatic Corps, no matter how well connected his father. So Max's dad pulled a few other strings and managed to find his disappointing son an entrée into Christie's. He worked there for seven years lugging around furniture and learning a lot about antiques. Still living just off the King's Road with Adam from Balliol, he danced, took drugs and got laid at weekends, while maintaining some sort of work ethic during the week. It was all going well, until Adam decided to get married and Max had to leave.

It was panic that brought Max to Henley-in-Arden. At thirty-two he was rapidly about to become the oldest swinger in town. He had a notion to buy a shop and set up on his own, but not in Oxfordshire, which would simply be too embarrassing. He had saved some money but not nearly enough to buy anywhere chichi in London. So Henley-in-Arden was one of his increasingly few options. Close enough for a bit of family support when it came to guiding rich and influential friends towards his shop, but not too close. It was also an affluent area, full of rich people with no taste. Max's plan was simple and about the same length as one of Stalin's. He wanted to pile his furniture high, ship it out and make enough money to start up somewhere off Bond Street, or perhaps if he weren't so lucky somewhere like Kensington Church Street or the top of the Portobello Road. Returning to London at thirty-seven, he'd pick up a wife and that would be it.

At first it went well. All these women with their sports cars and husbands' credit cards kept turning up. All it took was a bit of constructive flirting before they left with a nest of tables, or some cabinet thing and then a week later they came back. With lower necklines and more gold dripping off their wrists and fingers, they stayed a little longer in the shop and spent a little more. There were two in particular who were quite insistent, Liz and Valerie. But Max knows how to work women like that. It is all water off a duck's back to him. He has been dealing with that sort of strident female attention since about the age of seventeen or eighteen. He has it down to a fine art. Flicking the hair, laughing at their jokes, maintaining eye contact, occasionally glancing at their lips like they are ripe cherries that he wants to taste. It works like a dream.

Liz and Valerie were very lucrative customers. Liz even invited him to Sunday lunch. It was the perfect way to meet the husbands and persuade them to part with more money. Women usually only ever buy the smaller things in his shop; male support is required to shift the larger pieces. It was a barbecue. A great networking opportunity. He might also meet a few more people, put his feelers out. He'd been in the area six months, he was settled, he had his supply routes organised and what he really needed was to expand his client base. The lunch invitation could not have come at a more opportune moment. It was just Madeleine Johnson he had not banked on.

Madeleine was exactly what Max did not need, and he knew

it. He tried his best to avoid her, to have nothing to do with her. He tried not to see her and put her out of his mind. That Sunday put a terrible spanner in his works but he recovered. After the Conservative dance, however, it became apparent to him that there was no turning back.

Max thinks that sex with Madeleine is a mere formality. He gets the feeling from nearly every other woman in the area that extra-marital intercourse is more or less freely available. Fidelity, or so it seems, is not something highly prized in Solihull. But he is wrong. Madeleine doesn't come to the shop the next Monday as he expects. He waits all day on tenterhooks. Whenever the doorbell rings in the shop he makes a mad dash to the front, a faux relaxed smile on his face, expecting her to be wearing the same. But she never shows. Plenty of other women he'd spoken to that night do. Their large dark glasses perch nonchalantly on the back of their heads as they come in to finish off conversations they started the Saturday before. They breeze in as if they were old friends. But Madeleine does not come.

Tuesday is the same. The same tension, the same keen sweeping out of the back of the shop, the same casual smile. But still she stays away. So on the third day Max goes looking for her.

Meanwhile Madeleine has no idea what to do. She is sure that Larry suspects something is going on, because on the Sunday after the dance, he is particularly attentive. Instead of his usual monosyllabic day spent in the company of newspapers, he suggests that they all go out to lunch and then punting on the Avon. Larry never normally makes suggestions of any kind. Larry never has ideas. It is Madeleine's job to organise things, and Larry's to complain. Even his own daughters are surprised and ask what is the occasion. 'If I can't enjoy my own family once in a while what sort of bloke am I?' he replies. So they keep quiet and in the end they all rather enjoy themselves. Ham rolls in the pub garden, a splash around on the river: they all agree it is a lovely day out.

So on the Monday, Madeleine is racked with guilt. It takes over her whole being and eats away at her soul. She feels sick, can't look her children in the eye and is sharp and bad-tempered with their questions. She blames it on slimming pills even though she hasn't taken one. Tuesday and the feeling is unbearable. The longing to see Max, just to pass him by in the street, catch a glimpse of his smile, makes her short of breath. Never one to understand what they mean in cheap romances about young ladies who swoon, Madeleine suddenly feels genuinely unwell and has to take to her bed. On Wednesday she finds any excuse to drive into Henley.

They have just parked outside the bakery when Sophie sees him.

'Mummy, Mummy, it's Max,' she says, running up the street towards him. He stands in the bright morning sunshine in the same black T-shirt and blue jeans that he'd been wearing when they first met. He is smiling, his arms outstretched waiting for Sophie to run into them. Madeleine just stands watching and holds the car door for support. He picks up Sophie; her red sundress bunches up almost around her waist, and walks towards her.

'Aren't you going to say hello?' says Lara, looking at her mother with a puzzled expression.

'Um, yes, of course,' says Madeleine, running her hands nervously through her hair, looking down at the pavement.

'Hello,' he says as he approaches the car. 'I saw you drive past and ran up the street to meet you. Um . . .' Max's lack of cool manages to embarrass even himself and he blushes as he puts Sophie down on the ground. 'Um . . .' he repeats, holding his head with both hands. He had planned so many times what he was going to say when he next saw her and now it has all gone clean out of his head. 'Um, anyway,' he says finally. 'I think we need to talk.'

'Talk,' repeats Madeleine. She has not moved from behind the car. She has come to Henley to see him but has not really thought about what she was going to do after that. 'Talk,' she says again. 'Of course.' She is coming slightly more to her senses. 'I know,' she says. 'Lara, can you prove what a big girl you are and take Sophie to the ice cream shop and buy some ice creams and meet Mummy back at Max's shop at the end of the road?' Lara looks thrilled at such a request, for not only is there ice cream involved, she gets to boss her little sister around and walk through town on her own. 'Do you see where Max's shop is?' says Madeleine.

'I know where it is,' replies Lara, with an affected jadedness beyond her eight years. 'It's simple – down there and on the right.'

'Here's a whole pound note,' says Madeleine, 'and don't be long.'

'Oh, my God, I've missed you,' says Max across the car as soon as they have gone.

'I've missed you too,' whispers Madeleine, taking herself by surprise.

They walk down the street together about a foot apart. It is almost as if either of them were to touch the other they would not be responsible for their actions.

As soon as the shop door slams Max has Madeleine up against the wall. He kisses her neck, her cheeks, her face. His hands go up and down her back, her hips, her arse, her thighs. He pulls her shirt off, taking a button with it, and, cupping her breasts, he buries his face between them. His urgency surprises and shocks her for a second. She leans against the wall unable to move. In only moments, however, she is kissing him back and tearing at his T-shirt, running her hands up his arms and under the sleeves. He starts to move her away from the wall, walking her backwards towards his office, pulling her skirt up with one hand as he tries to unbuckle his trousers with the other.

'What are you doing?' she mumbles, her mouth against his cheek.

'I don't think I can wait any longer,' he says, steering her through the door.

'Wait any longer for what?' she says, stopping his hand on her thigh.

'To make love to you of course,' he says, sounding surprised.

Madeleine immediately pulls away. Closing up her shirt and smoothing down her skirt and her hair, she looks at him, her eyes shining with lust, her mouth pink. 'Max.' She sighs. 'I don't think I can. I'm married, and my children are about to walk in any minute. I'm just not ready for all this yet.'

'Of course,' he says. 'I was moving way too fast,' he continues, buckling up his belt. 'I don't know what I was thinking. I'm sorry, I'm sorry,' he says. 'You're right, of course you're right. It's just that you've been driving me insane and to be honest I'm finding it quite hard to cope. I really am. Can I see you again?' he says, sounding slightly panicked like he might have totally blown the whole thing. 'Can we do lunch or something civilised . . . anything . . . Christ, please say yes.'

As he stands with his hands limply by his sides, his hair dishevelled, his trousers half undone, his T-shirt hanging out, he looks so worried and vulnerable that Madeleine would have had him there and then if her children weren't about to arrive.

'Of course we can.' She smiles.

His relief is instant and obvious. 'Thank God for that.' He laughs.

'I think we should put our clothes back on before my children arrive,' she says.

'Yes, right, of course,' he replies.

It is the same story when she returns on Friday. Snatched gropes in the office while her children are sent off to buy and eat ice creams. Max can't believe how quickly they walk the length of the High Street and eat an ice cream. It seems to him that they have some teleport and Hoover technique that brings them through the front door just when Madeleine might possibly be weakening.

Max finds the whole process so sexually frustrating that he almost contemplates ringing up one of the furniture-philes from the Conservative dance for some foxy fun and games but actually – and this makes him even more livid – all he wants is Madeleine.

Madeleine decides that Monday will be the day she'll have sex with Max. Liz has got her tennis coach back and has offered to have Lara and Sophie round for a day of swimming and tennis with Chantal and Christian. It is the only way she can think of keeping her difficult children entertained in the hot weather. She did invite Madeleine to stay for lunch and lie by the pool drinking wine, but Madeleine said she had things to do.

So it's all planned and Madeleine thinks about nothing else over the weekend. In fact, she is quite light-headed and giggly at the prospect. She keeps running the fantasy scenario over and over in her head, imagining what he will do to her, where his tongue will go, what he will say, what the initial deep thrust of penetration will be like. She lies in the sun, on her green plastic sunbed, occasionally rubbing herself with oil and dreams about it all weekend. For some reason the guilt has gone. The children love Max. She smiles as she lies there, a whole future mapping itself before the present is even secure. He loves them back, she laughs.

'What?' says Larry. 'What are you laughing at now?'

Larry is particularly irritable all weekend. He wakes up on Saturday with a cracking hangover and has not really been able to shift it. No matter how many big fizzy pills he pops into pints of water his head still feels like a dried-up walnut and his tongue like a cotton-wool trampoline. And the heat isn't helping. It is an airless heat. A heat that you cannot escape, even if you sit inside with curtains closed, which Larry does. There is not a breath of air, no breeze to disturb the atmosphere; it is like being smothered in a thick, heavy blanket. Madeleine seems to be able to deal with it. In fact she is revelling in it. While Larry sits inside, the curtains drawn, watching cricket with the sound down, she lies outside basking and browning herself, occasionally stretching herself out like one of Liz's Persian cats. The children aren't enjoying themselves too much either. Shuttling backwards and forwards between their parents, the small blue plastic paddling pool in the garden isn't large or deep enough to keep them cool. They get short-tempered and fight over a Pippa doll. Madeleine cannot be bothered to intervene.

Finally Monday comes and Madeleine is up at the same time as Larry, which he finds surprising. She explains she has a lot to do today but then spends the whole morning in a rather agitated state waiting until midday when she can drop off the children. Turning round in Liz's gravel drive, she insists she has no time for coffee, and very nearly forgets the children's tennis racquets in the boot of the car, such is her haste to leave. Liz is too wrapped up in her tennis coach flirtation to remark on the strangeness of Madeleine's behaviour, but her children are unusually quiet and Sophie hardly eats anything for lunch.

Madeleine drives at speed to Henley-in-Arden. The car windows are down and the radio up loud. She feels young again and extremely over-excited, the adrenaline coursing through her veins like she's overdosed on Apesate. Her mouth is dry and her hands are sweating. She is nervous. She parks the car a bit further up the street away from the shop just in case anyone drives past and recognises it. As she walks towards Wright Furniture, she realises how nervous she is. Unsteady on her feet, she has to pause for breath by a tree to try and steady herself. She hasn't told Max that she was coming. She hasn't told him of her plan. What if he isn't there? Closed for the day? What if he's gone on a furniture-buying trip and won't be back until tomorrow? What if he's changed his mind about sex?

The shop door says 'Open'. He is there and the look of delight on his face as she walks in tells her he hasn't changed his mind.

'Madeleine,' he says with large smile, as the bell announces her arrival. 'I'll be with you in a minute. I just have the customer to deal with.' He motions with his head towards a woman *d'un certain âge* who walks out from behind a bookcase dressed in something floaty and comfortable that she hopes hides the width of her hips. 'Why don't you wait in the office and I'll have the paperwork ready for you in a minute.'

'Oh, well, if you are busy,' says the woman, her mouth puckering unpleasantly, 'I can come back later?'

'No, no,' replies Max. 'You take your time.'

So she does. For another ten minutes, Madeleine paces around in the office, mulling her decision over and over in her head, contemplating leaving with her marriage vows still intact, while Max tries to sell a secretaire. Eventually he appears in the doorway, his cheeks a little flushed with excitement. He smiles.

'She's gone,' he says, walking towards Madeleine.

'Have you shut the shop?' asks Madeleine, slightly panicking about practicalities.

'I've closed it,' says Max.

'You'd better lock up,' says Madeleine with a playful smile. 'You've got me all afternoon.'

'All afternoon,' he repeats, standing in front of her, tracing the line of her collarbone with his index finger. 'All afternoon,' he mumbles. 'Well, we had better make it count then, hadn't we?'

And he does. Such is the build-up of tension between them over the last week or so, that Max makes love to Madeleine eight or nine times that afternoon. Once on the stairs before they even make it to the bedroom, twice in his bed; they even try to have some late lunch, but get distracted by the kitchen table. Madeleine has never experienced sex like it. She has only had sex once before Larry and that had been a fruitless, pleasureless grope in the back of some army officer's car after a dance in Norfolk when she was eighteen and didn't really know what she, or even he, were doing. Other than that it has simply been a series of half-hearted penetrations by her drunk or uninterested husband.

But Max is incredible. The way he loves her body. The way he plays with it, and strokes and licks it. The way he brings her to the point of orgasm and then keeps her there before finally letting her come is something she hasn't even read about in *Cosmopolitan*. She wants to have sex with Max all the time. She wants to have sex with Max all day, every day. She finally understands what all the fuss is about: the reason for those giggly boasting conversations between Valerie and Liz that she has never been able to join in; those surveys that Angela's tennis ladies read out loud over a couple of glasses of wine. She has laughed with the rest of them for fear of being shown up, but now she can hold her own. She sighs and relaxes back against Max's chest.

'What?' he says.

'What?' she replies.

'What was that for?'

'What?'

'I heard you sigh. What were you thinking?'

'Oh, God,' she says. 'So many things . . . but mainly how happy I am.'

Max is too. Madeleine is unlike all the liberated Scandinavian girls he slept with on the ashram. She is also a totally different type of lay from the pot-head birds he'd had in London. She is much more inhibited and shy but, the more he sleeps with her that afternoon, the more amazing she gets. It is as if there were some great untapped passion in her soul that is desperate to be released. And he enjoys that feeling of power.

They spend the whole afternoon together in Max's flat, tucked away in the eaves above the shop. Surprisingly empty, it bears the stamp of someone who isn't planning to stay long. There are two rooms and a bathroom above the shop and an office and kitchen on the ground floor, all connected by a narrow staircase with a rather scratchy threadbare carpet with which Madeleine is already intimate. His bedroom contains a large, dark wood double bed, with an intricately carved base, plus some sort of bedside table and chair. A sitting room is next door. A short two-seater sofa is stuffed along one wall, with a small black and white television in the corner opposite. Some ethnic rugs obviously picked up in India lie on the floorboards, and an old school trunk covered with a printed fabric serves as a table. For someone who knows and likes furniture Max has remarkably little of it.

So they lie naked on the bed together all afternoon. It is so hot neither of them ventures under the sheets. They talk and doze and make love until about four or five o'clock. Max tells her about India, about his time in London, about his family and friends. He misses out many of the women, the drugs and his general impecuniousness; instead he ups the culture and the philosophy and the great adventure of it all. Madeleine is impressed. In fact she is more than impressed – she is in love.

People notice immediately. Not that she is in love, of course, because that requires a certain amount of perception, but that she is looking well. In fact everyone keeps remarking on how well Madeleine is looking to such an extent that it becomes embarrassing. She tries to hide it. She wears less make-up and her old clothes. But still the comments keep on coming. Even Larry notices.

'You're looking very well, these days,' he remarks one morning as Madeleine was humming, making breakfast.

'It's the weather,' she replies. 'You know how much I like the heat and the sun; they bring out the best in everyone.'

'Not in the bloody drivers stuck in a traffic jam on the way to work they don't,' he mutters, spreading some marmalade on his toast.

It is eight days since Madeleine first spent the afternoon with Max. She has only managed to see him on two other occasions. On Thursday when Candida took a whole group of kids to the cinema for fat Robert's birthday, and Saturday when Larry took his girls into Stratford for some new shoes. The second time she only just made it home with about five minutes to spare. But Max is all she can think about. Like some addict in need of a fix, her plans to meet him are becoming more elaborate and more complex.

It's Tuesday and ladies tennis day at Angela's. During the school holidays Angela normally puts on some sort of lunch for the children who are left to run loose in her expansive garden, while their mothers try and beat each other at tennis.

'So what time are you turning up today?' says the rehabilitated Val on the telephone.

'Um, I don't know exactly,' says Madeleine, sounding uncharacteristically evasive.

'What do you mean you don't know?' says Val, sounding puzzled. 'You are coming, aren't you, because I was rather hoping you'd be my partner.'

'Course I am,' breezes Madeleine. 'I've just got to . . .'

'To what?'

'Um . . . got to go to a gynaecologist's at around lunchtime for an hour or so,' she says. It's the best excuse she can come up with at such short notice.

'Can't you change it?'

'Um, no.'

'Don't be ridiculous,' insists Val. 'Ring them up and tell them you are playing tennis and ask them to reschedule later in the week . . . actually better still, have mine; he's a total sweetheart and will fit you in at any time.'

'I can't,' says Madeleine quickly.

'It's not urgent, is it?' asks Val, sounding worried.

'It could be,' says Madeleine, crossing her fingers and curling her toes as she lies herself into a corner.

'Well, in that case . . .'

By the time Madeleine arrives at Angela's, the whole tournament group seems to know about her appointment. Val has been there all of ten minutes before her and has obviously shared her problem with everyone. Quite what they think is wrong with her, Madeleine has no idea. But by the looks she is getting they all presume it to be quite serious. Pregnancy, the clap, whatever it is she is obviously in need of urgent assistance to have to leave during one of Angela's lunches.

Madeleine is beginning to wish that she had never gone down this route. Why had she chosen such a lousy excuse? Why couldn't she have come up with something less controversial like her car needed servicing? Or she had to collect her mother from the train station or something infinitely more innocuous. Eventually she decides to bite the bullet and be done with it.

'Angela,' she says, lighting a B&H so she doesn't have to look anyone in the eye. 'So sorry about later on today.' She inhales. 'But it's one of those annual check-up things with my gynaecologist, and I've cancelled twice already. I don't know what I was thinking when I said yes to a Tuesday lunchtime.' she laughs. It sounds hollow to her but no one else seems to notice. 'Everyone knows that we nearly always play tennis on a Tuesday.'

'Oh, don't be silly,' says Angela, bouncing a ball on her crazy-paved path. 'FBM, fine by me, darling, fine by me. It's that we'll miss you for the lunch, that's all.'

'Can I leave the children here while I go?' asks Madeleine, as nonchalantly as she can.

'Course,' says Angela. 'Don't be ridiculous.'

As the atmosphere around Madeleine dissipates, everything appears to get back to normal. Angela picks teams as usual. Liz for once is not partnered with Madeleine and is handed on to Candida instead.

'Shit. Right, Liz,' commands Candida, pulling her large white pants out of her large white arse. 'What we are going to do today is concentrate.'

'Concentrate,' nods Liz, looking down at her wrists. 'Do you think I should play in all this jewellery, or not?'

Candida exhales loudly and takes Liz up to the other end of the court. Angela and Patricia are already at the near end vigorously serving Apesate-fuelled balls into the net. Among the various groups of children hanging around some are reading books, riding bikes or sitting in the shade waiting for their turn at the net as ball boys or girls, for money of course. Angela has promised them a pound each, just so long as they do it diligently and without complaining.

While the four battle it out on court, Madeleine and Val sit on the bench smoking cigarettes and chatting.

'So how have you been?' asks Val, flicking her ash on the grass. 'I haven't spoken to you for ages.'

'What, about three days?' laughs Madeleine.

'Yeah, precisely.' She smiles. 'Ages. So?'

'So?'

'So what have you been doing, who have you been talking to when you haven't been talking to me?'

'Oh, God.' Madeleine shifts in her seat. 'You know – this and that. It's school holidays and I have very little time to myself as per usual. It's the same old story.'

'Like what?'

'You know, trying to fill up the days as interestingly as possible before they go back to school.'

'Have you seen anything of Max?' she asks.

'God, no!' says Madeleine, overcompensating. 'God, him!' She laughs. 'Why?'

'Oh, no reason really,' says Val, flicking her ash again. 'Only you were very pally on the dance floor the other day.'

'Oh, God that.' Madeleine smiles, her shoulders relaxing. 'That was all Larry's fault. He made Max dance with me because he wanted to do the tombola. He's tombola-obsessed, Larry; it's almost the only reason he goes to those Conservative dos.'

'Right,' says Val. 'He's a good dancer.'

'Who?'

'Max.'

'Oh, my God, isn't he just?' Madeleine enthuses. 'He's amazing. I have never danced with anyone like that. He really is good. I mean—'

'He's not that good,' Val says with a laugh.

'No, no, you're right,' says Madeleine, pushing her hair behind her ears and looking at the floor. 'Um . . . so, have you seen him?'

'No,' says Val.

'Oh.'

'Well, yes,' she adds.

'You have?' Madeleine spins around in her seat to face her friend.

'Well, no, but I have tried to,' says Val. 'It's very odd. I've only been a couple of times and he's been closed.'

'Really?' says Madeleine, glancing sideways.

'Last Monday afternoon,' says Val. 'Very weird, because I'm sure I've bought stuff there on a Monday before. And when I drove past this Monday afternoon he was open.'

'Oh.'

'Anyway . . .'

'Anyway.' Madeleine smiles. 'How have you been?'

'Oh, God, so-o-o exciting,' she starts.

Ever since the incident at Liz's lunch and Val's subsequent ostracism, she and Christopher have been getting on ever so well. Apparently, or so it transpires, Christopher can be unpleasant to his girlfriend, but when everyone else is he comes over all protective. Val actually squeals out loud at this point in her story. So by way of a show of support he has bought her this fabulous new Mercedes convertible and given her another of his credit cards. He is apparently doing rather well financially at the moment and Val admits to being happy with him. She has decided to calm down on the rich man-hunting front and make do with what she has, for the time being.

127

'Give it a few months and we'll see,' she says, stubbing her cigarette out on the lawn.

'So have you stopped seeing Xander Paul?' Madeleine grins, with a conspiratorial look.

'I still get pills from him,' she replies nonchalantly.

'No-o-o,' smiles Madeleine. 'You know what I mean.'

'No, I have no idea what you mean,' she replies, her face totally blank.

They sit in silence and watch the tennis. They both smoke and stare straight ahead. When people in a relationship that is built on sharing secrets, stop sharing secrets, there is often very little else to say. As they sit, not saying anything, Val somehow manages to exude an air of detached superiority and makes Madeleine feel so uncomfortable that she makes an excuse of going to the loo to escape.

She has this awful feeling that Val knows she is lying. But she is not ready to share her affair. For that is what she is having with Max, an affair. She is not ready to share it with anyone. She doesn't really know what she is doing herself, risking everything for a man she hardly knows. She looks at her watch: it is 12.20. In ten minutes she is allowed to go.

'Are you all right?' comes a concerned-sounding voice, complete with Stepford smiling tones. 'You look a little tense.'

Anne is sitting so neatly on the grass in her smart tennis dress that Madeleine doesn't notice her as she paces the small patch of lawn to the left of the tennis court.

'Oh, my God,' she says, caught by surprise. 'Um.' She laughs. 'I am a little tense, yes. I have an appointment at lunch and they always upset me,' she lies again.

'Oh, I heard,' smiles Anne, full of empathy. 'I'm the same.'

Madeleine can't bear it any more. She can't take the sympathy. The concerned smiles. The keep-your-chin-up-girl sort of sisterhood that is suddenly emanating from the tennis group. She is about to go and sleep with a man who is not her husband, while they look after her children. Not one of nature's liars, Madeleine keeps thinking that they can all see she is not telling the truth.

'D'you know,' she says as breezily as she can to Anne, 'I think I might go early to . . . you know, get the whole thing over and done with.' She smiles. 'I'll just slip off now. I don't really want to make a fuss, upset the children.'

Anne smiles. 'Absolutely,' she says. As Madeleine turns to walk away, 'Good luck,' she adds. Madeleine breaks into a run.

Max can't understand what she is on about when she walks through the door. 'Stop being so paranoid,' he says, taking her in his arms as he closes up the shop. 'No one knows anything,' he mumbles. 'No one suspects anything. Come to bed.' He smiles, his forehead leaning against hers. 'The only thing they do think is that I have mighty strange opening hours.' He laughs.

Madeleine does not. 'That's been remarked upon already,' she says. 'I'm sure Val knows.'

'How can she possibly know?' sighs Max, turning to lead Madeleine up the stairs. 'How could she possibly know anything?'

'Oh, I don't know,' she says. 'You can't keep secrets round here for long.'

Madeleine feels morose, depressed and weighed down by deceit and lies. She had no idea how many people she'd have to involve in her dishonesty when she started down this adulterous path. So far today she has lied to Val, Angela, Candida, Patricia, Liz, the whole of the ladies tennis set, Lara, Sophie and Anne. Oh, God, Anne. Anne even felt sorry for her. Anne had wished her 'Good luck' as she went off, leaving her children, for lunchtime sex with a furniture-shop owner in Henley-in-Arden.

But Madeleine can't help herself. She really can't. It's an illness, an affliction, a terrible disease, she concludes, as she climbs the stairs. She is in love and there is nothing she can do about it. It would stand up in a court of law. On the grounds of diminished responsibility, her responsibility is definitely diminishing. But she loves Max. The way he smiles at her when she walks into the shop. The way he smells when he takes her in his arms. The way his mouth tastes when he kisses her. The way he makes love to her over and over again in the hot heat of the afternoon. The way his hair sits flat on the side of his head when he wakes up after sex. She loves the whole thing. She loves it all.

Max appears to be just as obsessed. He has reached the stage where he barely dares leave the shop just in case she might turn up. He sits around all day putting off trips to the post office and the shops for fear her might miss her. The rest of the time he is listlessly selling furniture to mature married women, with whom he is finding it increasingly difficult to flirt. Even as recently as a couple of weeks ago he would have been able to muster a hair flick, a wink, a wide white smile, a rakish raising of an eyebrow, but since Madeleine it all seems a bit hollow. Not – and he is the first person to admit this – that it was terribly profound before, but now he can't even manage the eyebrow thing without feeling a total fraud. He is sure that his income is suffering, quite apart from his spontaneous closing policy, because his heart isn't in it. Selling anything, he has always maintained, is like bringing in a fish, teasing it from the bank, toying with it, letting it run and then finally bringing it in with your big strong rod. But Max's big strong rod is otherwise occupied and his fish are getting away.

★   ★   ★

Madeleine risks staying another half an hour and it's quarter to three by the time she makes it back to the tennis. Val is furious as she has had to partner Anne in Madeleine's absence and stomps around, exhaling cigarette smoke like a teenager. Everyone else, however, is horribly sympathetic. There are weak smiles from Anne. Nods from Angela. And a couple of 'How ghastly to be kept waiting so long's from Liz. Plus a 'Shit, I hope he warmed up the bloody silver thing,' from Candida. And inevitably a 'Mummy, where have you been all afternoon?' from her children.

'I never knew there was a gynaecologist in Henley,' pipes up curly blonde-haired Barbara, from the bench.

'There isn't,' says Madeleine, looking the other way.

'Oh,' says Barbara. 'That's odd. I could have sworn I saw your car there at lunchtime today when I went to pick up a prescription.'

'No-o-o?' says Madeleine, feeling her cheeks redden and her hands start to sweat. 'You must be mistaken.'

'No,' corrects Barbara. 'Well, it looked very like yours. It was parked outside the bakery. It was still there when I left. I was half expecting you to bring us all a load of doughnuts for tea.'

'It's a popular car,' laughs Madeleine.

'It had the same sticker on it like yours and everything.' She smiles. 'Isn't that strange?'

'Bizarre,' laughs Madeleine again.

'I'm not being funny but that is quite odd, isn't it?' Barbara says, trying to continue her discussion.

Barbara is not gifted enough in the brains department to be malicious. She is quite genuinely fascinated by Madeleine's vehicular doppelgänger, and muses about it for the rest of the afternoon. 'The sticker and everything,' she mutters every so often. And Madeleine digs her nails deeper and deeper into the palm of her hand.

★   ★   ★

But Madeleine does not learn from the apparent closeness of this shave, and a few days later she is so starved of Max that she sees no other option than to invite him round. Everything tells her that this is not a sensible idea. But who is going to find out? Their driveway is sufficiently hidden that anyone driving past would have to strain their neck seriously while avoiding a sharp corner and a swiftly oncoming tree to be able to see that he was there. And, anyway, the children adore him. They would love him to come to lunch and she would simply say that she'd bought a bedside table for their bedroom and that Max was kind enough to deliver it in person.

So he does. Max arrives for lunch at the Johnson household, bedside table in tow, and Madeleine cooks for him as she does for her husband. She and the two girls sit on the terrace under the green and white striped umbrella eating ham and salad and potatoes covered in mayonnaise. It's another hot sunny day and Lara and Sophie show off, running and jumping into their paddling pool. Max applauds and laughs and holds their mother's hand and caresses her thigh underneath the white plastic table.

They open a bottle of wine and begin to relax. Children don't notice such things, Madeleine tells herself as she and Max lie back together on the large checked picnic rug on the lawn. She leans against him as he plays with her hair. They drink some more wine. As she laughs and smokes her cigarettes and throws her head back, he steals kisses at the nape of her neck. The children say they are tired of their pool, and the sun, and want to go inside. They want to watch television. *Blue Peter* will be on soon and they both like that. Madeleine thinks this is a marvellous idea and pops them on the sofa with pints of milk. She and Max are going to go upstairs to discuss where they should put the new bedside table. The children listen to their mother giggle all the way up the stairs, and they sit and watch television as the rest of the house goes quiet.

They have nearly finished making the desktop penholder out of an empty bottle of washing-up liquid and double-sided sticky tape for speed when Madeleine and Max finally come down. Madeleine seems distracted and her eyes are sleepy. She stands in the doorway to the sitting room, smoothing down her hair.

'Where are you going to put it?' says Lara, swinging her legs on the sofa.

'What's that, darling?'

'The bedside table, where are you going to put it?'

'Oh, right, that,' says Madeleine, barely able to disguise her ambivalence. 'Max, darling, where are we going to put it?'

'Oh, that,' says Max, poking his head around the door. 'Hi, kids,' he says with a grin.

Neither of them replies.

'I think it's in your kids' room, isn't it, Madeleine?'

'That's right,' she replies. 'Come on, you two,' she says, appearing slightly more together. 'Say goodbye to Uncle Max, he's leaving now.'

They mumble something from the sofa without turning their heads from the screen.

Madeleine laughs. '*Blue Peter*.' She shrugs. 'It's their favourite programme.'

Max smiles. 'Bye, then, girls. I'll see you later.'

As they turn to leave the room, there's the sound of a car on gravel and then a door slamming.

'Daddy!' say both girls together, leaping off the sofa.

'Larry!' says Madeleine at exactly the same pitch as her daughters. Her eyes widen, she grins. 'Back home early for the first time in ten years.'

Max is rooted to the spot. He has no idea what to do.

He has in the past made it his business to stay clear of other men's wives, finding it too complicated a combination. This is not a situation he has been in before. The girls run past him.

Madeleine springs in to action. 'Look,' she hisses. 'The bed is made upstairs. As far as he need know, you've been delivering furniture.'

Max nods.

'Larry, darling,' she says, as Larry comes through the open front door. 'You know Max?'

Larry stops dead in his tracks as soon as he sees Max, like he's just encountered a brick wall.

'Ma-a-ate,' he says slowly. 'Haven't seen you in a while. What are you doing here?'

'Ma-a-te,' says Max, walking forward ready to shake Larry's hand. 'I've just dropped off a bedside table for your kids' bedroom.'

'You have?' Larry looks puzzled. 'I wasn't aware we'd bought one?'

'It was supposed to be a surprise.' Madeleine smiles.

'Who for?' says Larry.

'Um, you.'

'Well, you sure as hell got me there.' He laughs, pushing past Max, getting inside his own hall.

'I'll be off now,' smiles Max, in as boy-bonding a manner as he can muster, shooting Larry with his right index finger and clicking his teeth as he goes.

'Yup, see you,' mumbles Larry, walking into his kitchen and slowly putting down his briefcase. 'So how long has he been here?' he says lightly, his small eyes darting round the room trying to glean as much information as he can before the scene is disturbed.

'Oh, not very long,' lies Madeleine.

'Oh?'

'Just got here,' she lies again, moving to stand between Larry and the pile of washing up.

'Oh, that's okay then,' smiles Larry. Lying right back.

6

Larry is no fool and it suddenly dawns on him what is going on. All the signs are there, he thinks, why hadn't he noticed before? It would take someone truly mentally deficient not to realise that they had been made a cuckold, he berates himself. When you catch a man leaving your house in the middle of the afternoon and there's the high sweet smell of sex in your bedroom when you go upstairs to change, there are no other conclusions to draw. But there are other signs, he thinks: Madeleine's distance, her mood swings, her hysterical good humour, her sudden flowering. Good Lord, Larry has slept with enough married women himself to see what it does to them. Strangely, the only one who didn't flower was Liz. But then again, she is in a permanent state of infidelity so it is no wonder no one ever notices.

If Larry has finally noticed what has happened to his wife, it is surely only a matter of time before the rest of the county finds out? As he drives to work the morning after the night before, so to speak, he considers his options.

He had played it cool last night for numerous reasons. The first was shock. The idea that Madeleine, reliable, meek Madeleine, would be unfaithful to him disorientated him to such an extent it was like someone had rapidly removed the shagpile from under his feet. He had mulled that one over with a gin and tonic at the bottom of the garden. But during his coronation chicken supper he had moved on to stage two. Having, somewhat reluctantly, come to terms with what was going on, he wasn't going to limit his options by acknowledging the affair just yet. So he carried on with a normal evening, eating his food, drinking his wine, watching the *Nine O'Clock News*, keeping the conversation as banal as possible, scrutinising Madeleine for any reaction or any twinges of guilt.

The longer he left it before he confronted her, the more avenues were open to him. There is always the possibility that, like most of the affairs in the area, the various cuckold partners remain atrophied by their lack of emotion and everything carries on as before. Some go through a genteel period of separation before the rehabilitation process, and others have in the past organised a whole-hearted swapping of wives and husbands for the comfort and convenience of both parties involved. But Larry isn't sure how far the whole thing has gone. One lusty grope in the marital bed? Regular afternoon sex? The occasional screw? Who knows?

Driving up the Hagley Road, he concludes he'll play his cards close to his chest and see what happens. Why rock the boat if it doesn't need to be rocked? After all, he has his secretary on Tuesdays and Fridays, and he's been through various women in the county to little ill effect. Madeleine has always been none the wiser and his marriage is swimming along just fine. Maybe he can pretend and do the same? Allow her the occasional dalliance and turn a blind eye?

But Madeleine's dalliance turns out to be more than occasional. Under the misguided impression that she got away with her home visit from Max, she asks him round again and, while her children have lunch downstairs she entertains above them. Max and Madeleine both feel terrible about it, they discuss it, but they decide that their need is too great and children don't really notice such things.

★   ★   ★

Madeleine doesn't go to Tuesday tennis any more. Well, she does, merely to drop off her children. But she always has some very pressing appointment that she can't cancel. No one is fooled. Her car has been spotted too many times in Henley for anyone to think otherwise. One only has to mention Max's name and witness Madeleine's faux indifference and uncomfortable body language to understand exactly what is going on. Not that any of them cares particularly, or so they say. Anne is slightly shocked but she has been living in the area long enough not to dwell on it too much. It's just the inconvenience of it they find irritating. Dumping her children left and right, lying to everyone. It's just so inconsiderate, they all agree. The fact that Max is the only handsome man in the county has got nothing to do with it.

'I mean, really,' said Val one Tuesday between puffs. 'You would think that she's the only person in the world to have discovered sex, the way she's round there all the time. Nearly every time I drive through town I see her car there, parked outside the post office or something. Like no one is going to notice it. Who is she fooling?'

'I know,' replied Angela, rolling her eyes. 'Who the hell is she fooling? I don't know why she doesn't just park it outside the shop and be done with it. The amount of times it's nearly there anyway is ridiculous.'

They are both lying of course. Max tends to go to Madeleine a bit more these days and she is very aware of people seeing her car in town so she tries to park it quite subtly. But Val is annoyed that Madeleine hasn't confided in her and Angela is irritated by anyone else having sex when she patently is not. If you listened to the two of them you'd think that Madeleine was at the shop every day of the week, which of course she is not. But that's how the rumours start. Val exaggerates to Angela. Angela embellishes to Liz. Liz relishes telling Geoff, and Geoff jokes with Larry.

Larry's position is now increasingly impossible. He really has no idea what to do. He has heard from numerous sources that his wife is playing around and that she is not being subtle about it. 'Flaunting it,' he's heard. 'All over him,' someone said. 'Quite a goer apparently,' someone else let slip. He is getting pitying looks at parties, hearty slaps on the back at golf, and the conversation lulls when he goes in to the Bull of a Saturday lunchtime. And these are people who don't even know what his children are called, yet they all seem to know his business. Either that, he thinks, as he speedily downs his pint, or he has become paranoid. But there is only so much of this a man can take. His wife has changed from a little miss prim 'n' proper perfect into a madame yo-yo pants almost overnight and he can't cope.

She never likes it much when he's around but with that Max bloke she can't seem to get enough. He drinks another pint. It's strange, he thinks as he leans on the bar; how come he can sleep with Liz for nearly two years on and off and no one really seems to mind? But when his wife starts tarting around with some furniture salesman the whole county is interested?

By the time Larry arrives home from the pub, he has lost count of how many drinks he has had. But it's obvious as soon as he walks into the house that he's had a skinful. Anger and alcohol have worked their alchemy and his normally pink face is fuchsia. His skin is sleazy with sweat and his gestures are large and out of control. As he leans against the doorway to the kitchen, his stance is threatening, and the atmosphere menacing.

Turning around from her washing up, Madeleine is frightened. Her stomach is tight, her legs are shaking; she instinctively knows that the moment she has been pushing for has arrived. In the last ten days or so, consciously or unconsciously, she has been taking greater and greater risks. Not being there when he gets back from work, not bothering to have a story about how she has filled her day, daring Larry to react, dangling Max in front of his eyes, compelling him to bring this suffocating situation to some sort of conclusion.

'This,' he says, his eyes scarlet with fury, every pore on his nose open with frustration. 'This,' he repeats slowly and deliberately, 'has got to stop.'

'What has?' says Madeleine, trying to buy some time, not quite knowing what to do with the situation that she has so actively been seeking.

'You know what the fuck I'm talking about,' he whispers, spheres of spittle firing out of his mouth. 'The whole county thinks you are a whore, my family is a laughing-stock and my children can't even look their own mother in the eye.'

His venom is formidable. Madeleine clutches her orange Formica unit for support. Her knuckles are white.

'Well, I can't stop,' she says, shaking her head in defiance. 'I love him.'

'Love him?' Larry snorts. His whole body shakes so violently he looks as though he has been electrocuted. 'Don't . . . make . . . me . . . fucking . . . laugh.' He laughs. 'I love him,' he imitates. 'He's the first bloke who has ever given you more than the time of day and you're so fucking desperate for a bit of attention that you leap into bed with him at the drop of a fucking hat. He must be pissing himself. Having a good old laugh down the pub with the rest of them. Little Miss Ice Queen is a loose old tart the same as the rest of them. He can't believe his fucking luck. I love him,' he parrots again. 'God, don't tell me that he loves you too because then I might just have to crap myself, it's so funny . . .'

'Stop it, stop it,' shouts Madeleine, covering her ears. 'He does love me, he does love me, he's told me so.'

'Jesus fucking Christ.' Larry is now really enjoying himself. 'You didn't fall for that load of old tosh did you? Oh dear, oh dear, oh dear.' He shakes his head. 'When will you learn, Madeleine? Any man will say anything to get a bird into bed and saying I love you is the oldest fucking trick in the book. I should know,' he adds exuberantly. 'I wrote the fucking manual!'

Madeleine feels like she has been kicked in the stomach. Her legs are weak. She feels faint. Time and time again Larry does this in arguments. He asks the questions and answers them in such a manner that she feels powerless and totally stupid. Her three-week deeply passionate love affair with Max has been debased to a fling of teenage proportions. In about three cruel sentences Larry has managed to sully something that was previously romantic, pure and full of profundity. In the space of less than a minute, all her private thoughts and dreams about flight, escape and a future with Max are lying covered in spittle on the floor.

Madeleine is undone. She feels destroyed, decimated, foolish even. What was she thinking? Girls like her don't find happiness. Girls like her don't find love like they do in films and romantic novels. It is stupid and naïve to think that such a thing even exists. Everyone else knows it is pure fiction, why doesn't she? Her life is here, taking her children to school, playing tennis at Angela's, cooking dinner for her husband, playing bridge, getting drunk, taking more Apesate. It is arrogant in the extreme to think that she is any better than anyone else, that she is above such things. She should stop thinking beyond her abilities, her ordinariness and be happy with her lot. The world may be divided into ordinary and extraordinary people, as Max says, but she is ordinary. Or at least that's how Larry makes her feel.

As Madeleine stands at her orange Formica kitchen, a dusty spider plant behind her on the shelf, the spirit seeps from her soul. Her eyes shine less brightly and her shoulders stoop. She visibly crumples in front of Larry's eyes.

'He does love me,' she whispers so quietly her mouth barely moves.

'Yeah, sure he does,' laughs Larry. 'And every other women he's currently screwing in the county.'

'He's not sleeping with anyone else,' she says, her cheeks flushing pink.

'Right, of course he isn't,' says Larry, throwing his arm in the air like some over-excited punter at a fight.

'He isn't,' she hisses.

'How do you know?' jeers Larry. 'How the fuck do you know? I know you are with him a lot of the time, half the county tells me that, but are you with him twenty-four hours a day? Are you? I think the answer is no.'

'He isn't sleeping with anyone else,' she says.

'How do you know?' asks Larry.

'Because . . . because he told me,' she replies.

'He told me . . . he told me.' Larry is almost hysterical. 'Well, that's all right then.' He is laughing theatrically as he turns to walk out of the kitchen and into the sitting room. 'God,' he says as he goes. 'You're even more pathetic than I thought.'

Madeleine turns round immediately and throws up in her sink. Her blonde hair falls over her face, sticking to her mouth as she retches and retches. Her future is now all too clear. All the escape routes have been blocked. The life-raft that was Max has been punctured and is deflating before her very eyes. Hot tears of fear and rage slowly burn tracks down her cheeks and drip into the sink. She stands there for about five minutes, her shoulders collapsing into the occasional sob. Then finally she lifts her head and, tucking her hair behind her ears, she breathes in, wipes her nose on the back of her hand and walks into the sitting room.

There is sport on television, but Madeleine is too emotional to pay any attention. Her husband is sprawled in his favourite red armchair while her two daughters are sitting on the custard-yellow sofa in bare feet. Lara, her chin in her hand, is avidly watching the screen. Sophie has her thumb in her mouth, and is simultaneously picking her nose with the same hand, while twirling her hair with the other.

'Hi, Mum,' she mumbles with her mouth full.

Lara looks round. Larry doesn't bother to move.

'Um, shepherd's pie all right for everyone tonight?' she says.

'Mmm,' says Sophie. No one else replies.

Madeleine doesn't see Max for a week. It is the longest they have been apart since they first met and it drives them insane. Madeleine paces her house like some caged animal. Sighing and smoking and drinking pot after pot of black coffee, she is short-tempered with her children and keeps throwing up. All the colour has drained from her cheeks. Her eyes are haunted and hollow. She is unable to concentrate, but keeps going maniacally through the motions of a housewife. She obsessively scrubs and pours bleach everywhere, she keeps cooking extravagant three-course meals with opulent puddings none of which she eats. She is driving Larry mad but he refuses to give in. Instead he sits in silence ostentatiously enjoying his supper, and then retiring to bed early. There they lie side by side like cold corpses in the morgue, neither moving for fear of touching the other.

Meanwhile Max has no real idea what is going on. He received one hysterical telephone call in the middle of the night that Saturday, and between the whispering and the sobbing he managed to work out that it was over. She could never see him again and he wasn't to call or come round. It was the terror in her voice that had really upset him. He lay in bed, sweating and staring at the ceiling, shivering at imagined events in her house. He thought of Larry shouting at her, screaming at her, making her cry. He thought of Larry hitting her about the head, raining punches down on his unfaithful wife. He walked past her house a couple of times during the week just to make sure that she was still alive.

Max is miserable. Everyone notices it. It is the way his face falls when someone comes in to the shop that makes it so obvious that they are not the person he is hoping for. In the end he calls Val.

'Oh, hello you,' she purrs down the receiver when she realises it's him.

'Um, hi,' he says, sounding slightly embarrassed. 'Look, Val, I wouldn't normally ask this of anyone, but I am actually quite desperate and have no one to turn to. Can I ask you a favour?'

'Course you can,' she replies, thrilled to be taken into his confidence. 'Whatever you want.' She giggles.

'It's Madeleine,' he says.

'Oh.' Val could not sound more disappointed if she tried. 'Um . . .'

'No, go on,' she says, clawing back some dignity.

'I just don't know what to do,' he says. 'She won't see me. She has cut off all forms of communication. Whenever I call she puts down the phone.'

He carries on and on. Desperate to talk to anyone about the situation, he releases a tidal wave of emotion down the telephone. Val, for all her shiny brass qualities, does have a heart made of a more valuable metal and appears to be genuinely moved by Max's emotion. She has never heard a man speak that way before, and she finds it rather beguiling. Together they hatch a plan.

★　　★　　★

Saturday night and Madeleine could not feel less like going to Val's for dinner. It is one of those last-minute invitations.

'It's been so beautiful all week, and the weather is never this good in England,' she'd said on the telephone. 'I just really fancy a bit of a relaxed supper outside.'

Madeleine wasn't keen but Larry had insisted.

'I don't want my wife hiding away,' he'd warned.

So she'd accepted but is really going through the motions. Brushing her hair, putting on something nondescript and casual. Madeleine is like a lobotomised schizophrenic preparing for a day in the community.

'So who else is going?' whistles Larry, looking in the mirror as he flattens down his ginger hair.

Madeleine doesn't answer.

He repeats the question with a hardened edge.

'She didn't say,' she replies, brushing her hair with her elbows still on the dressing-table. 'But I should imagine the usual sort of crowd.'

She is right, of course. As she walks into the drawing room extension at the back of the house, with double French windows at either end of the room leading into the garden, she smiles at the familiar faces. She collects a colourless drink, as every single pair of eyes in the room is trained on her, then walks around the room.

Candida and Alan. 'Good evening.' She smiles. Angela and James. 'Hello.' She nods. Oh, God, she thinks, Liz and Geoff. 'Hello.' Two people she has never met before. 'Hello.' And Max . . . Max. What the hell is Max doing here? Why is he here? What is going on? Why is he smiling at her pretending they are old friends? The room falls quiet. How does one greet Max? 'Hello,' she says, her eye almost falling on to the shagpile in shock. She grips the stem of her glass like a vice. It shakes and dribbles on the carpet.

146

'Max,' she says loudly enough for them all to hear, which they do, because they are all listening. 'Gosh, Max.' She clicks her teeth. 'What a surprise, I wasn't expecting to see you here.'

'Yeah,' says Larry dryly. 'Neither was I. I would have thought you would have better things to do with your time than hang out with a whole load of married people on a Saturday night.' Larry's grin is fixed, his manner confrontational, yet very obviously polite.

'I know,' says Val, swanning in, dressed in some cream silk jersey number with shoestring straps and a handkerchief front that plunges and then gathers just under her breasts. Her hair is piled high on her head with tonged curls snaking down from her temples. She is holding a tray of sausage rolls. 'But isn't he a dear. There I was with a dinner planned and Christopher away and no one to host it. So I rang Max up, and begged him to help me out.'

Val herself is taking a huge risk. Bearing in mind her recent ostracism for fooling around with the very same man whom she has just invited, as soon as her boyfriend's back is turned, she herself can't quite believe she has done it. But Max was very persuasive on the telephone and she has always enjoyed creating a bit of stir. She only hopes that Christopher will see the funny side when he comes home. Anyway how could she refuse? Madeleine is her best friend and she has always rather disliked Larry. He is far too pleased with himself for such an unattractive man and one with so little cash.

Angela is so enjoying herself, her cigarette is slowly turning to ash in her left hand. Candida, on the other hand, like a machine-eating spectator at an event, has eaten five sausage rolls without noticing. It's Madeleine who is the most uncomfortable.

'Well, that was nice of him.' She smiles at Val, her eyes

totally spherical as she gestures towards the kitchen. 'D'you need some help in there, Val?'

'Do you know that would be nice,' she says, putting down her tray and following her friend into the kitchen.

'Jesus Christ,' says Madeleine in a screaming whisper as she downs her drink in one and leans against the pine units. 'What are you doing?'

'It's Max's idea,' grins Val, delicately sucking on her cigarette out of the far corner of her mouth so as to avoid smudging her lipstick. 'He made me do it.'

'No one makes you do anything,' hisses Madeleine.

'Oh, for God's sake calm down,' replies Val. 'Everyone knows that you have been sleeping with him for weeks.'

'They do?'

'Well, you haven't exactly been very subtle about it, have you?'

'I suppose not.'

'He is really desperate to see you.' She shrugs. 'And this is the only way, since you have cut off all forms of communication. Anyway,' she laughs. 'What's Larry going to do? Start a fight?'

'Course not.' Madeleine sighs. 'That's the last thing he's likely to do. He can't stand the idea of losing it in front of other people. But it's more complicated than that.'

'How?'

'I think I'm in love with him,' says Madeleine. The weight of her confession makes her lose an inch in height. She leans against the pine units for support.

'Oh,' says Val, looking stunned and beginning to regret her Cupid involvement in what she presumed to be rather an amusing game. 'I didn't think it was that serious. Um, are you sure?'

'I don't think I can live without him, if that's what you are asking,' says Madeleine, pouring herself what looks like

148

a glass of cheap cooking sherry that is sitting on the side. 'I've worked that one out in the last few days.' She knocks the whole thing back.

'Well,' says Val, thinking for a second, then adds with the characteristic optimism of someone who has totally reinvented themselves, 'You had better go for it then.' She smiles, picking up a plate of pineapple and cheese. 'Nothing ventured nothing gained, as my mother used to say. As I keep telling you, I fully intend to marry a millionaire and I haven't given up that one yet now, have I?' She smiles again. 'Everything all right in here,' she says loudly as she leaves the kitchen and makes her way into the sitting room. 'We're eating in the garden tonight if that's all right with everyone.' There is a general murmur of approval.

For someone who had not been to a dinner party until their early twenties, Val is extraordinarily good at them. She has set up the table across the wide flat lawn just next to the pool house by her steamingly warm turquoise mosaic swimming pool. A hot, heady, breathless evening, the sky is a deepening shade of purple as the guests troop across the lawn, drinks in hand, towards the pool. It's the same lawn where the Conservative dance marquee had been just over a month before. Out of the corner of her eye Madeleine glimpses the elm tree where she and Max had sat and kissed and fallen in love.

'That is an elm, isn't it?' says Max, pointing off to his right with his cigarette.

Madeleine stares at the ground.

'Is it?' replies Val, concentrating hard on preventing her stratospherically high heels from sinking into the grass. 'Don't ask me.' She laughs. 'I wouldn't know an elm if it fell on me.'

'I thought they were all racked with disease,' says Liz, punctuating each word with a steady stream of smoke. 'Some grubby little beetle from India or something.'

149

'Yeah,' says Larry. 'Some wog beetle has had the lot. All except that one, it seems.'

The whole pool area is lit by small round candles. Balanced all the way along the edge of the pool, on the low side walls, around each of the ten or so pots of geraniums, the effect is ostentatious, yet magical. The air is warm with the sweat smell of chlorine, clematis and pine from the new Swedish sauna-effect pool house. Swallows are flying overhead, dipping their wings in the water as they dine on the aphids buzzing above the pool.

'Wow, Val darling,' says Angela, her heels clicking on the paving as she walks towards the table. 'QDD,' she says, stubbing her cigarette out in a geranium pot. 'Quite divine, darling. I have never seen anything so . . . so much like a Hollywood film set in my life.'

'Gosh, thanks,' says Val, genuinely thrilled with the compliment. 'Um,' she continues. 'I did have a table plan but it has gone clean out of my head.' She giggles. 'So what I shall do is put Larry next to Liz over there, Geoff next to Angela there, James next to Madeleine and Keith next to Candida, Belinda next to Alan with Max and me at either end.' She throws her hands in the air for dramatic gusto effect.

Val has been subtle enough to put Madeleine and Max almost at opposite ends of the table from each other, but the tension as they all sit down is palpable. It is a tight squeeze around the table and everyone apologises to each other for rubbing legs, touching elbows and taking the wrong glasses. The half avocado pears packed with plump prawns and mayonnaise are already on the table.

'Do tuck in, everyone,' announces Val, holding up her teaspoon as a serving suggestion. 'Oh, silly me,' she says, covering her mouth. 'Max, we haven't served the wine.'

Max is up, out of his seat and rummaging around in the pool house before anyone else can offer. Choosing a bottle of white wine from the fridge he takes it round the table, pouring each glass in turn. As he goes from Larry to Liz to Keith to Candida, Alan asks Belinda where she lives and where her children go to school, Angela talks to Geoff about her idea for a rose garden like his and Larry talks to Liz about money. But when Max reaches Madeleine, the table is instantly silent, as it there were a prearranged plan to eavesdrop on whatever private conversation might ensue. Max stops as he prepares to pour.

'Um,' he says. 'Would you like some white wine, um . . . Madeleine?'

'Yes, please,' she says, staring down at the half-shredded paper napkin on her lap.

'Aren't these prawns great,' announces Val to the group. 'I know you're not supposed to applaud your own cooking but aren't they just wonderful? They're from that great little fishmonger in Stratford, you know.' She pops a couple in her mouth. 'Mmm,' she says.

'Mmm,' the whole table mumbles keenly in agreement.

'For chrissake, Max,' she nannies, with exaggerated efficiency. 'Hurry up with that wine, will you, half the table is dying of thirst.'

Max doesn't say anything. He simply smiles as he walks behind Madeleine, making sure that his thigh rubs against her back as he passes.

His touch is so exhilarating, Madeleine digs her fingernails deep into her palms in an effort to control herself. She picks up her glass of wine and downs half of it in one. Reaching down into her beaded handbag she picks up a packet of cigarettes and lights one, pulling the smoke deep into her lungs.

'So, Val,' she says breezily. 'Where is Christopher this weekend?'

'Christ . . . Do you know.' She laughs. 'I'm not entirely sure. He did say where he was going but I wasn't really listening. I know you can't drink there, that's for sure, because he packed himself a bottle of whisky. Somewhere "archy".' She purses her lips.

'Karachi?' ventures Max.

'God! Yes! That's the one.' Val claps her hands with delight. 'Max, you're amazing,' she says, pretending to swoon. 'I had quite forgotten how clever you are.'

'He's not that fucking clever,' mutters Larry into his starter, loud enough for only his end of the table to hear. They all shift in their seats.

'How long is he away for?' asks Candida, pushing her starter to one side and plucking a cigarette from her packet with her long pink nails.

'A week or so,' says Val. 'He might come back via Munich, who knows? Anyway, enough of boring old Chris. Who's going to help me clear?'

'I will,' says Madeleine, probably a bit too quickly but she doesn't care.

The atmosphere at the table is unbearable and she is desperate to escape. She has already finished her glass of wine and feels no better for it. Perhaps some time on her own in the loo would improve things? She walks around the table collecting the plates. Larry hands his over with barely a glance in her direction. She notices that he has his hand very obviously placed on Liz's thigh. Angela passes hers up with two butts already in the prawns, and Geoff gives her what he hopes is a winning smile. She stands next to Candida, with her back to Max. As she stacks the plates he runs his fingers slowly and gently up and down her legs. Madeleine shivers with excitement while Max looks the other way and pretends to engage in conversation with Belinda.

'So, children at Pankhurst,' he says, nodding away like he cares. Madeleine can't really move. Like a cat petrified through pleasure, she stands frozen, gripping on to her plates, head down engrossed in the avocados.

'Get a move on, Madeleine,' shouts Val over her shoulder as she teeters along by the pool. The blue subaqua light shines up through her dress and announces to her own dinner party that she isn't wearing any knickers. (Larry gets an erection. Liz thinks that it is her breasts that have turned her neighbour on so much and proffers them up some more.) Madeleine manages to pull herself together enough to hurry along after her friend. Meanwhile Belinda is still talking Max through the extra facilities in the new school art labs.

Back in the kitchen, Madeleine deposits her pile of plates on the side, and leaning against the units she rolls her eyes. 'Oh, my God,' she says. 'Val, what the hell am I going to do? I want to sleep with him right here and now.' She laughs. 'Have him in the loo, on the lawn, anywhere. It's insane, but do you know I have almost reached the stage where I don't care any more. My whole life is collapsing around me and all I can think of is him.' She laughs again and, turning round, she looks up and down the side to find the same bottle of cheap sherry she had drunk earlier. 'It's obviously madness,' she says, shaking as she pours herself a wine glass full of the stuff and knocks it back in one, her whole body shaking in revulsion as she does so. 'What am I supposed to do?' She is shaking her head, looking at the empty glass. 'Stay in my miserable marriage for the sake of my children or chuck the whole thing in for Max. What am I supposed to do? What am I supposed to do?'

Val is suddenly quite nervous about her friend's state of mind. Madeleine's cheeks are burning red and her eyes are glazed and focused on the middle distance. She is rocking slightly against the sideboard.

'Do you know,' she says as lightly as she can. 'I think I'll go and get Max.'

'You can't,' whispers Madeleine, her eyes staring. 'Everyone will know what is going on.'

'No, they won't,' says Val. 'Anyway fuck them. It's my house. I can do what I want. Go upstairs to my room and wait there,' she orders as she minces her way out of the kitchen.

Madeleine walks up the wide Fred Astaire staircase laid with red carpet and marble tiles and makes her way into Valerie's bedroom. A riot of pink and white with a giant four-poster bed, it is every little girl's dream princess room. The walls are covered with rosebud wallpaper, the carpet is white and thick with even fluffier, thicker, whiter rugs either side of the bed. The bedside tables are piled with fashion magazines, a copy of *Jonathan Livingston Seagull* and a well-thumbed volume of *The Joy of Sex*. The bed itself is beclouded in cushions. Hundreds of them, all with frilly edges made of lace or broderie anglaise, they make it almost impossible to climb on to the thing. Her dressing-table is also festooned with white lace, tiebacks, bows and pink cotton balls. She has a collection of silver hairbrushes. The whole effect is whore meets Barbara Cartland.

Madeleine doesn't know what to do or where to put herself in this perfectly manicured environment. She thinks about sitting down at the dressing-table. She contemplates lying on the bed. She wants to throw up, but she ends up pacing the length of the room, carving a path in the carpet as she waits for Max. Her five-minute wait feels like an hour until she finally hears him running up the stairs. She stands in the middle of the room rather like a weak and lost-looking child. He doesn't say a word as he enters the room. Instead he walks straight up to her, takes her in his arms and kisses her. Madeleine starts to cry.

In the ten minutes that his wife has been away from the table, the whole of Larry's life has changed. But he doesn't know it

154

when Madeleine returns. She has no idea what Val has said to explain her absence with Max but no one seems to notice or care that the two of them have been away, together, for so long.

'. . . and then I said, "No fucking way, mate,"' exclaims Larry, recounting some hilarious tale. '"You've got to be bloody joking," and he said, "D'you know, mate, I am!"'

The whole table rocks with laughter. Liz is almost hysterical. She laughs so much her eyes water and her eyeliner streaks down her face. It is not a good look. Angela is flicking her ash with amusement and Candida is so tickled that she has to get a comb out of her handbag to smooth down her hair.

Val serves the chicken fricassee and a big bowl of salad. Max pours some more wine, leaving bottles at either end for everyone to help themselves to, which they do, generously. By the time the raspberry pavlova is finished and they are on to coffee and liqueurs everyone is really rather drunk indeed. Liz has consumed an off-licence of wine and cigarettes and ceased to make sense about half an hour ago. In an effort to impress Larry, she has undone her shirt so far you can see her front-fastening push-up bra. Lolling back in his chair, Larry is telling one lewd anecdote after another, while Angela is trying to light the wrong end of a cigarette. Val is boring Geoff about how terrible her childhood was. Geoff, snout down, is only concentrating in case her nipple falls out of her dress like it did ten minutes ago. Candida is barking nonsensical orders at her husband. Keith is sitting on his own playing conversational ping-pong. Madeleine is nodding along to James's story that she has failed to comprehend from the outset. And Belinda is still talking to Max about Pankhurst School.

'Right,' says Val, in a manner that suggests she has bored even herself into submission. 'Who's for skinny-dipping?'

It is like an east wind has suddenly blown the length of the table. Everyone falls silent. Belinda appears so appalled that she looks up and down the table as if trying to ascertain who has farted. Angela looks down and chain-smokes into her plate; there is no way she's showing off her figure no matter how small and thin she is.

'What?' says Val, heaving her shoulders in an effort to look surprised. 'No one is coming skinny dipping? Crikey,' she says exhaling, her drunken lips flapping like a horse. 'You lot really have lost your edge. I thought you were all quite a laugh, you know, liberated and swinging. In fact it turns out you're all bourgeois and suburban.'

'Right, that's it,' says Larry, standing up and tearing off his navy short-sleeved shirt to reveal a pair of white breasts covered in a faint ginger down. 'No one accuses me of being suburban without me getting my cock out.'

'Me neither,' giggles Liz, continuing the undressing process she had started earlier. Unbuttoning her shirt, she releases her front-loaded breasts all over the table.

Val needs no more encouragement. She peels off her cream silk jersey dress and leaves it like a puddle beside the pool. Stark naked except for her high-heeled shoes, she parades like a porn star towards the diving board at the top of the pool. Larry sings the striptease music as he stands in his white Y-fronts at the shallow end of the pool. Liz suddenly sprints with a high-pitched squeal towards the pool. Clutching her bosom, her behind in a heavy-duty state of flux, she hurls herself into the shallow end. Val's on the diving board, her luxuriant long-legged figure bathed in the blue light from the pool. She moves her hips in time to Larry's tuneless accompaniment, her breasts round and plump, her pubic hair waxed into what looks like a strip of Velcro. Everyone around her dinner table is staring at her. She prepares to dive and then, suddenly remembering her expensive silver shoes, bends down to take them off.

'Sorry, everyone,' she slurs. 'Bruno Magli. Can't have them going in the pool.'

Larry resumes his tune and within a second Val is in the pool swimming towards the shallow end like some Bond Girl fantasy. As she nears the end Larry whips his pants off and is in there, quick as a flash, ready to frolic and play silly buggers at the shallow end.

'Who else is coming in?' she says, rising out of the water like a mermaid, trying to keep Larry at arm's length. 'Max, come on, you're co-hosting this evening.'

'Yeah, come on, Max,' encourages Liz, bouncing around in the pool. 'Get your pants off.'

'Come along now, Max,' says Candida, standing up at the other end of the table. 'I'll show you mine, if you show me yours.' Candida starts to remove her T-shirt, revealing a thick white bra of industrial proportions. Ever practical, Candida, although frightfully rich, is one of those women who hates wasting money on underwear. She parades to the end of the pool in her huge white bra and even larger, whiter up-to-the-navel pants. 'Shit, for chrissake, Max, hurry up will you,' she complains, her marble white foot with pink toenails preparing to dip into the water. 'I don't bloody ruin my hair-do for anyone, you know.'

'Seeing as you put it that way.' Max smiles as he stands up and walks towards the pool peeling off his black T-shirt, down to his brown muscled body.

Madeleine stares, and starts to bite her thumb. He walks to the edge of the pool and, unbuttoning his jeans, he pulls them down. He is not wearing any underwear. Larry lets out a fake groupie scream.

'Aaah, Max.' He waves his hands in the air from half-way up the pool. 'Get your skinny brown arse in here,' he shouts.

Max executes a neat dive, arriving halfway up the pool,

almost next door to Larry. He surfaces and shakes his head, flicking his long dark hair about his shoulders.

'Right?' He grins. 'Who else is coming in?'

Madeleine sits and smiles.

'Not a chance in hell from me,' says Angela, flicking her ash on to her saucer.

'I suppose I could be persuaded,' says James, standing up and loosening his belt buckle. He drops his blue and yellow checked trousers to reveal a pair of pale blue tight briefs, and a pair of yellow calf-length socks. All of which he leaves, along with his blue shirt, in a well-folded pile by the edge of the pool before he walks in calmly, completely naked.

By now the pool is quite full of naked and cavorting adults. Liz is standing in the shallow end splashing anyone who comes near her. Val is doing elegant lengths like something out of a fifties Hollywood movie. Larry is treading water next to Max, commanding the whole pool to look at him and pay attention. Candida is attempting some backstroke. And James, having made his grand entrance, is standing by the steps hugging himself, looking distinctly cold.

'Okay, who else is coming in?' shouts Larry, his hands cupped round his mouth.

'Me-e-e-e,' yells Madeleine uncharacteristically, getting out of her chair and preparing to take off her clothes.

'About bloody time too,' says Val, finally stopping underneath the diving board.

'Quite right,' says Candida, still on her back, her bosom shifting from side to side with each stroke like an overly mobile life-jacket.

'Hurrah,' says James, quickly shaking his fists in the air before returning them around his waist.

'Oh, no, you bloody well won't,' yells Larry from the middle of the pool.

Madeleine freezes in her tracks.

'Put your fucking knickers on,' continues Larry as he starts to wade towards the shallow end.

'Larry, don't be silly,' says Val. 'We're all naked in the pool. What difference does it make? It's just a bit of fun. Where's your sense of humour?'

'No one apart from me gets to see my wife naked,' announces Larry as he climbs up the steps. His ginger hair stuck in streaks to his body like melted toffee, he walks dripping wet and naked to his white Y-fronts. He puts them on without towelling himself and they immediately turn transparent across the crotch.

'Oh, God, Larry, you're such a spoilsport,' says Val, swimming down to the other end of the pool. 'What does it matter if Madeleine gets her clothes off? You can see me for free.' She laughs, trying to execute a star jump at the shallow end of the pool.

'Don't you fucking call me a spoilsport,' says Larry, shaking a finger at Val in the pool.

'Don't you be so fucking rude to your hostess,' says Max, striding through the water to the steps.

'Don't you fucking get involved with things that don't concern you,' says Larry, standing at the tops of the steps as the naked Max climbs up them.

'Listen, mate,' says Max, standing in front of Larry with his hands on his hips, his nude behind pointing towards the dining table. 'You apologise or you leave.'

'Apologise to the local fucking village bicycle? Everyone has had that old tart, every which way they please,' he says, defiantly smoothing down his moustache, staring Max in the eye.

Max punches Larry so hard that it is not until he hits the paved terrace that he realises what has happened to him. The one clean belt isn't hard enough to break Larry's nose, but it is certainly strong enough to make it bleed. Yet Larry doesn't react. He staggers to his feet, glutinous blood spitting and splattering down his chest, and walks towards his pile of clothes.

'Larry,' says Val eventually. 'Don't be silly, there's no need to leave it like this.'

'Yes, darling,' says Madeleine. 'I only wanted to have a swim.'

'Well, that's as may be,' hisses Larry, walking towards his wife. 'But that's the problem with whores like you. You don't know when to stop, do you?'

7

That night, for the first time ever in her life, Madeleine Johnson stands up for herself. With the bronzed and totally naked Max beside her, she refuses to go home. So what could have ended up as a vicious and uncoordinated drunken fight, with slapping wet fists and sprays of blood turning green-black in the swimming pool, turns into something strangely dignified.

After insulting his wife, Larry simply sits quietly down on the wet flagstones next to the pool and puts his socks and shoes on. Rather like a fastidious schoolboy he pulls each sock high and smooth along his shin and slips on the side-buckled leather pumps that he'd bought on holiday in Spain. With a silent group of stunned guests watching, the only noise is the occasional loud splash as the gobs of blood from his nose hit the deck. Eventually he stands up, runs his hands down the damp trousers that cling to his sodden crotch and wet thighs and quietly asks Madeleine if she is coming home.

'I don't think so,' Madeleine mutters almost inaudibly. Staring at the paving, her left hand is fisted by her side, while her right seeks Max's.

'What?' whispers Larry, swaying slightly with the debilitating cocktail of exhaustion and inebriation.

'I don't think so,' she repeats more loudly. Her chin rises with defiance, her right hand clasps Max's.

And with that, Larry simply staggers towards the house and his parked car, leaving his wife and his marriage behind him.

He drives home, opens a bottle of whisky and drinks a large part of it staring at the wall, incapable of thought.

Madeleine, on the other hand, lets out a long exhausted sigh and collapses into a chair. She puts her head in her hands and stares at the ground, as large silent tears roll slowly down her cheeks. She has no idea what do, where to go, or who she is any more.

The rest of the group becomes a mass of activity. The balmy evening has suddenly turned quite chilly. Val and Liz's teeth begin to chatter as they wander around in the shadows looking for their clothes. Angela smokes and spectates as her husband grovels around, hirsute arse in the air, under the sunbeds in search of his yellow socks and pale blue pants. Belinda is rendered so inert by the scene that for a full three minutes she forgets to close her mouth or let go of her husband's hand. While Candida, with tight pink-lipped efficiency, wanders around in her huge white pants, exposing her huge white breasts, looking for her huge white bra. The only person not interested in immediately covering himself up is Max. In fact, he's quite forgotten that he is naked and continues to march about as if fully clothed. First he goes into the Swedish sauna pool house and picks up a warm dry towel. Instead of using it on himself, he wraps it around Madeleine's shivering shoulders. He doesn't say anything. Words like 'It'll be okay,' and 'There, there,' seem patronising to him. So he stands by her side, and simply strokes her hair.

Eventually everyone leaves. The carnage of the dinner party remains, like some atrophied scene at Pompeii: half-drunk glasses of wine, half-eaten rolls, scrunched-up paper napkins and the occasional waft of a still smoking cigarette emanating from a serving of raspberry pavlova. The candles still burn round the pool and Candida's bra swims slowly in the deep end like a giant ray.

'Shall I take you home?' says Max, after the last voices disappear into the night.

Madeleine nods, as she draws the towel tighter around her shoulders. Max looks for his jeans. Finding them in a pool of water, he notices they are flecked with blood as he puts them on. Larry's blood, he thinks, as he puts his arms around Larry's wife and takes her home.

For two days Madeleine remains locked away in his small flat. He does not open the shop. They spend most of the time lying in bed together, the curtains drawn to the rest of the world.

That night she makes almost no sound or movement at all. She lies there, curled up tight in his bed like a traumatised child. She rocks from side to side, occasionally shaking uncontrollably, occasionally clinging on to him for dear life. To say he is worried is an understatement. He thinks of calling out the emergency doctor to get her some tranquillisers, but every time he threatens to get out of bed to make the call she whimpers and cries for him to return.

The next day, Sunday, she is mildly improved. He makes love to her as soon as she wakes up. Max doesn't dare suggest it, but she climbs on top of him and is really rather insistent. In fact, she makes him do it three times that day. It is almost as if the more they have sex the more she seems to justify her decision and situation. Making love to Max brings her alive, she keeps saying. He is in no position to refuse.

By Monday afternoon the hysteria seems to have left her. She clings to him less and is less sexually demanding. He even manages to make her eat some food. He cooks pasta with a tomato sauce and audibly exhales when he sees her put five or six tubes of macaroni in her mouth.

Today, it's Tuesday morning and Madeleine is still sleeping soundly when Max wakes. She looks fragile and beautiful as she lies, her plump lips slightly parted, breathing on his pillow. Max props himself up on his side watching her, for the first time thinking how wonderful it is to wake up lying next to her. For the first time since she has moved in, all the trauma and pain and agony seem worth it. As he runs the back of his hand over her soft pale cheek, his lips curl into a languid smile as he contemplates his victory.

Max had never punched anyone before, let alone fought over a woman. The sudden rush of masculinity excited him. The hunter-gatherer that had lain dormant in him had roared to the fore and he'd found it all rather exhilarating. Back in his pot-fuelled hippy days sitting tantrically in India, he'd been somewhat more of a natural coward, preferring to charm, not fight, his way out of trouble. There had been a few incidents where Max had been hit, but he'd never managed to throw a punch himself. The first had been a plain old head-butting in a pub just off the King's Road around closing. Max had been pissed and posh and probably deserved it. The second was over some Norwegian girl and a bloke called Craig in the ashram near Bodhgaya. Max couldn't really remember all the details, he'd been on LSD at the time. But Craig blamed Max for something to do with this Norwegian bird with whom Max had slept, but was no longer interested in. Anyway, Craig was upset because whatever-her-name-was had left the village and he used Max's face and stomach to vent his anger. Craig was inevitably asked to leave the group, and Max got three sympathy fucks for his trouble. So it had all turned out rather nicely for him in the end.

But Madeleine has changed all that. It hadn't really been Val's honour that Max had been protecting the other night. Both he and Larry knew that, as indeed probably did Val. They'd been getting at each other all evening, Larry with his snide little asides, and Max by sleeping with Larry's wife between the starter and the main course. The confrontation was inevitable. Truth be known, Larry hated Max as soon as he set eyes on him at Liz's that Sunday afternoon. Not only was he handsome and long-limbed – two qualities the Lord had not seen fit to grace Larry with – but also he commanded the attention of every female on the lawn, which was something that Larry – despite his surprisingly high success rate – longed and prayed for. So even if Max hadn't slept with his wife, Larry's jealousy would never have let them be friends. They each had something the other wanted; yet Max was the only one man enough to go out and take it in the end.

And that's what Max loves most about Madeleine as he strokes her cheek at 8.30 a.m. She makes him feel like a man. Alive and virile like a real man. All he wants to do is protect her.

Madeleine rolls, stretches and wakes with a sudden start. Her whole body is rigid and tense as she gasps.

'Oh, my God, thank God it's you,' she says as she sits up and sees Max lying next to her. 'For one terrible second I thought it was all a dream and I was going to wake up in my own bed . . . with him.'

Her eyes are huge and round with fear. Max hushes her as he takes her in his arms, cradling the back of her head with the palm of his hand. The smell of dried sweat emanates from his armpits; Madeleine inhales it deeply as she starts to calm down.

'What are we going to do with you today?' says Max, as he plays with her hair. 'Do you think that we should try and leave this room and greet the world head-on? Do you think you could manage that?' he cajoles, half playfully but half slightly wondering how much longer he can cope with being cooped up in this small, darkly furnished, airless bedroom that he has never particularly liked.

'Do we have to?' says Madeleine, her bottom lip pouting like a child. 'It's just that when I leave here reality is going to hit me. What I have done? You know, my children: what am I going to do with them? How are they? I should see them. I want to see them. Oh, Lord, what a mess.'

She sighs and starts to cry. Large, slow, fat tears of despair roll down her cheeks. Max squeezes her tighter and strokes her hair.

'We'll sort it out, we'll sort it out . . . don't worry,' he says, kissing her on the forehead. 'But we should get out of here.'

'Oh, I don't know,' says Madeleine, tears still on her cheeks.

'We have to some time,' says Max, raising his eyebrows as if it's not such a bad suggestion. 'For a start I'm very, very, very low on food,' he continues, running his index finger along the curve of her shoulder. 'Very, very low on food . . . and, um, and,' he adds, tracing the line of her hip slowly down towards her thigh. 'And – we – I should really try and open up the shop at some stage in order to keep you in the manner to which you are accustomed.' He leans in to kiss her already parting lips.

'First, take me in the manner to which I am rapidly becoming accustomed,' she whispers in his ear.

Almost an hour later it is hunger that finally forces Max out of bed. Madeleine is not far behind. The smell of hot buttered toast beckons her down the stairs as she pulls on one of Max's crumpled old shirts that is slightly in need of a wash.

'Put another one of those in there for me.' She smiles as she stands in the doorway watching him wander barefoot around the kitchen, holding slices of bread in his hand, dressed only in his hip-hugging jeans.

'That is my favourite shirt.' He winks across the table. 'It looks wonderful on you.'

'It certainly smells like one of your favourites,' says Madeleine.

'You don't have to wear it,' he replies, holding his breaded hands up in protest.

'Actually I don't have anything else.'

'Ah,' says Max. 'But I do.'

'True.' She smiles. 'But I always thought that washed-out green rather suited me.'

'And you would be right,' he replies with a nod. 'One or two?' he asks, holding up the bread.

'Um.'

'Two it is then. You haven't eaten properly in days.'

Madeleine sits down at the small round table in the kitchen and pulls her knees up under her chin. She lets out a blissful sigh as she watches Max make toast, humming along to some tinny track playing on the cheap transistor radio perched on the windowsill. Both the kitchen windows over the sink are open. The thin white curtains with a faded red tulip motif flutter in the light breeze. The mid-morning sun is pouring in, melting the butter on the table.

'Are you a tea or coffee person in the morning?' asks Max. His bare foot squeaks as he spins on the brown plastic faux-tiled floor.

'Tea?' punts Madeleine.

'Oh, I'm a coffee bloke myself.' He smiles.

'Oh, so am I really.' She laughs. 'I just thought maybe with the family thing . . . you know, loyalty and all that.'

Max looks puzzled for second. 'Oh, that,' he says finally. 'God, no.' He looks at her strangely. 'I can't wake up without a cup of the strong black stuff.'

'Neither can I,' she replies quickly.

'Well, that's settled then.' He smiles. 'Large pot of coffee it is then.'

'Great.' She smiles back.

They sit and eat. Max reads the *Guardian* with one hand, while using the other to play with Madeleine's bare feet which are nestled in his lap. Madeleine nods her head in time to the music, occasionally moving her shoulders from side to side, as she reaches over for more marmalade from a jam jar boasting a 1975 vintage.

'Where did you get this?' she asks, indicating a knife loaded with orange peel.

'Get what?' replies Max, his forehead furrowed, his head full of thoughts about the drought and the continued hosepipe ban story he has just been reading.

'This?' she says, waving her knife again.

'Um.' He shakes his head and shrugs his shoulders, unable to understand the question.

'The marmalade.'

'Oh, that,' says Max distractedly. 'Christ, I don't know. My mum probably. She always gives me bags of the shit whenever I go and stay for the weekend.'

'Oh.'

'Mmm.' Max returns to his newspaper.

'How often do you go?'

'Go where?'

'Home.'

'Oh.' He pauses as he tries to remember when he was last there. 'Not that often,' he says, turning his pale eyes towards the ceiling as he thinks. 'I am about due for a visit.' He smiles and then leans over to touch her hand. "We should go together. It's about time the rest of the family met you.'

'Great,' she replies, her smile strangely tight.

The mention of the word 'family' sends a cold bolt down Madeleine's spine that grips her stomach like a vice. The daughters she has left behind, the parents she hasn't told, even the husband she abandoned at a dinner party. She slowly drops her piece of toast on to her plate and steadies herself on the table, as the heavy shroud of guilt quietly overwhelms her. It's her daughters who weigh heaviest on her shoulders. What are they doing now? Where are they? What are they thinking? Do they hate her? Will they ever forgive her? She feels sick to the very depths of her soul. Like some jilted lover, she half closes her eyes and inhales, remembering the smell of their hair and the touch of their skin. She can hear their voices, their burbling laughs. Her knuckles turn white as she grips the table even harder.

'In fact,' continues Max breezily, 'I think that's a fantastic idea. You and me and a trip to Oxfordshire. An open-topped car, the wind in our hair, a fabulous weekend with my parents. I know they'll love you as much as I do, they have to. I mean, who couldn't? You're wonderful.' Max gets up from the table and kisses Madeleine on the top of her head as he clears away her plate. 'Mmm.' He inhales. 'Everyone loves you.' He walks over to the sink, his body silhouetted by the sun. 'I think I might open up the shop today, darling, what do you think?'

'Don't you think that it's a bit soon?' says Madeleine, sounding panicked. So many things happening at once. Everything so out of control. Her children. What would they think and say? What if they came into town with their father and saw her in the shop? Would they ever forgive the betrayal? Her and Uncle Max together in the shop. It doesn't bear thinking about. 'You know, people might think we're flaunting it a bit?' she says eventually.

'Flaunting what?'

'Oh, I don't know,' she says, shaking her bowed head, fighting the terrible wave of nausea that is still churning her stomach.

'Flaunting the fact that we love each other?' announces Max proudly with his hands on his hips. He walks up and leans over her. 'This is going to be fun.' He shakes her shoulders. 'You and me against the rest of the world. Fun,' he insists. 'Let them come in and stare if they want to.' He grins, looking at her, sounding quite theatrical. 'Let them come for a good old gawp at total and utter happiness; see how uncomfortable and jealous it makes them.' He laughs. 'Actually, if they're coming to stare we'd better get you some clothes. Come along, Madeleine,' he announces loudly. 'We've got some flaunting to do,' he adds, as he pulls her reluctantly out into the shop.

Stratford-upon-Avon is packed with tourists and shoppers by the time Max and Madeleine arrive around lunchtime. Its black and white half-timbered houses converted into fudge shops, Portmeirion outlets and Shakespeare-themed tearooms are an irresistible combination for large-arsed, comfy slack-sporting Americans in search of history and culture. The pavements are heaving with the sounds of twanging vowels, frotting nylon thighs and the snapping of camera shutters. There is little squatting room left in the park, where one northern coach party after another sit in regional groups on the grass, tucking into Tupperware boxes of flaccid sandwiches, fending off the increasingly audacious swans. There's a queue for punts by the theatre, and a large group of foreign-looking students compares fistfuls of coins as they hang around the ice cream van, trying work out how much they can afford.

Max and Madeleine trawl round and round the streets in the interminable oneway system, looking for somewhere to park. Roof down, music up, Max is posing at the wheel of his sporty single man's MG, while Madeleine is more subdued as she passes the group of students for the third time. What if she sees anyone she knows? What if she sees her children? She sinks lower and lower into the car.

But Max's ebullient mood is contagious. Eventually they manage to dump the MG just past the theatre on the right and, leaving the roof off, they walk, swinging their clasped hands like schoolchildren. They make their way up Sheep Street to the main shopping area and on towards the roundabout, past Barclays Bank and the fishmonger where Val bought her prawns for that dinner. They pause outside what can only be described as a chic boutique.

'What do you think?' asks Madeleine, pressing her face up against the window, thinking that only the likes of Liz can afford such glamour.

'What do I think?' replies Max. 'Of course, is what I think.' He grins, taking hold of her hand as they both tumble into the shop.

To the fat-ankled county lady minding the boutique, Madeleine could not have looked more bizarre. Max's flared jeans are gathered round her waist, held by some orange plastic string and his faded green shirt is tied in a knot at the front underneath her bosom. Not only is she flashing her midriff, but also a pair of semi high-heeled flip-flops – her concession to glamour the last night she and Larry had gone out together as husband and wife. Yet the clothes in the shop could not have looked less like the fat-ankled county lady's speed either: long patchwork wrap-over skirts, scoop-neck T-shirts, hot pants, chiffon tops and lots of floaty cheesecloth. In the far corner there is even a pure white flared trouser suit with tie belt and elegant long lapels. Madeleine walks up and down the racks, running her hand along the fabrics, breathing in the high, sweet smell of new clothes. Her eyes shining in anticipation of imminent retail, she cannot stop smiling.

'Um, I'm not overly familiar with the stock,' announces the fat-ankled lady. 'My niece is away for a few days and I'm looking after the shop. It's all from London, that I do know,' she continues, her voice disappearing further up the back of her nose with irritation the more Max and Madeleine continue to touch each other and giggle. 'She makes regular trips to the capital, Biba, all those sort of designers. You might, therefore, find some of the prices quite dear,' she adds, with a short shift of a smile.

There is nothing that winds Max up more than being told he might not be able to afford something. Brought up in a big house with no furniture, he has spent his whole life the wrong side of flush. The result being that if he has money he will spend it, and if he has no money he will still spend. A generous fool fond of the *grande geste*, with little or no regard for tomorrow, Max is the sort of man credit cards were made for.

'Now, darling,' he says loudly. 'Let's think about this logically. You'll need three or four outfits just for this weekend, alone.' Max is showing off, and amusing only himself really, but he doesn't care.

'Three or four you say?' replies Madeleine, joining in.

When Larry used to buy her clothes, it made her feel cheap and rather like a whore. He would always turn up drunk with something stiff and wholly inappropriate in the back of his car – like the hard, scratchy baby doll nightie he'd brought for her birthday. It was actually a means of Larry assuaging his guilt at having spent the afternoon with his secretary, but Madeleine, of course, did not know that. Yet his vulgar gifts always left her with a foul taste in her mouth; that and the whole-hearted inability to be grateful. But with Max it is different, she thinks, as she walks up and down the shop choosing outfits. With Max this is a hoot. Spending money, being spontaneous and young: with Max everything is fun.

Much to the annoyance of the fat-ankled woman, Max stands in the doorway of the shop, smoking a B&H, flicking the ash in the street. He leans against the door, one foot either side of the threshold. His dark hair is bathed in the white lunchtime sunshine as he applauds every time Madeleine materialises from behind the changing-room curtain.

'Now, that . . . that is gorgeous,' he repeats at each turn, pointing with his cigarette. 'You know when I said you had lovely legs.' He nods, keenly. 'Well, your tits are great as well.'

Madeleine giggles. The fat-ankled woman doesn't know where to put herself. Becoming increasingly uncomfortable in her role as spectator, she busies herself clearing up the clothes from the floor of the changing room, exhaling a lot as she does so.

Half an hour later, Madeleine has modelled almost all of the shop.

'Do you know what sir will be taking?' asks the woman, a certain amount of sycophancy creeping into her voice as the moment of payment approaches.

'Um,' says Max, flicking his butt into the street and walking back into the shop. 'All of that there, I suppose,' he says, feeling in his back pocket for his Visa card. His cheeks pink slightly at the recklessness of his decision but he snaps it on to the counter just the same. At this point, he is not backing down.

'What, all of that pile?' says Madeleine, swallowing for dramatic effect.

'Absolutely,' breezes Max. 'You deserve it, darling.' He stoops and, lifting up a bunch of her long blonde hair, kisses the nape of her neck.

It's three o'clock in the afternoon by the time they arrive back at Wright Furniture. While Madeleine unpacks her new clothes into a corner of Max's old wardrobe, he opens up the shop downstairs. On the way back in the car he'd explained as simply and as gently as he could that although the first couple of days would be difficult, the sooner they got some sort of normality back in their lives the better. And Madeleine, much to his surprise, had agreed.

So while she potters upstairs admiring her reflection and pressing each new outfit against her body before she hangs it up, Max wanders around downstairs. She smiles as she hears him opening drawers, cracking ring-pull files and generally going about his business. She stares at herself in the full-length mirror clutching a scarlet scoop-neck T-shirt.

'It's all going to be fine,' she assures her reflection, which assures her right back. 'You are going to be fine. The children are going to be fine. Max loves you,' she affirms, determinedly tapping her thighs. 'And he loves them. Everything is going to be all right.'

But outside Wright Furniture, everything is far from all right. Larry is in a terrible state. Quite apart from the hangover that greets him that Sunday morning when he wakes (one of the heinous nearly-whole-bottle-of-whisky variety where your tongue becomes sandpaper and your head a dry cup with a stone), he had rather hoped that Madeleine might have come to her senses and returned in the middle of the night. Either that, or Val's soirée had been just some appalling dream brought on by too much blue cheese and pudding wine. But the lack of warm buttocks and sweet-smelling skin next to him tells him otherwise.

He can hear the children playing downstairs. The television is on. Something they know they can only get away with when their parents are too hungover to care. The sweet, innocent, happy cadences of their chatting voices make him feel sick. Larry lies in bed staring at the ceiling wondering what on earth to do.

Fucking bitch, he thinks, with an uncharacteristic lack of selfishness. Why has she left me to tell them the single most shattering thing in their young lives? 'Girls,' he rehearses. 'Your mother has left you – the bitch.' 'Your mother has left you – the whore.' 'Your mother has left, because she was fucking that bloke who sells furniture in town. You may both be familiar with him? You know, the smug fuck who's been round here a lot, eating my food, drinking my wine and sleeping with my wife.' Uncle Max. Maxie. That tosser . . . Well, she's left you and me for him!'

Larry isn't so much upset as bloody furious. His anger isn't even directed at Madeleine. She's too inert and weak-willed to have brought any of this on herself. It is Max whom he hates. Max who has pinched his wife. Max who has fucked up his life and made everything so damned inconvenient. He gnaws at his bottom lip, his left leg jigging in irritation. He wants to go to the bathroom for a piss, but instead he sits up in bed and telephones Val. Quite why he's chosen Val he doesn't really know. But he sure as hell needs to speak to someone. And Val – hostess of the party, Madeleine's best friend, and a woman who has already humiliated herself over Max – seems the most involved and his best bet.

Sleepy, muffled fumbling answers the phone.

'Val?' says Larry.

'Mmm? What? Yes.'

'It's me, Larry,' says Larry.

'Oh, hello. Um . . . are . . . are you okay?' mumbles the stirring Val.

'Well, it depends exactly how you define okay. If okay means am I still alive, then yes, I'm okay. But if okay means am I okay about my wife running off with another man then I'm not okay. In fact I'm far from fucking okay. Okay?'

'Oh,' says Val. As someone who looks her natural best in artificial light, this is all rather too much for her so early in the morning. 'Calm down, Larry, it's 10.30, you're going to have to be a bit less . . . um . . . aggressive.'

'Um, yes, sorry, of course,' replies Larry. 'It's just that I'm a bit all over the shop and I don't quite know what to do . . .'

'Oh, right,' says Val, propping herself up with one of her extensive range of white frilly cushions. She has never heard Larry speak that way before.

'What do you think I should do? Should I tell the children? I can hear them downstairs.'

'No, absolutely not,' responds Val immediately. 'Don't tell them anything. You know she might well come back any minute and then what would have been the point in that?'

'Do you think she will?'

'What?'

'Come back.'

'Of course,' lies Val, suddenly feeling slightly guilty about the rather naïve part she played in the break-up of Larry's marriage. 'I bet that if not this afternoon, then in a couple of days she'll come to her senses and come crawling back.'

'Yeah.' Larry laughs. 'Crawling back.' He laughs again. 'I mean it's not as if it's serious or anything . . .'

'No,' lies Val once more, the ramifications of her romantic meddling beginning to dawn on her. 'It's not as if she loves him or anything . . .'

'Now that would be stupid!' Larry chortles. 'I mean for fuck's sake everyone knows not to do that in this day and age. Anyway how could she? The bloke hasn't got any money!'

'Exactly,' agrees Val.

'So what do you think then? What should I do?'

'Just say that she's gone away for a couple of days, and leave Madeleine alone. She'll come round.'

'And what if she doesn't?' says Larry, suddenly losing confidence.

'Then I'll talk her round,' promises Val.

'Really?'

'Yeah.'

'Could you do that?' asks Larry, swinging his feet out of bed at this sudden ray of hope.

'Oh, yes,' says Val, wondering what on earth she is saying.

'Thanks, Val,' says Larry. 'Thanks a lot. Speak to you soon.'

★   ★   ★

So for the past couple of days Larry has been coping, putting a brave face on things. Lara and Sophie think their mother is at a health farm losing weight. It was the first thing that came into Larry's head and he is sticking to it. He has taken the week off work and has so far reheated three lasagnes out of the freezer and spent the rest of the time with the girls in the garden, waiting like some over-hormoned teenager for any sound at the front door or the slightest ring of the telephone.

It's Tuesday afternoon and he has still not heard anything. The girls are beginning to wonder how long telephones stay out of order at Forest Mere, while Larry is becoming snappier by the hour and developing a habit of pacing and staring at the front door. Eventually he decides enough is enough and gives Val another call.

'Val? Look, it's Larry. Still no word.' He's rambling slightly. 'So would you, you know, would you . . . Would you mind doing what you said you would?' he asks.

'Oh,' says Val, her forehead furrowing at his rambling. 'Really? Still nothing?'

'No, nothing.'

'Not even silent phone calls or anything along those lines?'

'No.'

'Oh.'

'So would you . . . you know?'

'Okay, I'll call,' says Val. 'But I can't promise anything . . .'

'Phone,' shouts Max from behind a grandfather clock at the back of the shop. 'Madeleine, darling, can you get that please.'

'What do I say?' she asks, almost excited at the responsibility.

'Wright Furniture will do,' says Max.

177

'Hello, Wright Furniture. How can I help you?' says Madeleine, with exaggerated efficiency.

Max laughs.

'Hello, Madeleine, is that you?'

'Hello, Wright Furniture,' she says again.

'Look it's me, Val. Don't hang up.'

'Wright—'

'Stop it,' says Val. 'We need to talk.'

Madeleine says nothing.

'Tomorrow? Lunch? The Black Bull? One o'clock? I'll be there.'

'Sorry, wrong number,' says Madeleine and hangs up. 'Wrong number,' she repeats more loudly to Max.

'Oh, right,' he says, infinitely more interested in winding up his clock.

Neither Max nor Madeleine can sleep. It's a hot, airless night; the breeze of the past couple of evenings has dropped and the atmosphere is close and heavy. With only a sheet on top of them, they lie side by side, their eyes closed, pretending to be dead to the world.

Max is worried about his shop. He suspects – actually if he's honest, he knows – that the gossip about him and Madeleine has done the rounds and for some reason or another there's a bit of a boycott going on. The first week in August is not normally the time of year for a rush on nests of tables, but no one, not one person came into the shop this afternoon. Granted he hasn't got the school-run ladies who always stop off, if only for some gratuitous flirting on the way to pick up their children. But around this time of year, or so the last lease-holder informed him, there is the passing tourist trade, who like nothing more than picking up something old and quaint from Shakespeare's county. Max turns over, wondering how long he can afford to sustain this financial cold-shouldering. Such a bunch of hypocrites, he concludes. They're all at it, sleeping with each other's wives. Why does his relationship matter so much? He turns again and comes across Madeleine's smooth, soft, naked body lying next to him. What does he care, he thinks, as he edges himself alongside her, burying his face in the nape of her neck. The love of his life is lying right next to him.

All Madeleine can hear is the sound of Val's voice, asking her out to lunch, asking her what she is doing, asking her where she thinks she is going. All she can see are the faces of her two children as they spin round and round in the air above her head like the petals of a flower. Her children are crying. Their noses are running. Their eyes are rubbed red raw and miserable. They shout her name, hold out their arms and she can't get to them. Val is saying meet me, meet me, and all the time the bed is too hot and Max is breathing down her back. His hands are running up and down her side. It's irritating not erotic. Madeleine moves on to her front, pretending to be fast asleep. He takes the hint and turns the other way.

The next morning Madeleine is resolved to meet Val. She walks downstairs in the new cream silk negligée, to find the table already laid with coffee and toast and Max sitting there, reading the paper.

'Sleep well, gorgeous?' He smiles, looking up, toast crumbs sitting in the corner of his mouth.

'Great,' she lies.

'Me too,' he lies back. 'So what are you going to do today?'

Madeleine sits down next to him as he leans over to kiss the curve of her naked shoulder.

'How are we going to keep you occupied today?' He smiles.

'Actually, I rather thought I might have lunch with Val,'

she replies. Her tone is sharper as she blurts out her secret. Well, his question had felt patronising and Larry had always patronised her.

'That's wonderful,' Max smiles. His guilelessness is disconcerting.

'Um, yes,' she replies.

'Give her a call.'

'I will.'

'Well, that's sorted,' says Max, getting up from the table, running his hands through his long dark hair.

'And what will you do?' asks Madeleine, buttering her toast.

'Oh, Lord.' Max laughs, putting his finger to his mouth in jest. 'Let me see . . .' He winks.

'Shop?' Madeleine smiles.

'Oh, don't mind if I do,' he replies.

Val is already sitting in the Black Bull by the time Madeleine arrives. A ten-minute drive from Wright Furniture, Max had insisted that Madeleine borrow the car. Uninsured and unused to driving it, she is tense and slightly neurotic even before she arrives. Val is in the corner in a pale pink vest top that is so low at the front that at first glance she appears to be almost entirely naked, simply resting her bare breasts on the table. An enormous pair of spherical sun specs are perched on top of her blonde Farrah Fawcett hair, and she is smoking.

'Co-o-ey,' she calls and waves as Madeleine walks into the dark Elizabethan pub and waits for her eyes to become accustomed to the gloom after the bright sunshine outside. The smell of spilled beer and stale cigarettes is all-consuming. The maroon carpet with dramatic textured swirls is tacky to walk on and the collection of horse brasses randomly displayed around the fireplace is in need of a polish. Madeleine always maintains that she hates pubs and, walking towards her waving girlfriend, she is reminded why.

'Hiya,' says Val, standing up to reveal the tightest pair of pale pink flared trousers Madeleine has ever seen. She appears to be straddling some rather vicious-looking barbed wire.

They hug. Val smells strongly of Charlie. 'Sit down, sit down,' she adds, patting the dark wooden chair with maroon tapestry cushion next to her.

'Hi.' Madeleine smiles. 'Don't you think it's nicer in the beer garden out the front?'

'Someone might see us,' replies Val. 'It's way more discreet in here.'

'Oh,' says Madeleine. New to the mistress stakes, such subtleties had passed her by. 'I suppose you're right,' she says, sitting down.

'Anyway . . . You look great,' says Val, closely inspecting her friend. 'New clothes?'

'Um, yes.'

'Where from?'

'Oh, you know, that place opposite the fishmonger in Stratford.'

'Christ.' Val coughs into her gin and tonic. 'He must really love you. That place is expensive. Stand up again so I can have a proper look.'

Madeleine duly stands up and does a *Generation Game* twirl. Val stops her halfway round to rootle down the back of her red hipster A-line skirt with buttons up the front, so she can read the label.

'Biba,' she says, sounding impressed. 'So when did you get all this?'

'Yesterday,' says Madeleine. 'I'm just going to get a drink at the bar. Do you want one?' she adds.

'G and T,' says Val. 'And make it a double.'

★　　★　　★

'So?' says Val as her friend rejoins the table.

'So?'

'So . . . God!' says Val, squeezing her hands between her knees with excitement. 'So what's it like? Um, what's he like? Is he a good fuck? Are you in love with him? Is he in love with you? God!' She shivers again. 'So many bloody questions.'

'Well,' says Madeleine, sparking up a B&H, throughly enjoying the attention. 'I truly love him and he truly loves me. He's my soul mate. My life. My world. I just don't think I can live without him. He's wonderful, kind, beautiful, considerate, the best lover I have ever had. Well, the only lover I have ever had,' she amends. 'But he is amazing . . .' The more she speaks about Max the more romantic their story becomes. The longer she is apart from him the more remarkable he appears.

'I'm so happy for you,' says Val, stubbing out her cigarette slightly too thoroughly. 'So . . .' She smiles, knowing the answer to her question. 'Um, have you spoken to the girls?'

'No.'

'Have you thought what you might do?'

'Well, they can come and live with me and Max, of course,' says Madeleine, with exaggerated confidence.

'Where? In that small flat?' Val sounds incredulous.

'To begin with. Then we'll buy a big house. You know, all four of us together like a big happy family. Max loves the girls and the girls really love Max.' She smiles and drains her drink to the point where all the ice slides down to hit her on the nose. 'Do you want another?'

'Um?' Val is only a third of the way down her glass. 'Oh, go on then . . .'

'I've spoken to Larry,' starts Val, when Madeleine returns.

'You have?'

'Almost every day, actually,' adds Val, slightly over-emphasising her role.

'Really? Why?' says Madeleine, leaning in, intrigued.

'Well, he doesn't know what to do really,' she says, taking a drag on her cigarette. 'So he calls for advice and stuff, you know, about the children and things.'

'But you don't have any children,' says Madeleine, slightly more sharply than she intended.

'I know, but I'm female and that's what Larry needs right now.'

'But you're *my* friend,' says Madeleine. 'You're supposed to be on *my* side. You helped set the whole thing up.'

'Yes, well,' she says, slightly embarrassed. 'It's not a question of sides; and anyway I have known Larry much longer than you.' She smiles. 'We're almost childhood friends.'

Madeleine swallows half her double gin and tonic in one and lights another cigarette from the one she has still lit. 'So have you seen my girls then?' she asks quietly.

'No, I haven't.' Val smiles. 'But Liz has . . . a lot.'

'Liz?'

'And Angela.' She flicks her ash. 'Larry's been, um, farming them out a bit. Well, it has been five days since you left and he has been going a bit mad.'

'Oh,' says Madeleine, inhaling. 'Are they all right?'

'Oh, Liz says they're doing very well, considering . . .'

'Considering what?'

'Well, you know . . . considering.' Val smiles.

'Considering their mother has run off with another man.' Madeleine laughs ironically and starts to scratch vigorously behind her right ear. 'I suppose you're all talking about me?'

'Oh, no; not really,' says Val ever so lightly, flicking her ash again.

'Don't lie.' Madeleine smiles, leaning on her elbow. 'Go on, please tell me.' She grins again. 'It's not often in one's life that one gets to play the scarlet woman, so please tell me what they're saying.' She puts her hands together in prayer.

'If you're sure,' says Val, raising her eyebrows.

'Certain.'

'Okay then.' Val grins, taking a steeling swig of her drink. 'Well . . .'

As it, somewhat unsurprisingly, turns out, Madeleine's dirty linen has been the focus of all gossip and intrigue for the past few days. And Val, as she delights in telling, has been the font of all knowledge. Not only was her place the scene of the break-up, but her regular conversations with Larry keep her firmly in the picture. The first person on the telephone after Larry that Sunday had been Angela. Eager for the gossip, she wanted to know if Madeleine had really gone home with Max? How long had they stayed before leaving? Was it really love? And did Val think that Madeleine would ever go back to Larry? Angela had seen it all coming from a long way off, she'd assured Val. Quite why Larry hadn't was a different matter, or actually probably part of the problem. Anyway, or so Angela said, she'd give the affair a week before Madeleine came home, her tail between her legs.

'She didn't?' squeals Madeleine.

'She did.' Val grins. 'But Liz was worse . . .'

Liz, frustrated by the constant engaged tone on Val's phone, had driven round for an update. Pretending to her husband that she'd left something of vital importance in the swimming pool area, she arrived at Val's with a fresh packet of cigarettes ready for a blow-by-blow account. Val, of course, told her very little. But Liz was quite persistent. How long had the affair been going on, exactly? Why had Madeleine actually left? Was Larry going to kick her out? Surely they could patch things up, it was only an affair after all? Nothing that out of the ordinary. They can't possibly be in love, can they? Did Val know?

'Everyone else had the decency to phone,' says Val, flicking her ash. 'But do you know the one person who wasn't that interested was Candida.'

'Really,' says Madeleine, now on her third double gin and feeling quite drunk. 'What do you think that means?'

'Maybe she's in love with Max herself?'

'Ah,' says Madeleine, tapping the side of her nose. 'That'll be it.'

'But I tell you, I have never been so popular,' says Val with a smile. 'Ever since Saturday my phone has not stopped ringing. Even Geoff and James have called.'

'No-o-o!'

'Oh, yes, rubbish excuses both of them, asking when Christopher is coming back, but both ended up asking about you. I don't know why they're so bloody interested; neither of their wives is going to run off and leave them. They're both too rich.' She laughs. 'Oooh, the tidal wave of trouble you have started, Madeleine, you can hardly imagine.'

They laugh and chink glasses. Leaning back into their chairs, they both sigh.

'Yeah,' says Madeleine.

'Yeah,' says Val and half smiles. 'Tell me, are you really all right?'

'I love him,' whispers Madeleine, looking like she is about to cry. 'There is nothing I can do about it. I wish there were but there isn't. I can't live without him. I just can't.'

'And your children?'

'My darling girls,' she says. Her head drops into her hands. Her face crumples easily with alcohol-assisted emotion, and she starts to cry. Fat tears quietly splash on to the complimentary beer mat. 'They're coming with me, my girls are coming with me,' she repeats over and over again like some mantra that if repeated often enough would come true. She looks up. 'How are they? Have you seen them? Where are they now?' Madeleine is shaking as she tries to take a cigarette out of the packet and light it. 'Val, Val,' she implores. 'Tell me where they are. Are they at home?'

'I think Liz has got them this afternoon,' she says. 'Larry's got some work thing he had to go to despite saying no. So I think Liz has them; in fact, I know Liz has them.'

'She does?' The look of joy on Madeleine's face makes Val immediately regret her indiscretion. 'What are we waiting for? Let's get over there,' she says, standing up and walking mechanically towards the door.

'Do you think this is a good idea?' badgers Val on the way out. 'I mean they think you're at a health farm, they don't know anything about what is going on. I really don't think this is a good idea.'

But Madeleine is deaf. Brushing off Valerie's remarks with a wave of her hands, she climbs into Max's car and over-revs the engine. She spins it around the pub car park, spraying all the other vehicles with a hail of pebbles, and sets off down the road towards Liz's house. Valerie is in hot pursuit. *Jesus Christ Superstar* at full volume on her stereo, she has to floor the accelerator in her new Mercedes to keep up with Madeleine. It's something that she is rather loath to do, but needs must, she says to herself, taking yet another corner at speed.

The look on Liz's face as she spots Madeleine marching across the lawn towards the pool is something that Val will never forget. Total and utter shock is the only way to describe it. Her eyebrows are so raised that they practically vanish into her hair. She is standing astride a sunbed in the largest, shiniest beige pair of pants that Val has ever seen, clutching her loose bosom, her mouth wide open. Madeleine fails to notice Liz in her state of unreadiness and shock. She can hear shouts and screams from the swimming pool and that's exactly where she is headed.

'Larry will be here any minute,' warns Liz, holding her bosom with one hand as she cups the other around her mouth. 'He's just phoned. He's on his way.'

Madeleine doesn't hear. Her focus is on the rose-scented path and the swimming pool where she first met Max.

'Christ, what is she doing here?' says Liz to an out-of-breath Val as she approaches.

'Oh, God, it's just me and my big mouth,' says Val, her hands pressing against each side of her face with worry.

'What are we going to do?' says Liz, looking for her T-shirt to cover herself up. 'I mean, Larry is on his way, I'm not joking when I said that, and he sounds like he's been drinking.'

'Oh, God, so has Madeleine,' says Val.

'Really,' replies Liz. 'How much?'

'Just enough for her to be totally irrational.'

'Shall we call Max and get him to come and collect her?'

'He doesn't have a car.'

'Fuck.'

'Yeah, fuck.'

'Mummy!' The loud scream can be heard even on the lawn. 'Mummy! Mummy!' Val and Liz look at each other.

'Look,' says Liz. 'You go up there and persuade her to leave. I'll head Larry off at the pass.'

By the time Val reaches the pool, Madeleine has both her daughters out of the water and is attempting to get them dressed without the aid of a towel.

'Quickly, quickly, girls,' she says, trying to hurry them up. Her red skirt has turned a dark maroon with water, her white

T-shirt is transparent. 'Come along, come along, Mummy is in a rush.'

'Oh, hi, Val,' says Sophie, trying to put her shorts on over her wet bikini bottoms.

Val smiles. 'Madeleine, what do you think you are doing?' she says, slowly and calmly.

'What do you mean what am I doing? What do you mean?' replies Madeleine, sounding increasingly hysterical. 'I'm collecting my children. My children. I'm collecting my own children.'

'And where are you taking them?'

'Home,' replies Madeleine, brusquely pulling a T-shirt over Lara's head.

'Whose home?'

'Jesus, I don't know,' barks Madeleine, squatting down on the ground looking increasingly like a cornered dog. 'I'm just taking them.'

'No, you're fucking well not.' Larry's voice is low and slow and deeply aggressive. His eyes are shining, his cheeks flushed, he is drunk. His moustachioed top lip is curling full of hatred.

'They're my children,' says Madeleine, standing up, defiantly flicking her blonde hair as she tugs Lara towards her.

'Well, you should have thought of that before.' Larry enunciates each word with increasing emphasis. He smiles. 'Shouldn't you?' he adds, taking a step towards her. 'Girls,' he says, looking down at his daughters. 'Go back to the house.'

'But, Daddy,' says Lara. 'We want to see Mummy.'

'Just do what I fucking well say, all right,' he shouts with such ferocity that Lara starts to cry, and Sophie runs down the path taking her sister with her.

'Look, Larry,' says Val, edging between the couple.

'Why don't you just fuck off, Val,' says Larry through

gritted teeth, taking another step closer. 'This is between my wife and me . . .'

'But—' she tries.

'Just leave us a-fucking-lone,' shouts Larry.

'I think I'm coming with you,' says Madeleine, scurrying towards her friend.

'You . . . you are staying right fucking here,' hisses Larry, grabbing her by the arm. 'You, my darling, are staying right fucking here.'

8

The bruise across Madeleine's face horrifies Max. He has never seen anything like it before. Even after his pissed and posh punch-up, his face looked nothing like as bad. The welt across her left cheekbone is huge and red. With cloudy purplish hints and dark black overtones, it already possessed a luminous quality all of its own. As Max stands there, open-mouthed, it takes all Madeleine's powers of persuasion to stop him from leaping into his car, there and then, and driving over to commit first-degree murder. Gathering her up, a crumpled heap on the doorstep of the shop, he finds himself crying hot tears of anger and frustration at his inability to look after her. Why wasn't he there? He hates himself. Why hadn't he been able to protect her from that shit of a husband? God, he hates himself. It is time they got away from here. Somewhere they can be together until things calm down a bit.

Max rings his mother, and the next morning Max and Madeleine leave to spend the weekend at the Wrights' in Oxfordshire.

'You'll love it,' insists Max, as he leans over to squeeze Madeleine's knee. 'It's quiet and beautiful and my family will love you.'

Madeleine smiles weakly as she rests her chin on the frame of the open car window, and stares at her bruise in the wing mirror. Her face is more swollen than it was last night. She seems to have an extra bag under her eye. Or could it be two?

The colours are still at the pale blue, red and bright purple stage; the yellows and greens have yet to arrive. It hadn't actually hurt that much. It was more of a shock than anything else. Valerie screamed. Larry collapsed to his knees, crying and begging for forgiveness and Madeleine simply walked across the lawn, clutching her face and drove slowly and in a bit of a haze back to the shop. It was Max's reaction that had made her buckle in front of him and start to cry. She doesn't think she's ever seen anyone that distressed before. He must really love her, she thinks, smiling as she leans further out of the window. Really, really love her.

It takes over an hour to drive to Max's family home near Charlbury, just north of Oxford. The air is dry and blissfully warm. During this longest, hottest summer on record, the countryside is parched. All along the roadside the earth is cracked. Gaping fissures fork off into the distance like the root structure of a tree. Long grasses wave stiffly in the breeze. A brittle yellow, those no longer pliant enough lie snapped at the side of the road to eddy and flow with the whirlpools of dust. Some of the fields have already been harvested. Mechanically recovered Swiss rolls of straw sit among acres of stubble, waiting to be collected. Others play host to giant red combine harvesters that trawl up and down, churning out arrows of straw and chucking up dust.

Passing through a cloud of dandelion clocks, Max and Madeleine turn into his parents' drive. The simple square gate posts in honey-coloured Cotswold stone mark the beginning of a long and heavily potholed drive.

'Fuck,' says Max, as his car bounces and the exhaust scrapes the road for the third time. 'I'm going to fix this drive myself one day.'

Madeleine holds on to her breasts.

Eventually they pull up outside a large and well-proportioned

Queen Anne house, with a dry fountain in the middle of a circular gravel drive. Set in what looks like acres of parkland, there is a croquet lawn over to the right-hand side of the house where two girls, in long floral-print dresses, are bent double over their mallets. Deep in conversation, it takes the sound of the car doors slamming to make them react.

'Max, Max, Max,' they both squeal with delight as they drop everything and run barefoot across the gravel.

Max stands, like some sort of benevolent Jesus, arms outstretched, as he receives them into his embrace. 'Hey, you two.' He smiles, hugging them both firmly against his chest. 'How are my two kid sisters doing?'

Both are freckled and ginger blonde, with transparent eyelashes and honey-coloured skin. One of them is tall, willowy and rather attractive, the other is not, with short legs, big head, sloping shoulders and small dark eyes like a myopically challenged mouse. She is obviously the youngest and by far the most affectionate, squeezing Max as if her life depended on it.

'Holly, Holly.' Max laughs, feeling the last vestiges of oxygen leaving his body. 'Steady on, steady on.'

'We haven't seen you in ages,' she trills, losing herself in his armpit.

'My turn,' insists the other, who has been standing back letting her younger sister go first.

'Nicola.' Max hugs her, kissing her on both cheeks. 'You look great. School treating you well?'

'Oh, stop it.' Nicola smiles, her eyes rolling. 'You know perfectly well that I'm at Durham.'

'So you are.' Max winks, clicking his tongue and pointing his finger. 'Oh, by the way everyone, this is Madeleine.'

They all turn to face her, standing alone by the car.

'Hi,' she says, shrugging her shoulders. Distinctly uncomfortable in her tight white flares that have cut off the circulation around her thighs, she feels gauche and particularly overdressed. Somehow the gold rings on her fingers and the dark pink nail varnish she'd put on this morning to try and appear smart seem totally inappropriate when confronted by these barefoot girls.

'Hi,' they both reply in a manner that implies sizing up and disliking all in one.

'Mum here?' asks Max, opening the boot of the car and bringing out one small suitcase.

Nicola and Holly look from one to the other and then at each other.

'Yup,' replies Nicola. 'The whole gang is here. Constance, Heather, Martha's even over from Paris. Dad's splashed out on new batteries for his hearing aid. They're *that* excited. They've killed the fatted calf and everything.'

'As long as it was just the calf, I can live with that.' Max smiles at Madeleine as he takes her hand to walk her up the steps to the front door.

'What's happened to her face?' whispers Holly as soon as their backs are turned.

Inside, the hall is cold and cavernous. Their footsteps echo on the black and white marble tiled floor, as they move towards the shiny mahogany table in the middle of the room. On it stands a large vase of pale pink roses. A dramatic staircase curves around the edge of the hall, rather like the faux number in Val's house, except this red carpet is threadbare and bleached pink. The dull brass banisters need polishing. Above hangs a rather sparse chandelier which, like a tree in winter, seems to have lost most of its appendages. Pushed up against the walls and into corners are various chairs, each different, each in need of a bit of love, care and attention.

'Darling!' comes a theatrical voice from the top of the stairs.

Both Max and Madeleine look up.

'Mum.' Max beams.

'Darling,' she repeats, before starting to swirl her way down the stairs, her dark and light green silk kaftan billowing in her wake. With a scarf wrapped tightly around her head and knotted at the front like a boiled sweet, Max's mother knows how to make an impression. A long nose, huge blue eyes and thick shoulder-length dark hair, she looks amazing for a woman who has had six children and must be knocking sixty. Her skin is smooth, white and extraordinarily unlined. She has full lips and one of those delicately arched browbones that suggests fine breeding.

'Sweetheart,' she says, puckering up her lips, yet proffering up her earlobes. 'Give Mummy a kiss.'

Max rubs cheeks with his mother and then stands back a pace. 'Mum,' he says. 'This is Madeleine.'

'Hello.' Max's mother smiles in a manner that implies both total pleasantness and total froideur. 'How lovely to meet you.' She offers a hand, bird-like in its slimness.

Madeleine takes it and shakes it as confidently as she can. 'Lovely to meet you too . . . um, Mrs Wright,' says Madeleine.

'It's actually Lady Wright,' she replies with a special generous smile. 'But Alice will do.'

'Oh, right, sorry,' stammers Madeleine. 'Um, Max never told me.'

'I'm sure there are many things Max has never told you.' She smiles. Her eyes flicker rapidly over the bruise on Madeleine's cheek, but she says nothing. 'Darling,' she says to Max, turning towards the door at the back of the hall. 'I have put you in your old room, and Madeleine is in the yellow room.'

'Oh,' says Max. 'I was rather hoping—'

'Really?' Alice replies, sounding surprised. 'As you wish,' she says, with a wave of her hand. 'Madeleine,' she continues without missing a beat. 'Come with me; you must be in a need of a drink.'

'Oh, yes, thank you,' says Madeleine, feeling sixteen all over again. As she trots along behind the formidable Alice, she turns to see Max walking slowly up the stairs with his suitcase, like a schoolboy returning on exeat.

Madeleine follows Alice into a huge and delightfully warm kitchen. A large sixteen-seater pine table dominates the middle of the room. There are French windows at one end, leading straight out on to a paved terrace and a flowerbed full of rosemary. Along the right-hand wall is a fat cream Aga, pumping out heat. An industrial-size kettle sits steaming on top of one of the silver hob covers. The opposite wall is completely covered in curling, dusty photographs and framed childhood achievements.

'Pink gin?' asks Alice. 'Old Indian habit.' She smiles. 'Find it terribly hard to lose.'

'Please,' says Madeleine, wandering over to the photo wall. There are hundreds of them. Mostly black and white, some formal, some not, group shots, some close-ups. A wavy-haired child in the grass, with a cricket bat, with a fishing rod, with a fish, on the beach, hanging upside down out of an apple tree, wearing school uniform, winning a cup. The longer and the closer she looks, the more it occurs to her that nearly all the photos are of Max. Give or take a few tutu shots and a couple of family groups, they are almost all, without exception, images of Max, in various stages of growing up.

'Admiring the shrine to Max?' comes a jovial, yet obviously sarcastic voice.

Madeleine turns round to be confronted by a tall, slim, dark-haired girl with the same eyes as Max. In fact, she looks almost exactly like him. The same features, straight nose, curled mouth, pale blue-green eyes, yet feminised. It is a stunning combination.

'It is a bit,' says Madeleine with a laugh.

'A bit!' says the girl. 'I think I appear in one of those,' she says, walking over to search for herself in the mêlée. 'There,' she says, pointing. 'It's with Max, of course.'

'Of course,' smiles Madeleine, looking at a photograph of two small children on the beach dressed in identical swimming trunks, both with the same pudding-bowl haircuts. It is difficult to tell which is male and which is female. In fact, they look so similar you could mistake them for twins.

'Stylish? Don't you think?' says the girl.

'What are you complaining about now?' asks Max, standing in the kitchen doorway.

'You!' says the girl, with a wide grin. 'God, it's lovely to see you,' she announces. 'What has it been? Two years?'

'And three months,' adds Max. 'Come here.'

They stand and hug so tightly and so long right in front of Madeleine that she doesn't really know where to put herself. So she stands leaning against the photos, a fixed smile on her face.

'Oh, sorry,' says Max, taking hold of Madeleine's hand. 'This is Madeleine . . . Madeleine, this is Martha, number two.'

'And Max's favourite,' adds Alice, handing over a pink gin. 'Hope it's not too strong for you.' She smiles. 'Old habits . . .'

'She's only his favourite because he's such a vain bastard and she's the one who looks most like him,' laughs someone else, whom Madeleine recognises as Heather from the Conservative dance. 'How are you, Madeleine?' she says, flicking her long red hair as she walks over with a trug full of lettuce and strong-smelling tomatoes. 'Ouch,' she says, pulling herself up before exchanging kisses. 'What happened to your face?'

'Oh, God,' says Madeleine, quickly covering her left cheek with both her hands. 'I fell.'

'Bumped into a wall,' says Max at the same time.

'Fell *and* bumped into a wall?' says Heather. 'How awful. Are you sure you're all right?' she asks, staring her brother in the eye. 'Ghastly thing to have happened.'

'No, I'm fine, honestly,' says Madeleine, taking a huge slug of her drink.

'Good,' says Heather, turning round and putting her vegetables down on the table. 'Who's for some drinks? Mum, did you just make those gins for you and Madeleine or are there any left for us?' she breezes.

'No, no,' insists Alice, standing aside. 'I made a rather large jug right here.'

She has indeed made a rather large jug. It is also a rather strong jug, as Madeleine discovers. The whole family, bar one of the daughters and Max's father, congregate around a large wooden table outside. Each with a pink gin in hand, including the youngest, Holly, who must be all of sixteen, they lounge like lizards turning to face the sun, soaking up its midday rays. Alice is the only one sitting in the shade. Her huge sunglasses disguise the direction in which she is looking. Madeleine is hot and sweating in her tight white trousers. She can feel the alcohol start to numb her legs. Beginning with her calves, by the time she is half-way down her first drink, the warm feeling is already up around her knees. She is smoking a lot of cigarettes and keeps wiping beads of sweat off her top lip, while skinny rivers of the stuff snake like eels down her sides.

'God, it's hot,' exhales Martha, hitching up her skirt, tucking the loose cotton material into the legs of her pants. Lounging back, her eyes closed, she crawls her feet forward and balances her drink on her smooth, flat stomach. 'So, Madeleine,' she says, not bothering to move. 'What do you do?'

'Um, what do I do?' says Madeleine, flicking her hair and cigarette at the same time. 'Um . . .'

'Darling,' says Alice, from the cool of the shade. 'Haven't I told you before about asking personal questions?'

'Madeleine's a mother,' says Max, finishing his drink and putting it down on the table with a rattle of ice.

'A mother?' queries Holly. 'But I thought she was your girlfriend.'

'She is,' says Max, getting out of his chair with a slow and exaggerated stretch. 'Darling?' he asks with a yawn. 'Do you want a tour?'

'A tour?' says Madeleine, sounding a bit too relieved. 'That would be lovely.' She smiles, getting out of her chair at speed. 'Could I also go and change?'

'Quite right,' says Alice. 'Get out of those city clothes, and into something more appropriate.'

As Max and Madeleine walk back inside the girls move closer together. Alice stays in the shadows, drinking her gin.

'So what do you think?' asks Holly in rather a loud whisper.

'Well, I've met her before and I think she is rather charming,' announces Heather, pouring herself some more gin.

'Really, where was that?' asks Nicola, helping herself to one of Madeleine's cigarettes that she left behind in her haste.

'Oh, at this black tie do thing that I went to with Max,' says Heather, sitting down again. 'Full of the most hideous sort of people,' she continues. 'I have never seen such a vulgar display of wealth in my life. Designer dresses, big hair, the lot. Short men with trophy wives; it was quite interesting.'

'It sounds ghastly,' says Martha, her eyes still closed. 'What the hell is Max doing hanging out with those sort of people?'

'Yeah. What is he doing?' agrees Nicola. 'Ghastly.'

'Do you know,' replies Heather, her head cocked to one side in thought. 'I think he enjoys it. Well, they all certainly know how to have a good time. The amount of food and wine on offer was amazing, and Max has always liked that sort of life, hasn't he?'

'What? Decadence?' asks Alice.

'Precisely,' agrees Heather.

'Do you think that's what he sees in her?' asks Nicola.

'There must be something,' mutters Martha. 'Because I sure as hell can't work it out.'

'She is very pretty,' admits Holly.

'That's true,' agrees Nicola.

'Not that pretty,' says Martha, taking a swig of her drink. 'Anyway, how do you think she got that bruise?'

'It looks like a punch to me,' says Heather, moving her chair a bit closer to the table. 'You don't think Max did it?'

'No-o-o,' they all reply at the same time.

'How could you?' says Martha, sitting up and turning round to look at her sister. 'Max would never do such a thing. He loves women. Anyway,' she adds, 'we all know he's far too much of a hippy to do something like that.'

'It was probably her husband,' says Heather, putting her legs in the sun.

'Husband?' asks Martha.

'Oh, yes,' says Heather. 'I've met him. Not a very nice man,' she adds. 'Well, at least I didn't think so. Boorish is the word to describe him.'

'How come you didn't mention this before?' asks Martha.

'Well, I don't know,' replies Heather.

'When Max said that he was coming home with a woman, why didn't you say something? We could all have been a bit more prepared,' she continues.

'Oh, you know,' shrugs Heather. 'When Max says he's bringing someone with him, you never know who he might turn up with. I know he's been talking about this one for a while, but he might well have moved on, frankly.'

'Now that's true,' agrees Martha.

'He changes his women like he does his shirts.' Nicola laughs.

'Yeah,' agrees Holly.

'Do you think this one will last?' asks Martha.

'Mmm,' muses Alice from the shade. 'He is sailing pretty close to the wind with this one if he isn't serious. Someone else's wife. With children. That's a lot of noses out of joint for a bit of local frivolity.'

Meanwhile Max takes Madeleine upstairs. He leads her along a dank, musty-smelling corridor, lined with glaring, bewigged ancestors. Florid and syphilitic with chins like testicles and eyes like crows, they don't bode well for future generations of the Wright family. At the end of the moss-coloured carpet, Max opens a door into a bedroom. It is dark as they walk in; the air hangs thick and undisturbed. Max pulls back the white wooden shutters to reveal a pale yellow room, dominated by a white art deco four-poster bed with coloured inlays. The counterpane is made of the same pale yellow silk as the wallpaper. Bleached and faded by the sun, what was probably quite garish and racy in its time has become soft and subtle and deliciously romantic.

'I've always loved this room,' smiles Max and he studies Madeleine's face for a reaction. 'But I have never been allowed to sleep here until now.' He collapses back into the cushions on the bed with an expansive sigh, and stares up at the yellow silk rosette in the canopy above him. 'Come on.' He grins, leaning up on one elbow and patting the space next to him, his rapidly consumed pink gin getting the better of him.

'Do you think we should?' says Madeleine, taking off her shoes and giggling as she falls on to the bed.

'This is my one and only chance in over three decades,'

laughs Max, as he starts to try and peel off her sweaty trousers. 'And I am sure as hell going to make it count.'

'Don't you think we should close the door?' asks Madeleine, wiggling her hips to help her out of her trousers.

'Nah,' says Max, pulling off her T-shirt. 'They're all outside in the sun.'

'Anyway,' he grins, leaning in to kiss her. 'Let's live dangerously.'

The silence that greets Madeleine and Max when they finally come downstairs almost an hour later is frosty to say the least.

'Nice tour?' asks Martha eventually, smoking another of Madeleine's cigarettes. 'Max thorough enough for you?'

'God.' Holly sighs. 'Finally. We've been waiting ages for you to have lunch. I'm starving.'

'Max,' says Alice, finally getting up out of her cool shady place. 'A word.' She says it in such a manner that there is no way the man can refuse.

'Mother,' he says, standing to attention.

They disappear off into the kitchen. Alice speaks too low for the rest of the group to hear, although they all lean forward to try and listen. Max is heard to say 'sorry' a lot and, 'yes' repeatedly.

'Do you think he's getting a bollocking?' asks Holly, her eyes wide with an obviously intimate knowledge of such a scenario.

'Stop being so nosy,' says Nicola.

'Who's being nosy?' announces a booming voice.

'No one,' says Nicola.

'Oh, right,' replies a tall short-haired girl, with strong thighs encased in a pair of denim shorts. 'I'm Connie,' she announces confidently, moving to shake Madeleine's hand. 'Been out in the fields with Dad,' she apologises. 'We thought you were arriving this afternoon. Or at least, that's what I was told, but then' – she laughs – 'no one ever tells me anything.'

'They certainly don't, do they,' says a rather tall, lean man with a full head of thick grey hair and a wide generous grin. 'I'm Max's father,' he says unnecessarily. The similarity is striking. Not so much physically because Max definitely has his mother's eyes, but the charm, and the charisma and the broad smile are all his father. 'Ouch,' he says, embracing Madeleine with an all-encompassing hug. 'That looks nasty. You should put some witch hazel on that, shouldn't she, Alice? Holly, get some from the cupboard will you? There's a love.'

Minutes later he is sitting next to Madeleine, dabbing a cold compress on her face.

'Probably a bit late,' he says. 'But worth a go, don't you think?'

'Thank you,' says Madeleine, enjoying the feeling of the cold liquid against her hot face.

'I don't hear terribly well,' says Max's father. 'The war.'

'Right,' says Madeleine.

'Just shout at me like an idiot and we'll get along fine.' He smiles. 'Christ, I'm starving,' he announces, rubbing his hands together. 'What's for lunch?'

'What, flirting already?' says Alice as she comes out of the house, putting her huge sunglasses back on. 'Alexander, you are terrible. The poor girl has only just arrived and you're all over her like a rash. What will she think?'

'What was that, dear?' says Alexander, winking at Madeleine. 'I'm afraid I didn't quite catch that.'

'Lunch is on the south terrace,' announces Alice. 'And don't tell me you didn't hear that.'

The spread on the long trestle table, parked under the canopy of purple and white passion-flowers, is impressive.

A whole ham with a ginger breaded coat is the centrepiece. There are wooden bowls of green salads and hand-made pottery platters of tomatoes from the garden. A mountain of minted new potatoes glistens with melted butter and a garish collection of home-made pickles and chutneys, each dated like the marmalade at Max's breakfast table, stand in a smart line like soldiers from the United Nations.

'Wonderful,' announces Alexander before taking his place, slowly and stiffly, at the head of the table, puffing up a thin floral cushion as he does so. 'Right now,' he says. 'Madeleine, you should come and sit next to me, here' – he indicates. 'On the right, next to my good ear, Holly on my left. I have had nothing but turgid conversation from you all for weeks about how you want a new this, and a new that, for birthdays and Christmas put together, so that'll be a relief. And the rest of you . . . Well, Max, you're next to your mother, you know how much she enjoys that, and that's it.' He exhales as he sits down.

Madeleine, in her wrapover skirt and vest top, is beginning to feel slightly more comfortable. But her pink polish looks plastic compared to Constance's rough red fingers, which adeptly pick up potatoes next to her and pop them in her large and accommodating mouth.

'Um,' ventures Madeleine. The whole table stops what they are doing as she speaks. 'I know an old girlfriend of yours, Constance.'

'Oh, do you?' she replies, helping herself to a hearty serving of cheddar. 'Who's that?'

'Patricia . . . I think Woodland was her maiden name?'

'Oh, my God!' shrieks Connie. 'Patsy Woodland! Do you remember her, Mum?'

'Unfortunate-looking child,' says Alice, cutting the fat off her ham.

'God.' Connie sighs. 'Patsy Woodland.'

'Is she from that family who sold their home to a country hotel chain?' asks Martha.

'Yup, yup, that's the one,' says Connie, waving her fork. 'We were such good friends at one time.' She adds, sitting back in the sun, 'I think she was a bit in love with Max.'

'Isn't everyone?' Martha sighs.

'Actually, none of my friends is,' replies Holly. 'They all think he's too old.'

'Old!' says Max, putting his head in his hands. 'How old?'

'Well, you're over thirty.' Holly shrugs. 'And in my book that's ancient.'

'Ancient!' Max rolls his eyes. 'Mum,' he whines, slouching across the table like a small child. 'Stop her from being so mean.'

'Now, Holly,' says Alice, wagging her finger. 'Stop calling your brother old. You know very well how much it upsets him. Any more ageism from you and you will have to go to your room.'

Nicola and Heather are laughing. Their mouths curl in the same way when they're amused. Max smiles a 'that's-you-told' smile and ruffles up Holly's hair. She immediately straightens it. Alexander sits at the head of the table like some mafia don, simply enjoying his own family.

'How long is it since we have all been together?' he asks. He looks the length of both sides of the table. No one, or so it appears, is sure of the answer. 'Last Christmas?'

'No, I was in Paris with Jean-Luc,' says Martha.

'Oh, God, him,' says Nicola, making as if to vomit on her plate.

'The year before then?'

'Um.' Alice thinks.

'Nope,' says Heather, leaning back in her seat. 'I was trekking in Africa.'

'Oh, yes.' Her father nods. 'Easter then?'

'No,' says Martha. 'Max was with—' She stops. The rest of the table look at their plates.

'But the Easter before, we were all definitely together,' chips in Heather, breaking the silence.

'Really?' says Alexander. 'How interesting. Well, let's have a toast then, shall we, seeing as we are all here now.' There's a general rummaging and pouring out of wine. 'Come along, Madeleine,' he says, noticing her reticence. 'Hold back in this place and you'll die of thirst and starvation.' He pours her a huge glass of wine. 'Right,' he announces, getting rather slowly out of his chair. 'To my wonderful family and many more occasions like this.' He smiles.

'To us,' they all say in a mad mêlée of chinking glasses.

'To you,' smiles Madeleine raising her glass and taking a sip on her own.

Lunch clatters on. Max chats to his mother as she positively glows with pride at the attention. Alexander makes polite conversation to Madeleine about her two children. Martha listens. Constance eats fourteen potatoes while Madeleine has some salad and a slice of lean ham. Nerves are certainly a better appetite-suppressant than Apesate. Heather entertains her two younger sisters with stories of London and the property magazine she works for. It is four o'clock by the time all the fruit and cheese and coffee plus an additional naughty box of chocolates have been consumed.

Holly is lying on the check rug, half asleep in the sun. The wine and the earlier pink gin have obviously got the better of her. Alexander keeps threatening to join her but eventually elects to go and have a lie down inside. The other sisters start to clear the table, refusing Madeleine's offer of help, while

Max and his mother sit firmly ensconced at the far end of the table, talking. Madeleine sits on her own, smoking. It's Heather who eventually comments.

'Max,' she says. 'Do you normally invite people away for the weekend and leave them on their own, or is this a new fashion that I'm unaware of?'

Max is effusively apologetic as he leaps out of his chair and comes to the other end of the table. Standing behind Madeleine, he puts his arms around her and kisses her behind her left ear.

'Yuk,' says Martha, as she piles up some empty plates. 'Max, we have just eaten, you know?'

'Stop being so jealous,' says Heather, holding a salad bowl. 'Just because you're an embittered old spinster at the moment.'

'Girls, girls, girls,' says Alice, ushering them along. 'Max,' she adds, shaking her head. 'Couldn't you possibly do that elsewhere? It really is quite vulgar.'

Max offers to take her on a proper tour of the gardens and Madeleine, desperate to escape his increasingly claustrophobic family, is only too keen to accept. Not that Max's family are unpleasant because they're not. It's just that they are a bit overwhelming and very confident of themselves, thinks Madeleine, as she follows Max into a formal and highly scented rose garden. They seem to operate very happily on their own and have little need for outsiders. Coming from a small family with only one other sister, Madeleine finds such a verbose and assured gathering rather intimidating. All Max's sisters are also frighteningly educated, with jobs. Heather works for some property magazine in London, where, as far as Madeleine can work out, she seems to run the whole advertising section single-handed. Martha is the artistic one, living in Paris and working in an art gallery specialising in modern art. Connie works on the farm, helping to run the estate with her father. Nicola is at Durham University reading history or art or both, and Holly, although still at Cheltenham Ladies College, has plans to follow in her sisters' footsteps. The product of a family that failed to educate its daughters, Madeleine finds it hard to handle such intellect in so many women all at the same time.

And she can tell they disapprove of her. Not in any malicious way, but they seem disappointed with Max's choice. The golden boy, handsome and charismatic, the bloke who has the pick of the bunch when it comes to girlfriends and look who he brings home. A neurotic blonde, with a black eye, who is married to someone else and has two children. It's not even as if she has any money. It's easy to presume they don't understand the attraction.

'I don't think your family approves of me,' says Madeleine, placing her arm through Max's as they walk down the box-tree-lined path that dissects the rose garden.

'Don't be silly,' says Max, squeezing her arm. 'They just don't know you yet, and when they do, they will find you as irresistible as I do.'

Madeleine is not convinced. 'Do you really think so?'

'Of course. Mother is the one to get on-side,' he says. 'She pretends to be tough but really she's a sweetheart. Talk about me, that usually does the trick.' He laughs.

'It's Martha who I find the most terrifying.'

'Yes.' He nods in agreement. 'It has been said before. She's a complex person. We were the closest when we grew up. She just gets a bit protective, that's all.'

'Your father is great,' adds Madeleine, desperately trying to sound positive.

'Isn't he?' Max smiles. 'He's responsible for all this.' He spreads his arms expansively. 'It was a total mess when he inherited the place. He's built the rose garden up from scratch, almost. Well, not entirely from scratch but it was falling apart, full of weeds, looking very sad and it's his pride and joy.'

It is indeed beautiful. The grey flagstones covered in soft green lichen blend perfectly with the dusty pink of the roses. The garden is divided into triangles, neatly bordered with box, each with a different variety of rose in a subtle dusty colour. The different sections blend together in a symphony of good taste. And the scent, sweet and heady, rising from the heat of the afternoon, is overpowering.

'He has done the most wonderful job, it's quite beautiful,' says Madeleine, as she walks over to a border of pale purple petals and inhales.

'Tell him,' beams Max. 'Tell him you love his garden, and I bet you a quid he cries. He nearly always does.'

Beyond the rose garden, the parkland attached to Horsely House extends almost as far as the eye can see. Cedars stretch their arms against the sky. Tall pines, and the odd oak, dance in the acres of long, long grass.

'I used to spend whole afternoons in that grass.' Max smiles. 'Lying on my back staring at the clouds, working out the shapes of faces and animals and monsters in the sky. No one ever knew where I was. I'd spend hours flat on my back, solving the problems of the world, worrying about what it would be like to be grown up.' He sighs quietly. 'I always used to think it looked like the sea, especially when the wind blows.'

'It's beautiful.' Madeleine smiles, enjoying Max's smile.

'Come on,' he says brusquely, pulling himself together. 'Haven't shown you the pool or the tennis court, or Mother's arboretum. So much to pack in before dinner.' He slaps his own thigh. 'We'd better get a move on.'

'God, dinner,' exhales Madeleine. 'We've only just had lunch.'

'I know,' he says, taking hold of her hand. 'It's endless socialising chez the Wrights, I should have warned you. We've got dinner for twelve tonight.'

'My God, have we really?' asks Madeleine, her eyes spherical with surprise. 'Who?'

'Oh, you know,' says Max, sounding vague as he walks along the gravel path towards the swimming pool, kicking an imaginary Coke can. 'A few people whom I used to know very well when I was a child . . . sort of neighbours.'

'Don't be stupid,' says Madeleine briskly. 'There aren't any bloody neighbours around here, Max.'

'Well, family friends sort of people.'

'People with a bloody history of "do you remember when" stories, and all I'll be able to do is sit and smile like some stupid piece of fluff at the end of the table, which is what everyone already thinks I am, a piece of fluff.'

'Don't be so ridiculous,' says Max, taking a step backwards, trying to look Madeleine in the eye. 'You're not a piece of fluff.'

'Well, that's how it feels,' says Madeleine, probably more curtly than she intended. The combination of the alcohol at lunch and the baking afternoon heat is making her feel bloated and irritable, verging on the morose.

'Well, you're a very attractive piece of fluff,' says Max, roguishly tweaking her chin. 'Come on, there's more of the estate to see.'

Estate? thinks Madeleine, as she follows along behind. Who is he kidding? It's not as if Horsely House is some baronial hall. It's a house, for Christ's sake. Her shoes start to rub at the back of her heels as she slips on the sweaty sole of her sandals. Max is holding forth about the extra-special marble from just north of Pisa where his family went one summer to buy the poolside urns, when she hears the sound of Holly laughing somewhere in the garden. The sound immediately makes her think of Lara and Sophie.

'Do you think your parents would mind if I made a phone call?' Madeleine asks suddenly, as she stops by the entrance to the pool, her sweaty panicked hands rigid by her side.

'Why?' says Max, looking confused. 'Have you been listening to a word I've been saying?' he says, offended.

'Yes, yes,' says Madeleine, shaking her head and cupping her forehead in her right hand.

'I mean is it really necessary?' Max sighs, placing his hands on his hips. 'Because Mother is quite strict about the telephone. The telephone and wrapping paper, for some reason. Wrapping paper has to be saved, folded up and put in a drawer for future use and the telephone is for emergencies only. There is a phone box in the village if it's really urgent,' he says by way of an afterthought.

'No, no,' says Madeleine. 'If it's really that difficult . . .' Her voice trails off. 'I just wanted . . .' She digs her fingernails into the palms of her hands and stares at the ground. 'Lara and Sophie . . .' she whispers.

'Obviously, you couldn't get urns like these, nowadays. Not for love nor money.' He chortles, carrying on his talk, oblivious to Madeleine's mood. 'And believe you me, we've had offers.' He stops and turns round to smile. 'Marvellous, isn't it?' Moving on towards the arboretum, Max's enthusiasm grows. 'Anyway, some of these trees are worth between two and three thousand pounds each,' he lies expansively, impressing himself. 'Did you know that mature trees are very expensive?' he asks like a bragging schoolboy.

Madeleine shakes her head.

'They are, you know. Mother does really rather well out of something that is a bit of a sideline for her.'

★   ★   ★

The noise, when Max and Madeleine eventually make it back into the kitchen, is deafening. Max's sisters are all sitting around the kitchen table shelling peas, slicing beans and squawking with hilarity at some shared joke. Sounding like a group of particularly boisterous geese, they fail to notice the arrival of the other two. Connie is doubled over she is laughing so hard. Nicola is shouting loudly that she might have to go and pee if this carries on much longer, while Heather is simply crying. The tears roll down her cheeks to such an extent that at first glance it is difficult to work out whether she is amused or upset. But the upward curl to her mouth gives the game away. Finally it is Martha who speechlessly beckons them both in and, shifting along the bench, makes just enough room for Max. He slips in buttocks first, swinging his legs over after him and immediately starts to shell peas. Madeleine stands. The conversation continues.

It is obviously a scene that has been repeated again and again around this very table, thinks Madeleine, aware of what little bearing her presence has on the proceedings. She wants to vomit on their *Brady Bunch* perfection. Instead she makes an excuse that she needs a bath, and is irrationally curt when Max suggests he comes up and runs it for her.

Walking into the relative calm of the yellow bedroom with its crumpled sheets, she collapses back on the pillows and starts to weep.

It's not a hysterical type of crying. Just a gentle bit of self-pitying as she lies there, letting the tears trickle down the sides of her cheeks into her ears. What is she doing here? Who does she think she is kidding? Running off, and leaving her children for this man? She sighs. And what does Max think he is doing? Does he really think she is impressed by his overt display of wealth? He's supposed to be a beatnik hippy who wore beads and hung out in India. The bloke who left the rat race behind to open a shop in Henley-in-Arden, for Christ's sake. Like she really gives a shit? She has just left a man who flashed his cash around as if his masculinity depended upon it.

Anyway, she smiles thinking of Val; as country stacks go, it's not much to write home about. The swimming pool is falling apart. The rose garden is nice. But the tennis court has more fissures than the San Andreas Fault. The house needs repointing and, as she gets off the bed and walks next door to run a bath, she takes mental bets on the plumbing being crap.

Sure enough it is. Wailing and screaming like a petulant child, the piping shakes and rattles in some sort of orgasmic frenzy along the peeling damp walls of the bathroom. After a couple of minutes of high-pitched protestation, the tap eventually judders into action and releases a load of russet-coloured water into an enormous roll-topped free-standing bath. Madeleine leans over to dip her hand in and is greeted by a mass of floating debris. Old hair, dust, dead spiders curled up like tomato tops and discarded woodlice skin form a floating film on the top. Madeleine pulls a face and, with her toes firmly curled, empties the bath and swills it clean before going through the whole filling process again.

Returning from the bedroom naked save for a stiff towel the size and texture of Ryvita wrapped tightly around her stomach, she climbs into the ankle-deep water, only to find it tepid, almost cold.

Emotionally drained and feeling very much alone, Madeleine sits down in the cool water, and proceeds to wash herself in a manner that is both rapid and efficient. She had been looking forward to washing her hair, shaving her legs and maybe de-hoofing her feet. But a quick once-over with a flannel is about all she can bear. With her damp hair curling at the back of her neck, dressed in a towel the size

213

of a postage stamp, Madeleine wanders back into the yellow bedroom and decides to have a sleep. It is only 5.30 p.m. she concludes, so it is either a sleep or a couple of hours spent in jolly conversation with the Wright girls, asking her whether she is employed or not, what her intentions are towards Max and whether she might go back to her husband at any stage. Sleep is by far the more preferable option.

It is gone 7.30 p.m. by the time Max comes upstairs to wake her.

'Darling,' he says, stroking her hair to stir her. 'Wakey, wakey.' He leans in and kisses her on the mouth, his tongue running the length of her lips. He tastes of gin.

'Mmm.' Madeleine wakes and stretches. Her whole body shivers as she tries to come round. 'What time is it?' she asks, her eyes half open.

'Time you woke up,' says Max, walking around the room, unbuttoning his shirt. 'You don't fancy a quick one before dinner?' he asks, falling on to the bed. 'You know, just the quick once over?' He is snaking his way up the bed towards her. He seems to be quite drunk.

'No, piss off, Max,' she says, struggling out from underneath him. 'Are you pissed?'

'A bit.' He grins. 'Can you tell?'

'Yes,' she says, sounding more irritated than she intended, because he actually looks quite sweet. All brown, his toned chest, his dishevelled hair, his shirt unbuttoned, his trousers halfway down his legs, as tipsy men go Max didn't look bad. 'What have you been doing?'

'Oh, God,' Max puffs. 'I've been mixing martinis with Martha.'

'Oh.'

'Well, we thought we'd make them for tonight, you know,

for the dinner thing. Anyway, she made them and I tested them. She made a few mistakes on the way but I think we might have the recipe sorted out now.'

'So she didn't drink any?'

'No, no, just me.' He giggles. 'God, I must sober up a bit. I know.' He raises his finger in the air. 'I'll have one of those nice cold baths. The speciality of the house.' He smiles. 'And you,' he says, hitting her hard on the behind, as he makes his way towards the bathroom, 'you had better get ready for dinner.'

Half an hour later Madeleine, plus a surprisingly sober Max, make it downstairs for dinner. Everyone else, plus the guests, are already having drinks on the terrace. However, when Max announces they are having dinner for twelve, with such a large family it actually only means there are three other people joining them.

'Darling, there you are!' declares Alice expansively. She has exchanged her green kaftan and sweet-wrap headscarf for another diaphanous outfit of dark purple silk that floats voluminously in the warm evening breeze. Her dark shoulder-length hair is carelessly chic and she wears large pendulous earrings that rattle as she moves. 'Jennifer, George and Felicity have been wondering where you were. The food is nearly ready,' she adds, walking into the house.

Jennifer, George and Felicity stand in a row, all holding their martinis in their right hands, smiling at Max.

'Maxi,' hails George, the loose flesh under his chin chattering as he speaks. 'Put it there, old boy,' he demands, putting his glass down as he proffers up his clammy right hand, thwacking Max on the back as they bond manfully. 'Great to see you, old boy, it's been far too long, far too long. It really has.'

'Max, darling,' says Jennifer, her small orange-lipped mouth puckering up as she stands, craning forward, looking somewhat constipated, waiting for Max to approach and trade cheeks. 'Delightful to see you, simply delightful.'

Felicity stands back. Cool, long and languid-looking, with buttock-length hair, elegant ankles and wrists, she sports high heels and an open-necked shirt-dress. She has tits like apples, looks better then her gene pool and has obviously slept with Max. There is something in the way that he slips his arm around her waist, and she leans in to him as they kiss, rubbing herself up against his thigh, that sends a frisson of jealousy and fear down Madeleine's spine. She takes a hearty swig of her cocktail.

'I'm Madeleine,' she says, shaking George's limp hand, soliciting a weak smile from Jennifer.

'Lovely,' says Jennifer eventually. 'What on earth happened to your face!'

'Oh . . . I . . . um.'

'She fell,' says Max assertively.

'How ghastly,' Jennifer responds in a manner that implies more of a comment on the injury itself than any form of sympathy. 'So, Max,' she says without missing a beat. 'We haven't seen you round our neck of the woods since you moved out of the cottage.'

'No, yes, indeed,' says Max, taking a swig of his martini.

'Max and Felicity have been very close friends for years,' says Jennifer, sounding extremely pleased with herself.

'Oh, really,' says Madeleine. 'That's nice.'

'A lot of people used to say that they were the perfect couple,' announces Martha from across the garden table.

'Well . . .' says Heather.

'They did,' insists Nicola.

Felicity smiles and smugly flicks her long hair.

'That was a long time ago,' laughs Max, walking over to take Madeleine's hand, kissing her on the cheek as he does so. 'Anyway, did I hear mention of dinner? Another one of these and I'm afraid I'll be arseholed.'

'Who's arseholed?' asks Alexander, clutching a fistful of salted almonds.

'Me, Father,' replies Max, pointing at his own chest.

'Quite right too.' He grins. 'Best state to be in on these occasions.'

Jennifer hoots with hollow laughter. 'Always knew we could count on you!' she shouts into his good ear. Alexander winces in pain.

'Dinner everyone,' announces Alice, wafting back on to the terrace. 'Oh, Madeleine,' she says. 'I quite forgot to say how nice you look. Dear little outfit,' she adds, checking her long cream cheesecloth dress up and down. 'Have you met Felicity properly?' she goes on. 'She and Max have been very close friends for years.'

Dinner for Madeleine, as she sits in the badly lit, hot, blue dining room, at a long mahogany table with high-backed chairs riddled with woodworm, is a living nightmare.

'Okay, quiet everyone,' commands Alice, tapping her hands together like a rather elegant master of ceremonies. 'I have a seating plan.'

'Oh, God.' Holly yawns. 'I hate it when you do those. I always get the shit seat.'

'Shut up, darling,' dismisses Alice, flapping out a piece of paper and holding it at arm's length. 'You,' she says, looking down, pretending she is unable to remember exactly where she has placed everyone. 'You, darling, I think, are down at the far end with George and Madeleine.'

'Great,' says Holly, her arms sulking by her sides as she drags herself to the other end of the room.

'Madeleine, you're down there, between George and Holly.'

She points distractedly, as Madeleine makes her way across the room. 'Alexander, dear, you are over that side. Now, Max.' Alice beams at him. 'You're up here next to Felicity, so you can have a good old chat. Such close friends and you haven't seen each other in a long while.'

'Um, actually,' ventures Max.

'Don't argue,' retorts his mother, exchanging smug smiles with Jennifer. 'It's my party.' She laughs. 'Connie and Martha, you are there and there,' she indicates. 'God, there are too many women in this house,' she says, flicking her hair. 'And Heather, you are here, next to Jennifer. Marvellous,' she adds, sitting down. 'Thank God that's all sorted.'

While Holly hands round the bowls of vichyssoise, Madeleine tries to be pleasant to the sexist bore George.

'So you're a housewife?' he says, his moist mouth straining towards the chilled soup on his silver spoon.

'Mmm,' replies Madeleine, not really concentrating, unable to do little else but watch Felicity in operation.

The girl could almost be a professional, concludes Madeleine, as she observes the competition in action. She flicks her hair and laughs enthusiastically at Max's jokes. She pouts and preens. She pushes her bosom together and proffers it up on an underwired platter in Max's general direction. In short, she gives him her undivided attention. And Max, or so it appears, is flattered. Initially, he is embarrassed. He keeps constantly checking the end of the table, smiling at Madeleine, mouthing: 'All right?' But by the main course – a rather dry lasagne with a lettuce and pea salad that Alice laboriously tells everyone how to make – Max has his back to Madeleine and is hunched conspiratorially with Felicity. Occasionally they whisper, they giggle and then laugh uproariously at some shared joke. Alice and Jennifer look pleased and appear to marvel at the fruits of their divine intervention. Meanwhile George bores on.

'I mean I do find this women's lib thing amazing,' he

says. 'I mean what do they want to be liberated from?' He chortles, a long hard piece of snot hanging from his left nostril by a hair.

'Well, plenty of things actually,' says Madeleine.

Martha is also obviously irritated by this boozy display of chauvinism and smiles at Madeleine for the first time since she arrived. Together they watch George opine on, electing to say nothing about the nodding nasal appendage that seems to agree with his every word.

'Okay, everyone.' Alice taps her hands again. 'Who's for some pavlova with fresh raspberries from the garden?'

'Oh, yes, lovely,' says Madeleine, leaping out of her seat, offering to clear. Her dress clinging to her shoulder blades, thanks to the close heat in the room, she walks the length of the table collecting plates. Approaching Max, she notices Felicity's hand firmly gripping his thigh. 'Darling,' she says forcing herself between them. 'Are you all right up here?' She presses a possessive thigh up against his side.

'Bearing up, bearing up.' Max smiles, brushing off Felicity's predatory hold. 'Let me help you with those,' he adds, making as if to stand up.

'No, no, you stay there!' insists Alice with a wave of her angular hand. 'What is the point of having so many daughters, if one has to clear away as well as cook?' She laughs, leaning forward with a cigarette in her mouth, gesturing for Max to light it.

Madeleine passes on the pavlova in favour of more wine that she mistakenly pours into her water glass. But fortunately no one notices, as no one is paying her any attention. Holly has not addressed a word to her since she sat down. Martha is gazing out of the window, thinking of something else. And everyone else seems otherwise engaged; including Max, or indeed especially Max. Such is the charm of his dinner companion that he has stopped bothering to look down the table at Madeleine, and appears to have his nose surgically taped down Felicity's cleavage. While the airlessness of the evening is making Madeleine break out in beads of sweat all over her forehead, Felicity still looks as cool and smooth as an ice cube, flicking her hair, pouting her lips and telling terribly interesting stories. Madeleine drinks some more. The cognac makes a tour of the table. She tucks in.

'Max?' she says suddenly. There is no break in the conversation. 'Max,' she repeats. His back remains turned towards her and everyone carries on talking. 'Max?' she says, slightly louder.

'He can't hear you, dear,' says Jennifer, leaning across Holly's plate. 'He's talking to someone else.'

'Max!' says Madeleine, hammering her fist so hard on the table that the Wrights' two-hundred-year-old set of dining silver leaps in the air with fright. The table falls silent.

'Yes?' says Max, slowly extricating himself from Felicity's pair of Cox's pippins.

'Um.' She smiles as everyone turns to stare. 'Do you have a cigarette?' She blushes.

'But you have—' says Holly, picking up a golden box of B&H from underneath Madeleine's napkin.

'Of course,' says Max, loudly interrupting his sister. 'How rude of me not to notice.' He passes a packet down the table. Madeleine takes one and, leaning forward, lights it from a candle flame, taking extra care not to set fire to her hair.

The conversation takes a good two or three minutes before it returns to its previous volume. Madeleine inhales and exhales, trying to look busy, studiously ignoring Little Miss Cucumber at the other end of the table.

'So?' she says to George finally, slurring her words a bit. 'What is it about feminism that you find so offensive?'

'I'm surprised you need to ask.' He chortles. 'A housewife

like you . . . can't really see you burning your brassiere with the rest of them, now, can we?' He leans over and pats her on the knee.

'Well, yes,' replies Madeleine, draining her glass of cognac for want of a reply.

'Actually you might find that motherhood is not excluded from the feminist ethic,' pipes up Martha. 'The thing is that we feel it should be recognised along with a lot of other things, like for example wages for housework, the mantra of the socialist feminists.'

'So you're one of them then, are you?' asks George, looking down his fleshy nose.

Martha and George start to argue. As intelligence battles with belligerence, it is a painfully obvious no-win situation. Madeleine, unversed in her Greer and de Beauvoir, smokes and spectates as she has done for most of the evening. She looks down to the other end of the table to find Max building a map with his napkin, knife, fork and the silver saltcellar by way of explaining something deeply fascinating to the ever-attentive Felicity. He takes hold of her hand, she smiles into his eyes and Madeleine scrapes her chair along the flagstone floor as she stands up.

'I think I might turn in,' she announces, holding on to the table for support.

Jennifer and Alice exchange glances.

'I'm really quite tired.'

'Well, yes, indeed you must be,' says Alice, smiling not quite generously enough. 'You have had quite a time of it recently, haven't you? Leaving your husband and children is enough to make anyone a little over-tired.'

'Yes, quite.' Madeleine smiles tightly as she watches her dirty linen waft gently around the room.

'What, off already?' says Alexander, standing up as

221

Madeleine leaves the table. 'That's a shame. I thought you might partner me in Trivial Pursuit.'

'Don't be foolish, darling,' says Alice. 'We're socialising, we don't play games when we have guests.' She nods towards Felicity who is whispering something coquettish and obviously frightfully funny into Max's ear.

'Right you are then,' says Alexander, looking confused.

'Right, then,' says Madeleine, standing by the door. 'I'll be off to bed then everyone.'

'Yes, yes,' says Alice. 'Off you go.'

'Um, thank you for a lovely dinner,' she says, smiling at Alice.

'Fine, yes, fine,' she replies.

'So, 'night then, everyone,' Madeleine announces more loudly as she stands by the door. She waits a second longer. 'Um, bye then . . .'

'Oh, darling!' says Max, sounding surprised, looking up from his DIY cutlery charts. 'Are you off to bed?'

'It looks like it,' she replies.

'Oh, okay then.' He nods. 'I'll see you in a minute.'

Alice and Jennifer smile. Felicity flicks her hair.

'I'll make some more coffee,' sings Alice, floating off towards the kitchen.

'Absolutely,' preens Jennifer. 'Coffee all round for everyone; the night is still young as they say.'

'Very young indeed, don't you think, Max?' purrs Felicity, licking her top lip with her tongue and running her hand along his thigh.

'Yes,' says Max.

'In fact,' says Felicity, leaning over, 'it's terribly hot in here. Do you fancy a stroll outside?'

'Do you know?' announces Max, suddenly glancing towards Madeleine who is still standing in the doorway. 'Do . . . you . . . know,' he says determinedly, staggering somewhat unsteadily to his feet. 'On second thoughts . . .' He belches through the back of his teeth. 'I think I might come up with you, darling.' He coughs. 'You know, um, upstairs to bed. I'm suddenly rather over-tired myself.'

9

The argument they had that night was apparently so shrill you could hear it in the neighbouring county. The next day Alice took her son to one side and told him exactly how mortified she was. For all her kaftan-wearing, Bohemian pretensions, Alice finds shouting and stamping and other such emotional outbursts 'undignified' and quite frankly a bit 'common'.

'I mean who the hell does she think she is?' she hissed at her son when they discussed the whole rather sordid incident in the rose garden. 'She sounded like a bloody fishwife. The whole thing was so embarrassing, with Felicity downstairs. It's fortunate for you that your father is so frightfully deaf because otherwise he would have been up there like a shot, sorting the two of you out.' She shivered. 'Actually, I find the whole thing too upsetting to talk about. Don't you ever,' she stressed. 'Ever, do that to me again.'

Max, on the other hand, revelled in the whole thing. In fact, he'd loved it. There he was, standing, drunk, flat up against the wall, facing a firing squad. There she was, drunk, standing stark naked in the middle of the room, throwing things at him, shouting, screaming obscenities at the top of her voice, her hair wild, her body taut and shaking with anger. It was better than sex.

'You . . . bloody . . . bastard,' she shouted, slurring her words somewhat through alcohol and anger. 'You bring me here, to this bloody shit-hole of a bloody house . . . With more bloody witches in it than bloody Mac-bloody-beth . . . and you leave me down the end of the table to talk to some horrible bastard . . . while you – you – have your tongue firmly stuck in some tart's cleavage . . . while she sits, with some smug carrot up her arse . . . and you, you're probably giving her one under the table for all I bloody know! I mean, I left my children for you. I left everything for you. I gave it all up for you . . . and now look. You drop me for some dolled-up tart with tits like zeppelins. I ha-a-a-te you! I bloody ha-a-ate . . . I do . . . I ha-a-te you!'

Max had never seen a woman spit in anger before. The whole scene was one of the most exhilarating and alive performances he had ever witnessed. The raw emotion of it all, the total and utter loss of control; he never really thought that Madeleine had it in her to behave like that. He had always rather hoped that she might. Not that he had had any evidence of it in the past. She had always been quite middle class in her approach to everything. But he had seen something in her when he first laid eyes on her. Something in her smile that day at Liz's barbecue that made him think she could possibly be a bit different. Unlike other cipher females he had met before, this woman was obviously capable of real unadulterated passion. And he had never loved her more than that night in the yellow room, shouting at him, threatening to throw her hairdryer out of the window, so wound up by jealousy. It was delicious.

Eventually, it was the loud shattering of glass that brought Madeleine to her senses. What was she doing? She had never behaved like this before in her whole life. She actually looked horrified, standing there with her hands over her mouth, in total shock. It was as if, in the silent aftermath, when all the shouting stopped and all the glass finished fracturing on the terrace below, the true force of her actions hit her.

'Jesus,' she said quietly, as she dry-retched into her hands.

'Jesus,' she repeated, as she took in the broken window, the black marks made by her shoes as they hit the yellow silk wallpaper, the broken pot of face cream sprayed, like projectile vomit, all along the skirting board. And Max standing flat against the wall, his legs and arms splayed like some knife-thrower's assistant, awaiting further instructions. 'God,' said Madeleine as she collapsed on to the bed. 'Max,' she muttered, her huge brown eyes whipped even wider with adrenaline. 'I am so-o-o sorry.' She looked around the room, her hands gripping the bed, her mouth aghast. 'What have I done? My God.' She held her temples in disbelief. 'Max, I'm sorry, I don't really know what came over me.'

'I don't know either,' he said, peeling himself away from the wall. 'But it was excellent to watch.'

'What?' she replied.

'It was amazing.' He started to laugh. 'The hairdryer through the window was quite spectacular.' His laugh became looser. He sat down next to her on the bed and kissed her bare shoulder. 'Are you all right now?' he asked with gentle sympathy.

'Um.' She looked up, still puzzled.

'Are you all right now?' he repeated.

'Um, I think so,' she said. 'God, Max, I am so sorry. Do you think they heard it downstairs?'

'Every word.' He grinned.

'How do you know?'

'We're directly above them,' he said, lightly tapping the floor with his foot.

'Oh, my God.' She covered her nose and mouth with both her hands and stared at him in terror. 'What?' she whispered, shaking her head. 'Everything?'

He nodded.

'All the stuff about how ghastly they all are?'

'Yup.' He grinned, falling back on to the bed. 'Fuck it, if they can't take a joke.'

Max and Madeleine got up the next morning and left before lunch. Max had gone down early to receive his rose garden bollocking, while Madeleine stayed rather sheepishly in the bedroom. He'd announced to his mother that he no longer cared what she thought of his choice of girlfriend. He also declared that no matter how many times Felicity was paraded in front him, he was not going to marry her. He'd had her, and she was boring, and no amount of her father's money could make her any more interesting. So as Max and Madeleine drove up the drive, in their heavy sunglasses, only Martha and Alexander waved them goodbye.

All that happened a month ago and Max and Madeleine have not been back since. Not that they have been invited. But then again, they don't get invited anywhere that much any more. Madeleine is not sure whether their dearth of invitations has more to do with loyalty to Larry rather than any moral judgement on her behaviour. He has, after all, been living in the Solihull and Redditch area for a lot longer than either she or Max, and in suburbia longevity, or so she suspects, is everything.

So they have slipped into a bit of a routine. Max works at selling furniture all day and Madeleine plays house. On Tuesdays and Thursdays each week she see her daughters. The situation is not ideal, it is anything but ideal but Madeleine tells them over and over again that things will improve soon. She finds the emotional rollercoaster of her own excitement and tears hard to handle. The girls themselves seem a lot braver and more grown-up about their parents' separation than she ever imagined they would be. She keeps talking to Larry about getting them an au pair, instead of relying on the

228

daily for help. He keeps pretending to listen. In the meantime Max and Madeleine love each other and wonder when the rest of Solihull society will let them in.

'I hear Liz had another one of her Tory fund-raising supper parties,' announces Madeleine, having just put the telephone down on Val.

Max doesn't answer. Sitting in the shop with his feet up on the desk, he is engrossed in the small ad section of the *Stratford Herald.*

'Val just told me,' continues Madeleine, lighting a cigarette and leaning on the kitchen door frame. 'It just slipped out. She was telling me about some massive row Liz and Geoff had, and just happened to mention that every single person you and I know was round at their house on Thursday.'

'Mmm,' says Max.

'Are you listening to me?'

'Course I am, darling,' he says, lowering the paper on to his thighs. 'We haven't been invited somewhere again: so what's new?'

'But I don't understand why,' says Madeleine, her brow creasing. 'People break up and swap partners around here all the time. I mean, for Christ's sake, Angela and Geoff were engaged at one time.'

'Were they?' Max smiles.

'A long time ago, when they were teenagers, but they were still engaged.'

'I can't see that myself,' says Max, shaking his head.

'Liz stole him, after some party,' she continues. 'And they are still best friends.'

'Maybe it's me they don't like?' suggests Max.

'Don't be stupid; they were all over you like a cheap suit when you first tipped up here,' says Madeleine, flicking her ash.

'But that was when they thought they could have their wicked way with me.' Max winks. 'Now I am a taken man, they are no longer interested.'

'Mmm,' says Madeleine, thinking. 'Possibly. Who knows? Do you know, if they won't come to the mountain, then the mountain is moving of its own free will, so to speak.'

'What are you on about?'

'Let's have some people round for dinner.' She smiles sunnily, suddenly energised by her own idea.

'Where?' says Max, dramatically shrugging his shoulders.

'Round the kitchen table.'

'But we don't have any room.'

'Don't be ridiculous, we can squeeze six round the kitchen table.'

'You are joking; we can only just get you and me round it,' laughs Max.

'Stop being so damned practical,' she replies. 'I'm off to make some calls.'

'On your own head,' says Max, shaking his finger. 'I think you are making a great mistake.'

Four days later and Madeleine is steaming up the kitchen, cobbling together something she spent over an hour choosing in her Elizabeth David cookbook. While the clipped-toned Radio 4 presenter drones on about the nationwide drought, Max props open the shop door, trying to get the air to circulate. Sporting a smock-fronted top with trumpet sleeves, flared jeans and a shoe lace wrapped around her head like some quasi Maid Marion hair-do, Madeleine is halfway through her second gin and tonic in an attempt to calm her nerves.

'Oh God,' she says, turning away from the small gas stove to grimace wildly at Max. 'What the hell are we doing?'

'I have no idea.' He laughs, walking towards her and putting his arms around her waist, kissing her collarbone. 'But it was your idea so let's just go with it, darling. We can pull it off!'

'Oh, sorry,' comes a cold, curt voice from the direction of the shop. 'We could come back later if you two lovebirds are busy?'

'Oh, hello.' Madeleine smiles, pulling away from Max. 'Angela . . . James, come in, come in. How lovely to see you.'

'Likewise,' says James, running his hands through his thin blond hair and loosening his tie as soon as he notices Max's open-necked shirt. 'Phew,' he says as he files himself on the transparent plastic fold-up chair in the tight corner furthest from the stove. 'It's um, very cosy in here, isn't it, dear?'

'Yes,' agrees Angela, resting her bony behind against the white Formica sideboard as she lights a cigarette, and flicks her long cream nails through her smooth, blonde, salon-coiffed hair. 'I had no idea these cottages were so . . . um, neat.' She smiles.

'Oh, I know, I know.' Madeleine laughs with exaggerated breeziness. 'They are terribly small.'

'Snug is the word you are looking for,' adds Max, distractedly planting a kiss on the top of Madeleine's head as he walks past on his way to the fridge.

Angela coughs and shifts position on the Formica sideboard, while James turns his head and looks through the open back door.

'So do you have much of a garden then, mate?' he enquires.

'I think garden is probably putting it a bit too grandly.' Max laughs, handing over a glass. 'Gin and tonic all right?'

'Perfect,' replies James.

'G&T for me too please,' says Angela, flicking her ash into the sink.

'Darling?' asks Max as he runs his hands over Madeleine's denim-clad buttocks on his way back to the fridge.

'Oh, the same,' she replies.

'Shall we go outside?' suggests Angela, halfway towards the door. 'It really is quite hot in here,' she adds, tugging at her long peach-coloured T-shirt dress and golden hooped hip belt.

Angela and James leave the kitchen with uncharacteristic speed and, on finding nowhere else to sit, plant themselves side by side on the one green and white plastic slatted sunbed prostrate in the yard.

'Jesus,' whispers Angela, forcing a slim column of silver smoke out of her frosted mouth. 'They can hardly keep their hands off each other. It's so bloody . . . bloody teenage.'

'I know,' agrees James, finding the sensation of his wife's thigh frotting against his own mildly irritating. 'Talk about rubbing our noses in it.'

'Quite,' she replies.

'It's revolting.'

'Co-o-ey! Hello!' comes a voice accompanied by a loud banging from the other side of the yard door. 'Madeleine? Max? Is this you two? I think we might have come in the wrong way.'

'Liz? Geoff?' says Max, coming out of the kitchen. 'On my way. One second, I'll just go and get the key.'

'Sorry, mate,' comes Geoff's voice. 'I did say we should come in through the front, but the wife—'

'Don't bloody blame me,' huffs Liz from behind the fence. 'You're always blaming me; we've only just arrived and already you're picking a fight.'

'I'm not.'

'Oh, shut up.'

Max eventually finds the key and lets Liz and Geoff into the yard, serving them a gin and tonic each and then setting up another plastic sunbed as a seat. The two couples sit opposite each other, tightly and precariously balanced on the beds, while Max and Madeleine float backwards and forwards from the kitchen into the yard, bringing bowls of Ritz biscuits, peanuts and anchovied eggs to accompany their drinks.

'Well, this is nice,' says Liz, her glossed lips just managing a smile in the evening sun before she knocks back her entire drink. Her rolled stomach is clearly visible in her tight uncomfortable-looking burgundy top and she is sweating slightly around the armpits.

'Yes,' agrees Angela. 'Very nice.'

They both smile at each other and take a drag on their respective cigarettes.

'Absolutely,' says Geoff, after a minute or so. 'Nice.'

'Mmm,' says James, shifting slightly as one of his buttocks slips slowly between the slats. 'Quite,' he adds. 'Um . . . cheers, everyone.'

'Absolutely. Cheers to you lot,' says Max, dragging the transparent plastic fold-up chair outside with him and sitting down on it. 'Darling,' he shouts. 'Come out and cheers with all of us.'

'Oh, right. Cheers,' says Madeleine, tripping out through the door with a large gin and tonic in her hand. Clinking glasses with everyone, she giggles before she sits down on Max's knee. 'I would just like to say that I am thrilled you have all come tonight.' She smiles, pushing strands of damp hair behind her ears. 'Actually we're both thrilled, aren't we, darling?' she adds, leaning back into Max's chest and turning to kiss his cheek. 'This is like a new beginning for us, and we're glad that you . . . um, that you're . . . our friends. Aren't we, Max?'

'Absolutely.' Max smiles, squeezing Madeleine on his knee.

'To friendship!' she announces, standing up, her face flushed.

'To friendship,' they all repeat, sitting solidly on their sunbeds.

'Great.' Madeleine smiles looking down on her guests. 'Dinner won't be much longer.'

'Terrific,' says Liz, draining her already empty glass and ostentatiously placing it on the ground next to her feet. Her dark hair is frizzing slightly in the heat.

'I'll get you another one of those,' says Max, leaping out of his seat and walking straight inside.

The two couples sit in silence. Angela smokes, Liz polishes off the plate of eggs, Geoff points his short nose at the floor and looks for patterns in the crazy paving and James slips further between the sunbed slats.

'Dinner is served,' comes the call from the kitchen and the group dutifully file inside.

'Sit where you want, sit where you want,' smiles Madeleine. 'It's very informal tonight. I mean, there's no starter and Max has only just found the candles at the back of a drawer,' she adds, pointing to a pair of the turquoise tapered variety that flicker in the centre of the table. 'Also please excuse the non-matching anything, Max is not used to entertaining!'

'Very far out,' says Geoff, sitting down on a stool and comparing his purple side plate with the rest of the green and white service.

'And I will also admit to this being an experiment,' she continues, bending down to take the main course out of the oven. 'Duck à la tinned peaches.' She smiles, placing three pairs of rather pink-looking breasts on the table.

'Darling,' says Max, inhaling deeply above the dish, while running his hand over her hair. 'Those look delicious.'

'They look wonderful,' agrees Angela, lighting up another cigarette.

'French beans,' adds Madeleine, wafting from oven to table and back again. 'And croquette potatoes. I know that it's not terribly summery but . . .' She shrugs.

'Delicious, darling,' agrees Max.

'Please,' says Madeleine, flopping down next to Max, her left hand resting on his thigh, as she leans back and wipes her forehead with the back of her right hand. 'Serve yourselves.'

'Have you closed the shop door?' asks Angela.

''Fraid so,' smiles Max.

'It is very hot in here,' she adds, rattling her gold belt against her hard hips.

'It's been hot for weeks,' says Liz, lunging forwards, helping herself to a large glass of wine and another serve of potatoes.

'Our lawn has been brown for nearly a month,' informs Geoff.

'Has it?' says Madeleine. 'How terrible.'

'We haven't been able to fill up the pool,' adds Geoff. 'Or anything. I should have invested in water futures not aluminium after all,' he chortles.

'Poor you,' says Madeleine.

'At least you've got no problem with the hosepipe ban here, have you?' asserts James. 'Yard like that . . . with all my lawns it's been a terrible problem. The conservatory has overheated as well. But with your small little space . . . what is it: six by six?' He laughs. 'Well, apart from those few pots in the corner, you have no need for water at all.'

'No,' agrees Max, standing up to pour another bottle of wine. 'I suppose that is something to be thankful for. Wine? Liz?'

'Please. Right to the top.'

'Angela?'

'Oh, pretty please.'

'James?'

'Thank you,' he says, looking up from his plate. 'Nice and cheap this South African stuff, isn't it?' He nods.

'So . . .' Madeleine smiles, looking round at her guests. 'This is nice.'

'Very nice,' says Liz, taking a slug of wine. Her mouth full of croquette, her face flushed and shining, she suddenly looks strikingly like a tomato. 'So, what have you two been up to?' she goads, her head wobbling.

'Oh, God,' gushes Madeleine. 'That's a question!' She laughs. 'Gosh, what have we been up to? You know, this and that.'

'Well, no actually.' Angela smiles, tearing at her under-cooked breast. 'You two have kept yourselves so much to yourselves we're all dying to hear what you've been up to, aren't we, dear?' She smiles at James, prodding him in the elbow.

'Sorry, what?' he replies, running his finger uncomfortably round the back of his shirt collar. 'I wasn't listening.'

'We're all dying to hear what Madeleine and Max have been up to, aren't we?' she repeats, her eyes narrowing slightly.

'Well,' says Madeleine, running her hands through her hair. 'Max works in the shop most days, obviously.' She giggles. 'And I do the books.'

'And then I re-do them.' Max laughs, running his finger over her cheek.

'No, you don't!' she smiles.

'Yes, I do.'

'Don't be mean.'

'Oh, I'm sorry,' he says, leaning in and resting his forehead against hers, kissing her on the mouth. 'You are very good at . . . books.'

'Well, that sounds nice,' says Angela, pushing her almost full plate towards the centre of the table and lighting up a cigarette. 'Have you seen Larry?'

'Um,' says Madeleine.

'No, not really,' says Max, leaning back in his chair, sounding loudly relaxed.

'He's got a new au pair, I hear,' says Angela.

'Conchita,' adds Liz, tapping the table with a short maroon nail. 'I helped him choose her.'

'You did?' interjects Madeleine, unable to disguise her surprise. 'Because I have been asking him to . . .'

'Oh, yes,' interrupts Liz, putting her fork down and, leaning over, plucking a cigarette from James's packet across the table. 'Did Lara and Sophie not tell you?'

'Um . . .'

'No, that's right, you haven't seen them since she arrived, have you?' continues Liz, lighting her cigarette and taking a large sip of wine. 'What is it? Tuesdays or Thursdays, you have them for the afternoon? I can never remember which. And they have been in Cornwall with me for the weekend. So, anyway . . .'

'With the new au pair?' asks Angela.

'Oh, yes,' replies Liz. 'She's terribly nice.'

'Really?' says Angela.

'And actually quite attractive. Larry insisted he couldn't have something ugly, as he had to look at it every day.' Liz laughs.

'Typical,' laughs Angela.

'Yeah,' agrees Geoff. 'Good old Larry . . .'

'Would anyone like some pudding?' says Madeleine, quickly leaving the table to look busily in the fridge.

'Oh, God, leave that door open, will you?' says Angela, turning round. 'It's so hot and poky in this place.'

Max springs out of his seat and picks up a couple of plates, stacking them on the side. While Madeleine continues to look animatedly in the fridge, he walks up behind her and, pushing all her hair to one side, kisses the back of her neck. Liz stares as Madeleine arches her back and leans against Max. Flicking her cigarette into her food, she places her hand on her husband's knee. Geoff immediately moves it away.

'So, James,' says Liz, undeterred, lowering her bosom on to the table. 'How have you been?'

'Who, me?' says James, sounding surprised.

'Of course, you.' Liz smiles. 'There isn't another James here, is there?' She giggles. Her ample chest ripples.

'I'm fine,' he replies.

'He's fine,' insists Angela, taking hold of her husband's hand.

'You know me,' says James, removing his hand and running it through his blond flyaway hair.

'Well, I could do,' says Liz, raising her eyebrows.

'Did you say there was some pudding?' says Angela, stubbing out her cigarette.

'Just some chocolate roulade,' replies Madeleine, still staring into the fridge, looking at a jug of cream. Madeleine is starting to regret her dinner party. Max was right. What is she doing? This is a foolish idea. It is curiosity, not friendship, that has tempted these people here. How did she ever think things could be different? Of course they are all going to be Larry's friends; how she ever expected otherwise, she doesn't know. 'Maybe, as it's so hot, we could serve the roulade in here and then drink coffee outside.' She smiles, trying to sound relaxed.

'That's an excellent idea, darling,' says Max, giving Madeleine a gentle wink of encouragement.

'God, Geoff, why can't you be more like him?' exhales Liz, standing half out of her chair, helping herself to some more wine.

'Who?' says Geoff.

'Max, you idiot.'

'I don't know what you mean.'

'You know, be a bit more supportive,' she says, rolling her eyes as she collapses back in to her chair.

'I am supportive.'

'No, you're not,' she continues, taking a large sip of wine. 'He's not, is he? Angela?'

'Don't get me involved in your domestic.' She laughs.

'Yes, quite.' Madeleine laughs, desperately trying to keep her show on the road. 'I know, shall we move outside for pudding as well as coffee? It'll be a bit cooler.'

'Why aren't you more supportive?' continues Liz, a whine developing in her voice.

'Liz, please . . .' hisses Geoff.

'But you could be, couldn't you? A bit more supportive?' she adds, draining her glass again.

'I don't know what you're talking about.' He laughs, pulling up his trousers as he stands up. 'Do you, James?'

'No idea, mate.' James laughs back.

'By being supportive do you mean financial support? Because I don't know of a more supported lady round these parts, do you?' laughs Geoff, snorting through his retroussé nose like an over-exerted Pekingese.

'Shall we go through?' suggests Madeleine.

'What do you know?' says Liz, her eyes shining, as she randomly turns on her hostess.

'What do I know about what?' says Madeleine.

'About people's domestic arrangements?'

'Nothing,' says Madeleine quickly. 'Nothing at all.' She smiles tensely. 'Shall we go outside?'

The party moves into the yard and sits down on the sunbeds. Geoff takes Liz inside for a moment and obviously gives her some sort of a talking-to, because after five minutes of hushed argument in the shop she comes back looking contrite and hardly speaks again for the rest of the evening. Madeleine serves her chocolate roulade and coffees and offers a round of brandy. They all refuse.

'That's unlike you, James,' she says, her hand ruffling Max's hair.

'To be honest with you,' he says, getting up off the sunbed, pulling his sweaty trousers out of his groin. 'I don't think I could manage a brandy.'

'Something else then?' She smiles encouragingly.

'No, no, really.'

'Geoff?'

'Not tonight,' Geoff replies. 'I have a feeling Liz is very tired.'

'Oh, I am . . . very tired,' she agrees, her mouth smiling, her eyes furious.

'But it's only quarter past eleven,' says Madeleine.

'It's the heat,' says Geoff. 'It tires you out and, you know, we have a babysitter.'

By 11.30 p.m. they are all gone. Max and Madeleine are left with a yard full of butts, a kitchen full of dirty plates and a distinctly unpleasant taste in their mouths.

'Well,' says Max, as they start to clear up. 'That went well . . .'

'Stop it,' replies Madeleine. 'I really don't want to talk about it.'

Neither, or so it appears, does anyone else. For in lieu of the usual after-dinner-party thank-you cards, or notes, or long, languid post-prandial telephone calls dissecting the soirée, Madeleine receives nothing. It is as if her duck à la tinned peaches has secured her a position mining salt in social Siberia, rather than saving her from such a fate. Even Valerie, who is rapidly becoming her only link with the outside world, is not returning her messages with any speed or diligence. Like a teenager with a heavy hormonal crush, Madeleine religiously rings Val, leaves a message with her cleaner and then trips to the phone every time it rings, announcing, 'I'll get it!' But to no avail.

The frost is beginning to bite in Siberia. However, neither Max nor Madeleine ever really mentions it. Instead they try to create as much normality and routine in their abnormal lives as possible. Max throws himself into the running of the shop. He makes trips to arts and antique fairs around the county, toying with the idea of buying more stock. He organises the odd day trip to London, but Madeleine's mood in the lead-up to these sorties is so odd and unpleasant he only makes that mistake twice. In the meantime, Madeleine keeps herself busy doing so-called essential jobs around the cottage, anything and everything to occupy her and to stop her missing her children. She runs up some new curtains for the kitchen, replacing the faded tulip print with something abstract in lemon and lime from Winter's in Stratford. She takes to cooking all day, pickling red cabbage, making chestnut puddings; she spends whole mornings perusing her Connie Spry and Elizabeth David cookbooks. She has always heard that the days are longer in Solihull when you don't have children and now she realises exactly what they mean.

Not that she doesn't have children, because obviously she does. But Larry continues to ensure that she isn't allowed to see them anywhere near as much as she wants. The charming Conchita, with her glossy hair, lush breasts and fecund behind, drops them off on Tuesday and Thursday afternoons at the shop and collects them three hours later. The lack of space and Max's predilection for doing the accounts in the afternoons mean that the three of them invariably spend the time trawling the teashops of either Henley or Stratford. It is not an ideal situation, Madeleine realises that. But it is only temporary. After all, Max and she have talked about buying a house together – soon – somewhere along the line. In the meantime everyone has to be brave.

And they are being brave. Lara and Sophie are stoic to the point of silence. Madeleine is breezy to the point of flight,

Max is mute, and the only person to make any form of a fuss is Larry. He regularly calls 'war conferences' where his old mates Geoff and James turns up at Johnson Towers and consume copious amounts of Johnnie Walker Black Label, exchanging exaggerated and absurd anecdotes about the lascivious Max.

'I have heard that he's homosexual,' announces Geoff hilariously one afternoon when particularly inebriated. 'And that Madeleine is in fact a front for his other activities.'

'Now that wouldn't surprise me,' agrees Larry, tapping the side of his nose. 'You know the way he dresses and that, you know; like a poof really.'

'Yeah.' James nods, running his hands through his flyaway hair. 'Those tight trousers that show off his arse.' He hoots with laughter. 'I mean they say women find that attractive but we know who it's for.'

'Quite right, James.' Geoff sniffs, flicking imaginary fluff from his lemon-yellow sports jacket. 'You heard the one why God invented bent men?' He leans over.

'No,' they both reply.

'So fat birds get to dance!' announces Geoff before creasing up over his whisky. James does the same.

'But Madeleine's not fat,' replies Larry, somewhat puzzled.

'Er, no, mate,' agrees James. 'Geoff,' he adds. 'The bloke has got a point.'

However, despite her splendid isolation, Madeleine does occasionally have lunch with Val. They take a lot of organising and a particular persistence on Madeleine's part, but they do sometimes get round to it all the same. They are always in unpopular pubs, and always on a Monday or when Val can fit her in. What with tennis at Angela's and pedicures round at Liz's and the occasional girls' shopping trip to Birmingham and lunch afterwards, it is tricky to find the time. Madeleine understands and gratefully makes the most of these lunches. The only time she really manages to catch up on anything, she approaches these occasions with great excitement and gusto, drinking almost twice as many gin and tonics as Val, returning home rather the worse for wear.

It is at one of these lunches about three weeks after the disastrous dinner that Val suddenly makes a suggestion.

'Do you know,' she says. 'I'm fed up of all this cold-shouldering of you.'

'Ostracism,' adds Madeleine, already on her third gin and feeling quite drunk.

'Yes, yes, whatever.' Val smiles. 'But I am pretty pissed off with it now. I mean, for Christ's sake, it's not as if any of them haven't fucked around.' She sighs, stubbing her cigarette out in the huge black JPS promotional ashtray. 'I mean, Liz has been fucking your husband for years.'

Madeleine looks stunned, totally taken by surprise. A quiet 'What?' is all she can manage.

'Oh, yeah,' continues Val, lighting up another cigarette and exhaling in the direction of her friend. 'Oh,' she adds when she finally notices Madeleine's expression. 'Oh, I mean . . .' She smiles weakly. 'I can't believe you didn't know. I thought everyone knew.'

'Everyone apart from me, or so it seems,' says Madeleine softly, staring at Val, tapping around on the table looking for her cigarettes. 'But what about the tennis coach?'

'Oh, he's a summer thing. Larry's all year round. Well, anyway,' says Val. 'Um, so you see, no one is whiter than white, especially round here.'

'Who else?' asks Madeleine.

'What? Has slept with Larry? Oh, God.' She pauses. 'Um, hundreds. Where to start?'

'No, actually, I meant who else has been unfaithful?'

'Oh, God, sorry,' says Val, as she starts to giggle. She has reached the point of no return and knows it. 'Whoops!'

'Do you know?' says Madeleine, starting to smile. 'I don't think I care.'

'Really?' asks Val, relief writ large all over her face.

'No.' Madeleine sighs. 'They can all piss off.' She grins. 'Two-faced bastards the lot of them. So . . .' She leans in. 'Who else then?'

'Angela.'

'Oh, my God!' screams Madeleine. 'Not with Larry?'

'No-o-o,' she dismisses. 'Xander Paul, apparently.'

'But I thought you . . .'

'Oh, no.' Val swats the air with her hand. 'A couple of times in his surgery, so the story goes.'

'When?'

'I don't really know but I have a feeling it was when she was having all those "problems",' says Val, making quotation marks in the air. 'Last year some time?'

'Oh, yeah.' Madeleine nods. 'I remember: about eighteen months ago.'

'Mmm,' says Val, taking a sip of her gin. 'Anyway, the point is they're all bloody at it, so I think it's pathetic you're not invited to Angela's tennis lunches. After all you are the best player they've got. I mean Liz . . .'

'What? Still frying-panning them into the net, is she?'

'Oh, God.' Val yawns. 'And guess who's been lumped with her, now you're NFI – not fucking invited?' Her imitation of Angela is uncanny. 'So next Tuesday I'm going to insist that you be invited.'

'Do you think it'll work?'

'Of course it'll bloody work,' says Val, tapping the side of her nose. 'I can be very persuasive.'

'Of that I have no doubt,' laughs Madeleine.

*　　*　　*

True to her word, Val has obviously been very persuasive. On Monday afternoon Madeleine receives one of those 'just-checking-up-on-you phone calls' that women sometimes make when they are racked with guilt about another girlfriend. Angela breezes through various topics on her way to the tennis invitation: health, gossip about Liz and the departure of her tennis coach, the possibility that they might take a holiday in the south of France. Eventually she manages to make the invitation, asking in a vague tight-lipped manner that suggests she'd rather Madeleine refuse. But Madeleine not only surprises herself, but also Angela, with the enthusiasm of her acceptance.

It is now Tuesday and Madeleine is nervous. So nervous that she's thrown up twice already this morning. Max, on the other hand, is thrilled. Whistling to himself, he turns the radio up and makes coffee.

'About time you got out and enjoy yourself, hang out with the girls.' He grins, running his hands through his thick dark hair. 'Anyway I've always fancied you in a tennis skirt.'

'You've never seen me in a tennis skirt,' she says, going through one of the suitcases they still have piled in the hall. There's no room upstairs for all the clothes she collected from Larry's, so two suitcases of occasional-wear sit, perched one on top of the other, in the hall.

'Believe you me I have.' He smiles.

'Where?'

'In here,' he says, tapping his temple with his index finger.

'Pervert.' She laughs, throwing a T-shirt at him.

'You'd better get a move on,' he says. 'Aren't you due on court in half an hour?'

'Oh, my God,' says Madeleine, running up the stairs, clutching her short white dress.

★   ★   ★

Almost the end of September and the leaves are turning terracotta and slipping from the trees. The sky is clear, bright blue. It's warm in the sun, but chilly in the shade. Both Max and Madeleine are wearing their large sunglasses as they drive with the roof down to Angela's. Max looks handsome with the wind in his hair, the sun reflecting off his warm skin, and his thick sideburns tapering like two ends of a headscarf down his face. Madeleine smiles.

'What?' he says, as he catches her looking at him out of the corner of his eye.

'I'm just thinking how much I love you,' she says, as they turn the corner and crunch up Angela's heavily gravelled drive to be greeted by the yapping toy poodle. 'Oh, my God,' she says, putting her sunglasses on the top of her head, a wave of nausea surfing through her entire body. 'Look at all those cars,' she says, staring at the collection of Stags, MGs and of course Val's Mercedes sports. 'They're all here.'

'Course they are,' says Max. 'What did you expect?'

'Oh, I don't know. I feel really sick.'

'Don't do it in here,' says Max, pushing her out of the car with a friendly prod.

'Don't be mean.'

'I'm not mean,' he says. 'Go on.' He grins. 'Go and show them.' He spins the car round, and with a wave and hail of loose stones leaves her standing there like a small child, tennis racquet hanging limply by her side.

'Go and show them,' she says, biting her bottom lip. 'Right,' she adds, and turns towards the green door, now covered in the occasional hardy rose, surrounded by dead-heads still sporting the odd rotting pink petal. Walking towards the alcoholic gardener's topiary efforts, Madeleine can hear a couple of people knocking up on the court, accompanied by Patricia's loud heaving honking laugh like a goose in full-blown intercourse. As she walks up the path, a brave fixed smile emblazoned on her lips, the first person she bumps into is Candida. Sporting a new bright white nylon tennis outfit, Candida's heavily underwired breasts point forward like two enormous prying noses. Her stomach slouches over the top of her stiff skirt, as she smokes and pats a tennis ball up and down on the flagstone path. Looking the other way as Madeleine approaches, she is taken totally by surprise.

'Shit,' she shrieks, dropping her cigarette. 'Look who it bloody is!'

Everyone stops and stares, playing a sort of social musical statues.

'Darling,' she adds for good measure. Candida hates to be socially wrong-footed. 'How amazing. Angela didn't tell us you were coming. Angela,' she booms. 'You didn't tell us Madeleine was coming.'

'Didn't I?' says Angela, finally remembering to exhale her cigarette smoke. Her nonchalant swinging of her tennis racquet is not fooling anyone. 'Silly me.' She giggles. 'Madeleine and I had chats just yesterday. Anyway, we both decided that girls' tennis is not quite the same without her.'

'Hear, hear,' says Val from the other side of the court, halfway through a serving action.

'Christ, yes,' agrees Patricia, pulling her pants out of her backside.

'You look very well,' says Anne nicely, in the middle of serving coffee for all the women.

'Thanks.' Madeleine smiles, shrugging her shoulders. 'I don't feel that well. I think perhaps it's nerves at seeing all you lot again.'

'I can't imagine why,' says Liz, stubbing her cigarette out on the ground with a new pair of pink trimmed plimsolls.

'Anyway, it's lovely to see you,' announces Barbara, a cup

247

of coffee in one hand, a cigarette in the other and a wide-eyed glazed look in her eyes. No longer the pink plump teen, her arms are slim and her legs are decidedly thin. As Madeleine moves in to kiss her hello, she notices thick yellow down all over her cheeks and the beginnings of a rather coarse moustache.

'Gosh,' says Madeleine, smiling as casually as she can. 'You've lost weight.'

'Do you think?' Barbara smiles back, spinning on the spot while her skirt stays in the same position. 'Xander Paul.' She grins. 'He's a find and a half, isn't he?' She giggles. 'Those pills . . . I find two or three a day just aren't enough, how about you?'

'I haven't had them in a while,' replies Madeleine.

'Really?' says Barbara, looking her up and down. 'But you've lost ever such a lot of weight.'

'Right . . . thanks.' Madeleine smiles, moving towards Val who has taken up position in a patch of sun on the bench.

In Madeleine's absence, the pairs have already apparently been chosen and she is teamed with Liz, who seems to have disappeared almost as soon as Madeleine arrived.

'What's wrong with Liz?' whispers Madeleine out of one half of her mouth as she inhales with the other. 'She is being very unfriendly.'

'I know,' replies Val, watching as Angela and Candida prepare to take on Anne and Barbara.

'Do you know what her problem is?'

'Um,' replies Val, pretending to think.

'If you know,' hisses Madeleine, 'I really would rather you told me. Is it my fault or something?'

'Well, not exactly,' says Val quietly.

'Well, what exactly?'

'Oh, it's difficult . . .'

'I'm not exactly going anywhere, am I?' Madeleine replies.

248

'I have a set of Apesate-fuelled tennis to watch, haven't I?' she adds, watching Barbara sprint for a ball so enthusiastically that she runs past it altogether.

'It's a Larry thing,' Val finally admits.

'Don't tell me she finally feels guilty for sleeping with my husband all these years?' Madeleine smiles. 'Shot!' she shouts, as Candida whips the ball down the tramlines. Candida curtseys. Madeleine smiles and moves half a buttock closer to Val.

'Well,' sighs Val.

'Oh, no, do go on,' says Madeleine. 'I am all ears.'

'Well, since you left Larry he is now single, right?'

'Right.'

'And if you are single it changes things, right?'

'Um . . . like what?'

'Well, if you would normally go round and sleep with Liz of a Thursday afternoon, let's say, then suddenly it doesn't become that interesting.'

'Why?'

'Well, someone else's wife is all well and good when you have one of your own, but when you don't, what you actually want is a girlfriend. You know, someone to take out, go to parties with, that sort of thing.'

'God.' Madeleine sighs. 'Why have you always known so much more than me? It's so depressing . . .'

'So if you are going to have an affair with someone, it should always be with someone who has just as much to lose as yourself.'

'Like you and Xander Paul?'

'That wasn't an affair.' Val shrugs. 'Shot, Angela!' she shouts. 'That was sex.'

'It's the same deal, though, isn't it?'

'More or less, but he fucks lots of his patients, so that doesn't really count very much. But with the others, you know, you have to want the same thing; run the same sort of risks, as it were.'

'Right, so with Liz?'

'Oh . . . right, so with Liz and Larry, the stakes have changed. With you gone he's single now and needs, well, you know, a proper girlfriend to take out and I think – this is my theory, mind – I think he's rather stopped seeing her.'

'Oh,' says Madeleine, sitting thinking for a second. 'So let me get this straight. You think that she is angry with me because she is no longer sleeping with my husband, rather than feeling guilty at having slept with him in the first place?'

'That's about the sum of it,' agrees Val with a smile.

Madeleine takes in Val's theory. 'So what about me and Max then?'

'What about you two?'

'Well, he wasn't married.'

'That's entirely different.'

'Why?'

'You two are in love, stupid,' says Val, standing up and stubbing her cigarette out with her shoe. 'I'm desperate for a pee,' she says. 'Back in a sec.'

Madeleine sits and ponders Val's pearls. For a woman who had almost no education, Val isn't half bright, thinks Madeleine. If only she had been educated, imagine what she could have been capable of. She wouldn't be flailing around this place, looking for richer and richer men, occasionally doing the pill doctor in the NCP car park in Birmingham. She is much sharper than Larry and any of his insensitive friends. She is cleverer than Angela for all her night-school pretensions. Val could even give Max's sisters a run for their money. Madeleine smiles.

'Budge up,' says Patricia, using her ample behind as a battering ram. 'Now,' she says, pulling both her bra straps up and tugging down her tight Aertex shirt, stained with hard yellow circles under the arms. 'What's the goss?' she asks, rubbing her hands together in such a manner that the last thing Madeleine wants to do is share. Her long neck cranes round to get eye contact. 'A little birdie tells me you went to stay at Horsely House,' she adds, looking keen. 'So how are they all?'

'Um,' says Madeleine.

'Did they remember me?'

'Oh, yes,' says Madeleine. 'I asked Constance about you.'

'Oh, great.' Pat grins. 'Is she still a lesbian, because she was at school, you know?'

'Really,' says Madeleine, looking surprised but not shocked. 'Um, to tell you the truth, it wasn't the sort of thing that came up.'

'No,' says Pat. 'I shouldn't imagine it would.' She throws back her lack of chin and laughs. 'But, God, she did snog everyone. I mean, she was a few years below me but gossip like that travels.'

'I should imagine it does.'

'Yup,' says Pat, clapping her hands. 'Certainly does. So? Martha still dark and beautiful?'

'I have a feeling that will never change, don't you?'

'Yes, yes.' She smiles. 'And Max's father, is he still devilishly charming?'

'Oh, yes.'

'I think I was rather in love with him as a child,' she says, a long smile on her rather short mouth. 'In fact I have a feeling I was rather in love with the whole family. Max very much included,' she adds in a very friendly fashion. 'We've missed you round here, you know,' she continues, patting Madeleine on the knee like a child. 'No one is any good at tennis for a start,' she squawks. 'How's it going with the lovely Max, anyway?' she asks.

'Very well,' replies Madeleine with a smile.

'That's good,' she says. 'Because you have sacrificed a lot to be with him.'

'Like what?' says Madeleine defensively.

'Oh, no, don't get me wrong,' says Pat immediately. 'I didn't mean it nastily.'

'Well, how did you mean it, exactly?'

'Well, um, you know, your children, your husband, um, not being invited to things, that sort of thing . . .' Pat grimaces and stands up. 'I don't mean that negatively.' She is stammering now, realising perhaps she has gone a bit far. 'I just mean to say how brave you are . . . how wonderful to be so sure . . . to give it all up for love. Um, a lot of people round here are jealous,' she adds, hopping from one foot to the other, obviously trying to work out how to make amends. 'You know, um . . . you're in love, while they are, um, not . . .'

Madeleine sits motionless on the bench and stares at Pat. Her tactlessness is such that Madeleine can't quite believe what she has just heard. She knows that Pat is not being deliberately unpleasant. She is not a malicious person. She is simply honest. Madeleine has given up a lot. In fact, she has given up all that is dear to her for Max. The only thing is, she doesn't need it pointing out so blatantly. If Angela or Liz had said such things, Madeleine would have sensed the bitchy back-story behind the remarks. But Pat is a big fat whale of a person, a flat-footed insensitive soul, who considers herself very sensitive indeed, and good at discussing things that matter. So she wades in with flags, bunting and a full brass band at her disposal. She is the sort of person who would remark on Barbara's new hirsuteness in public, as a matter of general interest, and would then be amazed that the girl is at all offended. Patricia's other problem is that she is not fantastically bright. The product of many a cousin marrying many a cousin, the width of her shoulders is proportional to the diminutive size of her brain. So Madeleine concludes that Pat is simply parroting the topic on everyone's lips. She would never be able to think of those things herself.

'Are you upsetting my partner?' asks Val, immediately trying to defuse the atmosphere.

'Not really, am I?' asks Pat enthusiastically. 'Just having a gossip, weren't we?'

'Oh really,' smiles Val. 'Anything I should know about?'

'No, I don't think so,' says Madeleine, picking up her racquet.

'Thank God for that,' says Val. 'You know how much I hate to miss out.'

'Right,' says Angela with a sigh, smudging her eyeliner as she wipes the sweat off her face. 'Candida and I are through to the next round,' she says sounding unseemingly pleased for the hostess. 'So on you lot go. A bit of a change,' she adds. 'Liz and Patricia against Val and Madeleine. That'll be interesting. How out of practice are you, Madeleine? I can't imagine you've played much since . . . um . . . well, you know.'

'Well, actually,' lies Madeleine blatantly. 'I have played an awful lot. Max's parents have a wonderful court.'

'That's certainly true,' says Pat, for once coming up trumps. 'His mother was one of those Raj princesses with little to do so was rather a good tennis player. How is she now?'

'Oh, excellent,' Madeleine says, brazening it out. 'Still really rather excellent.'

'That's nice,' says Angela, blowing out a cloud of JPS. 'Where the hell is Liz?'

'Coming,' says Liz, jogging towards the court, her bosom hurling itself over the right and then the left shoulder as she moves. 'Sorry,' she says, removing crumbs from the cover of her mouth. 'I just had to make myself a piece of toast.' She smiles. 'I was starving. Nothing for breakfast,' she adds weakly.

'Chop, chop,' says Angela. 'Pat's waiting for you.'

Madeleine and Val win the toss and Madeleine elects to serve. All notion of a polite genteel game of tennis has totally evaporated. She is irrationally angry with almost everyone on and around the court. Angela, for suggesting she might be a little rusty, therefore blatantly pointing out that she and Max don't know anyone smart enough outside their circle to have a court. Pat obviously also feels sorry for her and thinks she has no friends. And Liz, well, Liz has not only been sleeping with her husband, but now seems to have some sort of axe to grind with Madeleine for leaving him.

Madeleine serves. It's hard and aggressive and on the line.

'Shot,' shouts Candida from the bench. A woman fond of aggressive behaviour, she likes to applaud it in others. 'Fifteen love.'

Madeleine serves again: like a bullet it fires into the far corner, bouncing high. Liz misses it as it rattles into the netting behind.

'Shot,' shouts Candida again. 'Thirty love.'

'Are you really trying to thrash them?' asks Val over her right-hand shoulder.

'Might be,' says Madeleine.

'Fair enough,' she replies.

Madeleine walks around the back of the court, shaking the tension out of her legs as she bounces the ball. Not only does she look determined, but really rather professional. Pat clears her throat and pulls her pants out of her behind one more time before squatting down and swaying from side to side to receive the ball. Madeleine serves again. It's fast and accurate and straight down the centre line.

'Christ,' says Angela, mouth all spherical as she exhales. 'You really have being playing a lot recently. Nice court?' she shouts, flicking her ash.

'Lovely,' lies Madeleine again. 'One of those new red and green ones.'

'Oh, very smart,' says Angela, boring her butt into the ground. 'Very smart indeed.'

After a succession of aces, Madeleine wins her game to love and feels slightly more relaxed. Liz and Patricia mutter something along the lines of how unsporting she is being and then proceed to huddle together for an unnecessarily long time. After a moment's more discussion between them, they decide Liz should serve next.

Despite her summer with the increasingly attentive tennis coach, Liz does not appear to have improved at all. Wade's off-court services were obviously more appreciated than his on-court skills, muses Madeleine, as she squares up for another of Liz's pancake serves that belly-flop into the net. As she stands, piped into her new tennis dress, in the glare of the unforgiving morning light, Liz appears to be a pale shade of Satsuma. In fact, as she bends over to pick up a tennis ball that she has failed to flick up with her foot, you can see gingery stripes down the back of her dimpled thighs. Not content to let her bronzage fade gracefully with the approaching autumnal tones, Liz looks like she has had a fight with a bottle of fake tan. Madeleine walks towards the net to take a closer look at her opponent's true colours, noticing a small white triangle between the thighs where the skin has rubbed together.

'Your tan has lasted well,' says Madeleine over the net.

'Thanks,' says Liz, shaking a gold bracelet down her arm as she prepares to serve. 'It was the long weekend in Puerto Banus that did it.'

'Will you get on with it?' shouts Val from the back of the court. Leaning on her racquet like a walking-stick, she is making small piles of grit on the court in her boredom.

The game drags on and on. Liz may as well be playing with a fishing net, the amount of impact she is having. Patricia, a perfectly adequate player at the best of times, is being pulled down to her partner's level, through overcompensation and irritation. Instead of relaxing and enjoying herself, her narrow shoulders are hunched in anger, and she is becoming increasing short with her yelling. 'Mine!' she shouts at the top of her voice at any ball that is remotely within her reach as she runs, her long neck out, like something you would happily serve at Christmas, before overplaying it wildly, sending it into the field next door.

From a spectator's point of view, the game is dull enough to turn what would normally be slacklustre offers to help with the lunch into firm and effusive proposals. Eventually, as the grey clouds begin to gather to the north towards Birmingham everyone, except Barbara, goes inside to make lunch. Finding the mere mention of the word food, or anything that involves touching it quite repellent, she feels the moronic side to side movement of her head in time with the rallies (no matter how short they are) more conducive to her mood.

With the score standing at four love and the drizzle just beginning to make everyone's hair frizz, they decide to call it a day and move inside. Angela isn't quite ready for them, standing behind her breakfast bar with a cigarette hanging from her mouth as she stirs the white sauce for her new special chicken dish. She ushers them on through to the sitting room to join the others. As they walk into the room, the other women fall silent.

'Oh, shit, is it raining?' asks Candida after a long pause. Glass of white wine in hand, she watches Liz walk straight over to the mirror above the fireplace and start combing her hair.

'Unfortunately, yes.' Liz sighs, sucking in her cheeks as she presents first the left and then the right side of her face to the mirror. 'I had my hair done this morning and I'm going out tonight. It's a bloody nightmare. Angela?' she shouts in the vague direction of the kitchen. 'Can I borrow your hairdryer? It's an emergency.'

'Course. In the bedroom,' comes the muffled reply.

As Liz hurries out of the room, the silence returns. Barbara sits in the cream leather, low-slung sofa, swinging her right leg over her left, while Anne sits in a nice neat kneeling position in front of the fireplace, her elbows on the glass-topped table, her calves nestling in the fluffy shagpile carpet. Patricia flops down on the cream leather sofa, throws her lack of chin in the air and pulls the toy poodle on to her lap, forcing it to sit there like unfortunate looking pubic hair.

'Phew,' she announces to the group. 'I'm exhausted.'

'Mmm,' agrees everyone.

'So?' says Candida, lighting a cigarette and pointlessly flicking it at the huge square brass and marble ashtray in the centre of the glass table. 'How have you been, Madeleine?' She smiles. 'Long time no see,' she adds, wiggling her shoulders.

'Oh, fine,' says Madeleine, trying to sound jolly. 'Quite busy actually.'

'Really?' says Candida, taking a drag. 'Doing what?'

'Well, this and that,' says Madeleine. 'Is there any of that wine left?'

'Shit, of course,' says Candida. 'You too, Val?' she asks, pointing a pink nail.

'Please,' says Val, sitting down on the floor, pulling out a maroon packet of Dunhill. 'Crikey me,' she adds. 'Angela hasn't half done this place up since I was last here. That settee is definitely new.'

'New sofas, new lots of things,' announces Angela, breezing in with another bottle of wine in her armpit, carrying two more ashtrays. 'Had a lot of it sent from Peter Jones's in London,' she says, sitting down in some yoga position, looking heavenward. 'Such a complicated business.

The sofas were a couple of thou' each. That glass table is Italian.'

'Oh, Italian,' repeats Val, gently caressing the top of it with the palm of her hand.

'Yes.' Angela nods.

'Was it expensive?' asks Val.

'Very.' Angela smiles.

'Like how much?'

'Oh, God . . . over a grand,' says Angela. 'I think.'

'Peter Jones?'

'Now, do you know, I can't quite remember exactly where I picked it up.' She smiles defensively, trying to put Val off the scent. 'Wine anyone?' She gets up to fill the empty glasses.

Madeleine is somewhat relieved that the attention has been diverted from her. What with Angela's sitting room make-over, and Val's need to know how much everything costs, everyone seems to have forgotten that she is sitting on the carpet. She is grateful to Val for such a distraction, but she is not sure whether her friend has done it on purpose or from a genuine desire to work out exactly how much Angela spent on her furniture.

'Anyway,' says Candida, marching up and down the room picking up various objects and inspecting them with indecent closeness. 'You've done jolly well.'

'Well, it really needed doing,' says Angela with a smile, filling up Barbara's glass. 'It had been four years, you know, since the last time I had a real go in here.'

'It looks smashing,' says Barbara, her eyes rapidly touring the room.

'Really lovely,' says Madeleine, joining in and immediately regretting her confidence.

'Thanks,' says Angela, smiling.

'I expect you'll be doing up Max's,' says Patricia, leaning forward, popping the dog on the floor, legs apart, showing her large white gusset to the rest of the room. 'I haven't been in there myself,' she says. 'But I should image the place needs a bit of a woman's touch.' She snorts.

All eyes are on Madeleine.

'Um,' she says. 'You're probably right. Not that I have done anything to it yet.'

'No?' says Angela, sitting down slowly, maintaining eye contact. 'So you are planning to stay there then?'

'Um, we haven't really thought about it yet,' says Madeleine, picking balls of fluff out of the shagpile.

'But you've discussed it?' Angela's concentration is total. Kneeling back on her heels, she is swaying slightly from side to side like a cobra.

'Um.'

'You must have discussed it,' she says.

'Well.'

'Thank God, that's a hell of a lot better, don't you think?' says Liz, mincing in to the centre of the room and bouffing her dark do with her left hand as she executes a quick game-show turn. 'Thanks, Angela, you're a star.' She smiles. 'So what are we talking about?' she says, bending over to steal one of Val's Dunhill.

'Interior decorating,' says Madeleine.

'Oh,' says Liz with a shrug. 'When are we having some lunch?'

'Right now if you want,' says Angela, realising her moment has passed. 'The croûtons should be crunched up by now.'

'Croûtons,' says Liz, following Angela into the kitchen. 'How delicious.'

As the women file into the kitchen to serve themselves on the breakfast bar, Madeleine hangs back. Not wanting to be the centre of attention again, she looks busy, smoking hard, waiting for everyone to leave. Hirsute and thin, Barbara is obviously as keen to get to the kitchen as Madeleine.

'Not hungry then?' says Madeleine.

'God, no.' Barbara sighs, lighting up another cigarette.

'I didn't know you smoked,' says Madeleine. 'You didn't when you were last here.'

'It's a new habit,' admits Barbara, inhaling like she really needs it. 'Can't think why I didn't take it up before.' She smiles. 'It helps ever such a lot with your weight.' She giggles through her nose. 'That and those pills, what's their name? From Dr Paul.'

'You've lost a lot of weight since I last saw you,' says Madeleine, sounding concerned, yet at the same time rather enjoying someone else's problem.

'Do you think so?' says Barbara, pulling up her tennis top to reveal a lot of loose skin, hanging off a very obviously defined and razor-sharp-looking ribcage. Her bosom has almost entirely disappeared. 'I can't see it myself.' She smiles.

'Well, I can,' says Madeleine, slightly horrified by what she has just seen.

'Trevor thinks I look great,' she says, standing up and smoothing down her skirt. 'In fact it was him who suggested I went to Dr Paul in the first place.'

'What, Xander Paul!' says Angela, returning to the room with a small serving of rice and a dessertspoonful of chicken in sauce on her plate and another bottle of white wine under her arm. 'He is QAD – quite a darling,' she adds. 'Look what he's done for your figure, Barbara. You're as thin as a pin. I mean, what would all we Warwickshire women do without him?'

Madeleine is extremely perturbed by Barbara's degeneration. From a lush young girl content to swig R Whites lemonade, in a little over four months she has metamorphosed into a chain-smoking, pill-popping, skeletal girl with enough facial hair to join the circus. Is that what a year and a half with a man old enough to be your father does to you? she wonders. Or is it a reaction to spending eighteen months in Solihull?

'God,' she says as she joins Val in the queue for food. 'I have just seen Barbara's stomach; it's amazing.'

'I know,' says Val, distractedly taking the croûtons off the top of the chicken dish. 'He's amazing, that Xander Paul.'

'I think he's evil,' says Madeleine. 'Barbara looks quite ill.'

'Oh, God,' says Val, rolling her eyes. 'Don't be so melo-dramatic.'

'I think someone should say something.'

'Look,' whispers Val, taking hold of Madeleine's arm so hard that it pinches. 'You're on borrowed time here,' she adds, remembering the hell of her own ostracism. 'So I'd be careful what you say, if I was you. Remember, I know what it's like to be cut out of life round here and let me tell you it's not fun. I got you back in to the tennis set, the one that you spent most of the summer using as a crèche, so don't let me down by causing an argument. Half the people here go to bloody Xander Paul. No, actually' – she glances around and rapidly reconsiders – 'everyone here except Patricia goes, so don't go alienating everyone. Anyway, you go there yourself.'

'Not any more,' says Madeleine, sounding suitably con-trite. 'Max threw them all away when he found out what they were.'

'What did Max do?' asks Candida over Val's shoulders, desperate for any titbit of Max information that she could share with the other group in the sitting room before Mad-eleine arrives.

'Oh, God,' says Madeleine dismissively. 'Nothing inter-esting.'

For all her laid-back appearance, Madeleine is slightly in shock. Standing over the salad, wooden spoon in hand, she realises that she is shaking. It has suddenly dawned on her that perhaps Val doesn't bat entirely for her team. Val, or so it seems, bats only for Val. In fact, as Madeleine serves herself an ostentatiously large portion of food, which she is surprisingly keen on eating, she feels totally alone in this snake-pit. For that's exactly what they are: a nest of vipers, slithering over each other, copulating with each other, moving in and out of each other's homes. Their amoral behaviour, their transparently selfish ideas and ambitions, their overt materialism make her feel ill. A nest of vipers and Val, to jolly up their jaded afternoon, has brought them a mouse to play with. Or at least that's what she imagines as she walks back into the sitting room to find them all sitting around the glass table together, toying with their food, drinking their wine, smoking their cigarettes and bitching. Madeleine stands for a second by the door, realising there's no space at the table.

'All right there?' says Angela, exhaling.

'Fine,' says Madeleine, lifting a forkful of chicken to her mouth.

'Gosh, look,' says Anne, moving along. 'Here,' she says. 'Here's some room.'

Sitting at the table is the last thing Madeleine wants to do, but short of throwing her lunch in the air, there is little she can do except join them. As she squeezes in next to Anne, the conversation steers round to the new shoe shop that has opened up in Stratford.

'Anyway, I bought three pairs there the other day, on Geoff's credit card,' announces Liz, her maroon glossy lips closing around her fork like some sort of marine beast. 'They're real fuck-me-up-the-arse shoes,' says Liz, like a woman who knows exactly what that feels like. 'Suitably expensive, of course.'

'Where is the shop?' asks Candida. 'I think I certainly need a pair of that sort of footwear in my life.'

'God,' honks Patricia. 'So do I.'

'I bought a pair there the other day,' announces Anne.

'You didn't!' says Candida, slamming her hand down on the table.

'Well, mine aren't quite as racy as Liz's. They have got some sensible navy pairs with nice flat heels too.'

'Oh, how disappointing. I thought you were going to announce your new-found deviancy in the bedroom.' Candida hoots. 'Have you been, Madeleine?'

'Oh, no,' says Madeleine. 'It sounds a bit expensive.'

'Of course, you don't have any money any more, do you,' says Candida, announcing what she considers to be rather a dull statement of fact.

'Well, it's not that bad,' says Madeleine, embarrassed at having to justify herself in such a way.

'No, no, I'm sure it isn't,' says Candida. 'When one's in love one can put up with anything.'

Madeleine simply smiles. She doesn't know what to say.

'You are in love, aren't you?' Candida carries on like a juggernaut.

This is after all the point of having Madeleine round for tennis: to pump her for information. That and, of course, because the new girl Lesley, who usually partners either Val or Liz, is in London for the day.

'Of course I'm in love,' snaps Madeleine, instantly regretting her confession.

Somehow, out in the open, for all to see and examine at close quarters, she has managed to sully their relationship. But there is no taking it back now.

'In love? Ah, that's so sweet,' says Anne, her head cocked nicely to one side, Stepford bonding.

'God, and there was I thinking only poor people fell in love.' Liz laughs.

'Well, that does explain everything,' says Angela, flicking her ash on to her untouched pile of rice.

'Go on, tell the story because it is so romantic, isn't it?' says Val, sitting up on her heels.

Madeleine does not reply.

'Oh, go on,' pleads Val, jokingly fluttering her eyelashes. 'Okay then if you won't say.' She sighs. 'Well, you all heard about the dinner at my house, didn't you?' starts Val, putting herself at the heart of the anecdote. 'Anyway, then he rang and said he couldn't live without her; and then she said she couldn't live without him; then there was this ama-a-zing naked fight by my pool . . .'

All the women in the room 'ooh' and 'ah' like Val hasn't told the story before, which of course she has, hundreds of times. But this time they get to see Madeleine's face close up and that's worth all the exaggeration and the embellishment she insists on adding.

'. . . So that's it really.' Val smiles, clapping her hands together.

'Ah, well, I think it's a wonderful story,' says Anne.

'Quite right too,' adds Patricia, now on her fifth or sixth glass of wine. 'God, I was in love with the man myself for years.'

'Yes,' says Liz, stubbing out her cigarette. 'So is he good in bed?'

'Yeah, great question,' says Candida, pointing with one of her pink fingers. 'So?' She pauses dramatically, like she's pretending to be Magnus Magnusson. 'Madeleine Johnson, is Max Wright a good fuck?'

Everyone shrieks with laughter at Candy finally having the audacity to ask the one question they've all been dying to ask all day. After they have finished kicking their legs with delight and tweaking their cigarettes with excitement, they calm down and lean in for the answer. Madeleine says nothing and stares at her legs through the glass table.

'Well?' says Angela, mouth circular, trying to work out

264

whether to inhale or exhale. 'Is he? A good fuck? Well, is he?'

Madeleine slowly gets up from the table, using her hands for support as she tries to stand. She stares at their upturned expectant faces, waiting to hear the answer. Is it worth giving it all up for romantic love? Is eroticism better than materialism? Can you live on love alone, in a small one-bedroom flat in Henley? Can you not mind if you don't get invited to Angela's for tennis? Or Liz's for dinner? Or Candida's for next year's Conservative ball? Is fucking the beautiful Max Wright better than all that?

'I feel a bit hot,' mutters Madeleine. The room spins, the faces whip round faster and faster in a kaleidoscope of lipstick, gold earrings and bouffed hair-dos. There is a sharp squeal and total group inertia as Madeleine slowly crumples to the floor in a dead faint, hitting her head on the corner of the glass table from Peter Jones as she falls. She cuts her forehead open, splattering Angela's thick, white, fecund shagpile with drops and gobs and one large puddle of blood.

'Oh, my God,' screams Val.

'Oh, my God,' screams Liz.

'Oh, my carpet,' yells Angela, running out of the room to get a cloth.

'Jesus Christ,' mutters Candida, flicking her cigarette into the marble ashtray. 'I do hope the stupid bitch isn't pregnant. Now that really would be vulgar.'

IO

The gossip spreads quicker than herpes. It is the ambulance crew who ask her if she is pregnant. They have to find a reason for sudden fainting and it makes a difference to what drugs they give her for the pain of her cracked head.

Entrusted with the job of calling Max, Angela holds back. Some belated, long-lost seed of sisterhood stirs in her soul and she doesn't tell him that Madeleine is pregnant. The fact that her whole tennis party is listening in on the telephone call could have something to do with her uncharacteristic tact. But she pats herself on the back nevertheless, and will tell the story endlessly in her favour at numerous dinner parties.

In the end Angela gives herself earache, from spending so much of that afternoon and evening on the phone. She couldn't be more thrilled: all that dark red blood over her white shagpile carpet, staining something horrid.

'She had to admit it,' Angela shares yet again in Liz's dining room surrounded by a brand-new audience of stockbrokers from Geoff's office in Birmingham. 'Otherwise, untold problems, I mean.' She exhales. 'The blood was all over the new shagpile. It was such a dreadful reminder, I had to have the whole place redone, didn't I, James?'

'You certainly had the whole place redone, my dear,' he announces. 'My bank manager can vouch for that!'

The whole table laughs.

'But it was very dramatic,' continues Angela, mildly put out. 'Liz was there, weren't you, darling?'

'She's right.' Liz nods. 'I was there. It was a terrible thing. But it's the husband I feel sorry for. He's such a nice man. Very big in tyres, you know,' she adds. 'You gentlemen must know him? Larry Johnson? Sells a lot to Leyland's, I think. His factory is in the north of Birmingham? Deputy MD?'

'You seem to know an awful lot about Larry,' says Angela rather sharply.

'Well, I have known him for ever such a long time,' agrees Liz.

'Indeed.' Angela smiles.

'I hear Max is none too thrilled about the pregnancy either,' continues Liz.

'Oh, yes?' Angela grins, egging her on.

'The story is that he has managed to put a few girls into that sort of state before and has always opted for, you know, a thingy.'

'Oh, I've heard that before too,' lies Angela. 'A friend of a friend of mine in London who met one of Max's ex-girlfriends said that he was very anti having children.'

'Maybe the bloke's had his potency proved one too many times before,' says Geoff with a laugh.

'Do you remember Larry when Madeleine first got up the duff?' James nods. 'How many times did we toast the fact that the bloke didn't fire blanks?'

'Too many times,' agrees James. 'Happy as Larry he was!'

The whole table laughs again.

'Val told me he didn't even smile when she told him the news,' shares Angela across the table.

'Who didn't?'

'Max,' says Angela. 'NPAA.' She smiles. 'Not pleased at all.'

★ ★ ★

It was true Max did pause before he smiled. Madeleine lay there in a white metal high-sided bed in Stratford hospital, her blonde head bandaged, feeling vulnerable and sick, scanning his face for a reaction and he didn't smile. He did eventually, but it was one of those over-egged wide ones that never reached his eyes.

'I'm sorry, I'm sorry, so, so sorry,' she repeated over and over, hot tears of utter uselessness slowly pouring down her panicked pink cheeks. 'I didn't do it on purpose.'

Max knew she hadn't done it on purpose. After all, he was just as much to blame. But he couldn't help himself from being annoyed. There was something about her total vulnerability that irritated him. The way she pawed his arm, the way her scarlet, tear-filled eyes begged his forgiveness made him slightly repelled. It was a brief moment. But it certainly wrong-footed him. His ensuing effusiveness was then, of course, overpowering. He pretended to be overjoyed. She was kept in for a couple of days for observation and most of the time Max was there by the bedside. He arrived every morning wearing a grin, hauling various baskets of fruit and bouquets of flowers in his wake. Madeleine's emotions swung from deliriously happy to fear, in the flutter of an eyelid; it was hard to keep up. But he finally convinced her that he was joyous and couldn't wait.

However, when Larry found out he was furious. Viewing it as her duty to an old friend and ex-lover, Liz rang and told him of the incident and the revelation as soon as she arrived home. Pouring herself a large gin and tonic with ice and a big fat slice, she proffered her cheeks to her children, who were inertly watching television, then went upstairs to lounge back on her excessively frilled bed to call Larry at work.

She has had his direct line for a couple of years. He'd slipped it down her cleavage after a particularly gymnastic trip to the utility room at one of Candida's South African wine tastings. Madeleine had always unquestioningly gone through his secretary. But the shiny red phone on his desk was for calls of an extremely personal nature only, so much so that Larry almost always got a hard-on as soon as it rang.

'Hello,' he said, trying to sound alluring through his hot custard-coloured moustache which was in desperate need of a trim.

'Um, Larry,' said Liz. 'It's me.'

'Hello, me,' purred Larry, not entirely sure who 'me' was.

'Are you sitting down?'

'I most certainly am . . . um . . . "me",' replied Larry, flipping back in his leather armchair, loosening the girth of his trousers. 'I'm almost horizontal.'

'Stop it, Larry,' said Liz in such a brusque and familiar manner that Larry's recall was immediate.

'Liz?' he said, flipping forward so quickly he nearly winded himself on the desk.

'I've got some news for you,' she announced, taking a sip of her gin, the ice rattling down the receiver.

'Oh,' said Larry, somewhat disappointed. The strain in his Y-fronts began to subside immediately. He couldn't work out whether it was that Liz no longer piqued his interest, or that she was ready with news, rather than phone sex, that disappointed him. Either way his nonchalance galled her.

'Um, Larry,' she said, lighting a cigarette, admiring her maroon manicure as she did so. 'There isn't really a very nice way of saying this,' she continued, enjoying his heaving silence down the phone. 'So I'll just come out with—'

'Go on then,' said Larry, spinning on his chair and, with some effort, launching one of his short legs at the top of the desk.

'Madeleine is pregnant.'

'What?' said Larry, leaning forward on his desk. 'Oh, fuck,' he shrieked, leaning right back, having giving himself vicious groin strain. 'Jesus fucking Christ.' He inhaled in agony.

'It's not that bad,' said Liz.

'It fucking is!' shouted Larry. 'I've fucking injured myself I'm so fucking furious. Jesus,' he continued, standing up and pacing slowly around his desk, trying to shake out his right leg and grabbing his inner thigh with his free hand. 'So Max has knocked her up then? The tosser.'

'Seems that way.'

'The bastard.'

'Oh, I know,' replied Liz, flicking her ash into her husband's bedside glass of water.

'The tart,' said Larry. 'I haven't even divorced her yet.'

'Oh, I know.'

'Why couldn't they fucking wait a decent length of time before . . .'

'Oh, I know.'

'God, what are people going to say?'

'Oh, I know.'

'She's already got two children. Why the hell does she want any more?'

'Mmm.'

'God, what am I going to do?' He sat down. 'Poor fucking me. It's always down to poor fucking me. At the end of the day, it's always up to me to pick up the pieces. Poor fucking me.' He sighed.

'Oh, I know,' replied Liz, puffing out her cheeks as she exhaled her cigarette smoke, slightly bored with the way the conversation was going. None of it was worth retelling at next week's tennis. 'What are you doing this week, Larry?' she teased.

'How do you mean?'

'You know . . .'

'No?'

'Oh, Larry, do I have to spell it out to you after all this time. I mean you and me . . . It's been a while . . .'

'Oh? Actually,' he stalled. Even he was shocked that she could think of sex at a time like this. 'I've got rather a lot on.'

'Oh,' replied Liz, her mouth pursing into an animal's orifice. 'If that's the case I'll leave you to your news.' She dropped the fake ivory and gilt telephone on its upright stand from quite a height and, extinguishing her cigarette in her husband's water, marched out of the bedroom.

By the time Madeleine comes out of hospital, the news of her predicament is not confined simply to their group of friends. In fact, as far as she can work out, the whole county knows.

Larry told almost everyone he came into contact with in the following twenty-four hours, including Alan in the pub round the corner from his office, where he went for a consolatory drink; Denise, the new girl, at his club where he went for a sharpener on the way home; and the regulars down the Nag's Head where he stopped off for a quick one for the road. Conchita heard an incomprehensible but apparently blow-by-blow account, but the children missed out. Larry was so inebriated by the time they got home from ballet lessons that he was fast asleep on the sofa in front of *Nationwide*. He slurred something incomprehensible at them, before demanding soup from the nanny, and then retiring to bed before she managed to heat it up.

Max is also heating up a lot of soups. With Madeleine back from hospital and instructed to lie low and rest for a couple of days, Max is beginning to enjoy his role of nursemaid. Having initially found Madeleine's vulnerability unattractive, he somehow slips into nurture mode. He is slowly but surely coming round to the role of being a father, not to the extent that he tells his family, but he notices that he finds himself unconsciously whistling on a couple of occasions and he thinks that he distinctly detects a spring in his own stride.

He is working harder in the shop, opening up on Sundays hoping to cash in on the day-trippers and the new 'leisure drivers' who are following the brown signs of suggested routes with 'lovely views' around the area. He even finds it hard to contain his enthusiasm when he bumps into Val in the delicatessen.

'So?' he says, clicking his teeth, checking Val up and down as she rests her heavily underwired bosom on the glass-fronted counter.

'So?' replies Val, a puzzled expression playing on her rather pretty face.

'So what do you think about my impending fatherhood?' Max grins, shaking his head with pride. 'A month and a half gone and counting . . .'

'Well, I'm obviously not as thrilled as you.' Val smiles somewhat weakly. 'Is Madeleine all right? I haven't spoken to her since, well, um, tennis.'

'She hasn't spoken to anyone actually,' says Max, propping his elbow on the counter. 'Except me, of course.'

'Of course. So you're pleased then?'

'Oh, very,' says Max quickly. 'Very, very, pleased indeed.'

'Right . . .'

'I was a bit shocked at first, but you know, now, it puts it all into perspective. It gives us a reason for everything. You know, Madeleine and I didn't really know what . . . Anyway,' he continues, exhaling. 'That small flat, the shop, now it all makes sense.'

'Right,' says Val, looking at him closely.

★　　★　　★

273

Max is a different man from the slightly sardonic matinée idol she'd met when he first moved here. Undoubtedly, he is still devastatingly handsome; the pink cheeks of the girl behind the counter are testimony to that. The hair is still long and dark, the sideburns are still thick and male and halfway down his face, his eyes are still that blue-green and his body is still worth humiliating yourself for in public. But he is different. She can't quite work out what it is but he seems a little manic, panicked, cornered, even, as he juggles the mini Edam cheeses he is holding in his hand. His foot taps as he speaks sometimes, and he seems to be drinking and smoking more than he used to. He is still extremely attractive, though, she thinks as she wraps herself around him to hug him goodbye. There are times when Val is very jealous of Madeleine.

By the middle of November, nearly six weeks since Madeleine came out of hospital, both she and Max have got back into some sort of routine. Madeleine spends the mornings pottering about. Sorting out the bedroom upstairs and the kitchen downstairs, she goes on to try and impose some sort of order into Max's paperwork. She then wanders up and down Henley High Street, getting lunch and supper and anything else either of them might need. On Tuesdays and Thursdays after school, she sees her daughters, who don't know about her pregnancy, although Madeleine thinks that Lara might have picked up on something someone said at school because she has asked the odd strange question. But she'll tell them a bit nearer the time. She doesn't want to upset them. Her hours with them are too precious to broach anything difficult. The look on their sad little faces as she hands them back to Conchita at the end of the day haunts her enough. She doesn't know if she could cope with tears. When they have got a bit more used to the situation, she concludes. When she and Max have hopefully found somewhere else to live. When she has worked out what they all should do for Christmas, which they keep hinting is rapidly approaching.

Meanwhile, Max stays in and spends more or less all day, every day, in the shop desperately trying to sell his furniture. When Madeleine is out, he flirts with the customers in an attempt to shift some of his stock: he runs his hands through his hair, he laughs a lot, he grins and stares at their breasts like he finds them desirable. But while she is around in the kitchen and the office area he refrains, as he knows it upsets her. He thinks she seems unreasonably sensitive about it. He's always telling her he loves her, that there is no reason for her to be so possessive. He knows that she has given up a lot for him and he sees how upset she is every time she comes back from her children's visits. She is always apologising for clinging so much, for asking him where he is going all the time, for checking up. But she says she feels insecure, like he is the only thing she has left. Being a separated woman with little access to her children and living in a one-bedroom flat above a shop is uncharted territory for her. So he tells her he loves her some more. He has tried to explain that it's good for business if he flirts with clients, but she doesn't believe him. So in an effort to maintain the peace, Max has more or less stopped doing it. His takings are down but then that is to be expected. It's the time of year, insists Madeleine. There are fewer tourists in Novemeber. Max always finds it simpler to agree.

It's a Thursday afternoon and Madeleine is out with her daughters when the telephone rings.

'Max, mate,' comes this voice down the phone.

'Hey,' says Max, trawling through his audio memory bank. 'This is never Adam, is it?'

'It is,' says Adam, his voice octaves higher in joyous delight.

'I'd recognise those tones anywhere.' Max laughs. 'How are you?'

'Missing you, you bastard. You have no idea how hard it was for me to track you down.'

'Well, if you will go and get married when we had a perfectly good life shagging birds in London, what do you expect?'

'Yes, well, there's no need to make it so complicated for me to find you that I have to ring your mother for your number.' Adam laughs. 'Only the most terrifying woman in the world!'

'Well, you did sleep with one of my sisters,' says Max. 'What the hell do you expect?'

'Only one?'

'Shut up, you bastard,' says Max with a laugh, his feet up on the desk, flicking his ash into his coffee cup. 'Where are you?'

'Closer than you think, mate.'

'No-o-o, where?'

'Stratford!' The triumph and enthusiasm in Adam's voice are contagious. 'Some bankers' conference.'

'You're a banker?'

'Afraid so.' Adam laughs. 'Anyway, you and me tonight, we're going to be the most pissed fuckers in the county.'

'Oh,' says Max.

'Don't you fucking "oh" me,' says Adam. 'You are my best mate and I haven't seen you in nearly two years. You are not going to stand me up, mate.'

'Oh, God, mate, I would if I could.' Max's legs are now off the table and he's doubled over the chair clutching his forehead. 'I can't, I just can't.'

'Course you fucking can. If you tell me it's a woman, I am hanging up right now.'

'No, no, no,' yells Max down the phone. 'Don't hang up. I'm coming. I'm coming. It is a woman, it's a very long story, but I am coming.'

★ ★ ★

Amazingly Madeleine doesn't seem to mind at all when he explains the problem. She is tired and needs a lie down, but seems to understand completely why, even though the call came out of the blue, Max must go and see his friend.

'He's the only man you really ever talk about.' She smiles sleepily halfway up the stairs. 'Of course you must go. And have fun.'

Max takes Madeleine at her word and meets Adam at the Dirty Duck pub near the theatre. In a black polo neck and denim flares, Max doesn't look that dissimilar to half the actors who frequent the place, both before and after the shows. Adam is slightly chubbier than he was a couple of years ago. Still essentially jovial-faced, with thick blond hair and full pleasure-loving lips, he yells, 'Ma-a-ate!' loudly across the room as Max comes in. Max walks halfway across the low-slung room and stands with his arms out, awaiting impact. Adam, with a pint and a half already inside after a very long day, in a very dull conference, runs and almost fells his friend in his enthusiasm. The pub is well used to more dramatic thespian behaviour, so no one bothers to react. It takes less than half an hour of drinking before they're mixing the pints with shorts and tearing at packets of crisps.

'So who is this bird, then?' asks Adam, slurping his pint with evident satisfaction.

'Her name's Madeleine,' says Max, doing the same.

'Sexy?'

'Oh, yeah.'

'What, blonde?'

'Yep.'

'Nice tits?'

'Oh, great tits.'

'Arse?'

'Yeah.'

'So how did you meet her then?'

'Well, I was at this party with her and her husband—'

'Husband?'

'Yeah,' says Max, raising his eyebrows.

'But you and I always had a rule about that,' says Adam, sounding horrified.

'I know, I know, I know,' agrees Max, shaking his head.

'Married women are always bad news,' says Adam. 'You want them young, pert, a good height and horny as hell.'

'That's why you're married, mate.' Max smiles, slapping Adam hard on the back.

'Not for much longer, mate,' says Adam, taking a large slurp.

'No, really?' says Max, genuinely surprised, leaning back on his bar stool, his jaw on his chest as he looks his friend in the eye. 'But Harriet is lovely.'

'She was lovely . . . she is lovely,' says Adam. 'So lovely she's been sleeping with someone else.'

'No-o-o way!'

'Yes, well . . .'

'Who?'

'Some bloke I work with, well, worked with. Now he's left the company.'

'Really?' Max is shaking his head. 'I'm so sorry, mate, I really am.'

'Fuck it,' announces Adam. 'Let's get pissed.'

'Absolutely.'

'Yeah,' says Adam, lost somewhere in his own head.

They go about their mission with gusto. Like the participants in some alcoholic relay, they take it in turns to go up to the bar, slapping five pound notes on its polished surface, returning, each time, with increasingly sloppy pints and a couple of whisky chasers tucked under the chin. By about ten o'clock Adam proudly announces that he is 'rat-arsed' and needs something to eat.

'Otherwise I'm passing out right here,' he declares.

'Well,' says Max, his index finger boring a hole in the air in front of him. 'We could go and have a Greek.'

'A Greek?' Adam's horrified head tries to leave his shoulders.

'Well, there isn't much else still serving, now,' says Max.

'Lumps of foul-smelling cheese and tomato it is then,' agrees Adam, using both his hands to support himself as he peels himself off the velvet bar stool.

The restaurant, simply called Costos' Taverna, halfway out of town on the Henley Road, is almost entirely empty when they arrive. A large, rather cavernous place, with a turquoise-cushioned meet-and-greet area, there's a brightly lit wooden bar decked out in permanently fecund plastic grapes. Towards the back, some thirty wooden tables frame a large open space, specially designated for drunken dancing and smashing plates. The walls are white and the floor is tiled in red. Apart from the occasional garlic plait and faded peach, the alcoves play host to troupes of male dancers, which on closer inspection turn out to be surprised-looking, blue-eyed lady dolls dressed in frilled dervish dresses with painted-on beards. The whole establishment smells of old onions and swimming pools.

'Nice,' says Adam, as he collapses on a turquoise meet-and-greet cushion.

'Well, we're not in London,' says Max.

'I think I can tell that.' Adam smiles. 'Actually, what the fuck are you doing here, mate?' he asks suddenly, trying to sit up straight. 'She must be quite something, this bird, for you to stay in this shit-hole.'

'Do you know?' says Max, slowly. 'I think I really love her.'

'Ah, ah,' says Adam. 'You think . . .' He taps the side of his nose.

'Okay, okay. I know, I know.'

'That's better,' replies Adam. 'That's better. Drink?'

'Absolutely.' Max grins. 'She's pregnant as well, by the way.'

'What?' Adam stops in his tracks.

'Yup,' Max smiles.

'Are you . . . ?'

'Pleased?'

'Yeah.'

'Yeah, I am.'

'Really?'

'Really pleased.'

'You're not just saying that because you're an old hippy?'

'Do you know, actually, I am delighted,' replies Max. 'I was a bit iffy about it to start off with. You know, what with all those close shaves in the past.'

'We've all had a few of those, mate.' He laughs. 'So why this time?'

'This time it seems to be right. I mean, she really is the love of my life.'

'You're pissed,' says Adam, grinning.

'I might be,' grins Max.

'Well, I'm very, very pissed,' admits Adam, lolling across the meet-and-greet cushion to hug his friend.

'So the hell am I,' says Max, hugging him right back.

'But you're going to be a dad!' Adam slaps him on the back.

'Do you think so?' asks Max, beaming slightly.

'I know so.'

'It's brilliant, isn't it?'

'Brilliant.'

'Brilliant,' they both agree.

It is gone one in the morning by the time Max finally makes it home. He and Adam have discussed everything from fatherhood, to the state of their relationships, to the state of Chelsea FC; they have laughed about girls they've had, and the women they wanted. In the end they decided they should marry each other, set up business together and move to the south of France. It has been a wonderful, magical night and somehow Max – who has no idea how he managed it – has driven home from Stratford. As he tumbles through the back door and fumbles about in the twilight of the kitchen, he throws his keys on to the table. Propping himself up slightly on the back of a chair, he feels like he is being watched. Looking up, he is greeted by the most terrifying sight. Madeleine is standing there, halfway up the stairs, back-lit from the bulb on the landing, dressed in some short white nightie. Her hair is wild. She looks certifiable, a lunatic.

'Where have you been?' she says in a slow, low voice that is obviously hoarse with hysteria.

'I've been out with Adam,' replies Max, desperately trying to understand the situation, as he stands feeling vulnerable and taken totally off guard.

'Until after one in the morning?' she hisses.

'God, is it really that late?' asks Max, his head spinning round trying to find the clock on the wall.

'I have been up for hours,' she says, her eyes narrowing as she hunches forward. 'Pacing around the house,' she whispers. 'Pacing around, wondering where you are. I went to bed at ten and woke at eleven,' she continues.

Max can see her slim legs, silhouetted against the light, visibly begin to shake. She holds on to the banister for support.

'It's eleven, I thought, the pubs close at eleven: he'll be home soon. It's a twenty-five-minute drive from Stratford. Five minutes to say goodbye, maybe ten, so he'll be home by twelve, at the latest. So I waited and waited and waited.

Sitting on the bed, lying on the bed, walking round and round the bed. Midnight . . . five past . . . ten past . . . Quarter past twelve . . . I'm thinking, maybe he's broken down? Poor bloke, poor thing. A puncture possibly? So I ring a couple of garages. Just to check. No one answers. No one takes my call. Half past twelve: maybe he's had an accident? Maybe he's hurt? I'm not his wife; they wouldn't ring me now, would they? They wouldn't tell me anything. I'm nothing. So I pace and pace some more. Maybe he's DEAD? Oh, my God! Maybe he's fucking DEAD? Lying there in a pool of blood and I'm the last person to know!'

She is starting to shriek now, in a tone and a voice that Max has never heard before. It is loud and high-pitched, diabolic. He is frightened. He holds his own head, wanting the noise to stop.

'Then it dawns on me,' she announces in a voice loaded with heavy sarcasm. 'He's fucking someone else.' She claps her hands. 'It happens all the time round here. Val is always talking about having other people's husbands while their wives are up the duff. I'm here, pregnant. He's somewhere else, fucking someone else. Of course he is! He's stolen someone else's wife before, he'll do it again. He's like a fucking cuckoo. Always in someone else's nest throwing out their darling babies. Making them leave their beautiful children behind. Leaving them with nothing . . . nothing at all. He can't fucking help it. It's in his nature.'

She starts walking towards him, slowly coming down the stairs one step at a time. Her eyes are hollow and haunted through delusion and lack of sleep. Her white skin shines with sweat. 'So, who have you been fucking?' she says, slowly and quietly. Her shoulders hunch further as she stares at him. 'Who?' she says. 'Who is it?'

She sounds like she is teasing, coquettishly moving her head from side to side. 'Go on,' she says, smiling and placing her forefinger on her bottom lip, pouting like a knowing Lolita. 'Come on, Maxy, tell me . . .'

'No one,' says Max in the weakest and quietest of voices. 'I've been drinking with Adam.'

'Liar,' she whispers. 'Come on, tell me; tell me, who was it? You've had me, you see, you've destroyed me. You've made me leave my children, everything I love for you. And now you're quite understandably bored. I'm used goods, you see, old goods, a little bit shop-soiled. I know . . . I know you wanted something new, so who was it?'

'No one.'

'Liar.'

'Honestly there is no one else. I don't know what you are talking about.'

'Liar,' she says, louder. Her eyes flash round and then narrow again. 'Liar . . . LIAR . . . LIAR . . .' she screams, her arms rigid by her side. She then runs towards him and starts to pummel his chest with tightly clenched fists, her head rocking from side to side, her hair whipping him across the face. 'Who were you fucking? Who were you FUCKING? Who were you . . . FUCKING?'

She yells so loudly and so closely in his face, he can feel the heat of her breath on his lips. Her cheeks turn scarlet and the whites of her eyes are on fire; she spits, before turning and shaking, as she vomits canary-yellow bile all over the floor. Her head stays down as she continues to retch and shake. The room is suddenly silent. Max is horrified and terrified; he stands rooted to the spot; with one hand he grips the back of the chair so tightly his knuckles stick out like lumps of chalk. Madeleine remains hunched; all they can hear is the drip, drip, drip of a tap. Madeleine starts to shake uncontrollably and violently, as the dripping becomes faster and more fluid, until there's a strange slapping thud like wet clothes hitting the floor.

'Max?' she says in a small, quiet voice, muffled by her hair.

'Yes,' he says, hardly daring even to move his mouth.

'Turn the light on, would you? I think I'm losing the baby.'

It is the amount of blood that terrifies Max. It is everywhere: on the chair legs, the skirting board, even splatter marks on the table. And there are great lakes of it all over the kitchen floor. Madeleine fortunately passes out immediately after her announcement. She lies motionless in the pool of black blood. Her white face – her dry mouth partly open, her shiny eyelids closed – is framed by her dank curls. Her thin white legs are covered in irregular skinny scarlet stripes, while her white nightie quietly absorbs a mass of it, soaking it slowly up off the floor.

And no matter how hard Max tries not to, that is how he will remember Madeleine: lying covered in blood on his kitchen floor. He comes with her in the ambulance, not that either of them really remembers the journey. He is distraught, fondling her hand all loose and slack like some smacked-up junkie; he thinks she is going to die. As she refuses to come round, they take her straight into surgery and tell him to go home. She won't wake until the following day, so what is the point of hanging around?

The next day Max oversleeps. The combination of emotional turmoil, alcohol, sleeping pills and exhaustion means that he doesn't make the early morning visiting hours and eventually turns up at about 2 p.m. By the time he walks into the women's ward with a huge bunch of flowers in his arms, she is gone. She's checked herself out apparently. At about midday. It was against the doctor's advice – he did try and stop her – but she said that she felt better and wanted to go home.

Max is distraught. He runs up and down the ward, tearing back privacy curtains, shouting out her name, until he is asked to leave. Escorted out of the building, he stands in the drizzle with his large bunch of red flowers, and, collapsing on to the steps of the hospital, he weeps. He doesn't really know who he is crying for: himself; Madeleine; or the baby they have lost. All he knows is that the tears and raw pain come from the very depths of his soul.

It is about an hour before he moves. Driving slowly back to his one-bedroom flat above his shop, he feels as if someone has turned the volume and colour down on the world. He can't hear anything any more. He can barely see anything any more and he certainly can't feel anything. He sits in silence in his sitting room, his large bunch of flowers slowly dying of thirst on the floor, staring at the telephone as he tries to work out where Madeleine might have gone for help. Who would she turn to? He sits with his head in his hands, mentally flipping through faces and numbers. Who would drop everything for Madeleine? Who would catch her if she fell? Who would come running at her call?

He realises there is no one at all. No one to whom she can turn. Ten years of living in the same place, and no one to call a friend: her husband has made his feelings perfectly clear; Liz and Angela might both have helped at one stage in her life but not now; Val – Val might well have been able to give her some money and send her off somewhere else but hasn't called once since the pregnancy was discovered. She and Madeleine have been on so-called 'non-speakers' for a month. Max knows that Madeleine has left various messages for Val, none of which has been returned. It is obvious what her feelings are. So if Madeleine has nowhere to go around Solihull, Max surmises, she must have gone home to her parents.

★   ★   ★

285

Madeleine's mother is tight-lipped and curt when she answers the telephone. She hasn't heard from her daughter in weeks, she lies. They aren't very often in touch. She hadn't heard that Madeleine was in trouble, she lies again. She will most certainly contact Max if Madeleine gets in touch. But it would be very unlikely. Max is beside himself with worry. He cannot think of anywhere else to look. The trail has run dry. Unfortunately, what he does not know is how economical with the truth Madeleine's mother can be, especially when her daughter begs her.

Madeleine had arrived on her mother's doorstep in such a state that her mother had little choice but to comply with her wishes. When Max failed to turn up at the hospital that morning, she lost all semblance of clear and rational thought. The longer she lay there, staring at the swing doors willing him to flip through, a comforting grin consuming his face, the more illogical she became. As far as she was concerned, in her time of real need, the man she loved was not there. And he should have been there, just like in the films, asleep, his face nuzzled into her lap, when she came round. He should have smiled and, half-asleep, bent over and kissed her, mumbling something along the lines that everything would be all right. Instead she woke up alone, only to be served breakfast by some frosty, starched nurse who informed her they'd managed to get everything nice and clean with the scrape.

By lunchtime, when all the other men were leaving their wives and girlfriends, exchanging lingering embraces and touching moments, Madeleine concluded that Max was either dead or had dumped her, and that whichever way she didn't care. She was leaving the hospital right then and there, and she never wanted to see him again. Freewheeling hormones and a general anaesthetic have never been the best of combinations. The doctors told her to stay in bed. But Madeleine knew best. She checked herself out and walked, as tall as she could, through the front door of the hospital, only to stop dead on the steps, wondering where the hell she intended to go.

Married off at nineteen, she thought, sitting there with her head in her hands, never employed, with no qualifications whatsoever, she had no options at all. She had married out of necessity. How else was she ever going to leave home? And she had chanced it all on love and now she was paying the price. She had always known that girls like her weren't allowed to be in love. They cooked, cleaned, had children, held the occasional dinner party and, round here, had an affair or two to stave off the boredom. But she wasn't supposed to fall in love. That only ever happened in films and books or to other people permitted to take risks, other women who had proper lives, who were equipped to make choices and decisions, who didn't have to rely on anyone for everything.

But Madeleine was incapable of looking after herself. She realised that as she sat there on the steps watching men in mackintoshes walk along the street, stooped against the rain. She had no ability to make any money, she had no friends to speak of, no one to help her, no one she could call on. What sort of mother did that make her? She had two children she was completely incapable of looking after. What example was she to them? A pathetic woman sitting on the steps of a hospital, not even able to carry a baby to term. They were better off with their father; at least he had money to look after them, at least he could put a roof over their heads, feed them, pay their school fees, take them on holiday. No one, and Madeleine knew this now, could survive on love alone. Devoid of resources, choices, any iota of self-worth, her only option was to go back to her parents.

I I

It takes Max about two or three months to realise that Madeleine isn't going to walk back through the door. Every time the front doorbell rings in the shop to announce another customer, his heart leaps and his blood runs as excited as it had done when he first met her. But still she doesn't come.

He spends afternoons at the police station begging them to take him seriously. He asks them to report her missing. He asks them to send out search parties. She wasn't of sound mind, he says. She loves me, he insists, she can't have left of her own free will. But the police aren't interested in so-called 'domestics'. She checked herself out of her own free will, they say. The doctors don't seem unduly concerned. What are we supposed to do? They quite rightly point out people are allowed to disappear if they want to. It's a free country. People can move around, change addresses as they like. They'll keep an eye out for her, they say, but tell Max not to hold his breath. They think she's run off with someone else. They even share a joke or two down at the station. But her daughters are distraught, says Max. There must be something wrong. Their interest is piqued for a while. It is odd, the police conclude, for a mother of two to disappear completely. But then Val receives a telegram shortly afterwards. It is brief and to the point. 'I am fine,' it reads. 'Don't worry about me, look after my girls – love Madeleine.' The police lose interest. Who can blame them? The woman is fine. She's told everyone as much. It really is time to give up. Except Max does not.

He buys her presents at Christmas, just in case she decides to come home. He drives to the post office in Oxford where the telegram was sent from; they have nothing to tell. He even drives down to her parents totally unannounced one afternoon. He swears that he smells her in the sitting room and feels her presence in the house, but her parents say she is not at home and although she is well, they insist, they hear from her quite regularly, but they are none too sure precisely where she is at the moment. She was thinking of travelling abroad. But as soon as they know anything for sure, they'll be very pleased to inform him. He is tempted to stand in the doorway and accuse them of lying. They're fobbing him off. He is tempted to shout and scream and demand to know where she is. But what good would that do? They are a link to Madeleine and when she finally comes to her senses and realises he cannot live without her, they might well be in touch.

The other even closer link, Lara and Sophie, hear nothing either. On the day of her disappearance, Max telephoned Larry, in case of the minutest possibility that she might have been there.

'Larry? Please don't hang up, please don't hang up,' he begged. 'It's Max.'

'I know,' Larry replied, an aggressive testosterone-filled silence in the air.

'I know you hate me.'

Larry did not even bother to deny it.

'But I am very worried about Madeleine. She has discharged herself from hospital and I have no idea where she might be.'

'Hospital?'

It was one of those rare bonding moments, where two people who hate each other forget what they are supposed to feel and, united in their love and worry for someone else, actually have a conversation.

So from that moment on Larry and Max keep in contact. Not that they have any news to share, because after Val's telegram Madeleine never gets in touch. But they spend evenings, occasionally, sitting together, talking about her.

Larry can't explain it at first, to himself, or to anyone else, and least of all to Liz whom he's found himself in bed with one rather cold and dank Tuesday afternoon. He had just ditched his last secretarial girlfriend the week before. She had become clingy and needy, demanding more presents and a weekend away, plus a show, in London. Larry considered this a bit much, seeing as he had barely begun to amalgamate her with the rest of his life and already she wanted to reap its rewards. Anyway, in a moment of blind sexual craving, he finds himself pulling in to Liz's gravelled drive and taking her on the sitting room floor, before they finally make it into bed.

'I can't believe you are now friends with Max,' says Liz, her loose bosom poured over his red chest hair.

'Neither can I really,' says Larry, scratching his crotch and flicking his long curling ash in Geoff's bedside glass of water. 'It just sort of happened. You know, the day Madeleine fucked off he rang me, like, all over the shop, and I felt sorry for him, really. I have seen him a few times since. Down the pub mostly. He has been over a couple of times to see the girls. I think he misses them.'

'Angela says he looks terrible.'

'Well, she's not far off. He looks shit. He's taken to drinking every night in the Nag's Head until closing, I've heard, and he seems to have lost a lot of weight.'

'We should have him round for dinner, introduce him to some women, get him laid again.' She giggles, curling her fingernail around his chest hair. 'Talking of which, Larry,' she purrs, taking his limp member in her left hand.

'Do you know,' says Larry, raising a buttock as he let out a long, low fart, 'I just don't think I could. Twice is enough for me in one day.'

Liz is not the only one who thinks that Max should get out and get laid. For the first couple of months after Madeleine left, he receives quite a few invitations, offering soufflé and sympathy over a bottle of blanc de blancs. Valerie is the first to try. No sooner did Christopher announce that he was off on a business trip than she is on the phone, offering to take him out to dinner at Lambs, suggesting an à deux in Henley. Max politely refuses, saying he'd rather stay in in case the telephone rings. Val finds out that he goes to the pub instead that evening and never offers again.

Angela is equally thwarted. Max comes round for dinner to one of her très relaxed lasagne, baked potato and salad evenings where everyone sits cross-legged on the floor. He turns up late, wearing a dirty tank top, stays till two in the morning, getting drunk and talking incessantly about Madeleine.

'I mean no one was bloody amused,' she complains to Liz the next day. 'On and on and on he went about her. I mean, I don't remember her being that marvellous myself. Do you?'

'God, no,' agrees Liz. 'A frigid bore if you ask me. After all, her husband had to have half the county, he was so unsatisfied.'

'I know,' shrieks Angela. 'But I'm afraid that Max has become a bit of a bore. How much mooning around can a man do?'

'You'd almost think that she was the love of his life!'

'Christ, I know, rather than some grubby little affair that went pathetically wrong.'

'Exactly.'

'It's all so banal.'

'I know.'

'Christ, you would have thought they were the only people to do it.' Angela laughs.

'What, round here!'

'It's all so ghastly and melodramatic.'

'And full of emotions.'

'Yuk,' they both agree.

Much to the surprise of his mother and the rest of his family, Max chooses to stay in Henley-in-Arden. He isn't sure whether it is a romantic gesture – if Madeleine ever wants him back she knows where to find him – or whether it is exhaustion that keeps him there. Emotionally drained and at the end of his tether, the idea of leaving, packing up the house where he was once so happy, makes him want to curl up into a ball and forget the whole thing. So he stays. He has become used to the area. There is a familiarity about it that proves to be some sort of comfort when everything else that he holds dear has crumbled to dust in his very hands. He likes the pubs where the landlord knows his name and exactly where he wants to sit down for his early evening pint of Ansell's. He likes the hassle-free ease of suburbia. But most of all he loves this small cramped cottage where every corner, every wall, chair and piece of furniture remind him of her.

There are times, early on in her absence, when he convinces himself he can hear her walking around upstairs. Deep down he knows that it is an illusion but he finds it strangely comforting. He often thinks that he sees her out of the corner of his eye. If he turns round suddenly, it is as if he just missed her. But her presence is everywhere and Max revels in it. He keeps all her perfumes and soaps so that he can inhale them in moments of abject loneliness. He plays some of her appalling Neil Diamond and David Dundas records to remind him of old times. There is one terrible occasion when, after a two-week-long bout of insomnia, he mixes alcohol with valium and wakes up near the wardrobe, rolling around in her old clothes, shouting her name. He never does drugs with alcohol again.

In the meantime Madeleine is doing nothing but drugs. Unable to deal with her relationship fallout and so-called 'baby blues', Madeleine's parents pack her off to a clinic that specialises in traumatised ladies. It isn't that they approve of the treatment, which involves heavy tranquillisers, and some sort of counselling. But they do not know what else to do. A couple not used to showing their emotions – the last time Madeleine's father shed a tear was when his friend, Derek, died in Egypt during the war – they find her excessive distress uncomfortable and extremely alarming. They hear her cry out in her sleep at night. They find it difficult to raise her in the morning. Getting so worked up about a man that she loses a baby and leaves her children is something her mother will never be able to understand. And it is really rather embarrassing. She can't stay where she is: the village is starting to gossip. The girl is obviously quite unwell and needs treatment. So they send her to some discreet clinic in Kent to get some help. It's a nice old manor house, that's actually jolly expensive for a couple on an army pension, but it's a place where she can calm down, get some rest and hopefully pull herself together a bit without the distractions of this Max person, her children and that ghastly Larry.

Their life was pleasant and ordered before she arrived on their doorstep; sending her away was the only option.

The afternoon that Max arrives, unannounced, Madeleine has only been home for a couple of weeks. After just over a month in the clinic and a fortnight's rest with her parents, she decides to spend that day in town, getting some new clothes and maybe a haircut. The salon is full, so she comes home early; it is only by a matter of minutes that she misses him.

It is also not out of malice that Sheila sends Max away. The pleading look on his face, his handsome eyes, his lovely long legs and square male shoulders are enough to melt any woman's heart, she thinks as she stands on the threshold, lying. She even lets him in and walk around downstairs to prove her point but she sticks to her story all the same. He may be persistent – a telephone call and now this surprise visit – but this man isn't good for her daughter. Look at the state she arrived in. How could any man leave a woman alone in a hospital like that? She would never be able to understand. Madeleine has only just turned the corner, the colour is beginning to return to her cheeks and she is not about to let it drain from them again. She wishes him good luck as he goes on his way, and keeps his visit a secret.

Madeleine's health gradually improves. And although she pines for her daughters and wonders on an almost hourly basis what they are up to, she tries to stop thinking about Max. He can't be interested, she concludes. He must feel well shot of her, she thinks, as she pads around her parents' garden in the spring. Why doesn't he try to find her? Why doesn't he come and rescue her from this hell? But then again, she doesn't know why she should be surprised. He abandoned her in the hospital, didn't he? He left her lying there, losing their baby and never cared. So why would he come looking for her now? He is a fair-weather lover. A selfish man only capable of loving when times are easy. Either that or maybe she isn't worth it. She is a useless mother, so maybe she was a useless lover as well.

Madeleine spends her time pacing, thinking and writing long letters to her daughters trying to explain herself to them in a way that they can comprehend. She asks for their forgiveness, their understanding. They are complex missives that she reads, rereads and never sends. She thinks about telephoning them all the time. She has dialled their number on numerous occasions but hangs up before she is connected. What would she say? How could she explain that she ran off and left them and yet loves them still, just as much as she did on the day they were born? She doesn't know what to say to make them understand because she doesn't understand herself.

By spring Madeleine is beginning to see straight. The mists are clearing, the numbness is easing and the stilted life at her parents' house is suffocating. The quiet and controlled existence that revolves around meals and the precise time they are served begins to irritate her and remind her of exactly why she left home in the first place. No one says anything they mean; in fact, they rarely, if ever, speak. Meals are eaten to the accompaniment of knife and fork scrapings and the occasional comment on the food.

'Do you know, I might try and get myself a job,' announces Madeleine over boiled eggs one breakfast at the end of April.

Neither of her parents replies. David, her father, digs deeper into the *Daily Telegraph* and Sheila reads 'Me and My Health' by Lulu in the *Daily Mail*.

'Did either of you hear that?' she continues, with more aggression than she has displayed in the last five months together.

Still they do not react.

'Jesus Christ, what does one have to do to get a bloody reaction in this house?'

'Well, swear, obviously,' says her father, putting down his *Telegraph*. 'So you're getting a job, are you?'

'Yes,' replies Madeleine, sounding increasingly childish.

'As what may I ask?' he queries.

'I don't know,' she says. 'I thought I might be a secretary or something.'

'But you can't type,' says her mother.

'I can learn.'

'How?' asks her mother.

'When?' asks her father.

'Soon,' she replies. 'I thought I might go up to London and go to one of those night-school things and . . . and teach myself book-keeping as well.'

'Might I point something out to you,' announces her father. 'You already have a career as a mother which, in case you haven't noticed, you have single-handedly managed to mess up. Might I suggest that you sort that one out before attempting anything so ambitious as book-keeping?'

'Quite,' adds her mother. 'You should really try and succeed at something before you take on anything else, dear. Know your place and all that—'

'Jesus Christ!' says Madeleine, standing up and slamming her fists so hard on the table that the china bounces. 'Listen to you two. It's no wonder I have turned out the way I am. It's no wonder I have been so weak and spineless and useless all my life. Every time I put my head above the parapet, you shoot me down. Every time I have an idea you laugh in my face. Every time I attempt to think big, you tell me I'm not capable. You tell me I'm too stupid, I'm not the sort of person who could do that. I'm too ordinary, I'm not special—'

'Honestly, dear,' interrupts Sheila.

'Shut up,' hisses Madeleine. 'I am not going to listen to you any more. I have had enough of being told that I am no good and that I can't do things. I have had enough of being told that I am ordinary and don't deserve any better. That I shouldn't take risks, that I can't try . . .'

'I have never heard anything so ridiculous in all my life,' says David. 'Such hysterical behaviour.'

'I agree. Dear, stop getting worked up over nothing; all we said is that book-keeping might be a bit tricky for someone like you.'

'Like me? Like me? What does that mean? Someone as boring as me, someone as dull as me, someone as stupid as me, someone as ordinary as me . . . My children don't think I am ordinary.' Madeleine stands and stares defiantly at her parents. 'I'm not ordinary.'

'Of course you're not, dear,' says Sheila with a pleasant smile.

'I'll show you,' says Madeleine. 'I'll get my life back on track, sort it out, get a job, earn the respect of my children, look after them properly, be a real mother to them, like I should have done a long time ago. I'll show you. I really will.'

'Of course you will, dear,' replies her father.

Folding his *Telegraph* neatly next to his plate, he rises from his usual head-of-the-table place and walks through the back door and out into the small walled garden. Unable to flounce her way out of the room, Madeleine is left with no option but to bow her head and pretend to read the announcements page in the paper.

And that's when she sees it. Halfway down the Forthcoming Marriages section, nestling in between a Peterson and a Thomas, the name Valerie Roberts leaps out at her. So Valerie is finally doing it, smiles Madeleine, picking up the newspaper. Val has given up on finding her millionaire and is making do with the wealthy boss's son, Christopher Ranger. Madeleine stares at the announcement. Here's her chance, she thinks. Val may well be giving up on her dream but she, Madeleine Johnson, will not. It is time for her to fight for what she wants and believes in. It's time for her to stand up for herself and finally be counted. If Val is getting married, then – she is prepared to lay money on it – Lara and Sophie will most certainly be bridesmaids.

Nearly six months to the day since Madeleine left, Val's wedding day is one of those fresh, May mornings when the air smells of flowers and the sky is the colour of cobalt. Wandering about in a push-up basque with transparent white lace pants and a pair of snowy stockings, Val looks more like a *Penthouse* centrefold than a bride about to get married. Angela is lying on the bed, her head propped up on Val's increasingly plump pillow collection, a full ashtray balanced on her flat stomach, smoking more voraciously than usual, lighting one from the other as she urges her friend to hurry up.

'Look, Val.' She exhales with such power it is like she is giving the surrounding atmosphere the kiss of life. 'You really are bloody BS – behind schedule – darling. I've got to do your face and bouffe your hair before you get down the aisle and we have to leave for Wootton Wawen church in about twenty minutes.'

'I know, I know,' squeals Val, running on the spot. 'Fuck, fuck, fuck, where's Liz with the blue garter? Liz? Liz?'

Liz runs in from the other room. Dressed in a pair of smoky ginger tights with no knickers on, she cups her own breasts as she lurches through the door. 'Mmm?' she says with a mouth full of hairgrips.

'Garter?' yells Val. 'Where the hell is the blue garter thing?'

'Mmm,' says Liz again. Taking hold of both her breasts with one forearm and palm, she points with her free hand in the direction of Angela and her behind.

'Oh, God, sorry,' says Angela, pushing her pelvic floor towards the ceiling as she balances the ashtray on her chest and searches under her buttocks for the garter. 'Here it is!'

she announces with a certain amount of triumph. 'How much longer for the girls?' she asks.

'Mmm,' replies Liz, making a five minutes sign with her free hand.

'Bloody get a move on, everyone,' says Angela, flicking her ash. 'Otherwise no one's bloody going to get married at this rate.' She stands up and kicks over a pink and white striped box. 'Jesus,' she declares. 'Have I broken a wedding present?'

'Don't worry,' replies Val, tweaking her hair in the mirror. 'I have got so much Queen's silver jubilee crystal I could open a shop.'

'Really?' says Angela. 'That'll be worth money some day.'

'Do you think so?' says Val.

'Oh, definitely. I have bought ever such a lot of memorabilia and put it away in the loft just in case.'

'Well I never,' says Val. 'Madeleine bought me a present, you know.'

'Which Madeleine?' says Angela, bending down to look inside the striped box.

'*The* Madeleine,' says Val.

'What, Max's Madeleine?'

'God, Jesus Christ, I wonder what has happened to her?' says Liz, walking into the room and taking the pins out of her mouth.

'No one's heard a thing about her in ages, have they?' says Val.

'Not since you,' says Angela.

'Amazing, isn't it?' says Val.

'I thought she was dead, but she clearly isn't now, is she?' says Angela, inhaling. 'Seeing as she sent you a gift.'

'Max never heard a thing, did he?' says Liz.

'Not a thing, I think,' says Angela. 'I wonder if he still carries a light for her.'

'Don't be silly.' Val giggles. 'I know he's been out with the girl who works in the delicatessen at least a couple of times. No one can keep their snake in their trousers that long.' She smiles. 'And I am a girl who should know.'

'Has he really?' asks Liz.

'Oh, yeah,' mumbles Val, pulling her breasts up in the basque.

'Actually I'd heard that too.' Angela nods, suddenly in the know again. 'About the deli girl. Two shop assistants together – how quaint!'

'I hadn't thought of that,' laughs Val.

'Oh, what a hoot!' Liz giggles.

Ten minutes later, amazingly, Val and her three bridesmaids appear ready on the tarmac outside Christopher's red-brick hacienda and pose for photographs by the white Rolls-Royce convertible. Val does look wonderful. Second time around, she carries off a white frock with consummated ease. Although the dress is indecently low at the front with a vulgar amount of cleavage on show, she insisted on long sleeves that taper into points along the back of her hand, by way of some sort of virginal compensation. Empire line with a flared skirt to the floor, the overall effect, with a bouquet of lily of the valley, is madonna whore and no one is more pleased than Val. She swears her face muscles are cramping she is smiling so much. Chantal, Lara and Sophie float around her like pink fairies in white satin ballet shoes and pink tulle dresses. With the same immaculately flicked and sprayed hair, they complement Val perfectly.

St Peter's Church in Wootton Wawen is packed. The atmosphere around the gravestones by the shiny black gates at the front of the church is that of a relatively glamorous cocktail party. Candida is shouting loudly and smoking ostentatiously in some trapeze frock that makes her look like a fuchsia lampshade as she moves between the plots. Angela is wearing a strange feathered hat that appears to follow her around like an exclamation mark. Liz is in a black and white number that is too tight over her breasts. Strained across the front, she is also sweating heavily at the armpits. The crème de la crème of Solihull society is here, frotting each other up, checking each other out. Angela doesn't think that she has seen such a gathering since the Conservative dance this time last year.

'I mean really QGS – quite a good show,' she opines to Liz.

'Not bad.' Liz nods, twisting around in her black and white jacket trying to loosen it around the armpits. 'I can't really think of anyone who's missing. Apart from the obvious of course.'

'Oh, yes. Shame,' Angela says with a smile.

Meanwhile the men, Geoff, James, Alan and Larry are all sporting variations on a morning-suit theme, with either pink or silver-grey kerchiefs tied at the neck. A couple of them have donned white carnations with a spray of baby's breath by way of buttonholes.

'I can't wait, can you?' Larry chortles, tugging at his crotch. His silver-grey trousers are so tight they have gathered in a Spanish fan formation around his balls.

'What for?' says James, flicking his ash over Maureen Little who died in 1879.

'For the undue impediment bit,' continues Larry, shaking his left leg.

'Oh, yeah?' says James, looking over Larry's shoulder.

'Can anyone think of any undue impediment?' Larry laughs. 'There's going to be a bloody Mexican wave around the church.'

'Yes, quite,' says James, flicking his blond flyaway fringe.

'I mean, I almost can't think of a man in Warwickshire who

hasn't had a good poke around her fireplace!' He snorts so hard that a slither of snot shoots down his left nostril, and whips immediately back up again.

'Indeed.' James laughs. 'I just wish they'd all get a bloody move on. I'm dying for a drink.'

'I think we should move on in,' says Larry.

'Absolutely,' replies James, leaving Maureen Little his butt as he spins on her grave, puts out his cigarette and goes into the church. 'I mean, we're late enough as it is. What time do you think the old tart is going to turn up?'

Val is half an hour late. Just enough to give Christopher the jitters as he waits by the brass altar rail. But eventually she shows. The relief on his strained white face is palpable. Silence falls in the church, there's an expectant shuffle of the order of service papers and Mrs Doyle strikes up a less then perfect rendition of 'Here Comes the Bride' on the organ.

While Val walks down the aisle, her chin in the air, her tits thrust forwards, Madeleine slips into the back of the church. Looking slim and glossy, there is a new confidence about her beauty as she stands quietly, shielded by a grey stone pillar. Her eyes are a darker brown than on the day of the barbecue, her skin glows in the sunlight. Her elegant lilac frock hugs her neat figure, while a large hat and sunglasses disguise the rest. She leans against the pillar and takes in the congregation.

There's Liz and Geoff, Angela and James, Candida and that small husband of hers, Alan; there's Patricia, and the even thinner and more hirsute Barbara, plus Chistopher and Val, of course, in her splendid white dress. There's Larry looking hot and pink in his ill-fitting morning suit. But it is the bridesmaids who capture her attention. Her daughters. The daughters she hasn't seen in six months. The daughters she was only ever allowed to see on Tuesday and Thursday afternoons. She searches every inch of their bodies for signs of change. Lara is taller, larger around the hips and chubbier on the chest and upper arm. She is no longer a little girl. Sophie is still relatively unchanged. A touch taller and plumper, she is still a child and stands with her stomach out and her thumb in her mouth to prove it. It's their hair that Madeleine finds shocking. All those battles she had, all those conversations about why they had to wait until they were older to have stripes and styles done to their hair have obviously come to naught. For standing alongside Chantal, there is now little or nothing to differentiate them.

But Madeleine doesn't really care. The joy at seeing them more than compensates for the change. Gently placing her elegant cheek against the cold hard stone of the pillar, she half closes her eyes and inhales. Her nostrils flare and she swears that if she concentrates hard enough she can smell their sweet, milky skin right the way down the aisle of the church. She feels high, like she is floating above the congregation. There is a blissful tightness in the pit of her stomach. She is concentrating so hard on her children that she fails to notice Max quietly slide in to the back of the church.

Dishevelled and disorientated by his own tardiness, he still spots her as soon as he walks in. In fact, the sight of her stops him in his tracks, as if he has walked slap-bang into a glass wall. Max is totally unprepared for his reaction. An extraordinary feeling of emotion courses through his whole body and he starts to shake. Unsteady on his legs, he reaches to grab hold of the pillar for support. He can hardly stand or breathe as he stares disbelieving at her obliviously leaning against the pillar on the opposite side of the aisle. He wants to cry out her name, to alert her to his presence, but he can't. The loud sigh he makes is drowned out by the congregation scraping to its feet. Instead, he leans against the pillar and watches her, watching her children. The six months she has been away have done little to stem his feelings for her; he realises that now as she stands so close to him. He had no idea how much he loves her until he sees her again. It is strange how he has managed to dull his emotions through gin and flirting with all the underwired ladies whom Liz and Angela paraded before him. But one glimpse of Madeleine in her stunning lilac dress and it is as if they have woken up together that morning. Max is beside himself. So unprepared for his own reaction, he is swooning like some sixteen-year-old girl.

And still Madeleine doesn't see him. Staring down the aisle, listening to the music, looking at Val's dress, picking out Liz and Angela and Larry, there is so much for her unaccustomed eyes to see and gorge themselves on, that she has no interest in turning her head to the right. As the choir belt out a rather flat 'Jerusalem', she gazes up at the medieval eaves of the church. With the final chords fading and the congregation sitting down again, she finally turns and looks towards the doors.

And there he is.

She is neither shocked nor frightened; in fact, she appears to be relieved. As soon as she sees him, she realises her children weren't the only reason she came back after all. Max. Max is the man she loves. Max is the person who stops her from feeling ordinary, who allows her to realise her dreams. Despite his unkempt ensemble, he looks better than she could ever remember, his dark hair resting on the shoulders of his morning suit, the sun flirting with the crown of his head as it pours through the stained-glass window above him. Madeleine is transfixed. All she can do is stare. All he can do is stare right back. She leans against the pillar, overcome and weak with emotion, not quite knowing what to do or say. She smiles. It is broad and gorgeous and makes Max's heart soar as soon as he sees it.

She loves him after all, is his only thought as he leans against his pillar, digging his nails into the palms of his hands in an effort to stop himself from crying out. They stare at each other. Max smiles.

'I love you,' he mouths.

She falls back against the pillar, clutching her hands to her heart. She half closes her eyes and smiles at him. 'I love you,' she mouths right back.

Epilogue

Madeleine and Max did not stay long at Valerie Rangers' wedding. They stood still and silently stared at one another throughout the whole service. Val saw them first. Turning down the aisle to face her friends, grinning in her moment of marital triumph, she saw her old friend and announced something along the lines of 'Oh, my God!' loudly to her own congregation. 'Madeleine Johnson,' she said, 'you look un-bloody-believably gorgeous. What have you done to yourself?'

Then the children joined in, yelping, 'Mummy! Mummy!' as they ran down the aisle towards their mother.

It was incredible. No one knew what to do or say. They just turned, slack-jawed, and stared. It seemed like an age until finally Max stepped in. Walking over towards Madeleine, he slipped his arms tightly around her waist. Then he took hold of the two girls and said, 'I think it's time we got out of here.'

'It was fabulous. No one could believe it. Best wedding we've had in ages.'

Or at least that's how Angela likes to tell the story, as she sits cross-legged smoking a cigarette, after one of her tennis party lunches. 'They're married now,' she adds with an authoritative flick of her ash. 'Another baby, the girls living with them, a house in Cornwall or somewhere like that. All very cosy. The shop's closed down, of course. But then a lot of the shops have closed down round here, haven't they? Anyway, can I offer anyone some more wine?'